Praise for #1 *New York Times*
bestselling author

NORA ROBERTS

"America's favorite writer."

—*The New Yorker*

"Roberts is indeed a word artist, painting her story
and her characters with vitality and verve."

—*Los Angeles Daily News*

"Roberts…is at the top of her game."

—*People* magazine

"Roberts has a warm feel for her characters and an
eye for the evocative detail."

—*Chicago Tribune*

"Her stories have fueled the dreams of twenty-five
million readers."

—*Entertainment Weekly*

"Roberts' style has a fresh, contemporary snap."

—*Kirkus Reviews*

NORA ROBERTS

SOMEDAY WITH YOU

Includes *Cordina's Crown Jewel* and
Unfinished Business

 *Silhouette Books*

SILHOUETTE™

Someday with You

ISBN-13: 978-1-335-14753-0

Copyright © 2020 by Harlequin Books S.A.

Cordina's Crown Jewel
First published in 2002. This edition published in 2020.
Copyright © 2002 by Nora Roberts

Unfinished Business
First published in 1992. This edition published in 2020.
Copyright © 1992 by Nora Roberts

Recycling programs
for this product may
not exist in your area.

This edition published by arrangement with Harlequin Books S.A.

For questions and comments about the quality of this book,
please contact us at CustomerService@Harlequin.com.

Silhouette
22 Adelaide St. West, 40th Floor
Toronto, Ontario M5H 4E3, Canada
www.Harlequin.com

Printed in Lithuania

MIX
Paper from
responsible sources
FSC® C021394
www.fsc.org

CONTENTS

CORDINA'S
CROWN JEWEL

To all the new princes and princesses in my family.
May you all grow up strong
and live happily ever after.

Prologue

She was a princess. Born, bred and meticulously trained. Her deportment was flawless, her speech impeccable and her manners unimpeachable. The image she presented was one of youth, confidence and grace all wrapped up in a lovely and carefully polished package.

Such things, she knew, were expected of a member of Cordina's Royal Family—at least in the public arena. The charity gala in Washington, D.C., was a very public arena. So she did her duty, greeting guests who had paid handsomely for the opportunity to rub elbows with royalty.

She watched her mother, Her Serene Highness Gabriella de Cordina, glide effortlessly through the process. At least her mother made it seem effortless, though she had worked as brutally hard as her daughter on this event.

She saw her father—so wonderfully handsome and steady—and her eldest brother, who was serving as her escort for the evening, mingle smoothly with the crowd.

A crowd that included politicians, celebrities and the very wealthy.

When it was time, Her Royal Highness Camilla de Cordina took her seat for the first portion of the evening's entertainment. Her hair was dressed in a complicated twist that left her slender neck bare, but for the glitter of emeralds. Her dress was an elegant black that was designed to accent her willowy frame. A frame both she and her dressmaker knew was in danger of slipping to downright thin.

Her appetite was not what it had been.

Her face was composed, her posture perfect. A headache raged like a firestorm behind her eyes.

She was a princess, but she was also a woman on the edge.

She applauded. She smiled. She laughed.

It was nearly midnight—eighteen hours into her official day—when her mother managed a private word by sliding an arm around Camilla's waist and dipping her head close.

"Darling, you don't look well." It took a mother's sharp eyes to see the exhaustion, and Gabriella's eyes were sharp indeed.

"I'm a bit tired, that's all."

"Go. Go back to the hotel. Don't argue," she murmured. "You've been working too hard, much too hard. I should have insisted you take a few weeks at the farm."

"There's been so much to do."

"And you've done enough. I've already told Marian to alert security and see to your car. Your father and I will be leaving within the hour ourselves." Gabriella glanced over, noted her son was entertaining—and being entertained by—a popular American singer. "Do you want Kristian with you?"

"No." It was a sign of her fatigue that she didn't argue.

"No, he's enjoying himself. Wiser to slip out separately anyway." And quietly, she hoped.

"The Americans love you, perhaps a little too much." With a smile, Gabriella kissed her daughter's cheek. "Go, get some rest. We'll talk in the morning."

But it was not to be a quiet escape. Despite the decoy car, the security precautions, the tedium of winding through the building to a side entrance, the press had scented her.

She had no more than stepped out into the night when she was blinded by the flash of cameras. The shouts rained over her, pounded in her head. She sensed the surge of movement, felt the tug of hands and was appalled to feel her legs tremble as her bodyguards rushed her to the waiting limo.

Unable to see, to think, she fought to maintain her composure as she was swept through the stampede, bodyguards pressed on either side of her rushing her forward.

It was so horribly hot, so horribly close. Surely that was why she felt ill. Ill and weak and stupidly frightened. She wasn't sure if she fell, was pushed or simply dived into the car.

As the door slammed behind her, and the shouts were like the roar of the sea outside the steel and glass, she shivered, her teeth almost chattering in the sudden wash of cool air-conditioned air. Closed her eyes.

"Your Highness, are you all right?"

She heard, dimly, the concerned voice of one of her guards. "Yes. Thank you, yes. I'm fine."

But she knew she wasn't.

Chapter 1

Whatever might, and undoubtedly would be said, it hadn't been an impulsive decision. Her Royal Highness Camilla de Cordina was not an impulsive woman.

She was, however, a desperate one.

Desperation, she was forced to admit, had been building in her for months. On this hot, sticky, endless June night, it had reached, despite her efforts to deny it, a fever pitch.

The wild hive of paparazzi that had swarmed after her when she'd tried to slip out of the charity gala that evening had been the final straw.

Even as security had worked to block them, as she'd managed to slide into her limo with some remnants of dignity, her mind had been screaming.

Let me breathe. For pity's sake, give me some space.

Now, two hours later, temper, excitement, nerves and frustration continued to swirl around her as she paced the floor of the sumptuous suite high over Washington, D.C.

Less than three hours to the south was the farm where she'd spent part of her childhood. Several thousand miles east across the ocean was the tiny country where she'd spent the other part. Her life had been divided between those two worlds. Though she loved both equally, she wondered if she would ever find her own place in either.

It was time, past time, she found it somewhere.

To do that, she had to find herself first. And how could she do that when she was forever surrounded. Worse, she thought, when she was beginning to feel continually hounded. Perhaps if she hadn't been the eldest of the three young women of the new generation of Cordinian princesses—and for the past few years the most accessible due to her American father and time spent in the States—it would have been different.

But she was, so it wasn't. Just now, it seemed her entire existence was bound up in politics, protocol and press. Requests, demands, appointments, obligations. She'd completed her duty as co-chair for the Aid To Children with Disabilities benefit—a task she'd shared with her mother.

She believed in what she was doing, knew the duty was required, important. But did the price have to be so high?

It had taken weeks of organizing and effort, and the pleasure of seeing all that work bear fruit had been spoiled by her own bone-deep weariness.

How they crowded her, she thought. All those cameras, all those faces.

Even her family, God love them, seemed to crowd her too much these days. Trying to explain her feelings to her personal assistant seemed disloyal, ungrateful and impossible. But the assistant was also her oldest and dearest friend.

"I'm sick of seeing my face on the cover of magazines, of

reading about my supposed romances inside them. Marian, I'm just so tired of having other people define me."

"Royalty, beauty and sex sell magazines. Combine the three and you can't print them fast enough." Marian Breen was a practical woman, and her tone reflected that. As she'd known Camilla since childhood it also reflected more amusement than respect. "I know tonight was horrid, and I don't blame you for being shaken by it. If we find out who leaked your exit route—"

"It's done. What does it matter who?"

"They were like a pack of hounds," Marian muttered. "Still, you're a princess of Cordina—a place that makes Americans in particular think of fairy tales. You look like your mother, which means you're stunning. And you attract men like an out of business sale attracts bargain hunters. The press, particularly the more aggressive element, feed on that."

"The royalty is a product of birth, as are my looks. As for the men—" Camilla dismissed the entire gender with an imperious flick of the wrist. "None of them are attracted to *me* but to the package—the same one that sells the idiotic magazines in the first place."

"Catch-22." Since Camilla was keeping her up, Marian nibbled on the grapes from the impressive fruit bowl that had been sent up by the hotel management. Outwardly calm, inwardly she was worried. Her friend was far too pale. And she looked like she'd lost weight.

It was nothing, she assured herself, that a few quiet days in Virginia wouldn't put right. The farm was as secure as the palace in Cordina. Camilla's father had made certain of it.

"I know it's a pain to have bodyguards and paparazzi surrounding you every time you take a step in public," she continued. "But what're you going to do? Run away from home?"

"Yes."

Chuckling, Marian plucked another grape. Then it spurted out of her fingers as she caught the steely gleam in Camilla's tawny eyes. "Obviously you had too much champagne at the benefit."

"I had one glass," Camilla said evenly. "And I didn't even finish it."

"It must've been some glass. Listen, I'm going back to my room like a good girl, and I'm going to let you sleep off this mood."

"I've been thinking about it for weeks." Toying with the idea, she admitted. Fantasizing about it. Tonight, she was going to make it happen. "I need your help, Marian."

"Non, non, c'est impossible. C'est completement fou!"

Marian rarely slid into French. She was, at the core, American as apple pie. Her parents had settled in Cordina when she'd been ten—and she and Camilla had been fast friends ever since. A small woman with her honey-brown hair still upswept from the evening, she responded in the language of her adopted country as she began to panic. Her eyes, a warm, soft blue, were wide with alarm.

She knew the look on her friend's face. And feared it.

"It's neither impossible nor crazy," Camilla responded easily. "It's both possible and sane. I need time, a few weeks. And I'm going to take them. As Camilla MacGee, not as Camilla de Cordina. I've lived with the title almost without rest since Grand-père…"

She trailed off. It hurt, still. Nearly four years since his death and it still grieved inside her.

"He was our rock," she continued, drawing together her composure. "Even though he'd passed so much of the control already to his son, to Uncle Alex, he still ruled. Since his death, the family's had to contribute more—to pull together. I wouldn't have wanted it otherwise. I've been happy to do more in an official capacity."

"But?" Resigned now, Marian lowered herself to perch on the arm of the sofa.

"I need to get away from the hunt. That's how I feel," Camilla said, pressing a hand to her heart. "Hunted. I can't step out on the street without photographers dogging me. I'm losing myself in it. I don't know what I am anymore. There are times, too many times now, I can't *feel* me anymore."

"You need a rest. You need a break."

"Yes, but it's more. It's more complicated than that. Marian, I don't know what I want, for me. For myself. Look at Adrienne," she continued, speaking of her younger sister. "Married at twenty-one. She set eyes on Phillipe when she was six, and that was that. She knew what she wanted—to marry him, to raise pretty babies in Cordina. My brothers are like two halves of my father. One the farmer, one the security expert. I have no direction, Marian. No skills."

"That's not true. You were brilliant in school. Your mind's like a damn computer when you find something that sparks it. You're a spectacular hostess, you work tirelessly for worthwhile causes."

"Duties," Camilla murmured. "I excel at them. And for pleasure? I can play piano, sing a little. Paint a little, fence a little. Where's my passion?" She crossed her hands between her breasts. "I'm going to find it—or at least spend a few weeks without the bodyguards, without the protocol, without the damn press—*trying* to find it. If I don't get away from the press," she said quietly. "I'm afraid—very afraid—I'll just break into pieces."

"Talk to your parents, Cam. They'd understand."

"Mama would. I'm not sure about Daddy." But she smiled as she said it. "Adrienne's been married three years, and he still hasn't gotten over losing his baby. And Mama…she was my age when she married. Another one who knew what she wanted. But before that…"

She shook her head as she began to pace again. "The kidnapping, and the assassination attempts on my family. Passages in history books now, but still very real and immediate for us. I can't blame my parents for sheltering their children. I'd have done the same. But I'm not a child anymore, and I need…something of my own."

"A holiday then."

"No, a quest." She moved to Marian, took her hands. "You rented a car."

"Yes, I needed to—oh. Oh, Camilla."

"Give me the keys. You can call the agency and extend the rental."

"You can't just drive out of Washington."

"I'm a very good driver."

"Think! You drop out of sight, your family will go mad. And the press."

"I'd never let my family worry. I'll call my parents first thing in the morning. And the press will be told I'm taking that holiday—in an undisclosed location. You'll leak Europe, so they'll hardly be hunting around for me in the U.S."

"Shall I point out that what started this madness was you being annoyed by having your face splashed all over magazines?" Marian plucked one from the coffee table, held it up. "You have one of the most famous images in the world, Cam. You don't blend."

"I will." Though she knew it was foolish, Camilla's stomach jumped as she walked to the desk, pulled open a drawer. And removed a pair of scissors. "Princess Camilla." She shook her waist-length fall of dark red hair, and sucked in her breath. "Is about it get a whole new look."

Horror, so huge it would've been comical if Camilla hadn't felt an echo of it inside herself, spread over Marian's face. "You don't mean it! Camilla, you can't just—just whack off your hair. Your beautiful hair."

"You're right." Camilla held out the scissors. "You do it."

"Me? Oh, no—absolutely not." Instantly Marian whipped her hands behind her back. "What we're going to do is sit down, have a nice glass of wine and wait for this insanity to pass. You'll feel better tomorrow."

Camilla was afraid of that. Afraid it would pass and she'd go on just as she was. Doing her duty, fulfilling her obligations, sliding back into the bright lights and the undeniable comfort of her life. The unbearable fleeing from the media.

If she didn't do something—*something*—now, would she ever? Or would she, as the media continued to predict, marry one of the glossy men deemed suitable for someone in her position and rank and just…go on.

She set her jaw, lifted it in a way that made her friend gasp. And taking a long lock of hair, snipped it off.

"Oh, God!" Weak at the knees, Marian folded herself into a chair. "Oh, Camilla."

"It's just hair." But her hand trembled a little. Her hair had become so much a part of her image, of her life, that one snip was like cutting off a hand. She stared at the long length of gilded red that dangled from her fingers. "I'm going in the bathroom to do the rest. I could use some help with the back."

In the end, Marian came through, as friends do. By the time they were finished, the floor was littered with hanks of hair and Camilla's vision of herself with long flowing hair had to be completely adjusted. A snip here, a snip there. A glass of wine for fortification. Another snip to even things up. And she'd ended up with a cap short as a boy's, with long spiky bangs to balance it out.

"It's awfully—well…different," Camilla managed to say.

"I'm going to cry."

"No, you're not." And neither, Camilla vowed, was she. "I need to change, and pack some things. I'm already behind schedule."

She packed what she felt were essentials and was both surprised and a bit ashamed that they filled a suitcase and a enormous tote to bursting. She put on jeans, boots, a sweater and topped them all with a long black coat.

She considered sunglasses and a hat, but decided the addition would make her *look* like she was in disguise rather than letting her pass unnoticed.

"How do I look?" she demanded.

"Not like you." Marian shook her head and walked two slow circles around Camilla.

The short hair was a dramatic change, and to Marian's surprise an intriguing one. It made Camilla's golden-brown eyes seem bigger and somehow more vulnerable. The bangs concealed the regal forehead and added a youthful edge. Without makeup, her face was rose and cream, maybe a bit paler than it should be. The high cheekbones stood out, and the long mouth seemed fuller.

Rather than cool, aloof and elegant, she looked young, careless and just a little reckless.

"Not like you at all," Marian said again. "I'd recognize you, but it would take me a minute, and a second look."

"That's good enough." She checked her watch. "If I leave now I can be well away before morning."

"Camilla, where are you going to go?"

"Anywhere." She took her friend by the shoulders, kissed both Marian's cheeks. "Don't worry about me. I'll keep in touch. I promise. Even a princess is entitled to a little adventure." Her long mouth bowed up in a smile. "Maybe *especially* a princess. Promise me you won't say anything to anyone before eight in the morning—and then only to my family."

"I don't like it, but I promise."

"Thanks." She hefted the tote then walked over to pick up the suitcase.

"Wait. Don't walk like that."

Baffled, Camilla turned back. "Like what?"

"Like a princess. Slouch a little, swing your hips a little. I don't know, Cam, walk like a girl. Don't glide."

"Oh." Adjusting the strap of the tote, she practiced. "Like this?"

"Better." Marian tapped a finger on her lips. "Try taking the steel rod out of your backbone."

She worked on it a bit, trying for a looser, easier gait. "I'll practice," she promised. "But I have to go now. I'll call in the morning."

Marian rushed after her as Camilla headed for the bedroom door. "Oh, God. Be careful. Don't talk to strangers. Lock the car doors. Um… Do you have money, your phone? Have you—"

"Don't worry." At the door, Camilla turned, shot out one brilliant smile. "I have everything I need. *A bientôt.*"

But when the door shut behind her, Marian wrung her hands. "Oh boy. *Bonne chance, m'amie.*"

After ten days, Camilla sang along with the radio. She *loved* American music. She loved driving. She loved doing and going exactly what and where she wanted. Not that the interlude had been without its snags. She knew her parents were concerned. Especially her father, she mused.

There was too much cop in him, she supposed, for him not to imagine every possible pitfall and disaster that could befall a young woman alone. Especially when the young woman was his daughter.

He'd insisted she call every day. She'd been firm on offering a once-a-week check-in. And her mother—as always the balance—had negotiated between the two for every three days.

She loved them so much. Loved what they were to her, to each other. What they were to the world. But it was so much to live up to. And, she knew, they would be appalled that she felt so strongly she had to live up to anything, anyone, but herself.

Other snags were more practical than emotional. It had struck her the first time she'd checked into a motel—and what an experience that had been—that she couldn't risk using a credit card. If any clever clerk tagged the name Camilla MacGee and realized who she was, with one call to the local papers she would be—as her brother Dorian would say—busted.

As a result, her cash was dwindling quickly. Pride, stubbornness and sheer annoyance at her own lack of foresight prevented her from asking her parents to front her the means to continue with her journey.

It would, after all, negate one of the purposes. A few precious weeks of total independence.

She wondered how one went about pawning an item. Her watch was worth several thousand dollars. That would be more than enough to see her through. Perhaps she'd look into it at her next stop.

But for now it was glorious to simply drive. She'd headed

north and west from Washington, and had enjoyed exploring parts of West Virginia and Pennsylvania.

She'd eaten in fast-food restaurants, slept in lumpy beds in highway motels. She'd strolled the streets of small towns and larger cities, had been jostled rudely in crowds. And once had been ignored, then snapped at by a convenience store clerk when she'd stopped for a soft drink.

It had been marvelous.

No one—absolutely no one—had taken her picture.

When she'd wandered through a little park in upstate New York, she'd seen two old men playing chess. She stopped to watch, and found herself being drawn in to their discussion of world politics. It had been both fascinating and delightful.

She'd loved watching summer burst over New England. It was all so different from her homes in Cordina and Virginia. It was all so…liberating to simply drift where no one knew her, where no one expected anything of her, or caught her between the crosshairs of a camera lens.

She found herself doing something she did only with family, and the most intimate of friends. Relaxing.

Each night, for her own pleasure, she recounted the day's events and her observations in a journal.

Very tired now, but pleasantly so, she'd written last. *Tomorrow I'll cross into Vermont. From there I must decide whether to continue east to the coast, or turn. America is so big. None of the books, the lessons, none of the trips I've taken with family or on official business had really shown me the size, the diversity, the extraordinary beauty of the country itself, or the people in it.*

I'm half American, have always found pride in that part of my heritage. Oddly, the longer I'm on my own here, the more foreign I feel. I have, I see, neglected this part of my blood. But no more.

I'm in a small motel off the interstate, in the Adirondack Mountains. They are spectacular. I can't apply the same description to my room. It's clean, but very cramped. Amenities run to a cake of soap the size of a U.S. quarter and two towels rough as sandpaper. But there's a soft drink machine just outside my door should I want one.

I'd love a good glass of wine, but my budget doesn't run to such luxuries just now.

I called home this evening. Mama and Daddy are in Virginia at the farm, as are Kristian and Dorian. I miss them, the comfort and reliability they represent. But I'm so happy I'm finding out who I am and that I can be alone.

I believe I'm fairly self-sufficient, and more daring than I'd imagined. I have a good eye for detail, an excellent sense of direction and am easier in my own company than I thought I might be.

I have no idea what any of this means in the grand scheme, but it's all very nice to know.

Perhaps, if the bottom drops out of the princess market, I could get work as a trail guide.

She adored Vermont. She loved the high green mountains, the many lakes, the winding rivers. Rather than cut through toward Maine, or turn west, back into New York state, she took a rambling route through the state, leaving the interstate for roads through tidy New England towns, through forest and farmland.

She forgot about trying to sell her watch and put off scouting out a motel. She had the windows open to the warm summer air, the radio up, and munched on the fast-food fries in the bag tucked in her lap.

It didn't concern her when the sky clouded over. It added

such an interesting light to the tall trees lining the road, and gave the air blowing in her windows a faint electric edge.

She didn't particularly mind when rain began to splatter the windshield, though it meant winding up the windows or getting soaked. And when lightning slashed over the sky, she enjoyed the show.

But when the rain began to pound, the wind to howl and those lights in the sky became blinding, she decided it was time to make her way back to the interstate and find shelter.

Ten minutes later, she was cursing herself and struggling to see the road through the curtain of rain the windshield wipers washed rapidly from side to side.

Her own fault, she thought grimly. She was now driving into the teeth of the storm rather than away from it. And she was afraid in the dark, in the driving rain, she'd missed— or would miss her turn.

She could see nothing but the dark gleam of asphalt, pierced by her own headlights, the thick wall of trees on either side. Thunder blasted, and the wind rocked the car under her.

She considered pulling over waiting it out. But the stubborn streak—the one her brothers loved to tease her about— pushed her on. Just a couple more miles, she told herself. She'd be back on the main road. Then she'd find a motel and be inside, safe and dry, and be able to enjoy the storm.

Something streaked out of the trees and leaped in front of the car. She had an instant to see the deer's eyes gleam in her headlights, another to jerk the wheel.

The car fishtailed, spun in a complete circle on the slick road, and ended up—with a jolt and an ominous squeal of metal—front-first in a ditch.

For the next few minutes, there was no sound but the hard

drum of rain and her own ragged breathing. Then a flash of lightning slapped her clear of shock.

She drew in breath slowly, released it again. Repeating this three times usually served to calm her. But this time that third breath came out with an oath. She slapped the wheel, gritted her teeth, then slammed the car in reverse.

When she hit the gas, her wheels spun and dug their way deeper. She tried rocking the car—forward, reverse, forward, reverse. For every inch she gained, she lost two.

Giving up, muttering insults at herself, she climbed out in the pouring rain to take stock.

She couldn't see any body damage beyond a scraped fender—but it was dark. Darker yet, she noted, as one of her headlights was smashed. The car was not only half on, half off the road, but the front tires were sunk deep.

Shivering now as the rain soaked through her shirt, she climbed back into the car and dug out her cell phone. She'd need to call a tow truck, and hadn't a clue how to go about it. But she imagined the operator would be able to connect her.

Camilla turned on the phone, then stared at the display. *No Service.*

Perfect, she thought in disgust. Just perfect. I drive into the middle of nowhere because the trees are pretty, sing my way into a vicious summer storm, and end up getting run off the road and into a ditch by an idiotic deer in the one place in the world where there's no damn mobile phone service.

It appeared the next part of her adventure would be to spend the night, soaking wet, in her car.

After ten minutes, the discomfort sent her back into the rain and around to the trunk for her suitcase.

Next adventure: changing into dry clothes in a car on the side of the road.

As she started to drag the case out, she caught the faint

gleam of headlights piercing through the rain. She didn't hesitate, but rushed back around to the driver's side, reached in and blasted the horn three times. She slipped, nearly ended up facedown in the ditch, then scrambled back up to the road where she waved her arms frantically.

No white charger had ever looked as magnificent as the battered truck that rumbled up, and eased to a stop beside her. No knight in shining armor had ever looked as heroic as the dark figure who rolled down the window and stared out at her.

She couldn't see the color of his eyes, or even gauge his age in the poor light and drenching rain. She saw only the vague shape of his face, a tousled head of hair as she ran over.

"I had some trouble," she began.

"No kidding."

She saw his eyes now—they were green as glass, and sharply annoyed under dark brows that were knitted together in a scowl. They passed over her as if she were a minor inconvenience—a fact that had her hackles rising even as she struggled to be grateful—and studied the car.

"You should've pulled *onto* the shoulder during a storm like this," he shouted over the wind, "not driven your car off it."

"That's certainly helpful advice." Her tone went frigid, and horribly polite—a skill that had goaded her brothers into dubbing her Princess Prissy.

His eyes flicked back to her with a gleam that might have been humor. Or temper. "I'd very much appreciate it if you'd help me get it back on the road."

"Bet you would." His voice was deep, rough and just a little weary. "But since I left my super power suit on Krypton, I'm afraid you're out of luck."

She sent him one long stare. He had a strong face, she could see that now. It was raw boned and shadowed by what seemed to be two or three days' worth of beard. His mouth was hard and set in stern lines. Professorial lines, she thought. The kind that might just lecture.

She was hardly in the mood.

She fought off a shudder from the chill, fought to maintain her dignity. "There must be something that can be done."

"Yeah." His sigh told her he wasn't too happy about it. "Get in. We'll go to my place, call for a tow."

In the car? With him?

Don't talk to strangers.

Marian's warning echoed in her ears. Of course, she'd ignored that advice a dozen times over the last week and a half. But get into the car with one, on a deserted road?

Still, if he'd meant her harm, he didn't need her to get into the car. He could simply climb out, bash her on the head and be done with it.

So, faced with spending hours in her disabled car or taking a chance on him and finding a dry spot and—God willing—hot coffee, she nodded. "My bags are in the trunk," she told him.

"Fine. Go get them."

At this, she blinked. Then, when he simply continued to scowl at her, set her teeth.

Shining knight her butt, she fumed as she trudged through the rain to retrieve her bags. He was a rude, miserable, ill-mannered boor.

But if he had a telephone and a coffeepot, she could overlook it.

She heaved her bags in the back then climbed in beside him.

It was then she saw that his right arm was in a sling strapped close to his body. Immediately guilt swamped her.

Naturally he couldn't help with the car, or her bags, if he was injured. And he was likely impolite due to discomfort. To make up for her hard thoughts, she sent him a brilliant smile.

"Thanks so much for helping me. I was afraid I'd have to spend the night in the car—soaking wet."

"Wouldn't be wet if you'd stayed in the car."

Something wanted to hiss out between her teeth, but she swallowed it. Diplomacy, even when it wasn't deserved, was part of her training. "True. Still, I appreciate you stopping, Mr.…."

"Caine. Delaney Caine."

"Mr. Caine." She pushed at her wet hair as he drove through the storm. "I'm Camilla—" She broke off, the briefest of hesitations when she realized she'd been about to say MacGee. The episode had rattled her more than she'd realized. "Breen," she finished, giving Marian's last name as her own. "How did you hurt your arm?"

"Look, let's just ditch the small talk." He was driving, one handed, through a wailing bitch of a storm, and the woman wanted to chat. Amazing. "We both just want to get out of the rain, and put you back on the road to wherever the hell you're going."

Make that ill-mannered swine, she decided. "Very well." She turned her head and stared out the side window.

One advantage, she decided. The man hadn't looked at her twice—had barely managed once. She wouldn't have to worry about him identifying the damsel in distress as a princess.

Chapter 2

Oh, he'd looked at her all right.

It might have been dark, she might have been wet and spitting mad. But that kind of beauty managed to punch through every obstacle.

He'd seen a long, slender, soaked woman in shirt and jeans that had clung to every subtle curve. He'd seen a pale oval face dominated by gold eyes and a wide, mobile mouth and crowned by a sleek cap of hair that was dark fire with rain.

He'd heard a voice that hinted of the South and of France simultaneously. It was a classy, cultured combination that whispered upper crust.

He'd noticed the slight hesitation over her name, and had known she lied. He just didn't happen to give a damn about that, or any of the rest of it.

She was, at the moment, no more than a nuisance. He wanted to get home. To be alone. To pop some of the medication that would ease the throbbing of his shoulder and ribs. The damp and the rain were killing him.

He had work to do, damn it, and dealing with her was likely to cut a good hour out of his evening schedule.

On top of it all, she'd actually wanted to chatter at him. What was it with people and their constant need to hear voices? Particularly their own.

The one benefit of having to leave the dig in Florida and recover at home was being home. Alone. No amateurs trying to horn in on the site, no students battering him with questions, no press wheedling for an interview.

Of course, the downside was he hadn't realized how problematic it would be to try to deal with paperwork, with cataloging, with every damn thing essentially one-handed.

But he was managing.

Mostly.

It was just an hour or so, he reminded himself. He couldn't have left the woman stranded on the side of the road in the middle of a storm. Okay, he'd considered it—but only for a couple seconds. A minute, max.

Brooding, he didn't notice her shivering on the seat beside him. But he did notice when she huffed irritably and leaned over to turn up the heat.

He only grunted and kept driving.

Baboon, Camilla thought. Delaney Caine was rapidly descending the evolutionary chain in her mind. When he turned into a narrow, rain-rutted, bone-jarring lane that had her bouncing on the seat, she decided he didn't deserve whole mammal status and regulated him to horse's ass.

Cold, miserable, fuming, she tried to make out the shape of the structure ahead of them. It was nestled in the woods, and looked to be some sort of cabin. She assumed it was wood—it was certainly dark. She caught a glimpse of an overgrown lawn and a sagging front porch as he muscled the truck around what was hardly more than a mud-packed path to the back of the building.

There, a yellow, unshielded lightbulb was burning beside a door.

"You…live here?"

"Sometimes." He shoved open his door. "Grab what you need, leave the rest." And with that, he stomped through the rain toward the back door.

Since she needed, more than breath, to change into dry, warm clothes, Camilla dragged her cases out and lugged them toward the cabin. She had to maneuver to open the door, as he hadn't bothered to wait for her or hold it open as any Neanderthal with even half a pea for a brain would have.

Out of breath, she shoved through into a tiny mudroom that lived up to its name. It was, in a word, filthy—as was everything in it. Boots, coats, hats, gloves, buckets, small shovels. Under a heap of pails, trowels and laundry were, she assumed, a small washer and dryer unit.

Cochon, she thought. The man was a complete pig.

The opinion wasn't swayed when she walked through and into the kitchen. The sink was full of dishes, the small table covered with more. Along with papers, a pair of glasses, an open bag of cookies and several pencil stubs.

Her feet stuck to the floor and made little sucking sounds as she walked.

"I see soap and water are rare commodities in Vermont."

She said it sweetly with a polite smile. He only shrugged. "I fired the cleaning lady. Wouldn't leave my stuff alone."

"How, I wonder, could she find it under the dirt?"

"Tow truck," he muttered, and dug out an ancient phone book.

At least he seemed to be fairly clean, Camilla mused.

That was something at least. He was roughly dressed, and his boots were scarred, but his hands and hair—though it was long, wet and unkempt—were clean. She thought his face might even be handsome—of a type—under that untidy beard.

It was a hard face, and somewhat remote, but the eyes were striking. And looked fairly intelligent.

She waited, with admirable patience, she thought, while he found the number. Then he picked up the phone, started to punch in a button. Swore.

"Phone's out."

No, she thought, fate couldn't be so cruel. "Are you sure?"

"On this planet, no dial tone equals no phone."

They stared at each other with equal levels of dismay and annoyance. Her teeth wanted to chatter.

"Perhaps you could drive me to the nearest inn, or motel."

He glanced toward the window as the next blast of lightning lit the glass. "Twenty miles in this—flash flooding, high winds." He rubbed his aching shoulder absently. Two good arms, he might have tried it, just to get rid of her. But with one, it wasn't worth it. "I don't think so."

"What would you suggest?"

"I'd suggest you get on some dry clothes before you end up sick—which would just cap things for me here. Then we'll see if we can find something to eat in this place, and make the best of it."

"Mr. Caine, that is incredibly gracious of you. But I wouldn't want to—" She sneezed, three times in rapid succession.

"Down the hall," he told her, pointing. "Up the stairs. Bathroom's all the way at the end. I'll make coffee."

Too chilled to argue or think of an alternative, she picked up her suitcases again, struggled with them down the short hall and up the stairs. Like a horse with blinders heading toward the finish line, she kept her gaze straight ahead and closed herself in the bathroom.

Locked the door.

There were towels on the floor, toothpaste—sans cap—on the counter of a small white sink that, while not gleaming, at least appeared to have been rinsed sometime within the last six months.

There was also, she soon discovered, hot water.

The minute she stepped into the shower, the glory of it wiped out every other sensation. She let it beat on her, flood over her head. She very nearly danced in it. When the warmth reached her bones, she simply closed her eyes and sighed.

It was with some regret that she turned off the taps, stepped out. Locating a reasonably clean-looking towel on the rack, she wrapped herself in it as she dug out a shirt and trousers.

She was standing in her underwear when the lights went out.

She screamed. She couldn't help it, and ended up ramming her hip sharply against the sink before she controlled herself.

Her hands shook and her temper spiked as she fought to dress herself in the dark.

"Mr. Caine!" she shouted for him as she inched out of the bath. The place was pitch-black.

"Yeah, yeah, don't blow a gasket."

She heard him tromping up the stairs, saw the narrow beam of light bobbing with him. "Power's out," he told her.

"I never would've guessed."

"Perfect time for sarcasm," he muttered. "Just stay put." He and the light disappeared into another room. He came

back with the flashlight, and offered her a flickering can-
dle. "You done in there?" he gestured with his head toward
the bathroom.

"Yes, thank you."

"Fine." He started back down, and the next boom of thunder had her hurrying after him.

"What do we do now?"

"We build a fire, drink coffee, heat up some soup and
wish you were someplace else."

"I don't see any reason to be rude. It's hardly my fault
there's a storm." She tripped over a pair of shoes and rapped
into his back.

"Damn it!" The jar had his shoulder singing. "Watch it,
will you?"

"I beg your pardon. If you didn't live like a pig, I wouldn't
trip over your mess."

"Look, just go in there." He pointed to the front room of
the cabin. "Sit down. Stay out of the way."

"Gladly." She sailed into the room, then spoiled the effect
by letting out a muffled shriek. "Are those…" She lifted a
hand weakly toward what her light had picked out on a littered table. "Bones?"

Del shined the flashlight over the bones sealed in air-
tight plastic. "Yeah. Human, mostly." He said it matter-of-
factly as he headed toward the fireplace. "Don't worry." He
crouched and set kindling. "I didn't kill anyone."

"Oh, really." She was edging back, wondering what she
might use for a weapon.

"The original owner died about seven thousand years
ago—but not in the fall that fractured a number of those
bones. Anyway, she doesn't miss them." He set the kindling to light.

"Why do you have them?"

"I found them—on a dig in Florida."

He set logs to blaze and stood. The fire snapped at his back, shooting light around him. "You...dig graves?" she managed to ask, the horror only a hint in her voice.

For the first time, he smiled. It was a flash as bright as the lightning that shot across the sky. "In a manner of speaking. Relax...what was your name?"

She moistened her lips. "Camilla."

"Right, well relax, Camilla. I'm an archaeologist, not a mad scientist. I'm going for the coffee. Don't touch my bones—or anything else for that matter."

"I wouldn't dream of it." She also wouldn't dream of staying alone in the dark room on a storm ravaged night with a pile of human bones. No matter how carefully packaged or old they might be. "I'll give you a hand." Because she wanted to cover her unease, she smiled. "You look like you could use one."

"Yeah, I guess." The injury still irritated him, in more ways than one. "Look, there's a spare room upstairs. You might as well figure on bunking there. We'll deal with your car in the morning."

"Thanks." She was warm, she was dry and the coffee smelled wonderful. Things might've been a great deal worse. "I really do appreciate it, Mr. Caine."

"Caine, just Caine, or Del." When he walked straight back to the mudroom, she followed him.

"Where are you going?"

"What?" He paused in the act of struggling into a slicker. He just wasn't used to explaining his moves. "We're going to need water. Rain, water, bucket," he said, picking up one. "And there's a generator in the shed. I might be able to get it going. Don't mess with my stuff," he added, and walked back into the storm.

"Not without a tetanus shot, believe me," she muttered as the door slammed behind him.

Afraid of what she might find, she eased open a cupboard. Then another, and another. As the first three were empty, she found what she assumed were the only clean dishes in the cabin in the last one.

She poured coffee into a chipped mug, and took the first wary sip. She was delighted and stunned that the man made superior coffee.

Braced by it, she took stock of the kitchen. She couldn't just stand around in this sty and do nothing. If they were going to eat, she was going to have to figure out how to cook under these conditions.

There were plenty of cans in the pantry, among them two cans of condensed tomato soup. It was something. Cheered, she cracked open the refrigerator.

While it wasn't filthy, perhaps worse, it was very nearly empty. She frowned over three eggs, a hunk of very old cheese, a six-pack of beer—minus two—and to her delight, a bottle of excellent pinot noir.

Things were looking up.

There was a quart of milk which—after a testing sniff—proved to be fresh, and a half gallon of bottled water.

Rolling up her sleeves, Princess Camilla got to work.

Fifteen minutes later, armed with a pail of her own, she stepped outside. She could barely make out the shed through the rain. But over its drumming, she heard plenty of cursing and crashing. Deciding Del would be busy for a while yet, she switched his half-filled pail with her own, and hauled the water back inside.

If he'd had some damn light, Del thought as he kicked the little generator again, he could see to fix the stupid son of a bitch. The problem was, to get some damn light he needed to fix it.

Which meant he wasn't going to get it up and running before morning. Which meant, he thought sourly, he'd wasted the best part of an hour fumbling around in a cramped shed, and had bumped his miserable shoulder countless times.

Every inch of his body hurt in one way or the other. And he was still wet, cold and in the dark.

If it had been just himself, he wouldn't have bothered with the generator in the first place. He'd have opened a can, eaten a cold dinner and worked a bit by candlelight.

But there was the woman to think about. He hated having to think of a woman under the best of circumstances—and these were far from the best.

"Fancy piece, too," he muttered, shining the flashlight around the shed to see if there was anything he could use in the cabin. "On the run from something. Probably a rich husband who didn't buy her enough sparkles to suit her."

None of his business, he reminded himself. She'd be out of his hair the next day, and he could get back to work without interruptions.

He turned, caught his shin on the generator, jerked. And literally saw stars as he aggravated his broken collarbone. Sweat slicked over his face so that he had to slap his good hand against the wall and wait for the dizzy sickness to pass.

His injuries were the reason he wasn't still on-site at the Florida dig—one that had been his baby since the beginning three seasons before. He could handle that. Someone had to do the written reports, the journals, the cataloging and lab work.

He preferred that someone be himself.

But he hated the damn inconvenience of the injuries. And the weakness that dogged him behind the pain. He could barely dress himself without jarring the broken bone, the dislocated shoulder, the bruised ribs.

He couldn't even tie his own damn shoes.

It was a hell of a situation.

Steady enough to brood over his unsteadiness, he picked up the flashlight he'd dropped and made his way back to the cabin. He stopped to pick up the pail of rainwater and swore viciously as even that weight strained his resources.

In the mudroom he set down the bucket, ditched the slicker, then headed straight for a mug in the kitchen.

When he reached for the coffeepot, he saw it wasn't there.

It took him a minute. Del didn't notice details unless he meant to notice them. Not only was the coffee missing, but so were all the dishes that had been piled in the sink, over the table and counters.

He didn't remember washing them. It wasn't a chore he bothered with until all options were exhausted. Baffled, he opened a cupboard and studied the pile of clean dishes.

The counters were clean, and the table. He snarled reflexively when he saw his notes and papers tidily stacked.

But even as he marched through the cabin, prepared to skin some of that soft, rosy skin off his unwelcome visitor, the scent of coffee—and food—hit him, and hit hard. It reminded him he hadn't eaten in hours, and buried the leading edge of his temper under appetite.

There she was, stirring a saucepot over the fire. He noted she'd jury-rigged a grill—probably one of the oven racks—bracing the ends of it with stacks of bricks.

He recalled the bricks had been piled on the front porch, but had no idea why.

Resourceful, he admitted—grudgingly—and noted that for a skinny woman, she had an excellent backside.

"I told you not to touch my stuff."

She didn't jolt. He clumped through the cabin like a herd of elephants. She'd known he was there.

"I'm hungry. I refuse to cook or to eat in a sty. The papers in the kitchen are relatively undisturbed. It's the filth I dispensed with."

And the papers, she thought, were fascinating. What she could read of his handwriting, in any case.

"I knew where everything was."

"Well." She straightened, turned to face him. "Now you'll have to find where it all is now. Which is in two ordered stacks. I have no idea how you—" She broke off as she saw the blood dripping from his hand. "Oh! What have you done?"

He glanced down, noticed the shallow slice in the back of his good hand, and sighed. "Hell. What's one more?"

But she was rushing to him, taking the wounded hand and clucking over the cut like a mother hen over a chick. "Back in the kitchen," she ordered. "You're bleeding all over the place."

It was hardly a major wound. No one had ever fussed over his cuts and scrapes—not even his mother. He supposed that was due to the fact she'd always had plenty of her own. Taken off guard, he let himself be pulled back into the kitchen where she stuck his bleeding hand into the sink.

"Stay," she ordered.

As she might have said, he mused, to a pet. Or worse—a servant.

She unearthed a rag, dumped it in the pail of water and proceeded to wash off his hand. "What did you cut it on?"

"I don't know. It was dark."

She clucked again, as she examined the cleaned cut. "Do you have a first-aid kit? Antiseptic?"

"It's just a scratch," he began, but gave up and rolled his

eyes at her fulminating stare. "Back there." He gestured vaguely.

She went into the mudroom, and he heard her slamming cabinet doors—and muttering.

"Vous êtes un espece de cochon, et gauche aussi."

"If you're going to curse at me, do it in English."

"I said you're a pig of a man, and clumsy as well." She sailed back in with a first-aid kit, busied herself digging out antiseptic.

He started to tell her he knew what she'd called him, then stopped himself. Why ruin what small amount of amusement he might unearth during this ordeal? "I'm not clumsy."

"Hah. That explains why your arm's in a sling and your hand is bleeding."

"This is a work-related injury," he began, but as she turned to doctor his hand, he sneezed. That basic bodily reaction to a dousing in a rainstorm had his vision wavering. He swayed, fighting for breath as his ribs screamed, and his stomach pitched.

She looked up, saw the pain turn his eyes glassy, his cheeks sheet pale.

"What is it?" Without thinking, she slid her arms around his waist to support him as his body shuddered. "You should sit."

"Just—" Trying to steady himself, he nudged her back. His vision was still gray at the edges, and he willed it to clear. "Some bruised ribs," he managed to say when he got his breath back. At her expression of guilt and horror, he bared his teeth. "Dislocated shoulder, broken clavicle— work-related."

"Oh, you poor man." Sympathy overwhelmed everything else. "Come, I'll help you upstairs. You need dry clothes. I'm making soup, so you'll have a hot meal. You should've told me you were seriously hurt."

"I'm not…" He trailed off again. She smelled fabulous—and she was cooking. And feeling sorry for him. Why be an idiot? "It's not so bad."

"Men are so foolish about admitting they're hurt. We'll need the flashlight."

"In my back pocket."

"Ah." She managed to brace him, shift her body. He didn't mind, not really, when her nice, firm breast nestled against his good side. Or when her long, narrow fingers slid over his butt to pull the flashlight out of his jean's pocket.

He really couldn't say he minded. And it took his mind off the pain.

He let her help him upstairs where he eased down to sit on the side of his unmade bed. From there he could watch her bustling around, finding more candles to light.

"Dry clothes," she said and started going through his dresser. He opened his mouth to object, but she turned with jeans and a sweatshirt in her arms and looked at him with a bolstering smile.

"Do you need me to help you…um, change?"

He thought about it. He knew he shouldn't—it was one step too far. But he figured if a man didn't at least think of being undressed by a beautiful woman he might as well be shot in the head and end it all.

"…No, thanks. I can manage it."

"All right then. I'm going down to see to the soup. Just call if you need help."

She hurried downstairs again, to stir the soup and berate herself.

She'd called him a pig. The poor man couldn't possibly do for himself when he was hurt and in pain. It shamed her, how impatient, how unsympathetic and ungrateful she'd been. At least she could make him as comfortable as possible now, give him a hot bowl of soup.

She went over to plump the sprung cushions of the sofa—and coughed violently at the dust that plumed up. It made her scowl again. Really, she thought, the entire place needed to be turned upside down and shaken out.

He'd said he'd fired his cleaning service because they—she—had touched his things. She didn't doubt that for a minute. The man had an obviously prickly temperament. But she also imagined finances could be a problem. Being an archaeologist, he probably subsisted on grants and that sort of thing.

She'd have to find a way to send him payment for the night's lodging—after she sold her watch.

When he came back down, she had bowls and cups and folded paper towels in lieu of napkins on the scarred coffee table. There was candlelight, and the glow from the fire, and the good scent of hot soup.

She smiled—then stared for just a moment. His hair was dry now, and she could see it wasn't brown. Or not merely brown as she'd assumed. It was all shot through with lighter streaks bleached out, she imagined, from the sun. It curled a bit, a deep and streaky oak tone, over the neck of the sweatshirt.

A gorgeous head of hair, she could admit, with a rough and tumbled style that somehow suited those bottle-green eyes.

"You'll feel better when you eat."

He was already feeling marginally better after swallowing one of his pain pills. The throbbing was down to an irritating ache. He was counting on the hot food smoothing that away.

He'd have killed for a hot shower, but a man couldn't have everything.

"What's for dinner?"

"Potage." She gave it a deliberately elegant sound. *"Créme de tomate avec pomme de terre."* Laughing, she tapped her spoon against the pot. "You had plenty of cans, so I mixed the soup with canned potatoes and used some of your milk. It'd be a great deal better with some herbs, but your pantry didn't run to them. Sit down. Relax. I'll serve."

Under normal circumstances, he didn't care to be pampered. At least he didn't think so. He couldn't actually remember ever having *been* pampered. Regardless, it wasn't what anyone could call a normal evening, and he might as well enjoy it.

"You don't look like the type who'd cook—more like the type who has a cook."

That made her frown. She thought she looked like a very normal, very average woman. "I'm a very good cook." She spooned up soup. Because it had interested her, she'd taken private lessons with a cordon bleu chef. "Though this is my first attempt over an open fire."

"Looks like you managed. Smells like it, too." It was his idea of praise—as his anticipatory grunt was his idea of thanks when she handed him his bowl.

"I wasn't sure what you'd like to drink. Coffee, or the milk? There's beer…and wine."

"Coffee. I took some meds, so I'd better back off the alcohol." He was already applying himself to the soup. When she simply stood in front of him, waiting, he spared her a glance. "What?"

She bit back a sigh. Since the man didn't have the courtesy to offer, she'd have to ask. "I'd enjoy a glass of wine, if you wouldn't mind."

"I don't care."

"Thank you." Keeping her teeth gritted, she poured his

coffee, then headed to the kitchen. How, she wondered, did a man get through life with no manners whatsoever? She opened the wine, and after a brief hesitation, brought the bottle back with her.

She'd have two glasses, she decided, and send him the cost of the bottle along with the money for lodging.

Since he'd already scraped down to the bottom of the bowl, she served him a second, took one for herself, then settled down.

She had suffered through countless tedious dinner parties, official events and functions. Surely she could get through a single stormy evening with Delaney Caine.

"So, you must travel considerably in your work."

"That's part of it."

"You enjoy it?"

"It'd be stupid to do it otherwise, wouldn't it?"

She pasted on her diplomat's expression and sipped her wine. "Some have little choice in certain areas of their lives. Their work, where they live. How they live. I'm afraid I know little about your field. You study…bones?"

"Sometimes." He shrugged slightly when she lifted an eyebrow. Chitchat, he thought. He'd never seen the point of it. "Civilizations, architecture, habits, traditions, religions, culture. Lapping over into anthropology. And bones because they're part of what's left of those civilizations."

"What're you looking for in your studies?"

"Answers."

She nodded at that. She always wanted answers. "To what questions?"

"All of them."

She rose to pour him another mug of coffee. "You're ambitious."

"No. Curious."

When her lips curved this time it wasn't her polite smile. It was generous and warm and slid beautifully over her face, into her eyes. And made his stomach tighten. "That's much better than ambition."

"You think?"

"Absolutely. Ambition can be—usually is—narrow. Curiosity is broad and liberated and open to possibilities. What do your bones tell you?" She laughed again, then gestured to the cluttered side table before she sat again. "Those bones."

What the hell, he thought. He had to write it up anyway. It wouldn't hurt to talk it through—in a limited fashion.

"That she was about forty-five years old when she died," he began.

"She?"

"That's right. Native American female. She'd had several fractures—leg and arm, probably from that fall—several years before she died. Which indicates that her culture was less nomadic than previously thought, and that the sick and injured were tended, treated."

"Well, of course, they would tend to her."

"There's no 'of course' about it. In some cultures, injuries of that type, the type that would incapacitate and prevent the wounded from pulling her weight in the tribe, would have resulted in abandonment."

"Ah well. Cruelty is nothing new," she murmured.

"No, and neither is efficiency, or survival of the fittest. But in this case, the tribe cared for the sick and injured, and buried their dead with respect and ceremony. Probably buried within a day. She, and others unearthed in the project, were wrapped in a kind of yarn made from native plants. Complex weave," he continued, thinking aloud now rather than talking to Camilla. "Had to have a loom, had to take considerable time. Couldn't have moved nomadically.

Semipermanent site. Plenty of game there—and seeds, nuts, roots, wood for fires and huts. Seafood."

"You know all this from a few bones?"

"What?"

She saw, actually saw him click back to her. The way his eyes focused again, clouded with vague annoyance. "You learned this from a few bones?" she repeated.

It was barely the surface of what he'd learned—and theorized. "We got more than a few, and findings other than bones."

"The more you learn, the more you understand how they lived, why they did things. What came from their lives, and what was lost. You look for—is this right—how they built their homes, cooked their food. How they raised their children, buried their dead. What deities they worshiped, and battles they fought. And in the end, how we evolved from that."

It was, he admitted, a nice summary for a layman. There was a brain inside the classy package. "That's close enough."

"Perhaps the women cooked soup over an open fire."

The glint of humor caught him, had him nearly smiling back. "Women have been copping kitchen duty since the start. You've got to figure there's a reason for that."

"Oh, I do. Men are more inclined to beat their chests and pick fights than see to the more basic, and less heroic tasks."

"There you go." He rose. Despite the coffee, he was dragging. It was the main reason he skipped the pain pills as often as possible. "I'm going up. Spare bed's in the first room, left of the stairs."

Without a thank-you, a good-night or even one of his occasional grunts, he left Camilla alone in front of the fire.

Chapter 3

I don't know what to make of my host, Camilla wrote. It was late now, and she'd opted to huddle on the miserable sofa in front of the fire as the spare room upstairs had been chilly and damp—and dark.

She hadn't heard a sound out of Del, and though she'd tried both the lights and the phone, she'd gotten nothing out of them, either.

I've decided to attribute his lack of social skills to the fact that his line of work puts him more in company with the long dead than the living. And to season this with some sympathy over his injuries. But I suspect he's every bit as brusque and unpardonably rude when in full, robust health.

In any case, he's interesting—and spending time with people who will treat me as they treat anyone is part of this experiment.

As a lovely side benefit of his, apparently, hermit lifestyle, there is no television in the cabin. Imagine that, an Ameri-

can home without a single television set. I saw no current newspapers or magazines, either. Though some may very well be buried in the refuse heap he lives in.

The chances of such a man recognizing me, even under these oddly intimate conditions, are slim to none. It's very reassuring.

Despite his odd choice of living arrangements when not actively working on a dig, he's obviously intelligent. When he spoke of his work—however briefly—there was a spark there. A sense of curiosity, of seeking answers, that appeals to me very much. Perhaps because I'm seeking something myself. Within myself.

Though I know it was not entirely appropriate behavior, I read through more of his papers when I was certain he was in his room upstairs. It's the most fascinating work! As I understand from the scribbles, he's part of a team which has discovered a site in south-central Florida. Deep in the black peat that was being dug for a pond in a development, the bones from an ancient people—tests show seven thousand years ancient—were unearthed.

His notes and papers are so disordered, I'm unable to follow the exact procedure, but the Bardville Research Project began from this discovery, and Delaney has worked on it for three years.

Their discoveries are amazing to me. A toddler buried with her toys, artifacts of bone, antler and wood, some of them inscribed with patterns. A strong sense of ritual and appreciation of beauty. There are sketches—I wonder if he did them himself. Quite intricate and well-done sketches.

There are so many notes and papers and pieces. Honestly, they're spread willy-nilly over the cabin. I would love to organize them all and read about the entire project from its inception through to the present. But it's impossible given the state of things, not to mention my departure in the morning.

For myself, I'm progressing. I'm sleeping better, night by night. My appetite's returned, and I've indulged it perhaps a little more than I should. Today, after a long drive, and a minor accident, I spent a considerable amount of time on elemental domestic chores. Fairly physical. Less than two weeks ago the most mundane task seemed to sap all my energy—physically, emotionally, mentally. Yet after this day, I feel strong, almost energized.

This time, this freedom to simply be, was exactly the remedy I needed.

I'm taking more, a few weeks more, before Camilla Mac-Gee blends back into Camilla de Cordina again.

In the morning, the bright, bold sunlight slanted directly across Del's eyes. He shifted, seeking the dark and the rather amazing dream involving a lanky redhead with a sexy voice and gilded eyes. And rolled on his bad side.

He woke cursing.

When his mind cleared, he remembered the lanky redhead was real. The fact that she was real, and sleeping under the same roof, made him a little uneasy about the dream. He also remembered the reason the classy dish was in the spare bed was that her car was in a ditch, and the power and phones were out.

That meant, rather than a hot shower, he was going to take a dip in a cold pond. He gathered what he needed, and started downstairs. He stopped when he heard her singing.

The pretty voice with its faintly exotic accent seemed out of place in his cabin. But he couldn't fault the aroma of fresh coffee.

The coffee was heating on the fire, and she was in the kitchen, rooting around in the pantry.

He saw that the floor had been washed. He had no idea it had any shine left in it, but she'd managed to draw it out. There were wildflowers stuck in a tumbler on the kitchen table.

She had opened the kitchen window, the door to the mudroom and the door beyond that so the fresh and balmy air circled through.

She stepped back, a small can of mushrooms in her hand—and muffled a short scream when she saw him behind her.

He hadn't clomped this time. He was barefoot and barechested, clad only in a ragged pair of sweatpants and his sling.

His shoulders were broad, and his skin—apparently all of it—was tanned a dusky gold. The sweatpants hung loose over narrow hips, revealing a hard, defined abdomen. There were fascinating ropy muscles on his uninjured arm.

She felt the instinctive female approval purr through her an instant before she saw the sunburst of bruises over his right rib cage.

"My God." She wanted to touch, to soothe, and barely stopped herself. "That must be very painful."

"It's not so bad. What're you doing?"

"Planning breakfast. I've been up a couple of hours, so I'm ready for it."

"Why?"

"Because I'm hungry."

"No." He turned away to find a mug. If he didn't have caffeine immediately, he was going to disintegrate. "Why have you been up a couple of hours?"

"Habit."

She knew most people's fantasies of a princess, and the reality of the life were dramatically different. In official mode, it was rare for her to sleep beyond 6:00 a.m. Not that Delaney Caine knew she had an official mode.

"Bad habit," he muttered and strode back to the coffeepot.

She got her own mug and went back with him. "I took a walk earlier," she began. "It's a gorgeous day and a beautiful spot. The forest is lovely, simply lovely. And there's a pond. I saw deer watering, and there's foxglove and wild columbine in bloom. It answered the question for me why anyone would live here. Now I wonder how you can bear to leave it."

"It's still here whenever I get back." He drank the first mug of coffee the way a man wandering in the desert drank water. Then closing his eyes, he breathed again. "Thank you, God."

"The power's still out. We have three eggs—which we'll have scrambled with cheese and mushrooms."

"Whatever. I've got to wash up." He picked up his travel kit again, then just stopped and stared at her.

"What is it?"

Del shook his head. "You've got some looks, sister. Some looks," he repeated with a mutter and strode out.

It hadn't sounded like a compliment, she thought. Regardless her stomach fluttered, and kept fluttering when she went back to the kitchen to mix the eggs.

He ate the eggs with a single-mindedness that made her wonder why she'd worried about flavor.

The fact was, he was in serious heaven eating something he hadn't thrown together himself. Something that actually tasted like food. Happy enough that he didn't mention he'd noticed that his papers in the living room had been shuffled into tidy piles.

She earned extra points by not chattering at him. He hated having someone yammering away before he'd gotten started on the day.

If her looks hadn't been such a distraction he might have offered her a temporary job cleaning the cabin, cooking a few meals. But when a woman looked like that—and managed to sneak into your dreams only hours after you'd laid eyes on her—she was trouble.

The sooner she was out and gone, the better all around.

As if she'd read his mind, she got to her feet and began to clear the table. She spoke for the first time since they'd sat down.

"I know I've been an inconvenience, and I appreciate your help and hospitality, but I'll need to ask another favor, I'm afraid. Could you possibly drive me to the nearest phone, or town or garage? Whichever is simpler for you."

He glanced up. Camilla, whatever the rest of her real name was, had class as well as looks. He didn't like the fact that her easy grace made him feel nasty for wanting to boot her along.

"Sure. No problem." Even as he spoke, he heard the sound of a car bumping down his lane. Rising, he went out to see who the hell else was going to bother him.

Camilla walked to the window. The instant she saw the car marked Sheriff, she backed up again. Police, she thought uneasily, were trained observers. She preferred avoiding direct contact.

Del caught her quick move out of the corner of his eye, frowned over it, then stepped outside.

"Hey there, Del." Sheriff Larry Risener was middle-aged, athletic and soft-spoken. Del had known him since he'd been a boy.

"Sheriff."

"Just doing a check. Whopping storm last night. Power and phones are out for most of the county."

"Including here. Any word when we'll have it back?"

"Well." Risener smiled, scratched his cheek. "You know."

"Yeah. I know."

"Saw a compact sedan in a ditch a few miles down the road here. Rental car. Looks like somebody had some trouble in the storm."

"That's right." Del leaned on the doorjamb of the mudroom. "I came along just after it happened. Couldn't call for a tow. Driver bunked here last night. I was about to drive down to Carl's, see what he can do about it."

"All right then. Didn't want to think some tourist was wandering around in the woods somewhere. I can radio Carl's place, give him the location. Save you a trip that way, and he can swing by and let you know what's what."

"I'd appreciate that."

"Okay then. How're you doing? The shoulder and all."

"It's better. Only hurts like a bitch about half the time now."

"Bet. You hear from your folks?"

"Not in about a week."

"You give them my regards when you do," Risener said as he strolled back to his cruiser. "My youngest still prizes those fossils your mother gave him."

"I'll do that." Del waited until the cruiser eased down the lane and out of sight. Then he simply turned, aware Camilla had stepped into the mudroom behind him. "Are you in trouble with the law?"

"No." Surprise at the question had her voice jumping, just a little. "No, of course not," she added firmly.

When he turned those green eyes were sharp, fully focused on her face. "Don't string me along."

She folded her hands, calmed herself. "I haven't broken any laws. I'm not in trouble with or wanted by any authorities. I'm simply traveling, that's all, and prefer not to explain to the police that I don't have any particular destination."

Her voice was steady now, and her gaze clear and level. If she was a liar, Del thought, she was a champ. At the moment it was easier to take her word.

"All right. It'll take Carl a good hour to get to your car and swing by here. Find something to do. I've got work."

"Delaney." She knew she should thank him for taking her word, but part of her was still insulted he'd questioned it. Still, she owed him for what he'd done—and she always paid her debts. "I imagine it's difficult for you to compile your notes and papers one-handed. I have two, and I'd be happy to lend them out for an hour."

He didn't want her underfoot. That was number one. But the fact was, he wasn't getting a hell of a lot done on his own. And if he had his eye on her, she couldn't go around tidying up his papers behind his back. "Can you use a keyboard?"

"Yes."

He frowned at her hands. Soft, he thought. The kind that were accustomed to weekly manicures. He doubted they'd do him much good, but it was frustrating to try to transcribe with only five working fingers.

"All right, just…sit down or something. And don't touch anything," he added as he walked out of the room.

He came back with a laptop computer. "Battery's good for a couple of hours. I've got backups, but we won't need them." He set it down, started to fight to open it.

"I can do it." She brushed him away.

"Don't do anything else," he ordered and walked out again. He came back struggling a bit with a box. He simply snarled when she popped up to take it from him. "I've got it. Damn it."

She inclined her head—regally, he thought. "It's frustrating, I'm sure, to be physically hampered. But stop snapping at me."

When she sat again, folding her hands coolly, he dug into the box and muttered. "You're just going to type, that's it. I don't need any comments, questions or lectures." He dumped a pile of loose papers, clippings, photos and notebooks on the table, pawed through them briefly. "Need to open the document."

She simply sat there, hands folded, mouth firmly shut.

"I thought you could use a keyboard."

"I can. But as you've just ordered me not to ask questions, I'm unable to ask which document you might like me to open, out of which program."

He snarled again, then leaned over her and started hitting keys himself. His nose ended up nearly buried in her hair—which annoyed him. It was soft, shiny, fragrant. Female enough to have the juices churning instinctively. He beetled his eyebrows and concentrated on bringing up the document he wanted.

Without thinking, she turned her head. Her mouth all but brushed his, shocking them both into jerking back. He shot her a fulminating, frustrated glare and stuck his good hand into his pocket.

"That's the one. There."

"Oh." She had to swallow, hard, and fight the urge to clear her throat. She took quiet, calming breaths instead. His eyes were so *green,* she thought.

"You have to page down to the end." He'd nearly stepped forward again to do it himself before he remembered he'd be on top of her again. "I need to pick it up there."

She did so with a casual efficiency that satisfied him. Cautious now, he circled around her for his reading glasses, then plucked from the disordered pile the precise notes he needed.

His eyes, she thought, looked even more green, even more intense, when he wore those horn-rims.

"Interred with the remains are plant materials," he began, then scowled at her. "Are you going to sit there or hit the damn keys?"

She bit back an angry remark—she would *not* sink to his level, and started to type.

"It's probable the plants, such as the intact prickly pear pad which was retrieved, were food offerings buried with the dead. A number of seeds were found in the stomach areas of articulated skeletons."

She typed quickly, falling into the rhythm of his voice. A very nice voice, she thought, when it wasn't snarling and snapping. Almost melodious. He spoke of gourds recovered in another burial, theorizing that the plant specimen may have been grown locally from seeds brought from Central or South America.

He made her see it, she realized. That was his gift. She began to form a picture in her mind of these people who had traveled to the riverbank and made a home. Tended their children, cared for their sick and buried their dead with respect and ceremony in the rich peaty soil.

"Chestnut trees?" She stopped, turned to him, breaking his rhythm with her enthusiasm. "You can tell from pollen samples that there were chestnut trees there nine thousand years ago? But how can you—"

"Look, I'm not teaching a class here." He saw the spark in her eyes wink out, turning them cool and blank. And felt like a total jerk. "Jeez. Okay, there's a good twelve feet of peat, it took eleven thousand years since the last ice age to build up to that point."

He dug through his papers again and came up with photos and sketches. "You take samples—different depths, different samples, and you run tests. It shows the types of plants in the area. Changes in climate."

"How does it show changes in climate?"

"By the types of plants. Cold, warm, cold, warm." He tapped the sketches. "We're talking eons here, so we're talking a lot of climatic variations. Leaves, seeds, pollen fall into the pond, the peat preserves them—it creates an anaerobic atmosphere—shuts out the oxygen," he explained. "No oxygen, no bacterial or fungi growth, slows decay."

"Why would they have buried their dead in a pond?"

"Could've been a religious thing. There's swamp gas, and it'd cause the pond to glow at night. Methane bubbles up, it gives the illusion—if you're into that stuff—that the water breathes. Death stops breath."

Poetic, she thought. "So they might have chosen it to bring breath back to their dead. That's lovely."

"Yeah, or it could've been because without shovels for digging, it was easier to plug a hole in the muck."

"I like the first explanation better." And she smiled at him, beautifully.

"Yeah, well." Since her smile tended to make his throat go dry, he turned away to pour coffee. And was momentarily baffled not to see the pot.

"It's in the other room," she said, reading his expression perfectly. "Would you like me to put on a fresh pot?"

"Yeah, great, fine." He looked down at his watch, then remembered he wasn't wearing one. "What's the time?"

"It's just after eleven."

Alone, he paced the kitchen, then stopped to glance over what had been transcribed. He was forced to admit it was more—a great deal more—than he'd have managed on his own with his injuries.

A couple of weeks at this pace and he could have the articles done—the most irritating of his tasks—while still giving an adequate amount of attention to organizing lab reports and cataloging.

A couple of weeks, he thought, giving his shoulder a testing roll. The doctors had said it would take a couple more weeks for him to have his mobility back. The fact was, they'd said it would be more like four weeks before he'd be able to really pull his own weight again. But in his opinion doctors were always pessimistic.

He should hire a temp typist or something. Probably should. But jeez, he hated having some stranger in his hair. Better to invest in a voice-activated computer. He wondered how long it would take him to get one, set it up and get used to it.

"Coffee'll take a few minutes." Camilla sat back down, placed her fingers over the keys. "Where were we?"

Staring out the kitchen window, he picked up precisely where he left off. Within minutes, he'd forgotten she was there. The quiet click of the keys barely registered as he talked of cabbage palms and cattail roots.

He'd segued into fish and game when the sound of tires interrupted. Puzzled, he pulled off his glasses and frowned at the red tow truck that drove up his lane.

What the hell was Carl doing here?

"Is that the garage?"

He blinked, turned. His mind shifted back, and with it a vague irritation. "Right. Yeah."

Carl was fat as a hippo and wheezed as he levered himself out of the cab of the wrecker. He took off his cap, scratched his widening bald spot, nodded as Del came outside.

"Del."

"Carl."

"How's the folks?"

"Good, last I heard."

"Good." Carl's eyes squinted behind the lenses of amber lensed sunglasses when he spotted Camilla. "That your car down the road a piece, miss?"

"Yes. Were you able to get it out?"

"Not as yet. Took a look at it for you. Got a busted headlight. Wrecked your oil pan. Left front tire's flat as a pancake. Looks to me like you bent the wheel some, too. Gonna have to replace all that before you're back on the road."

"I see. Will you be able to fix it?"

"Yep. Send for the parts once I get it in the shop. Shouldn't take more'n a couple days."

A couple of days! She readjusted her plans to drive on by evening. "Oh. All right."

"Towing, parts, labor, gonna run you about three hundred."

Distress flickered over her face before she could stop it, though she did manage to swallow the sound of it that rose up in her throat. Three hundred was twenty more than she had left in cash.

The interlude, she realized as she gnawed over it, was going to leave her flat broke. She couldn't call the car rental company as she wasn't on their records and that left her no option but to call home for funds. The idea of it made her feel like a failure.

Her silence, and the worried look in her eyes had Carl shifting his feet. "Ah… I can do with a hundred down. You can pay the balance when the work's done."

"I'll just go get the money."

She'd work something out, Camilla promised herself as she went back inside, and upstairs for her wallet. There had to be a way she could sell the watch—or something—within the next day or two. She had enough for a motel, for food until the car was repaired. As long as she was careful.

She'd figure something out in the meantime. She was good at solving problems.

But her stomach was busy sinking as she counted out the hundred dollars. It was, she discovered, lowering to need money. An experience she'd never had before—and, she acknowledged, likely one that was good for her.

A hundred-eighty and some change left, she mused, tucked into a wallet that had cost more than twice that. Let that be a lesson to you, she ordered herself, and went back downstairs.

Del was in the kitchen again, going through more notes.

"I thought I'd ask the tow-truck operator to give me a lift into town."

"He's gone."

"Gone?" She rushed to the window, stared out. "Where?"

"To deal with your car."

"But I haven't paid him yet."

"He put it on my account. Are you going to get that coffee?"

"On your account." Embarrassed pride stiffened her spine. "No. I have the money."

"Good, you can pay me when your car's up and running. I want some damn coffee."

He grabbed a mug and strode off. She marched right after him. "Here, take this."

He ignored her and the money she held out, instead going through the process of taking the pot off the fire, carrying it to the table so he could pour it into the mug, carrying it back again, then picking up the mug.

The woman was quivering with temper, he noted. Which was pretty interesting. He gave her points for being pissed. She wasn't used to being obligated, he decided. Or being in financial straights. There was money somewhere—she was wearing a few grand in that slim, Swiss efficiency on her wrist. But, at the moment, it wasn't in her wallet.

That was a puzzle, but he wasn't going to make it his business to solve it.

He'd felt sorry for her—not a usual reaction in him—when he'd seen all that worry cross her face. And he'd admired her quick control of it. She hadn't fluttered or whined, or used her looks to soften Carl up and cut a better deal.

She'd sucked it up. That he respected.

And it had occurred to him he could give her a hand, and solve one of his own problems without making either of them feel uptight about it.

"I figure you earned about twenty this morning," he told her. "Figuring ten bucks an hour for the work. I'll give you that for the keyboarding, and you can earn off the bed and meals by cleaning this place up, doing the cooking. If Carl says a couple days, you figure four. In four days, you'll have a place to stay and pay off the repair bill."

She stared at him, let it sink in. "You want me to work for you. To…do your housekeeping?"

"Been doing it anyway, haven't you? You get a bunk for four days, I don't lose time with my work, and we part square at the end of it."

She turned away, in what he assumed was embarrassment. He'd have been surprised, and confused, to see she had a huge grin and was fighting off laughter.

Oh, what the media would do with it, Camilla thought as she bit back chuckles. Camilla of Cordina paying for a roof over her head by scrubbing floors, heating up cans of soup and typing up notes on bones and elderberry seeds.

"How the princess spent her summer vacation." She could see the headline now.

She had to squeeze her eyes shut and bite her lip to keep the laughter from tumbling out.

She should refuse, of course. Give him the hundred dollars, beg a ride to town where she could contact her parents for a small loan or pawn the watch.

But, Lord, it was so *delicious.* And so wonderfully out of character. Wasn't that precisely the purpose of this quest?

No televisions, no newspapers with her image on them. Interesting work in a beautiful part of the country she'd never spent time in. Learning things she found far more compelling than anything she'd studied in school and knowing she was making a positive impact solely on her own skills. Not because of who she was, or any obligations or favors—but most importantly because it was her choice.

No, she couldn't possibly walk away from the opportunity that had just fallen into her lap.

"I'm very grateful." Her voice trembled a bit with suppressed humor—which he mistook for the onset of tears.

Nothing could have frightened him more.

"It's a fair deal, that's all. Don't get all sloppy about it."

"A very fair deal." She turned back, eyes shining, and struggled to keep her tone casual and brisk. "Accepted," she added, and held out a hand.

He ignored the hand because he'd added a personal stipulation to the deal. He would not, in any way, shape or form, touch her.

"I'm going to get the generator started, in case we don't get the power back. Clean something up. Just don't touch my stuff."

Camilla waited until she heard the rear doors slam behind him before she sat down and let the gales of laughter roll.

Chapter 4

An hour later, thoroughly appalled with the state of the cabin now that she had given it a thorough assessment, Camilla sailed into the shed. She was armed with a long list.

"You need supplies."

"Hand me that damn wrench."

She picked up the tool and considered herself beyond civilized for not simply bashing him over the head with it. "Your home is an abomination. I'll require cleaning supplies—preferably industrial strength. And if you want a decent meal, I'll need some food to stock the kitchen. You have to go into town."

He battled the bolt into submission, shoved the switch on. And got nothing but a wheezy chuckle out of the generator. "I don't have time to go into town."

"If you want food for your belly and clean sheets on which to sleep, you'll make time."

He used the wrench to beat viciously at the generator,

then gave it three solid kicks. Much too accustomed to the male response to irritating inanimate objects to be surprised, Camilla simply stood where she was, list in hand.

When he'd finished cursing, she angled her head. "I've always wondered why men refer to uncooperative machines with crude female euphemisms."

"Because they fit like a glove." He leaned over, slapped on the switch and grunted with satisfaction as the generator let out a loud belch and began to run.

"Now that you've accomplished that amazing feat, you'll want to clean up before you go fill this list."

Eyes narrowed on her face, he picked up the wrench again, weighed it consideringly in his hand.

The implication wasn't lost on her. She simply stuck out her chin.

He tossed the wrench aside, snatched the list and smeared it with the motor oil on his fingers. "I hate bossy women."

"I can't stand crude men. We'll both just have to live with it, since I'm currently washing your underwear."

The faintest glint of humor flicked into his eyes. "You've got plenty of starch. Just don't use any on my shorts."

They started for the door at the same time, and ended up jammed together. Her hand went automatically to his chest where she felt the surprised kick of his heart match hers.

"You're going to have to keep out of my way," he told her.

"You'll have to watch where you're going, then." She saw, with reluctant excitement, his gaze lower, and linger on her mouth. In response, her lips parted on one quiet and catchy breath.

"You got that right, sister," he muttered, and squeezed out of the door.

"Well." She breathed out, rubbing her finger experimentally over lips that felt just a little too warm. "Well, well."

She was angry, exhausted and energized—in a way she hadn't been in a very long time. Alive, whole, healthy and, she realized, interested. It was something to think about.

Del discovered, very quickly, he didn't care to be an errand boy. Shopping cut deeply into his day, and half the items on her list had him scratching his head in frustration.

What the hell was chervil, and why did it have to be fresh?

What the devil did she need with *two* dozen eggs?

And three gallons of bleach.

Maybe she was going to poison him with it, he mused as he drove back to the cabin. She'd looked mad enough to, behind that cool, queen-to-peasant stare she tended to aim at him.

That was some face she had, he reflected. The kind that kicked a man right in the gut. Then you added on the voice, those legs that seemed to go straight up to her ears, and you had one dangerous female.

He was starting to regret that he'd felt sorry for her.

Still, he knew how to be careful around dangerous packages. And she was, after all, no more than a handy tool for the next few days. So he'd give her a wide berth when they weren't actively working, keep his hands to himself at all times and do his best to think of her as a nonsexual entity.

Then when he pulled up behind the cabin and she came running out, his heart all but stopped. Nonsexual? A tool? The woman was a weapon—and a lethal one at that, he decided.

She was laughing, her face flushed with it as she pulled open the door and began to haul out grocery bags. "The power came back on. I never thought I'd be so delighted with something as basic as a working light switch. Still no phone service, but I'm sure that's next."

He snagged a bag and followed her inside. She walked across the dirt and gravel, he thought, as if she were gliding across the polished marble floor of a ballroom. He decided it had something to do with all that leg. Which he wasn't, of course, paying any attention to. Whatsoever.

"How many people are you planning to feed for the next few days?"

"Oh, don't be cranky." She waved him off and began to unload supplies. "I'll make you a sandwich as soon as these are put away."

She knew how to make a sandwich, he had to give her that. He ate, and ate well, in his now spotless kitchen, his mood improving as he scanned the next batch of notes. His ribs ached a bit, but the discomfort had eased to tolerable with just aspirin.

When he was done, he dictated for another three hours while she transcribed. She interrupted now and then, but her questions didn't bother him as much.

The fact was, they were good questions, the kind that made him think. He did classroom duty from time to time, though it was never his first choice. He was forced to admit that the majority of students professing a desire to make a career in the field didn't have as quick an understanding of the *point* as she did.

He caught himself studying the long line of her neck. The graceful curve and arch of it. Mortified, he turned away, pushed himself back into his notes and forgot her.

She knew he'd been staring, just as she knew he'd switched her off again as easily as a finger flicked a light from on to off.

She found she liked it—all the aspects. His interest, his annoyance with it and the focus that allowed him to dismiss it.

His interest had nothing to do with her family, her blood or her rank. It was the first time in her life she'd been utterly sure of that, and the response inside her was quick and pleased. As to the annoyance she could sense him feeling, that was purely satisfying.

He saw her as a woman, first and last. Not an image, not a title. And that made her feel like a woman. He was attracted to her and didn't want to be. That gave her a lovely edge of control—an essential female control that wasn't weighed down with royal command.

And his focus, well, that attracted *her*. It was a kind of skill she respected, and stemmed from willpower, intellect and passion for his work.

It also challenged her. Though she knew it would be wise to resist that challenge. She was, after all, essentially alone with him—a man she knew little about—and flirting with that focus, trying to undermine it for her own curiosity and satisfaction might have…consequences.

Then again, what was a quest without consequences?

When he paused long enough, she rolled her stiff shoulders, smiled over at him. "Would you mind if we took a break?"

She watched him come back to the present, back to the room, back to her. Felt his gaze, sexy and scholarly behind his reading glasses, slide over her as she rose to stretch.

"I'm not finished," he told her.

"We can pick it up again after dinner, if you like." She kept her smile easy. "I could use a walk before I start cooking. Do you ever walk in the woods, Del?"

There was the faintest hum of invitation in her voice. He

was sure—damn sure—it was deliberate. It packed a hell of a punch. He hated to think what she could do if she took a good, solid shot at a man.

"Go ahead, I've got stuff to do." He picked up more notes, dismissing her. He waited until she'd passed into the mud-room before he called out, "Watch out for snakes."

The hesitation in her stride, the faintest gasp, gave him a great deal of satisfaction.

He woke in the middle of the night with his ribs aching and his mind blurry.

He'd been dreaming of her again, damn it. This time they'd been in the kitchen working on his notes. She'd sat at the keyboard, stupendously naked.

The fantasy was juvenile enough to embarrass him.

The problem with women was they could get to you just by breathing.

He lay there a moment, willing his ribs to settle and his blood to cool.

He'd gotten through the day and the evening, hadn't he, holding on to his stipulation. He'd never touched her, not once. It would've been easy to. A finger trailed down that pretty nape while she'd typed. A brush of his hand when she'd passed him the salt over dinner.

Easy, as easy as grabbing her one-handed, diving in and finding out what that long, mobile mouth tasted like.

But he hadn't. Points for him.

Still, it made him a little nervous that he kept *thinking* about doing it.

And she was flirting with him. He'd ignored, evaded or moved in on flirtations often enough to recognize one. Especially when the woman wasn't being particularly subtle.

He'd had students—or the occasional groupie who hung

around digs—put moves on him. Mostly, in his estimation, because they'd dreamed up some romantic image about the field. He put the blame squarely on Indiana Jones for that. Though those movies had been so damned entertaining he couldn't be sore about it.

He dismissed the flirtations, or fell in with them, depending on the timing, the woman and his mood. But as far as serious relationships went, he'd managed to avoid that boggy complication. The redhead had complication written all over her, so fun and games were out of the question.

He should get her a room in town. Pay for it. Move her out.

Then he thought of the pile of neatly typed pages, and the intensity of his annoyance went way down. She was a miracle worker. Not only did her help mean he didn't need to fight his way through the material on his own, but her questions, her interest and her organizational ability was actually getting him to deliver the best material he'd ever done. Not that he was going to mention that.

He thought of the meal she'd put on the table. He hadn't a clue what she'd done to that humble chicken, but she'd turned it into a feast.

He began to revise his notion that she had a rich, irritated husband or lover stashed somewhere. She was too efficient, too clever in the kitchen to be somebody's spoiled and pampered tootsie.

Which was a good thing as fantasizing about another man's woman was too close to fooling around with another man's woman. And that was on his short list of unbreakable rules.

If he moved her out, he'd be back to square one. If he moved her out, he'd be admitting he couldn't keep his hands off her. If he admitted that, well, where was he?

Giving up, he rose—remembered at the last minute to tug on sweats—and went down the hall to the bathroom. He didn't notice the sparkling tiles and neatly hung fresh towels any more than he'd have noticed soap scum and damp heaps. But the scent caught him, because it was hers.

And it tightened every muscle in his body.

He yanked his pain medication from the cabinet, then shoved it back again. Damn pills made him stupid. He'd rather toss back a handful of over-the-counter stuff and a short, neat whiskey.

He didn't allow himself to so much as glance at her bedroom door, to think—even for an instant—of her lying in bed behind it. A minute later, he realized that fantasy would've been wasted because she wasn't in bed.

He heard her voice, the quiet murmur of it coming from the kitchen. Eyes narrowed, he paused, listened. He couldn't quite make out the words, but the tone was soft, full of affection. It set his teeth on edge.

Who the hell was she talking to? He moved forward and caught the end of her conversation.

"Je t'aime aussi. Bonne nuit."

The quiet click of the phone on the receiver came an instant before he hit the lights.

She stumbled back, bit off a scream and slapped both hands to her mouth. *"Mon Dieu! Vous m'avez fait peur!"* She let out a shaky breath, shook the French out of her head. "You frightened me."

"What are you doing down here in the dark?"

She'd crept down to check the phone, and finding it working, had called home to reassure her family. She kept the lights off and her voice low to avoid exactly what was happening now. Explanations.

"The phone's back on."

"Yeah. Answer the question."

Her shoulders went back, her chin went up. "I didn't realize I was meant to stay in my room like a child after bed-
time," she tossed back. "I'm repaying you for the lodging,
and assumed I was free to make use of the house."

"I don't give a damn if you dance a tango in the moonlight. I want to know why you're sneaking around and whispering on the phone in the dark."

She gave him the truth, and coated it with ice. "I couldn't
sleep. I came down for a drink and checked the phone. When
I discovered it was in order, I made a call. Don't worry, I
reversed the charges. If my mobile worked in this…back-
water, I wouldn't have presumed to use yours. And having
the courtesy to be quiet when another person in the house
was, *presumably,* sleeping isn't sneaking."

It was reasonable. It rang true. So he nodded, slowly.
"Fine. You want to check in with your husband or boyfriend,
go ahead. But don't prowl around like a thief."

Her color bloomed, her eyes went burning gold. "I was
not prowling, and I don't have a husband. If you must know,
I spoke with my mother to reassure her I was well. Is this
inquisition over?"

He hated feeling stupid so he said nothing and stepped
to the cabinet for aspirin.

"I should've known." With an impatient huff, she took
down a glass to fill it with water. "You're only more impossible when you're in pain. Here."

"I don't want water." He moved around her to root at the
bottle of whiskey from the pantry.

"Have the water first, you'll spoil the taste of the whiskey otherwise." She got down another glass, took the bottle from him and poured a tidy three fingers. "I imagine it
should help the discomfort. Is it your shoulder or your ribs?"

"Ribs mostly."

"I suppose they hurt more as they heal. Why don't you sit and I'll make you an ice pack for them."

"I don't need a nurse."

"Stop being such a hardhead." She filled a small plastic bag with ice, then wrapped it in a thin dishcloth. "Sit, drink your whiskey. Tell me about one of your other digs. Something foreign and exotic."

It amused her, pleased her, to hear her mother in her voice, the brisk indulgence of it, the tone she'd used to soothe and distract her children during illness.

"Go away." The order didn't have much punch behind it, and he sat down.

"When I was cleaning I noticed some correspondence to Dr. Caine. I was impressed." She sat, holding the cloth to her cheek and waiting for it to cool. "Where did you study?"

She was wearing a robe, the color of copper. He figured it had to be silk, and from the way it clung, shifted, that she had little to nothing on under it. In defense he closed his eyes and let the whiskey slide down his throat.

"Oxford."

"Now I'm more impressed. Delaney Caine, a doctorate degree from Oxford. How did you know you were an archaeologist?"

It was an odd way to phrase it, he thought. Not how did you become, or when did you decide, but how did you know. And it was exactly right. "I always wanted to know how and why and when. And who. Whenever I'd go on a dig with my parents—"

"Ah, they're archaeologists, too."

"Paleontologists. Dinosaurs." He kept his eyes closed, knowing between will and whiskey the ache would ease. "I liked the digs, but it seemed more exciting to me when they'd dig up something human. Pieces of pottery or tools or weapons. Something that said man walked there."

He hissed a bit through his teeth when the cooled cloth made contact with his ribs.

Poor thing, she thought sympathetically. So angry at the pain. "My brothers went through a fascination with dinosaurs. I think all boys do." She saw the strain go out of his face as the ice numbed the ache. "Were they disappointed, your parents, that you didn't go into their field?"

"Why would they be?" He let himself relax, inch by inch. An owl hooted, long, slow calls from the woods beyond the cabin. Her scent drifted over him like a gentle stroke of hands.

"Oh, tradition, I suppose. It's comforting, isn't it, to have parents who understand—at least try to understand—when you have to test yourself, try your own direction? Some of us wait too long to do so, fearing disapproval or failure."

He was relaxed, she thought, drifting toward sleep. Odd, he looked no less formidable now than he did when he was alert. Maybe it was the bones of his face, or that prickly shadow of beard. Whatever it was, it had a snake of arousal twining through her to look at him, really look at him when he was unaware.

Then his eyes opened, and that interesting face was very close to hers. She nearly eased back with instinctive courtesy, but there was a wariness in those deep green depths. An intriguing awareness that nudged her to test her power.

She stayed close, very close, and lifted a hand to give the rough stubble on his face a testing, and flirtatious, rub. "You need a shave, Dr. Caine."

He could smell her, all fresh and dewy despite the lateness of the hour. Her breath fanned lightly over his skin. And made his mouth water. "Cut it out."

"It'd be tricky to shave one-handed." She trailed a fingertip along his jaw. Down his throat. "I could do it for you in the morning."

"I don't want a shave, and I don't like you touching me."

"Oh, you like me touching you." Surely this lust that was curling around in her belly wasn't all one-sided. "You're just afraid of it. And annoyed that I'm not afraid of you."

He grabbed her wrist with his good hand, and his fingers tightened warningly. "If you're not afraid, you're stupid." Deliberately he raked his gaze over her, an insulting pass down her body and back up again. "We're alone out here, and you've got no place to hide. I may have only one good arm, but if I decided to help myself, you couldn't stop me."

Anger danced up her spine, but there was no fear in it. No one had ever laid hands on her unless she'd allowed it. She didn't intend for that to change. "You're wrong about that. I don't hide, I confront. I'm not weak or helpless."

He tightened his grip on her wrist, fully aware his fingers would likely leave marks. He hoped they did, and she remembered it. For both their sakes. "You're a woman, and I outweigh you by close to a hundred pounds. A lot of men would use that advantage to take a sample of you. Whether you were to their taste or not. I'm more particular, and, sister, you don't appeal to me."

"Really?" Her anger was full-blown now, a state she worked to avoid. When she was angry, overcome with anger, she knew she could be incredibly rash. She did her best to cool down, to take the reins of her temper in hand. "That's fortunate for both of us then."

She eased back, tugged her arm free when his grip on her loosened. She saw something flicker in his eyes—relief or disdain, she wasn't sure. But either way, it fanned the flames again.

"But it's a lie."

She was angry, rash—and, she supposed, incredibly stupid. But the reins of temper slipped, and she fisted both hands in his hair and crushed her mouth to his.

Her first reaction was satisfaction, pure and simple, when she heard his quick, indrawn breath. She went with it, using her lips and tongue to get a good taste of him.

And as that taste filled her, pumped inside her with an unexpected wave of heat, it led to her second reaction.

A slow and slippery meltdown.

She hadn't been prepared for it, not for need to burn through anger, every layer of it, and pull the hair trigger of her own passion. She made a little sound, both surprise and pleasure, and slid into him.

His mouth was hard, his face rough and his hair as thick and soft as mink pelt. She could feel the jackhammer of his heart, and the grip of his hand—this time vised on her nape. His teeth, then his tongue met hers. All she could think was: Give me more.

His reflexes were sluggish. It was the only excuse he could give for not shoving her away before she slid into him. And he was only human. That was the only reason he could find for his hand lifting—not to push her off, but to clamp over her neck, to keep her just where she was.

All over him.

The soft, greedy sounds she made had his blood surging, drove him to fight to deepen the kiss even as it reached depths he wasn't sure he could stand.

He wanted to swallow her whole—one wild, voracious bite. He wanted it, wanted her, more than he wanted his next breath.

He shifted, struggling to wrap his other arm around her,

drag her onto his lap. The sudden careless move had bright, blinding pain smothering passion.

She jerked back. She'd felt his body go rigid, heard him fight to catch his breath, knew she'd hurt him. Concern, apologies nearly fell off her tongue before his vicious glare stopped them.

"Stay the hell away from me." He couldn't pull in any air, and his head swam. He cursed because he knew it had every bit as much to do with his body's reaction to her as it did to the pain.

"Let me help—"

"I said stay the hell away." His chair crashed to the floor as he pushed himself upright. When his vision blurred he nearly swayed, and the weakness only added to his fury. "You want a quick roll, go somewhere else. I'm not in the market."

He strode out of the house, the two doors slamming like bullets at his back.

She was thoroughly ashamed of herself, and had barely slept all night for cringing every time she replayed the scene in her head.

She'd pushed herself on him. All but *forced* herself on him. It meant nothing that she'd been angry and insulted and aroused all at once. Why if a man had behaved as she had, Camilla would have been first in line to condemn him as a brute and a barbarian.

She'd made him kiss her, taking advantage of the situation and her physical advantage. That was unconscionable.

She would have to apologize, and accept whatever payment he wanted for the offense. If that meant booting her out of the house on her ear, he had a perfect right to do so.

She hoped it wouldn't come to that.

It might have been an embarrassingly female cliché, but she stationed herself in the kitchen, only an hour after dawn, and prepared to fix him a lovely breakfast to soften him up.

Of course, she might have to adjust that to lunch, as he hadn't come back into the house until after three in the morning. When she heard him come in, she hadn't started breathing again for ten minutes, half expecting him to burst into her room, haul her out of bed and pitch her out of the window then and there.

Not that he hadn't responded to her advance, she reminded herself as shame continued to prick. He'd all but devoured her like a man starving. And if he hadn't tried to drag her closer and caused himself pain…

Well, she supposed it was best not to think of that.

She had coffee brewed, juice chilling. She'd made batter and filling for apple-cinnamon crêpes from scratch and had a generous slice of country ham waiting. Now if the bear would only lumber out of his cave.

Minutes later she heard the creak overhead that told her he was up and about. She had to wipe suddenly damp palms on her slacks before she turned to heat the griddle for his breakfast.

Because Del was also replaying the scene in his head, he was in the foulest of moods as he showered. Part of him was furious with the woman for putting him in such an impossible position. The other stood back in amazed disgust at his reaction.

He'd had a beautiful woman come on to him in a staggeringly open and avid way. A gorgeous, sexy, unattached woman had grabbed him in the middle of the night and kissed his brains out.

And he'd stormed out of the house in a huff.

What was he, crazy?

Careful, he corrected, annoyed with the internal debate. He had no problem with casual, healthy sex between consenting adults. But if there was a casual bone in Camilla's body, he'd dance a jig naked in the middle of the road to town.

The woman breathed complications.

Besides the fact, he reminded himself as he dressed, he didn't have time for fun and games. He had work to do. And when he did have time, *he* made the damn moves.

Not that it hadn't been…interesting to have that step taken out of his hands, momentarily.

The woman had a mouth like a goddess, he thought. Hot, persuasive and potent.

Better not to think about it. Much better to decide what the hell to do about it. As far as he could see, there were two choices. He could pretend it never happened, or he could fire her, drive her into town and dump her.

The latter, it seemed to him, was the safest bet all around.

He was halfway down the stairs when he smelled coffee. The siren's scent of it weakened his resolve. He could count on the fingers of one hand the number of times in his adult life he'd woken to the aroma of fresh coffee.

Then he caught the scent of grilling meat.

Plays dirty, he noted. Just like a female.

The minute he stepped into the kitchen, she turned, coffee mug in hand. Rather than hand it to him, she set it on the table. She didn't smile, but her eyes met his and stayed level.

"I want to apologize for my behavior."

The tone, judge-sober, threw him off stride. He figured the best move was to keep his mouth shut—and drink the coffee.

"It was," she continued, "completely indefensible. I took

advantage of the situation and abused your hospitality. I couldn't be more sorry for it. You'd be perfectly justified in throwing me out. I hope you won't, but I won't argue if that's what you've decided to do."

Did he think she played dirty? he mused, eyeing her over the rim of his cup as she stood, solemn and patient with ham sizzling at her back. A heavyweight champ wouldn't last a full round with her.

"Let's just forget it."

Relief trickled through her, but she couldn't relax until she'd finished. "That's very generous of you." She shifted to pick up the kitchen fork and turn the meat. "I'd like to tell you I've never done anything like that before."

He thought of the kiss, the smoldering punch of it. "Like what before?"

"Pushed myself on a man." The memory of it had hot color washing into her cheeks, but she continued to cook with a steady hand. "It occurred to me afterward that if the situation had been reversed—if you had pushed yourself on me, particularly when I was incapacitated—"

"I'm not incapacitated." Irritated, he swallowed coffee, then went for more.

"Well…in any case, it occurred to me that it would've been contemptible, perhaps even criminal, so—"

"We locked lips. Beginning and end," he snapped out, growing more and more uncomfortable. "It's not a big damn deal."

She slid her gaze toward him, then away again. The deal, big or otherwise, had kept him out of his own house most of the night. So she *would* finish groveling. "A sexual act of any kind must be mutual or it's harassment. Worst, molestation."

"The day some skinny-assed woman can molest me is the day pigs go into orbit."

"I'm not skinny, assed or otherwise, but to finish. I was angry and I'm attracted to you—God knows why—and both those reactions, as well as the simple curiosity I felt, are my responsibility to control. I appreciate your acceptance of my apology. Now if you'd like to sit down, I'm going to make crêpes."

She stabbed the ham, dumped it on a plate. Before she could turn to the crêpe batter, he spun her around, clamped his hand over her throat. And lifting her to her toes closed his mouth over hers.

The fork she still held clattered to the counter. Her arms fell helplessly to her sides. It was an assault, a glorious one that made her weak-kneed, light-headed and hot-blooded all at once. Even as she started to sway toward him, he gave her a light shove. Stepped back.

"There, that clears the slate," he said, then picking up his coffee again, sat. "What kind of crêpes?"

Chapter 5

The beard irritated him. So did the woman. His ribs were a constant dull ache. As was his libido.

Work helped such nagging and unwelcome distractions. He'd always been able to lose himself in work—in fact he figured anyone who couldn't just wasn't in the right field.

He had to admit she didn't annoy him when she was helping transcribe and organize his notes. The fact was, she was such an enormous help he wondered how the devil he would get anything done when she was gone.

He considered playing on her gratitude and wheedling another couple of weeks out of her.

Then he'd be distracted by something as ridiculous as the way the light hit her hair as she sat at the keyboard. Or the way her eyes took on a glint when she looked over at him with a question or comment.

Then he'd start thinking about her. Who she was, where she was from. Why the hell she was sitting in his kitchen in the first place. She spoke French like a native, cooked like a gift from God. And over it all was a glossy sheen of class.

He hated asking people questions about themselves. Because they invariably answered them, at length. But he had a lot of questions about Camilla.

He began to calculate how he could get some information without seeming to ask the questions.

She was smart, too, he thought as she painstakingly filed and labeled on-site photographs while he pretended to study more notes. Not just educated, but there was plenty of that. If he had to guess, he'd say private schools all the way— and with that whiff of France in her voice, he'd put money on some kind of Swiss finishing school.

In any case, wherever she'd been educated, she was smart enough to let the whole matter of that little sexual snap drop.

She'd simply nodded when he'd said they were even, and had made her fancy breakfast crêpes.

He admired that, the way she'd accepted the tit for tat and had gone back to business as usual.

There was money—or there had been money. Pricey Swiss watch, silk robe. And it had been silk. He could still feel the way it had floated and slithered over his bare skin when she'd wrapped herself around him.

Damn it.

Still, she was no stranger to work. She actually seemed to *like* cooking. It was almost beyond his comprehension. Plus she'd sit at the keyboard for hours without complaint. Her typing was neat and quick, her posture perfect. And her hands as elegant as a queen's.

Breeding, he thought. The woman had breeding. The kind that gave you spine as well as a sense of fair play.

And she had the most incredible mouth.

So how did it all add up?

He caught himself scratching at the beard again, and was struck with inspiration.

"Could use a shave."

He said it casually, waited for her to glance his way. "I'm sorry?"

"A shave," he repeated. "I could use one."

Because she considered it a friendly overture, she smiled. "Can you manage it, or do you want help?"

He frowned a little, to show he was reluctant. "You ever shave a man?"

"No." She pursed her lips, angled her head. "But I've seen my father and my brothers shave. How hard can it be?"

"Brothers?"

"Yes, two." Thoughtful, she stepped to him, bending a bit to study the terrain of his face. A lot of angles, she mused. Dips and planes. There certainly wasn't anything smooth or simple about it, but that only made it challenging. "I don't see why I couldn't do it."

"It's my flesh and blood on the line, sister." Still he lifted a hand, rubbed irritably. "Let's do it."

She took the job seriously. After some debate, she decided the best spot for the event was the front porch. They'd get a little fresh air, and she'd be able to maneuver a full three hundred and sixty degrees around his chair as she couldn't in the tiny upstairs bathroom.

She dragged out a small table, and set up her tools. The wide, shallow bowl filled with hot water. The can of shaving cream, the towels, the razor.

Part of her wished it was a straight rather than a safety razor. It would've been fun to strop it sharp.

When he sat, she tied a towel around his neck. "I could trim your hair while I'm at it."

"Leave the hair alone."

She couldn't blame him. It was a marvelous head of hair, wonderfully streaky and tumbled. In any case her one attempt at cutting hair—her own—had proved she had no hidden talent for it.

"All right, just relax." She covered his face with a warm, damp towel. "I've seen this in movies. I believe it softens the beard."

When he gave a muffled grunt and relaxed, she looked out at the woods. They were so green, so thick, dappled with light and shadows. She could hear birdsong, and caught the quick flash of a cardinal—a red bullet into a green target.

No one was huddled in those shadows waiting for her to make some move that would earn them a fee for a new photograph. There were no stoic guards standing by to protect her.

The peace of it was like a balm.

"It's beautiful out today." Absently she laid a hand on his shoulder. She wanted to share this lovely feeling of freedom with someone. "All blue and green with summer. Hot, but not oppressive. In Virginia, we'd be drenched in humidity by now."

Aha! He knew he'd tagged a touch of the South in her voice. "What's in Virginia?"

"Oh, my family." Some of them, she thought. "Our farm."

As she took the towel away, his eyes—sharp and full of doubt—met hers. "You're telling me you're a farmer's daughter? Give me a break."

"We have a farm." Vaguely irritated, she picked up the shaving cream. Two farms, she thought. One in each of her countries. "My father grows soy beans, corn and so on. And raises both cattle and horses."

"You never hoed a row with those hands, kid."

She lifted a brow as she smoothed on the shaving cream. "There's been a marvelous new invention called a tractor. And yes, I can drive one," she added with some asperity.

"Hard to picture you out on the back forty."

"I don't spend much time with the crops, but I know a turnip from a potato." Brows knitted, she lifted his chin and took the first careful swipe with the razor. "My parents expected their children to be productive and useful, to make a contribution to the world. My sister works with underprivileged children."

"You said you had brothers."

"One sister, two brothers. We are four." She rinsed the razor in the bowl, meticulously scraped off more cream and stubble.

"What do you do, back on the farm?"

"A great many things," she muttered, calculating the angle from jaw to throat.

"Is that what you're running away from? Hey!"

As the nick welled blood, she dabbed at it. "It's just a scratch—which I wouldn't have made if you'd just stop talking. You say nothing for hours at a time, and now you don't shut up."

Amused, and intrigued that he'd apparently hit a nerve—he shrugged his shoulder. "Maybe I'm nervous. I've never had a woman come at me with a sharp implement."

"That is surprising, considering your personality."

"Tagging you as Rebecca of Sunnybrook Farm's surprising, considering yours. If you grew up in Virginia, where's the French pastry part come from?"

Her brows lifted above eyes lit with humor. "French pastry, is it? My mother," she said, ignoring the little twist of guilt that came from not being completely honest. Because of it, she gave him more truth—if not specifics. "We spend part of our time in Europe—and have a small farm there as well. Do this." She drew her top lip over her teeth.

He couldn't stop the grin. "Show me how to do that again?"

"Now he's full of jokes." But she laughed, then stepped between his legs, bent down and slowly shaved the area between his nose and mouth.

He wanted to touch her, to run his hand over some part of her. Any part of her. He wanted, he realized, to kiss her again. Whoever the hell she was.

Her thumb brushed his mouth, held his lip in place, then slid away. But her gaze lingered there before it tracked up to his.

And she saw desire, the dangerous burn of it in his eyes. Felt it stab inside her like the fired edge of a blade.

"Why is this, do you think?" she murmured.

He didn't pretend to misunderstand. He didn't believe in pretense. "I haven't got a clue—other than you being a tasty treat for the eyes."

She nearly smiled at that, and turned to rinse the razor again. "Even attraction should have more. I'm not sure we even like each other very much."

"I don't have anything against you, particularly."

"Why, Delaney, you're so smooth." She laughed because it eased some of the tension inside her. "A woman hasn't a prayer against such poetry, such charm."

"You want poetry, read a book."

"I think I do like you." She considered as she came back to finish the shave. "On some odd level, I enjoy your irascibility."

"Old men are irascible. I'm young yet, so I'm just rude."

"Precisely. But you also have an interesting mind, and I find it attractive. I'm intrigued by your work." She turned his face to the side, eased in close again. "And your passion for it. I came looking for passion—not the sexual sort, but for some emotional—some intellectual passion. How strange that I should find it here, and in old bones and broken pots."

"My field takes more than passion and intellect."

"Yes. Hard work, sacrifice, sweat, perhaps some blood." She angled her head. "If you think I'm a stranger to such things, you're wrong."

"You're not a slacker."

She smiled again. "There now, you've flattered me. My heart pounds."

"And you've got a smart mouth, sister. Maybe, on some odd level, I enjoy your sarcasm."

"That's handy. Why don't you ever use my name?" She stepped back to pick up a fresh towel and wipe the smears of shaving cream left on his face. "It is my name," she said quietly. "Camilla. My mother enjoys flowers, and there were camellias on my father's farm when he took her there for the first time."

"So, you only lied about the last name."

"Yes." Testingly she ran her fingers over his cheeks. "I think I did a fine job, and you have a nice, if complicated face. Better, by far, without the scraggly beard."

She walked to the table, wiped her hands. "I only want a few weeks for myself," she murmured. "A few weeks to *be* myself without restrictions, responsibilities, demands, expectations. Haven't you ever just needed to breathe?"

"Yeah." And something in her tone, something in her eyes—both haunted—told him that, at least, was perfect truth. "Well, there's plenty of air around here." He touched his face, rubbed a hand over his freshly shaved chin. "Your car'll be ready in a couple days. Probably. You can take off then, or you can stay a week or two, and we'll keep things the way they are."

Tears stung her eyes, though she had no idea why. "Maybe a few days longer. Thank you. I'd like to know more about your project. I'd like to know more about you."

"Let's just keep things the way they are. Until they change. Nice shave… Camilla."

She smiled to herself as the screen door slammed behind him.

To demonstrate her gratitude, Camilla did her best not to annoy him. For an entire day and a half. She had the cabin scrubbed to a gleam, his photographs and sketches labeled and filed. The neatly typed pages from his notes and dictation now comprised two thick stacks.

It was time, she decided, for a change in routine.

"You need fresh supplies," she told him.

"I just bought supplies."

"Days ago, and the key word is fresh. You're out of fruit, low on vegetables. And I want lemons. I'll make lemonade. You drink entirely too much coffee."

"Without coffee: coma."

"And you're nearly out of that as well, so unless you'd like to be comatose, we have to go into town for supplies."

For the first time, he spared her a look, taking off his reading glasses to frown at her. "We?"

"Yes. I can check on the status of my car as your Carl only makes mumbling noises over the phone when I call to ask about it." She was already checking the contents of her purse, taking out her sunglasses. "So. We'll go to town."

"I want to finish this section."

"We can finish when we get back. I'm happy to drive if your shoulder's troubling you too much."

In point of fact, his shoulder barely troubled him at all now. He'd put the hours he spent restless and awake in his room at night to good use by carefully exercising it. His ribs were still miserable, but he was about ready to ditch the sling.

"Sure, I'll just let you behind the wheel of my truck since you've proven what a good driver you are."

"I'm a perfectly good driver. If the deer hadn't—"

"Yeah, yeah, well you can forget driving my truck, kid." Since he knew her well enough now to be sure she'd nag and push for the next hour, he decided to save time and aggravation and just go. "I'll drive—but you do the grocery thing."

When he simply stood, frowning, she angled her head. "If you're trying to remember where you put your keys, they're in the ignition of your precious truck, where you left them."

"I knew that," he muttered and started out. "Are we going or not?"

As pleased as if she'd been offered a night on the town, she hurried after him. "Is there a department store? I could use some—"

"Hold it." He stopped short at the back door so that she bumped solidly into him. "No, there's not, and don't get the idea we're going on some spree. You want lemons, we'll get some damn lemons, but you're not dragging me off on some girl safari looking for shoes and earrings and God knows."

She had a small—and perfectly harmless—weakness for earrings. Her mouth moved into something perilously close to a pout. "I merely want some eye cream."

He tugged her sunglasses down her nose, gave her eyes a hard look. "They're fine."

She rolled them at his back as he continued toward the

truck, but she decided not to push the issue. Until they were in town. Now, it was better to distract him.

"I wonder," she began as she hitched herself into the cab of the truck, "if you could tell me how radio-carbon dating works."

"You want a workshop—"

"Yes, yes, take a course. But just a thumbnail explanation. I do better with the transcribing if I have a picture in my head."

His sigh was long-suffering as the truck bumped along the lane toward the main road. "Carbon's in the atmosphere. You got trillions of atoms of carbon to every one atom of radioactive Carbon 14. Plants absorb Carbon 14, animals absorb it by—"

"Eating the plants," she finished, pleased with herself.

He shot her a look. "And other animals. Absorbed, it starts to disintegrate. It gets replenished from the atmosphere or from food. Until whatever's absorbed, it dies. Anyway, in a plant or an animal it gives off about fifteen disintegration rays every minute, and they can be detected by a Geiger counter. The rest is just math. The dead source loses radioactivity at a rate… Why am I talking to myself?"

"What?" She dragged her attention back. "I'm sorry. It's just so beautiful. I missed so much in the storm. It's so green and gorgeous. A bit like Ireland, really, with all those hills."

She caught the glint that could only be sun flashing off water. "And a lake, all the lovely trees. It's all so still and quiet."

"That's why most people live in this part of Vermont. We don't like crowds and noise. You want those, you don't come to the NEK, you go west to Lake Champlain."

"The NEK?"

"Northeast Kingdom."

The name made her smile. So, she thought, she'd slipped away from a principality for a time, and landed in a kingdom. "Have you always lived here?"

"Off and on."

She gave a little cry of delight as they approached a covered bridge. "Oh, it's charming!"

"It gets you over the stream," Del said, but her pleasure was infectious. Sometimes he forgot to look around, to take satisfaction in the pretty piece of the world where he often made his home.

They rattled over the bridge toward the white church spires that rose over the trees. She thought it was like a book, some brilliant and deeply American story. The green roll of hills, the white churches and tidy houses with their tidy lawns. And the town itself was laid out as neatly as a game board with straight streets, a small park and weathered brick buildings tucked in with faded clapboard.

She wanted to stroll those streets, wander the shops, watch the people as they went about their day. Perhaps have lunch in one of the little restaurants. Or better, she thought, stroll about with an ice-cream cone.

Del pulled into a parking lot. "Grocery store," he informed her as he dragged out his wallet. He pushed several bills into her hand. "Get what you need. I'll go check on your car. You've got thirty minutes."

"Oh, but couldn't we—"

"And get some cookies or something," he added along with a meaningful shove.

Eyes narrowed behind her shaded glasses, she climbed down, then stood with her hands on her hips as he pulled out of the lot again. The man was a complete blockhead. Ordering her, pushing her, cutting her off before she completed a sentence. She'd never been treated so rudely, so carelessly in her life.

It was beyond her comprehension why she enjoyed it.

Regardless, she'd be damned if she wouldn't see something of the town before he hauled her back to the cave for another week. Squaring her shoulders, she headed off to explore.

The pristine and practical New England village didn't run to pawnshops, but she did find a lovely jewelry store with a fine selection of estate pieces. And the earrings *were* tempting. Still, she controlled herself and earmarked the shop as a possibility for selling her watch should it become necessary.

She wandered into a drugstore. Though the choices of eye cream didn't include her usual brand, she settled for what she could get. She also picked up some very nice scented candles, a few bags of potpourri.

An antique store proved a treasure trove. It pained her to have to pass up the crystal-and-silver inkwell. It would've made a lovely gift for her uncle Alex—but was beyond her current budget unless she risked the credit card.

Still, she found some interesting old bottles for a reasonable price, and snapped them up. They'd be perfect for wildflowers and twigs, and would perk up the cabin considerably.

The clerk was a woman about Camilla's age, with dark blond hair worn in a sleek ponytail and sharp blue eyes that had noted her customer lingering over the inkwell. She smiled as she wrapped the bottles in protective paper.

"That inkwell's nineteenth century. It's a nice piece for a collector—at a good price."

"Yes, it's lovely. You have a very nice shop."

"We take a lot of pride in it. Visiting the area?"

"Yes."

"If you're staying at one of the registered B & B's, we offer a ten percent discount on purchases over a hundred dollars."

"Oh, well. No…no, I'm not." She glanced back to the desk where the inkwell was displayed. Her uncle's birthday was only three months away. "I wonder, would you take a small deposit to hold it for me?"

The clerk considered, giving Camilla a careful measure. "You could put twenty down. I'll hold it for you for two weeks."

"Thanks." Camilla took the bill from her dwindling supply.

"No problem." The clerk began to write out a receipt for the deposit. "Your name?"

"My… Breen."

"I'll put a hold tag on it for you, Miss Breen. You can come in anytime within the next two weeks with the balance."

Camilla fingered her watch, and a glance at it widened her eyes. "I'm late. Delaney's going to be furious."

"Delaney? Caine?"

"Yes. I was supposed to meet him five minutes ago." Camilla gathered her bags and rushed toward the door.

"Miss! Wait!" The clerk bolted after her. "Your receipt."

"Oh, sorry. He's just so easily annoyed."

"Yes, I know." The woman's eyes danced with a combination of laughter and curiosity. "We went out once or twice."

"Oh. I'm not sure if I should congratulate you or offer my sympathies." So she offered a smile. "I'm working for him, temporarily."

"In the cabin? Then I'll offer you *my* sympathies. Tell him Sarah Lattimer sends her best."

"I will. I have to run or I'll be hiking back to the cabin."

You got that right, Sarah mused as she watched Camilla dash away. Del wasn't a man known for his patience. Still, she sighed a little, remembering how she'd nearly convinced herself she could change him—tame him—when she'd been twenty.

She shook her head at the idea as she walked back to put the hold tag on the inkwell. She wished the pretty red-head plenty of luck. Funny, she thought now, the woman had looked familiar somehow. Like a movie star or celebrity or something.

Sarah shrugged. It would nag at her until she figured out just who Del's new assistant resembled. But she'd get it eventually.

Juggling bags, Camilla made it to the parking lot at a full run. She grimaced when she spotted the truck, then just wrenched open the door and shoved her purchases inside. "Have to pick up a few things," she said gaily. "I'll just be another minute."

Before he could open his mouth—to snarl, she was sure—she was rushing inside the market.

Snagging a cart, she set off toward produce at a smart pace. But the process of selecting fresh fruits and vegetables simply could not be rushed. She bagged lemons, delicately squeezed tomatoes, pursed her lips over the endive.

The supermarket was such a novelty for her, she lingered longer than she intended over fresh seafood, over the baked items. She liked the colors, the scents, the textures. The big bold signs announcing specials, and truly horrible canned music numbers playing over the loud speaker, interrupted only by voices calling for price checks and cleanups.

She shivered in frozen foods, deciding the chances of talking Del into an ice-cream cone now were nil. So she bought the makings for them. Delighted with the variety of choices, she loaded the cart, then wheeled it to checkout.

If she were a housewife, she thought, she would do this every week. It probably wouldn't be nearly as much fun. Just another obligation, she thought, and that was a shame.

She came back to reality with a thud when she moved up in line and saw her own face staring out from the cover of a tabloid.

Princess Camilla's Heartbreak

Why, they had her in grieving seclusion, Camilla saw with growing irritation. Over an aborted romance with a French actor. One she'd never even met! *Imbéciles! Menteurs!* What right did they have to tell lies about her personal life? Wasn't it enough to report every move she made, to use their telephoto lenses to snap pictures of her night and day?

She started to reach for the paper, for the sheer pleasure of ripping it to pieces.

"What the hell are you *doing* in here?" Del demanded.

She jumped like a thief, and instinctively whirled around to block the paper with her body. Fury, which she'd considered a healthy reaction, became a sick trembling in her stomach.

If she was unmasked here, now, it would all be over. People would crowd around her, gawking. The media would be on her scent like hounds on a rabbit.

"I'm…waiting in line to pay."

"What is all this stuff?"

"Food." She worked up a smile as a cold sweat slid down her back.

"For what army?"

She glanced at the cart, winced. "I may have gotten a little carried away. I can put some of it back. Why don't you go outside and—"

"Just get through the damn line." He stepped forward, and certain he'd see the tabloid, she dug in her heels.

"Don't push me again."

"I'm not pushing you, I'm pushing the stupid cart."

When he moved past the newspaper rack without a glance, Camilla nearly went limp.

"Hey, Del, didn't expect to see you back in here so soon." The cashier began ringing up the things Del began pulling out of the cart and dumping on the conveyer belt.

"Neither did I."

The woman, a plump brunette whose name tag identified her as Joyce, winked at Camilla. "Don't let him scare you, honey. Bark's worse than his bite."

"Not so far," Camilla muttered, but was relieved that he was at the wrong angle now to see the grainy photograph of her. Still, she put her sunglasses back on before turning her face toward the cashier. "But he doesn't scare me."

"Glad to hear it. This one's always needed a woman with plenty of spine and sass to stand up to him. Nice to see you finally found one, Del."

"She just works for me."

"Uh-huh." Joyce winked at Camilla again. "You hear from your mom lately?"

"Couple weeks back. She's fine."

"You tell her I said hi—and that I'm keeping my eye on her boy." She rang up the total and had Camilla wincing again.

"I think I might need a little more money."

"Damn expensive lemons." Resigned, Del took what he'd given her, added more bills.

She helped him load the bags into the truck, then sat with her hands folded in her lap. She'd overreacted to the tabloid, she told herself. Still her initial spurt of anger had been liberating. Regardless, she'd recovered well, and a lot more quickly than she might have done just a week or two before.

That meant she was stronger, steadier. Didn't that serve to prove she was doing the right thing?

Now it was time to put that issue away again, and deal with the moment.

"I'm sorry I took so long, but I don't think it's unreasonable for me to want to see something of the town."

"Your car should be ready tomorrow. Maybe the next day seeing as Carl's claiming to be backed-up and overworked. Next time you want to play tourist, do it on your own time."

"Be sure I will. Sarah Lattimer at the antique store said to give you her best. I wonder that anyone so well-spoken and courteous could have ever gone out with you."

"She was young and stupid at the time."

"How fortunate for her that she matured and wised-up."

"You got that right." He caught her soft chuckle. "What's so funny?"

"It's hard to insult you when you agree with me." It was hard to brood about a silly photograph in a trashy newspaper when he was so much more interesting. "I like you."

"That makes you young and stupid, doesn't it?"

She grinned, then amused at both of them leaned over and kissed his cheek. "Apparently."

Chapter 6

I'm having the most wonderful time. It wasn't the plan to stay in one place so long, or to do one thing for any length of time. But it's such a beautiful place, and such an exciting thing to do.

Archaeology is truly fascinating. So much more interesting and layered to me than the history I enjoyed and was taught in school, or the sociology classes I took. More fascinating, I find, than anything I've studied or explored.

Who, where and why? How people lived, married, raised their children, treated their elderly. What they ate, how they cooked it. Their ceremonies and rituals. Oh, so much more. And all of it, society after society, tribe by tribe speaks, doesn't it, to our own?

He knows so much, and so much of what he knows is almost casual to him, in the way a true scholar can be. Not that knowledge itself is casual to him. He seeks it, every day. He wants to know.

I find that passion admirable, enviable. And I find it alluring.

I'm attracted to his mind, to all those complex angles. Working with—all right, for—him is hard and demanding, sometimes physically exhausting. Despite his injuries, the man has astounding stamina. It's impressive the way he can lose himself, hours at a go, in his work.

It's also an absolute thrill for me to do so as well. I've studied bone fragments that are centuries old. Sealed, of course, in plastic.

I wonder how they might feel in my hands. If anyone had told me I'd actually want to handle human bones, even two weeks ago, I'd have thought them mad.

How I wish I could go to the dig—or wet archaeological site—and actually see the work being done there. Though Delaney paints a very clear picture when he speaks of it, it's not the same as seeing it for myself.

This is something I want to see, and do, for myself. I intend to look into classes, and what Delaney somewhat disdainfully refers to as knap-ins (a kind of camping session on sites for amateurs and students) when I'm home again.

I believe I've found an avocation that could become a vocation.

On a personal level, he's not as annoyed by me as he pretends to me. At least not half the time. It's odd and very educational to have someone treat me as he would anyone else—without that filter of manners and respect demanded by rank. Not that I appreciate rudeness, of course, but once you get to know the man, you can see beneath the rough exterior.

He's a genius. And though courtesy is never out of place, the brilliant among us are often less polished.

I find him so attractive. In my life I've never been so

physically drawn to a man. It's exciting on one level, terribly frustrating on another. I was raised in a loving family, one which taught me that sex is not a game, but a joy—and a responsibility—to be shared with someone you care for. Someone you respect, and who affords you those same emotions. My position in the world adds another, complex and cautious layer, to that basic belief. I cannot risk taking a lover casually.

But I want him for a lover. I want to know what it's like to have that fire inside him burn through me. I want to know if mine can match it.

The tabloid in the supermarket reminded me of what I'd nearly let myself forget. What it's like to be watched, constantly. Pursued for an image on newsprint. Speculated about. The fatigue of that, the unease, the discomfort. Gauging how I feel now against how I felt the night I left Washington, I understand I was very close to breaking down in some way. I can look back and remember that hunted feeling, feel the nerves that had begun to dance, always, so very close to the surface.

Much of that is my own fault, I see now, for not giving myself more personal time to—well, decompress, I suppose—since Grand-père died, and everything else.

I'm doing so now, and none too soon.

My time here is, well, out of time, I suppose. I feel it's been well spent. I feel—perhaps renewed is an exaggeration. Refreshed then, and more energized than I have felt in so many months.

Before I leave and take up my duties again, I'll learn all I can about the science of archaeology. Enough that I might, in some way, pursue it myself. I'll learn all I can about Camilla MacGee—separate from Camilla de Cordina.

And I might consider seducing the temperamental Dr. Delaney Caine.

* * *

The cabin smelled like a woodland meadow. Since it was a nice change from the musty gym sock aroma he'd gotten used to before Camilla, it was tough to complain.

And he wasn't running out of socks anymore. Or having to scavenge in the kitchen for a can of something for his dinner. His papers—after a few rounds of shouts and threats—were always exactly as he left them. A good third of his notes were typed, and the articles needed for the trade journals and the site's Web page were nearly finished. And they were good.

The coffee was always fresh, and so were the towels. And so, he thought with some admiration, was Camilla.

Not just the way she looked, or the pithy remarks that she aimed regularly in his direction, but her brain. He hadn't considered just how much a fresh mind could add to his outlook and his angle on the project.

He liked the way she sang in the mornings when she cooked breakfast. And how rosy she looked when she came out of the woods after one of her breaks. Breaks, he recalled, they'd negotiated with some bitterness.

He couldn't say he objected to the candles and bowls of smelly stuff she'd set around the place. He didn't really mind the fancy soaps she'd put out in the bathroom, or coming across her little tubes and pots of creams in his medicine cabinet.

He'd only opened them for a sniff out of curiosity.

He even liked the way she curled up on the sofa in the evening with a glass of wine and grilled him about his work until he gave in and talked about it.

Alone in the kitchen, he did slow curls with a two-pound can of baked beans with his weak arm. It was coming back, he decided. And he was burning that damn sling. His muscles tended to throb at odd times, but he could live with that. Mostly it just felt so good to *move* his arm again. The ribs would take longer—the doctors had warned him about that. And the collarbone would probably trouble him for some time yet.

But he didn't feel so frustratingly helpless now.

Maybe he'd see if Camilla could give him a neck and shoulder massage, just to loosen things up. She had small hands, but they were capable. Besides, it was a good way to get them back on him again. She'd taken his orders to back off just a little more seriously than he discovered he'd wanted.

He paused, set down the can with a little thump. God, he was getting used to her, he realized with some horror. Getting used to having her around, and worse to *wanting* her around.

And that, he was sure, was the beginning of the end.

A man started wanting a woman around, then she expected him to be around. No more coming and going as you pleased, no more heading off to some dig for months on end without a concern about what you left back home.

Scowling, he looked around the kitchen again. Bottles of wildflowers, a bowl of fresh fruit, scrubbed counters and cookies in a glass jar.

The woman had snuck around and made the cabin a home instead of a place. You left a place whenever the hell you wanted. But home—when you left home it was always with a wrench.

When you left a woman, it was with a careless kiss and a wave. When you left *the* woman, he suspected it would rip you to pieces.

She came out of the woods as he thought of her, her face glowing, white wildflowers in her hand. How the devil had she come so close to becoming *the* woman? he asked himself with a spurt of panic.

They hadn't known each other for long. Had they? He ran a hand through his hair as he realized he'd lost track of time. What the hell day was it? How long had she been there? What in God's name was he going to do with himself when she left?

She came in, full of smiles. Well, he could fix that.

"You're late," he snapped at her.

Calmly she glanced at her watch. "No, I'm not. I am, in fact, two minutes early. I had a lovely walk, and fed the ducks who live on the pond." She moved over to the bottle, working her new flowers in with the old. "But it's clouding up. I think it's going to rain."

"I want to finish the section on brain tissue. I can't do if you're out feeding a bunch of ducks."

"Then we'll get started as soon as I pour us some lemonade."

"Don't placate me, sister."

"That would be beyond even my masterly capabilities. What's wrong, Del? Are you hurting?" She turned, the pitcher in her hand, and nearly bobbled it when she focused on him. "Your arm. You've taken off the sling." Quickly she set the pitcher aside and went to him, to run a hand along his arm.

He said nothing because, God help him, he wanted her to touch him.

"I suppose I expected it to be thin and wan. It's not." Her lips pursed as she tested the muscle. "A bit paler than the rest of you, and I imagine it feels odd and weak."

"It's all right. It just needs—ow!" The jolt made his eyes water when she pressed down firmly on his shoulder. "Hey, watch it, Miss de Sade."

"I'm sorry. Still tender?" More gently, she kneaded it. "You're all knotted up."

"So would you be if you'd had one arm strapped against you for the best part of two weeks."

"You're right, of course. Maybe some liniment," she considered. "My mother would rub some on my father when he overdid. And I've helped treat some of the horses that way. I saw some witch hazel upstairs. After dinner, I can put some on your shoulder. Then you'll get a good night's sleep."

He had a feeling having her rub him—anywhere—wasn't going to insure quiet dreams. But he figured it was a good trade-off.

"Laboratory tests proved that the substance found inside the recovered skull was, indeed, human brain tissue. In total, during the three six-month field studies, preserved brain tissue was found in ninety-five of the recovered skulls. Twenty-eight contained complete brains, albeit shrunken to approximately a third of their normal size. The find is completely unique, with significant scientific impact and potential. This will give scientists a never-before possible opportunity to study brain matter, which is more than seven thousand years old, with its hemispheres and convolutions intact. The DNA, the basic human building block, can be cloned from tissue older than any previously available."

"Cloned." Camilla's fingers stopped. "You want to clone one of the tribe."

"We can get into a debate on cloning later. But no, the purpose would be to study—disease, life expectancy, physical and intellectual potential. You can go back to your science fiction novel after we're done."

"They've cloned sheep," Camilla muttered.

He gave her a mild look behind the lenses of his reading

glasses. "That's not my field. DNA research isn't my area. I'm just outlining the potential and import of the find. We have intact human brains, seven millenniums old. People thought with them, reacted with them. Developed language and motor skills. They used those brains to build their village, to hunt their food and prepare it. They used these minds to interact, to raise their children, to find a mate and for survival."

"What about their hearts?"

"What about them?"

"Didn't their hearts tell them how to tend their children—how to make those children in the first place?"

"One doesn't happen without the other, does it?" He took off the dark-framed glasses and tossed them aside. "These people cared for their young and had interpersonal relationships. But procreation is also an instinct—one of the most basic. Without young, there would be no one to care for the old, no replacement for the dead. There'd be no tribe. Man mates for the same reason he eats. He has to."

"That certainly takes the romance out of it."

"Romance is an invention, a tool, like…" He picked up the scarred head of an old, crudely fashioned hammer. "Like this."

"Romance is a human need, like companionship, like music."

"Those are luxuries. To survive we need food, water, shelter. And to insure continued survival, we need to procreate. Man—being man—came up with tools and means to make meeting those needs easier. And often more pleasant. And being man, he devised ways to make a profit from those needs, to compete for them, to steal for them. Even to kill for them."

She enjoyed him like this—enjoyed the casually lecturing

mode when he discussed ideas with her as he might with a bright student. Or perhaps an associate. "That doesn't say much about man," she commented.

"On the contrary." He touched the jaw of a old, bleached-out skull. "It says man himself is a complex, ingenious and constantly evolving invention. He builds and destroys with nearly the same skill and enthusiasm. And is constantly re-making himself."

"So what have you made yourself?" she asked him.

He turned the hammer head over in his hand, then set it down again. "Hungry. When are we going to eat?"

She wasn't giving up on the discussion, but she didn't mind taking the time to think about it while she finished fixing dinner. She slid pasta into boiling water, tossed the salad. Sprinkled herbs on oil for the thick slices of bread.

She poured wine. Lighted candles.

And looking at the cozy kitchen, hearing the rain patter gently on the roof, she realized she had—unwittingly—employed a tool tonight. The scene she'd created was, unquestionably, a romantic one. She'd simply intended to make it attractive and comfortable. Instinct must have kicked in, she decided. Maybe for a certain type of person, particularly when that person was sexually attracted to another—creating romance was instinctive.

She found she liked knowing that about herself. Romance—to her thinking—was warm and generous. It took the other party's comfort and pleasure into account.

It was not, she decided as she drained the pasta, a damn hammer.

"A hammer," she declared to Del when he stepped in, "implies force or a threat."

"What?"

"A hammer," she said again, testily now. "Romance is not a hammer."

"Okay." He reached for a piece of bread and had his hand slapped aside for his trouble.

"Sit down first. Prove you've evolved into a civilized human being. And don't say okay just because you're bored with the subject and want to stuff your face."

"Getting pretty strict around here," he muttered.

"I'm saying that your tribe demonstrated human emotions. Compassion, love—hate certainly, as you did find remains that showed evidence of violent injury or death. Emotions make us human, don't they?" she demanded as she served the salad. "If it was only instinct that drove us, we wouldn't have art, music, even science. We wouldn't have progressed far enough that we'd build a village near a pond, create rituals to share and love enough that we'd bury our child with her toys."

"Okay. I mean okay," he insisted when she narrowed her eyes. He wanted the food in his belly and not dumped on his head. "It's a good point—and you could do an interesting paper on it, I imagine."

She blinked at him. "Really?"

"The field isn't cut-and-dried. It isn't only about facts and artifacts. There has to be room for speculations, for theory. For wonder. Edge over into anthropology and you're dealing with cultures. Out of cultures you get traditions. Traditions stem from necessity, superstition or some facet of emotion."

"Take our tribe." Mollified, she offered him the basket of bread. "How do you know a man didn't woo a woman by bringing her wildflowers, or a cup of fresh elderberries?"

"I don't. But I don't know that he did, either. No evidence either way."

"But don't you think there was a ritual of some sort? Isn't there always? Even with animals there's a mating dance, *oui*? So surely there had to be some courtship procedure."

"Sure." He dipped the bread, grinned at her. "Sometimes it just meant picking up a really big rock and beating some other sap over the head with it. Loser gets the concussion. Winner gets the girl."

"Only because she either had no choice, or more likely, she understood that the man strong enough, passionate enough to smash his rival over the head to win her would protect her and the children they made together from harm."

"Exactly." Pleased with the tidy logic of her mind, he wagged a chunk of bread at her. "Sexual urge to procreation. Procreation to survival."

"In its own very primitive way, that's romantic. However, the remains you've studied to date don't show a high enough percentage of violent injury to support the theory that head bashing was this tribe's usual courtship ritual."

"That's good." Admiring the way she'd spun his example back to prove her point, he gestured with his fork. "And you're right."

"Del, do you think, eventually, there might be a way for me to visit the site?"

He frowned, thoughtfully now, as she served the pasta. "Why?"

"I'd like to see it firsthand."

"Well, you've got six months."

"What do you mean?"

"In six months if the articles and reports I'm putting together don't beat the right drum and shake out a couple million in grants, the site closes."

"Closes? You mean you'd be finished with the dig?"

"Finished?" He scooped up pasta. "Not by a long shot. But the state can't—or won't—allocate more funds. Bureaucrats," he muttered. "Not enough media attention after three seasons to keep them smiling for the cameras and handing over grants. The university's tapped out. There's enough private money for another six months. After that, we're shut down and that's it."

The idea of the site closing was so appalling she couldn't get her mind around it. "That can't be it if you're not done."

"Money talks, sister." And he'd sunk all he could afford of his own into that dark peat.

"Then you'll get more. Anyone who reads your work will want to keep the project going. If not from the incredible archaeological significance of such amazingly rich findings, then for the completely unique scientific opportunities. I could—" She broke off. She was an expert fund-raiser. People paid, and dearly, to see Princess Camilla at a charity function.

Media attention? That was never a problem.

More, she had connections. Her thoughts went instantly to her godmother, the former Christine Hamilton, now the wife of a United States senator from Texas. Both were avid supporters of arts and science.

"You got an extra million or so weighing you down, just pass it my way." Del reached for the wine bottle, stretching his healing shoulder a little too far, a little too fast. And cursed.

She snapped back to the moment. "Be careful, you don't want to overtax yourself. I'm afraid I don't have a million on me." She smiled as she topped off his wineglass. "But I have ideas. I'm very good with ideas. I'll think of something."

"You do that."

She let it go, and he forgot about it.

* * *

When dinner was finished, he vanished. It was a talent of his to disappear when dishes were involved. Camilla was forced to admire it. She couldn't claim the washing up pleased her nearly so much as making the mess in the first place.

Cooking was a kind of art. Washing dishes a mindless chore she'd have been happy to pass along to someone else.

In the cabin, however, she was the someone else.

In any case, she knew he wouldn't come near the back of the house until they were done. It gave her the opportunity to call home.

She kept one eye and one ear on the doorway while the connection to Virginia went through. Her youngest brother, Dorian, answered, and though normally she'd have been delighted to chat, to catch up on family news, to just hear his voice, she was pressed for time.

"I really need to talk to Mama."

"You take off like a gypsy, and now you can't give me the time of day."

"When I get back, I'll bore your ears off with everything I've done. I miss you, Dorian." She laughed quietly. "I never thought I'd actually say that, but I do. I miss all of you."

"But you're having a great time. I can hear it in your voice."

"I am."

"So you're not pining away for the French guy."

She huffed out a breath. Dorian considered teasing a royal duty. "I take back that I miss you. Where's Mama?"

"I'll get her. But I'd better warn you, she's got her hands full keeping Dad from sending out a search-and-rescue. You're going to have to dance double-time to smooth things out with him."

"I know it. I'm sorry, but I'm not a child."

"That's what Mama said. And he said—at the top of his lungs—that you were *his* child. Keep that in mind. Hang on."

She knew he might tease, but Dorian was good as gold. He'd find a way to get their mother on the line without letting her father know.

Where would Mama be now? she wondered, and brought the image of the big, sprawling house in Virginia into her mind. In her sitting room perhaps. No, more likely out in the gardens, enjoying the evening.

Was it raining there, too?

Maybe she was entertaining. But no, Dorian would have said so.

As the silence on the line grew lengthy, Camilla began to fret.

Then she heard her mother's voice. "Camilla, I'm so glad you called. We were just talking about you."

"Is Daddy still very upset?"

"He's…adjusting. Slowly."

"I'm sorry, Mama. I just had to—"

"You don't have to explain to me. I remember what it's like. We just want to know you're safe, and happy."

"I'm both. I told you about the cabin, about Delaney. His work is so important, so interesting to me. Mama…" She reverted to French as English seemed too ordinary to explain her excitement in the project.

"You sound like a scientist," Gabriella laughed.

"I feel like a student. One who can't learn enough fast enough. Tonight I learned something distressing."

She explained about the project deadline as quickly as possible.

"That's difficult. Your professor must be very concerned."

"I'd like to help. I thought perhaps you could use your connections to find out what can be done, how much is needed. I was thinking—could you contact Aunt Christine? I'm good at raising money for causes, but she's even better. Finally I've found something that's really interesting—something that's personally important to me. I just need an idea of the right wallets to open."

"I can make some inquiries. Florida, is it? The Bardville Research Project, Dr. Delaney Caine. Give me a few days."

"Thanks. Thank you, Mama. You will be discreet? I'd just as soon he didn't know right now that Her Serene Highness Gabriella de Cordina had taken an interest in his work. It's so nice just being Camilla, I don't want to take a chance on anyone making the connection. Not just yet."

"Don't worry. The family's leaving for Cordina in a few days, Camilla. I'd hoped you might be ready to go with us."

"Another few weeks. Please. I'll contact you there and make arrangements to fly directly over when I...when I leave here."

"Take care of my baby. We love her."

"She loves you, too. I'll see you soon, Mama. I have so much to tell you."

After she hung up, Camilla hummed as she set the kitchen to rights. In so short a time, she thought, she'd accomplished much of what she'd set out to do. She was content with herself—and that had been something missing the past several months. She'd done ordinary things—too many of which had slipped away from her since adulthood.

And she realized much of that had been her own doing.

When she'd been a child, her parents had made certain she had a normal life, or as normal as possible. They'd done everything they could to keep her and her siblings out of the spotlight. But there had been duties, a gradual escalation of them as she'd grown.

Then the media had focused on her. Cordina's crown jewel, they'd dubbed her. And normality had begun to erode around the edges until the fabric of it was frayed. It had been flattering at first, exciting, even amusing. Then mildly annoying. After nearly a decade of constant attention, of speculative and outright fabricated articles, of being seen as a commodity, never as a human being, it had become smothering.

But now she could breathe again. And she knew she would go back to her life stronger, more capable and less vulnerable to the barrage.

She'd found a passion, and would now find a way to embrace it. This was the balance she'd seen and envied in her mother, in her aunts. Duty was never shirked, but each pursued a life full of interests and richness as a woman. So could she.

So *would* she.

One day she'd go on a dig and be part of a team that *discovered*. That sought knowledge and celebrated it. Let the media come, she thought as she prepared fresh coffee. The attention, while it lasted, would only generate interest in the field. And that meant funding.

It was unthinkable to allow their project to come to a premature end because of money. And it was their project now, she thought with a dreamy sigh. Hers and Delaney's. They shared it as they did the cabin, with each bringing their own stamp, their own mind, their own talents to the whole.

It was…marvelous.

Her excitement and passion might even be responsible for sparking the imagination of a generation of young women, bringing archaeology, the study of past peoples, cultures and customs into fashion.

She stopped, laughing at herself. Never satisfied with little steps, she thought. She always wanted more.

She filled two mugs and carried them into the living area. There he was, sitting on the horrible little sofa, his eyes intense behind his reading glasses, papers scattered over his lap and across the sprung cushions.

What leaped inside her was a wild and wonderful mixture of lust and longing, and, she discovered with a slow, warm sigh, love.

Why she was in love with him, she thought with surprise. Wasn't that...fascinating. Somewhere during this complicated and problematic interlude, she'd slid headlong into love with a bad-tempered, irritable, rough-mannered scientist who was more likely to snarl at her than smile.

He was rude, demanding, easily annoyed, impatient. And brilliant, passionate, reluctantly kind. It was a captivating mix that made him uniquely himself. She wouldn't change a single thing about him.

More, she thought, leaning against the wall to watch him. He had one of the most essential traits she wanted in a friend, and in a lover. He had honor.

They were alone here, yet he'd never tried to take advantage of that. In fact, he rarely touched her even in the most casual way. Though he was attracted—she knew she wasn't wrong about that—his personal code wouldn't allow him to exploit the situation.

Her lips twitched in a smile. That made him, under it all, a gentleman. How he would hate to be termed so.

So, she was in love with an ill-tempered gentleman who wouldn't allow himself to seduce his temporary assistant. That meant it was going to be up to her to seduce him.

The idea, only an interesting fantasy until now, became more intriguing, more exciting now her heart was engaged. Love, she thought, gave her a marvelous advantage.

You're going to have to deal with me now, she decided. And you, Dr. Delaney Caine, don't have a prayer.

She nearly went back to the kitchen to exchange the coffee for wine. But she reasoned the caffeine would be more... stimulating.

The plan of attack should be simple. And subtle.

She walked to him, held out the coffee. "Which area has you snagged?"

"Huh?"

"Which area," she repeated, gesturing toward the scattered papers, "has you snagged?"

"I just need to think it through. Get this damn paperwork done. I need to get back to the site." He rolled his shoulder, testing it. "Into the lab."

She felt the quick hitch in her throat. If he was starting to think about going back, she couldn't afford to be subtle for long.

Because when he went back, she intended to go with him. As his student, his associate. As his lover.

"The work you're doing here is just as important, just as essential. Though I'm sure it's not as rewarding for you."

"I'm not an administrator." He said it as though it were something foul, which made her smile.

"You'll soon be back in the field. You just need a little more time to finish here, and to heal."

He shifted, experimenting by stretching his torso. His ribs sang. An hour on the dig would have him crawling like a baby, he thought in disgust. But the lab...

"Let's get some of this down," he began, and rose too quickly. He had to grit his teeth as his body objected.

"Tell you what." Gently she took the coffee out of his hand. "I'll give you that rubdown first. It should help. You're always more uncomfortable first thing in the morning and after a long day. Let's loosen you up again. Then if you still want to work tonight, we'll work."

"I'm fine."

"You're not. And if you don't take care of yourself, you'll just delay your recovery and your return to the dig." Keeping her voice brisk, she started toward the stairs carrying both mugs. "Come on, we'll just consider it physical therapy."

He hurt, and that irritated him. He could take a pill—which would end up putting him to sleep and wasting work hours. He could put the damn sling back on, which would irritate him more. Or he could give the lubricant a try.

All he had to do was handle her rubbing her hands over him. And a man ought to have enough willpower to deal with that.

Besides, she had the coffee. He *had* to follow her upstairs.

"We can do it down here."

"Easier up here," she called back, smirking. "The sofa's a torture board, and too small in any case. No point in being uncomfortable. Just sit down on your bed. Take your shirt off."

Words, he thought, most men dreamed of hearing.

He wasn't going to think along those lines, he reminded himself. He was going to consider the entire experience a kind of therapeutic medicine.

Chapter 7

She made a quick detour into her own bedroom and dabbed on perfume. Undid another two buttons of her shirt. If the man thought of romance as a tool, she was going in fully equipped.

She gathered the witch hazel, some fresh towels and some of the scented candles.

It was conniving, she admitted, but surely a woman in love was allowed some ploys. Just as, she thought as she stepped into his bedroom and saw every available light blazing, a wary man was allowed to try for some defense.

She found his safety precautions wonderfully sweet. And easily foiled.

"Let's have a look." She circled around the bed where he sat, then instantly lost her calculation in her sympathy. "Oh, Del, you really did a job on yourself, didn't you?"

"It's better."

"I'm sure, but…" The shoulder which had been hidden

behind shirt or sling up till now was visibly swollen still. The bruising was a sickly yellow and green pattern that matched the clouds that ran along his ribs.

She wanted, more than anything else now, to simply nurse him, to ease his hurts.

"I didn't think about the swelling," she murmured, gently touching his shoulder.

"It's nearly gone." He moved his shoulder, as much to test it as to dislodge her hand. He wasn't, he realized, quite ready to have her touch him.

"Regardless. We should've been icing this down." Recalling what had happened before when she'd tried that particularly kind of medical attention had her pulse dancing.

She wanted to nurse him, and soothe. But that wasn't all she wanted, for either of them.

"Well, just relax, and we'll see what we can do about making you more…comfortable."

She turned away, started to arrange and to light the candles.

"What're you doing with those?"

The wariness in his voice had her lips curving. "Haven't you ever heard of aromatherapy? Just get as comfortable as you can, and we'll start on the shoulder first. You never told me how you were hurt."

"I was stupid enough to let some idiot kid drive from the lab. Some people just can't handle a wet road," he added with a bland stare. "He flipped the Jeep."

"Flipped?" Horror for him replaced any need to defend her own driving skills. "My God, you're lucky you weren't killed."

"He walked away with a couple scratches," Del said bitterly. "He's lucky I didn't snap his neck like a twig. This has put me on the DL over three weeks already."

She walked over to turn off lights. "DL?"

"No baseball in your world, sister? Disabled list." He'd just think about baseball—sports were good—or work, or world politics. Anything but the way she looked in candle-light.

"How're you going to see if you turn off the lights?"

"I can see perfectly well. You won't relax with lights shining in your eyes." She wished he had a radio, a stereo system. Something. But they'd just have to cope without it.

She climbed onto the bed behind him, knelt.

The give of the mattress had his stomach muscles fumbling into knots—and his body bracing as if for battle.

"Now don't be stoic," she said. "Tell me if I hurt you. I'd say you're healing remarkably well if it's only been three weeks. And that you've carved through an impressive amount of work while you've been here."

She rubbed the lubricant in her hands to warm it, then began to gently stroke it over the bruises. "I think we can all use a change of routine now and again, to step away from what we've become steeped in so that we can have a clearer vision of the whole picture."

"Maybe." It was true enough that since he'd come back to the cabin he'd been able to look at the project from angles he'd missed or ignored when he'd been in the middle of it. Such as the money problem.

"Don't tense up," she murmured. "Just close your eyes." Her fingers stroked, gently kneaded. "Let your mind drift. Did you play in the woods here as a boy?"

"Sure." Baseball, he was going to think about baseball. How was he supposed to keep a box score in his head when she kept talking in that exotic, sexy voice.

"Swim in the pond? Fish?"

"My mother likes to fish."

"Really?"

Because the image of her, wearing one of her ugly hats, stout boots, ragged shirt and trousers with a pole in her hand made him smile, he closed his eyes.

Surely thinking of your mother was as good a way to control your glands as sports. Probably better.

"She never could get me or my father into it. Bores both of us crazy."

"I'm afraid I have the clichéd girl response to fishing," Camilla confessed. "Fish are slimy and they wriggle. I prefer them sautéed in a nice herbed butter. You don't have brothers, sisters?"

"No."

"Feel this knot here." She discovered one at the base of his neck. "You carry too much worry. That's why you're so irritable."

"I'm not irritable."

"No, you've a sunny disposition. Candy sweet."

"Ow."

"Sorry."

Oh, the man had a back, she thought with sheer delight. Broad and tanned with intriguing scars marring any hope of perfection. A warrior's back, she thought. Strong and male. She wanted, badly, to slide her lips down the length of it, nibble her way along the ridges. But it wasn't quite the time to abandon subtlety.

In any case, she wanted to help, wanted to ease his discomfort. Then jump him.

Distractions, she decided. As much for herself as for him. "The book there, the mystery novel? I've read that author before, but not that book. Is it good?"

"Yeah, it's not bad."

"You have a small selection of books here, but it's quite eclectic."

Okay, they'd talk literature, he decided. Talking was fine. Books instead of baseball. Same thing. "Novels can relax the mind, or stimulate it."

At the moment, he couldn't decide which she was doing to him. Her hands were like heaven. Soft and strong, soothing and arousing. His blood warmed despite his efforts to control it. Yet at the same time the aches and stiffness eased, bit by bit.

The scent of candles, the scent of her, the sound of her voice—low and soft as she spoke of books—relaxed him until his mind, as she'd ordered, began to drift.

He felt the bed give as she changed position, then that smooth glide of her fingers, her palm, on the front of his shoulder. Her breast brushed against his back, pressed cozily against him as she worked.

He wondered, dreamily now, how it would feel in his hand. Firm, small, smooth. How it would taste in his mouth. Warm and sweet and essentially female.

Her free hand moved to his other shoulder, kneading until tension melted away.

The rain pattered quietly on the roof, and the candlelight flickered, warm and red against his closed lids.

"Lie down." It was a murmur in his ear.

"Hmm?"

Her lips curved. Maybe he was a little too relaxed, she thought. She didn't want him nodding off on her. The more she touched him, the more she looked at him, the more she wanted. Desire was a tightening ball in her belly.

"Lie down," she repeated, and resisted—barely—the urge to nip at his earlobe. She'd never in her life craved the taste of flesh so much. "So I can reach."

His eyes blinked open, his mind tried to focus. Lying down wasn't a good idea. He started to say so, but she was already nudging him back. And it felt so good, so damn good to ease down.

"Your ribs are still a mess, aren't they? We'll get to them. I suppose it's lucky you didn't break any."

"Yeah, it was my lucky day." He started to tell her she'd done enough—God, he was so stirred up he could barely keep two thoughts together—but when she leaned over him, stretching out for the bottle she'd set on the bedside table, those pretty breasts blocked his vision. And then even those thoughts scattered like ants.

"It would have been worse." She poured more lubricant into her palms, her eyes on his as she rubbed it warm. "But you're in such good shape. You have a strong, healthy body." She laid her palms on his bruised ribs.

She was counting on the healthy part.

"How old are you, Delaney?"

"Thirty. No, thirty-one." How the hell was he supposed to remember when she was smiling down at him?

"Young. Strong. Healthy. Mmm." She sighed, and it wasn't all calculation as she carefully straddled him. "That's why you've made such a quick recovery."

He didn't feel recovered. He felt weak and stupid. Tension, of a much different sort, was pumping through him. She had her weight on her knees and was, slowly, rhythmically moving in a way that made him imagine her naked, made him imagine himself inside her.

He curled his fingers into fists before he reached up and just grabbed that tight, sexy bottom. "That's enough." His voice was a croak, a thin one. God help him.

She just kept her eyes on his. His had gone dark, gone hot. And his breath had quickened. "I haven't finished."

She trailed fingers down to the waistband of his jeans, up again. And felt his stomach quiver. "There's a lot of you, isn't there? All hard and...tough."

He swore, but he couldn't work any venom into it. "Get off. You're killing me."

"Am I?" She only shifted. It was a very satisfying thing to hear the first time she set out, deliberately, to seduce a man. "I'll just kiss it, make it better."

Her gaze was a gold gleam under her lashes as she lowered her head, hesitated, then slowly rubbed her lips over his chest. She felt his heart kick like a stallion.

"Better?" She trailed her lips up his throat, over his jaw, then drew back, inches only when she heard him bite off a moan.

"This is nuts," he managed to say. "How long do you expect me to keep my hands off you when you're climbing all over me?"

"Who said I expect you to keep them off me?" She closed her teeth lightly over his chin. "Who said I want you to? I think..." She brushed her lips teasingly at the corner of his mouth. "I'm making it very clear what I expect. What I want."

"You're making a mistake."

"Maybe." She felt his hand grip her calf, then run firmly up to her thigh. And triumph lit her eyes. "So what?"

He couldn't come up with an answer, not when his system was screaming for her. He slid his hand over her hip until he could mold that lovely bottom. "You're taking advantage of me."

"I certainly am." She brought her mouth a breath closer. "Do you want me to stop? Now? Or do you want..." She nipped her teeth teasingly into his lower lip, chewed gently, released. "More?"

Either way, it was probably going to kill him. But if he was going to die, he'd damn well die happy. "All or nothing."

"All then," she agreed and closed her mouth over his.

The first flash of heat stole his breath. It bolted through him, a lightning strike of power and electricity. He'd have sworn he felt every circuit in his brain fry.

The hand on her dug in reflexively, then clawed up to her back and fisted in her shirt. Impatient, nearly desperate, he yanked. And the jolt of pain had him swearing.

"No, no, let me. Just let me." She all but crooned it, running her lips over his face, his throat, bringing them back to his for a deep and drowning kiss. "I'm mad for your body."

His groan had nothing to do with pain as she ranged hot kisses over his chest, down to his belly and back again. Her low, humming sounds of approval seemed to vibrate from her and into him until he was trapped somewhere between pleasure and pain.

Aching to touch her he worked his hands between their bodies to find her breasts.

Breath unsteady, she sat back, shivered once. Then that slow female smile spread over her face. Watching him watching her, she reached for the buttons of her shirt, flipping them open one, by one, by one.

"I'm in charge this time," she told him and slowly peeled off the shirt. "You'll just have to lie there and take it."

"You got me up here for this, didn't you?"

She tilted her head, reached behind to unclasp her bra. "Yes. So?"

As the bra fell away and those lovely white breasts spilled out, he let out a long breath. "So. I appreciate it."

"Good. Touch me. I've spent hours at night wanting you to touch me."

He skimmed his fingers over her, saw her eyes cloud. "I wasn't going to let this happen."

"I wasn't going to give you any choice. Oh, *mon dieu, tes mains*." His hands, his wonderful hands, big and strong and rough with calluses.

She was rose-petal soft, just as he'd imagined. He wanted to be gentle, careful with her. But he couldn't stop himself. And when she leaned over, bracing her weight on her arms, to mate her mouth with his again, his hands took more, took greedily.

He shifted, swore again as he fought against the protest of his ribs. "I need... I want..." His weight on her, his mouth on her. And though his side throbbed at the move, he managed to roll over.

"Wait. You'll hurt yourself."

"Shut up, shut up, shut up." Half mad for her, he scraped his teeth over the curve of her shoulder, breathed in her skin like a wolf scenting its mate. And had them both moaning when his mouth roamed down to her breast.

So hot, she thought as sensations battered her. His mouth, his skin, so hot against hers. As if they both raged with fever. His heartbeat was a gallop, and so was hers, as they raced to take more of each other. The weight of him was glorious, sinking her into the thin mattress and making her think of swimming beneath thunderous clouds.

To want and be wanted like this, for only herself, made her giddy and strong. And so very sure.

The thrill of it had her hands combing restlessly through his hair, digging urgently into his back as his muscles bunched.

Beneath them the bed creaked, overhead the rain drummed incessantly on the roof. Candlelight danced in the damp breeze that whispered through the open window.

And denim strained against denim as she arched beneath him. This time she quivered as he fought with the button of her jeans.

So soft, so tasty. And so ready, he thought, breathless as he fought her zipper down. She was already moving against him, those sexy little whimpers sounding in her throat. His mind was full of her, the scent, the shape, the flavor.

And he wanted more.

His fingers slid down, over the thin barrier of cotton, under it to the heat. Her whimpers became moans, and moans became quick, mindless gasps. When she erupted beneath him, he pressed his face to her belly and shuddered with her.

When his mouth roamed lower, she gripped the bedspread and prepared for the next onslaught on her senses. Her mind was hazed, her body a churning mass of needs and pleasures as sensations tumbled over and through her. It was staggering to *feel* so much, and still crave more.

He tugged the jeans over her hips, greedy for the next flash of flesh. And his bad shoulder gave out from under him. She let out a yelp of surprise when he collapsed on her. And while he cursed, violently, she began to laugh.

"It's all right, it's all right. *Merde!* My head's spinning. Let me help. Let me do it."

"Just a damn minute."

"I can't wait a minute." Still laughing, she wriggled, writhed and managed to drag herself free. Half naked and vibrating, she shoved and pulled until he rolled on his back again.

His face was fierce with frustration and temper, and only made her laugh harder.

"When I get my breath back, I'm going to whallop you."

"Yes, yes, I'm terrified." She scooted around on the bed,

then had saliva pooling in his mouth as she wiggled out of the jeans. Temper, he admitted as she slipped off her panties, seemed a waste of time. Under the circumstances.

"Come back here."

"I intend to. But now." She reached over, unbuttoned his jeans. "Let's just get these out of the way. My hands are trembling," she said with a half laugh holding them out. "It's yours that have made them unsteady. I love the way they feel on me."

She yanked and tugged, pulling off jeans and shorts at the same time. Then her gaze roamed over him. Lingered.

"Oh. My." She drew in, then let out, a long breath. "Well, I did say there was a lot of you." Her eyes glinted with a combination of amusement and desire as she slid her body over his. "Put your hands on me again. Del, kiss me again."

"Bossy, aren't you?" But he cupped a hand at her nape and brought her mouth down to his.

She wallowed in the kiss, and it went slow and soft and deep. And when his hands moved over her, she felt the kiss edge over to urgent. "Tell me you want me," she murmured. "Say my name. Say my name and that you want me."

"Camilla." Her name echoed again and again in his head. "I want you."

She shifted, rose over him. And with her pulse pounding, took him inside her.

The first jolt of awareness had her bowing back. Holding, holding to absorb every drop of sensation until her system felt it might burst from the glory of it. His hands slid up her, closed over her breasts. Pressing her hands to his, she began to move. To rock. To push them both toward madness.

She was beautiful. He didn't know how to tell her. Slim and white with that bloom of rose under the milk of her skin. Her hair was like a sleek cap of gold-shot fire. And the candlelight flickered, gold on gold, in eyes blurred with pleasure.

He couldn't breathe without breathing her.

He watched, unspeakably aroused, as she crested to another peak. And that long, lovely body pressed against his sparking sensation after sensation.

He wanted his arms around her, wanted to wrap them around her like chains. But he was pinned by his own injuries and the relentless demands of her body.

He fought to cling to reason another minute. Then one more. But his system screamed for the grand insanity of release. And his body plunged toward it, through it, as her head fell back on a low cry of triumph.

A cat, licking the last drop of a quart of cream from her whiskers, could not have felt more self-satisfied. That was Camilla's thought as she basked in the afterglow of lovemaking.

Everything about him, she decided, was completely delicious.

She wished she could stretch her body over his and just wallow. But he was lying so still, he might have been a dead man but for the regular sound of his breath.

She settled for slithering over to his good side and pressing a kiss on his shoulder. "Did I hurt you?"

He hurt, literally, everywhere. His bruises were throbbing like a nest of demons dancing under his skin. At the moment, pain and gratification were so mixed, he wasn't certain he'd ever be able to tell the difference. But he only grunted.

Arching eyebrows, she lifted herself on an elbow and stared down at his face. She should've helped him shave again, she mused. Though there'd been something oddly erotic about having that stubble rub over her naked skin.

He opened his eyes. "What?"

"You're trying to be annoyed this happened. It won't work."

Later, he decided, he'd think about if he were amused or uneasy that the woman read him so well. "Why not? I'm good at being annoyed."

"Yes, you should get an award. But you're going to want me again as soon as you've recovered, so you won't be able to be annoyed about it. Defeats the purpose."

"Awfully damn sure of yourself, aren't you?"

"About some things." She leaned down and kissed him. "About this."

"Well, it so happens, you're wrong, smart mouth." Because she was frowning at him, she didn't see the direction of his hand until it closed, possessively, over her breast. "I already want you again, and I might never recover from round one."

"I think you will. But I'm sorry you're hurting. I think I'll go down and make you an ice pack."

"I think you should settle down and be quiet for five minutes." To help her out, he pushed her elbow out from under her so her head bounced on his good shoulder.

"You have a body like a rock," she muttered.

"Don't try to get me going again, sister. I'm going to sleep for a half hour."

"Just let me—"

"Shh!" This time he solved the problem by wrapping an arm around her, and clamping a hand over her mouth.

She narrowed her eyes, considered biting. Before she could decide, his fingers went lax, his breathing evened out.

She saw, to her astonishment, that he was as good as his word. He was, in ten seconds flat, sound asleep.

Thirty minutes later, shortly after she'd drifted from consternation into sleep herself, he woke her with a mind-numbing kiss. She shot to the surface, floundered there, then was dragged under again.

Later, when she lay sprawled on the bed, feeling dazed and used and gloriously ravished, he rolled over onto his good side, muttered something about blowing out the damn candles, and went instantly back to sleep.

For a long time after, Camilla stared up at the ceiling, grinning foolishly. She'd found another passion, she realized, and his name was Delaney Caine. The man she was going to marry, whether he liked it or not.

She was, as always, up before him in the morning. Routinely she brewed coffee, then decided to take the first cup with her on a walk to the pond. She felt Del deserved to sleep in.

They would, of course, have to juggle their time between Vermont, digs, Virginia and Cordina. It was going to make for a full, busy and, she thought, very rich life.

He'd like her family, and they him. After they got to know each other, she thought, nibbling on her lip.

She didn't suppose he'd care for the protocol and formality demanded by her duties to Cordina as a princess and niece to the king. But surely he could adjust there. Marriage was, after all, give and take.

Naturally she was going to have to convince him he wanted to marry her first. And before that she'd have to convince him he was in love with her.

He *had* to be in love with her. She couldn't have all this

feeling inside her for someone who didn't return at least a part of it.

She wandered through the woods, watching the early sun slant quivering rays through the boughs. For now, she reminded herself, she would simply appreciate the moment. This time with him, and with herself, without a past or future. Time to enjoy the discoveries, the courtship and romance.

Just because she'd fallen in love quickly didn't obligate him to rush. And it didn't mean she couldn't drift a bit and savor the sensation of being a woman in love.

When she reached the pond, she sat on a stump. She'd have to see that they found a nice, weathered old bench to put here, she thought. And maybe she'd sink some containers of water lilies along the edge of the water.

Small changes, subtle ones, she mused. Nothing major. Just as she didn't intend to try to change anything vital and elemental where Del was concerned.

She'd put her mark on the cabin, hadn't she, while respecting its basic personality and charm. She would hardly afford the man less respect than she did his home.

No, she liked him the way he was. Her lips curved as she lifted the coffee cup. Just exactly as he was.

When they were both more accustomed to this new stage of their relationship, she'd find a way to tell him about her birthright. In another week, she decided. Surely she was entitled to one more week.

She'd have to find the right way to present things. She could start with her father, she mused. Casually mentioning that he'd once been a cop, and had gone into private security, buying the land in Virginia because he'd wanted to farm. How her paternal and maternal grandfathers had been friends. That was why, when her mother was in trouble, her grandfather had reached out to the son of his old friend for help.

A bit confusing, Camilla supposed, but it was a good start. Then she could say something like—oh, did I mention my mother's from Cordina?

That should, hopefully, open the door a bit wider. With any luck Del would comment, or have some minor question, so she could slide into a casual mention that her uncle, her mother's brother, was His Royal Highness Alexander de Cordina.

He'd probably laugh at that, say something like: *Sure, sister, and you're the queen of the May.*

She could laugh back, treating it all very lightly. *No, no, just a mere princess on a short, stolen holiday.*

And that, she decided, would never work.

She cursed in frustration, and in French, and propped her chin on her fist.

"You come all the way out here to swear at the ducks."

She yelped, spilling coffee onto the back of her hand. She sprang up and whirled to face Del. "I like it better when you clumped around like an elephant."

And he'd liked it better when he hadn't kept thinking how very beautiful she was.

He'd woken reaching for her. It seemed to him if the woman was going to slip into his bed, the least she could do was stay there. Then he'd panicked because she hadn't been in the house. The thought of her gone had sent him out in a rib-jarring run until he'd calmed himself down.

Now it was worse, a hundred times worse, because she wasn't gone. She was standing there, the sun and water at her back, looking like something out of a storybook.

The light played over that sleek cap of hair like jewels in a crown. Her eyes were more gold than brown, and seemed impossibly rich against the cool, clear skin. She had a half smile on her mouth—that long, lovely mouth.

He wanted, as he'd wanted the night before, to wrap his arms around her. To hold her exactly as she was.

And that was crazy.

"I didn't smell any breakfast."

"Because I haven't started it yet. I thought you'd sleep awhile longer."

"We said we'd start early today."

"So we did." Now she smiled fully. "I wasn't sure that still held, after last night." Since he wasn't coming to her, she stepped to him. Lifted a hand to brush at his hair. "How do you feel?"

"I'm okay. Listen, about last night…"

"Yes?" She rose on her toes, touched her lips lightly to his. And wound his stomach muscles into knots.

"We didn't lay out any of the… Look, there are no strings here."

A little bubble of temper rose to her throat, but she swallowed it. "Did I try to tie any on you while you slept?"

"I'm not saying—" He hated being made to feel defensive. "I just want us to be clear, since we didn't get into any of it last night. We enjoy each other, we'll keep it simple, and when it's over it's done."

"That's very clear." It would be undignified to strike him, and she didn't believe in resorting to physical violence. Particularly against the mentally deficient. Instead she smiled easily. "Then there's nothing to worry about, is there?"

With her expression pleasant, even patient, she ran her hands up his chest, lightly over his shoulders and into his hair. And fixed her mouth on his in a long, smoldering kiss.

She waited for his hand to fist in the back of her shirt,

then nimbly stepped away and left him vibrating. "I'll fix omelets, then we'll get to work."

Her eyes sparked with temper and challenge as she started up the path. And smiled in the friendliest of manners as she turned, held out her hand.

Baboon, she thought—with some affection—as he took her hand to walk back to the cabin. You're in for one hell of a fight.

Chapter 8

They had a week of relative peace. Camilla decided peace would always be relative when Delaney was involved. His grumpiness was just one of the things about him she'd come to count on. In fact, it was part of his charm.

She raided his books on archaeology. Though he muttered about her messing with his things, she knew he was pleased she had a sincere interest in the field.

When she asked questions, he answered them—and in more and more detail. It became routine for them to discuss what she had read. Even for him to suggest, offhandedly, another book or section she might want to study.

When he gave her a small Acheulean hand ax from his collection, she treasured the crude, ancient tool more than diamonds.

It was more than a gift, she thought. Much more than a token. It was, to her mind, a symbol.

He hardly complained at all about driving her back into

town to pick up her car. And he took it for granted that whatever her plans had been before, mobile or not, she was staying awhile.

They were, Camilla thought, making progress.

She'd managed to peel a layer or two away as well. She learned his father was English, also Oxford educated, and had met his mother, an American, on a dig the senior Dr. Caine had headed in Montana.

So he'd spent some of his childhood in England, some in Vermont, and the bulk of it in trailers and tents on various sites all over the world.

The hand ax he'd given her was from Kent, and one he'd unearthed when he'd been a boy. It made the gift doubly precious to her.

He could read Sanskrit and Greek, and had once been bitten by a coral snake.

The scar just beneath his left shoulder blade was from a knife wielded by a drunk in a bar in Cairo.

However foolish it was, Camilla found all of this fabulously romantic.

She drove into town to mail off the first of his reports and correspondence. *Their* reports, she corrected, smugly. She'd contributed more than typing skills and he'd managed to indicate just that with a few approving grunts when she'd suggested a change or another angle of approach.

They made a good team.

When they made love, it seemed there was nothing and no one in the world but the two of them. Past, future were distant and irrelevant in that intense and eager present. She knew by the way he looked at her when they joined, the way his eyes would stay so vivid on hers, that it was the same for him.

None of the men who had touched her life had brought

this kind of impact. To her heart, her body, her mind. She hoped—needed to know—that she brought the same to him.

No strings, she thought with a quick snort. Typical. If he wanted no strings why had he begun to take walks with her in the woods? Why did he answer patiently—well, patiently for him—when she asked questions?

Why did she sometimes catch him looking at her the way he did? So intense and direct, as if she were a puzzle he was trying to figure out?

And why did he, at the oddest moments, simply lean over and capture her mouth in a kiss that sizzled her brain?

The man was in love with her, and that was that. He was just too boneheaded to realize it. Or at least to admit it.

She'd give him a little more time, then she'd tell him she was in love with him. When he got used to the idea, she'd explain about the other part of her life.

It all seemed so reasonable as she ran her errands. Her mood was mellow when she strolled into the antique shop. She would try Sarah first regarding the watch, she decided. It was mortifying to be so low on cash, and have Del hand her money every time something was needed for the cabin.

Besides, if she could pay her way a bit more, she could fairly demand that he pull more weight on domestic chores. It was time he washed a few dishes.

"Good morning." She beamed a smile at Sarah as she wound her way through the antiques.

Sarah turned over the magazine she'd been paging through. "Good morning, ah… Miss Breen."

"I noticed you have a selection of secondhand jewelry and watches."

"Yes." Sarah answered cautiously as she studied Camilla's face.

"I wonder if you'd be interested in this." Camilla took off her watch, held it out.

"It's lovely. Um…" Hesitantly Sarah turned the watch over. She ran her fingers over the smooth gold, watched the tiny diamonds wink. "It's not the sort of thing we usually…"

She trailed off, then simply stared at Camilla.

"It's all right. I thought I'd see if you might be interested in buying it. I'll try the jeweler."

"You are her." Sarah barely breathed it, her eyes wide and dazzled.

There was a hard clutching in Camilla's throat, but her face remained perfectly calm. "I beg your pardon?"

"I thought…when you were in the other day… I knew you looked like somebody."

"Everyone looks like someone." With a steady hand, Camilla reached for her watch. "Thank you anyway."

"Princess Camilla." Sarah pressed her fingertips to her lips. "I can't believe it. Princess Camilla, in my shop. You're right here. And, and here!" Triumphantly now, she flipped the magazine over.

And there, Camilla saw with a sinking heart, was her own face being touted as one of the most beautiful in the world.

"You cut your hair. All that fabulous hair."

"Yes, well." Resigned, Camilla sighed. "It was time for a change."

"You look wonderful. Even better than—" Catching herself, Sarah paled. "Oh. Excuse me. Um. Your Highness." She dipped in a quick curtsy that had her blond tail of hair bouncing.

"Don't. Please." Struggling to smile, Camilla glanced toward the door and prayed no other customers would come

in. "I'm traveling very quietly at the moment. I'd really prefer keeping it that way."

"I taped that documentary on the Royal Family. After
you were in last week, I kept thinking and thinking, and
then it hit me. I watched it again. But I thought I had to be
wrong. Cordina's Crown Jewel doesn't just drop in to my
store for old bottles. But here you are."

"Yes, here I am. Sarah—"

"That Del." Overwhelmed Sarah babbled on. "I know
you have to pry news out of him with a crowbar, but this is
taking it too far. He's got royalty staying at his cabin, and
he doesn't say a word."

"He doesn't know. And I'd prefer to keep things that way
as well, at least until… Oh, Sarah."

Having a princess in her shop was one thing, having one
who looked so miserably distressed was another. "Golly."
Biting her lip, Sarah hurried around the counter, but stopped
short of taking Camilla's arm. She didn't think it was done.
"Would you like something to drink, Your Highness?"

"Yes. Yes, thank you, I would."

"I've got, jeez, I'm so flustered. I have some iced tea in
my office."

"That's very kind of you."

"It's nothing. Just let me, boy… I'll put the Closed sign
on."

She hurried to the door and back again, then wrung her
hands and couldn't stop herself from doing another curtsy.
"Behind the counter. It's not much."

"I'd love something cool." She followed Sarah into the little office and took a seat on a swivel chair while Sarah fumbled with the door of a small refrigerator. "Please don't be
nervous. I'm no different than I was the first time I came in."

"I beg your pardon, Your Highness, but you are. Of course you are."

"You needn't address me by my title," Camilla said wearily. "Madam or ma'am is sufficient, and in this case, I'd prefer you just use my name."

"I don't think I can. You see I've read about you and your family since I was a kid. We're almost the same age, and I used to imagine myself living in a palace, wearing all those beautiful clothes. Being a princess. I guess most little girls do."

She turned back to Camilla, eyes shining. "Is it wonderful?"

"It can be. Sarah, I have a great favor to ask you."

"Anything. Anything at all."

"Would you not tell anyone?"

Sarah blinked. "Anyone? At all?"

"Just for a little while. Please. Sarah, it can be wonderful being a princess, but there were times, you see, when I was a little girl, that I dreamed of being just that. Just an ordinary girl. I want time now to live that dream."

"Really?" It sounded beautifully romantic. "I guess we always want what we don't have." She handed Camilla a glass of iced tea. "I won't tell anyone. It'll kill me," she admitted with a wry laugh. "But I won't. Could you, would you mind, ah, madam, signing my magazine?"

"I'd be happy to. Thank you very much."

"You're nicer than I thought you'd be. I always imagined princesses would be, well, snobby."

"Oh, we can be." Camilla smiled, sipped. "Depending."

"Maybe, but, excuse me, but you seem so…normal."

The smile warmed, as did her eyes. "That's the nicest thing you could say to me."

"Classier of course. I noticed that right off, too, but…" Sarah's eyes popped wide again. "Del doesn't *know?*"

Guilt circled, nibbled at the back of her neck. "It hasn't come up."

"It's just like him. Oblivious." Sarah threw up her hands. "The man's oblivious. When we were dating, I think he forgot my name half the time. And forget noticing the color of my eyes. Used to make me so mad. Then he'd smile at me, or say something to make me laugh, and I wouldn't mind so much."

"I know what you mean."

"He's so smart about some things, and so lame about others." She picked up her own glass, then nearly bobbled it when she caught the dreamy expression on Camilla's face. "Holy cow. Are you in love with him?"

"Yes, I am. And I need a little more time to convince him he likes the idea."

It was just like a movie, Sarah thought. "That's nice. Really nice. And it's perfect, really, when you think about it."

"It is for me." Camilla admitted, then rose. "I'm in your debt, Sarah, and I won't forget it." When she held out a hand, Sarah quickly wiped her own on her slacks before taking it.

"I'm glad to help."

"I'll come in and see you again before I leave," Camilla promised as she started back into the shop.

When she picked up her watch from the counter, Sarah bit her lip again. "Your Highness, ma'am, do you really want to sell that watch?"

"Yes, actually. I'm embarrassingly short of liquid funds, just now."

"I can't give you what it's worth, not even close. But I could… I could lend you five hundred. And, well, you could have the inkwell you liked so much."

Camilla looked over at her. The woman, she thought, was nervous, intimidated and confused. But it didn't stop her from wanting to help. Another gift, Camilla thought, she would treasure.

"When I started out on this quest of mine, I wanted to discover... To find parts of myself as well as see... I'm not sure what now—maybe just things from a different perspective. It's such a wonderful bonus to have found a friend. Take the watch. We'll consider it a trade, between friends."

Del walked out on the front porch and stared at the rutted lane. Again. How long did it take to run a few errands? That was the trouble with women. They turned a couple errands into some sort of pilgrimage.

He wanted his lunch, and a fresh pot of coffee, and to answer the half-dozen emails that had come through his laptop that morning.

All of which, he was forced to admit he could handle for himself. Had always handled for himself.

What he wanted, damn it, was her.

His life, he thought jamming his hands into his pockets, was completely screwed. She'd messed everything up, scattered his focus, ruined his routine.

He should've left her stranded in the rain that night. Then everything would be the way it had been before. He wouldn't have some woman cluttering up his space. Cluttering up his mind.

Who the hell was she? There were secrets tucked inside that sharp, complicated brain of hers. If she was in trouble, why didn't she just tell him, so he could deal with it?

He needed for her to tell him, to confide in him, to depend on him to help her.

And when the hell had he started seeing himself as some

knight on a white charger? It was ridiculous, totally out of character.

But he wanted to fix whatever was wrong. More, he realized, much more, he needed her to trust him enough to tell him. Trust him enough to fix it.

Because he'd tripped over his own unspoken rule and fallen flat on his face in love with her.

And he didn't much care for the way it felt, he mused, rubbing a hand over his heart. It was a lot more uncomfortable than a few bruised ribs. And, he feared, a lot more permanent.

He'd had to go and say no strings, hadn't he? Of course, she'd had no problem with that, he thought now. Bitterly. That was just fine and dandy with her.

Well, if he was going to have to adjust, then so was she.

Besides, no strings didn't mean no faith, did it? If she didn't believe in him enough to even tell him her full name, where were they?

He paced into the house, then back out again.

Maybe he should go check on her. She'd been gone nearly two hours. She'd already had one accident, which meant she could easily have another. She might be sprawled over the wheel of her car, bleeding. Or…

Just as he was working himself into a fine state of agitation, he heard the sound of her engine. Disgusted with himself, he slipped back into the house before she could catch him keeping an eye out for her.

He circled the living room twice, then paused and considered. Adjustments.

Romance.

That was something she appeared to believe was vital in any culture. Cultures were made up of relationships, rituals and romance. Maybe he should try a small foray into that and see where it got him.

He strolled into the kitchen as she set a bag of groceries on the table. "I have your receipts for the overnight mail I sent," she told him.

"Good." Since he wanted to anyway, he brushed a hand over her hair.

She gave him an absent smile, and turned away to put a quart of milk in the refrigerator. "There were some letters in your post office box." Frowning, she rubbed at her temple where a tension headache nagged. "I must have left them in the car."

"No problem." He leaned down to sniff the side of her neck. "You smell great."

"I what? Oh." She patted his shoulder, reached for the bag of new potatoes she'd bought for dinner. "Thank you."

Determined to make an impression he dug a little deeper. What was it women always…ah! "Have you lost weight?" he asked, feeling truly inspired.

"I doubt it. Probably gained a couple if anything." She took coffee out of the cupboard and prepared to brew a fresh pot.

Behind her back, Del narrowed his eyes. Since words weren't getting him anywhere, he'd move straight to deeds.

He scooped her off her feet and started out of the kitchen.

"What are you doing?"

"Taking you to bed."

"Well, really. You might ask—and I haven't finished putting the groceries away."

Del paused at the bottom of the steps and stopped her mouth with his. "In certain cultures," he said when he eased back, "women indicate their desire for intimacy by stocking the pantry. I'm merely picking up on traditional signals."

Amusement nudged at the gnawing worry inside her. "What cultures?" she demanded as he continued up the steps.

"Mine. It's a new tradition."

"That's so cute." She nuzzled at the side of his throat. "I think you missed me."

"Missed you? Did you go somewhere?" When she huffed out a breath, he tossed her on the bed. When she bounced, he rolled his shoulder. "Got a twinge from hauling you up. Maybe you have gained a couple pounds."

She shoved herself up on her elbows. "Oh, really?"

"That's okay. We'll work it off." And he dived on her.

Her first reaction was laughter. Playfulness wasn't his usual style, and it caught her off guard. As he rolled her over the bed, she forgot to be worried.

"You're heavy." She shoved at him. "And you haven't shaved. You have your boots on my clean linens."

"Nag, nag, nag," he said, and dragging her hands over her head, took her mouth with his.

He felt her pulse jump, then race, and her hands go limp in his. Her body gloriously pliant.

He skimmed his lips over her jaw. "You were saying?"

"Shut up and kiss me."

He cuffed her wrists with one hand, used the other to unbutton her shirt. "So, are you indicating your desire for intimacy?" He trailed a fingertip down the center of her body, toyed with the hook of her slacks as he watched her face. "Just want to get my signals straight."

Her breath was already backing up in her lungs. "Your pantry's been stocked since I got here, hasn't it?"

"That's a good point." He lowered the zipper, brushing his knuckles over the exposed skin. "Had the hots for me all along, haven't you?"

"If you're going to be arrogant—"

"Maybe you were hoping I'd come into your room one night," he continued, and traced the dip between her center and her thigh. "And do this."

"I never..." Her hips arched, her breath hissed out as he cupped her. "Lord. Del."

"Let me show you what I thought about doing."

Keeping her hands pinned, he touched her, unerringly shooting her up into an intense climax, muffling her shocked cry with his mouth as her body bucked. When her breath sobbed, he closed his teeth over her breast, torturing the sensitized point through the cotton of her bra.

He nudged the straps down, nibbled his way over the slope of her shoulders, almost delicately, while his hand roamed, exploited and plundered.

She went wet and wild beneath him. Unable to find her balance, she shuddered, then spiked, then floated down again only to have him fling her ruthlessly over the edge one more time. Her hands strained against his grip. And the helplessness added a layer of panicked excitement over shattered senses.

Her body was molten, and she trembled from the heat that slathered her skin and burned in the blood. Still she arched to him, desperate for more.

She heard his voice, the words thick and soft.

"I'll owe you for this," he said and snapped the bra in two with one rough tug.

Then his mouth, his teeth, his tongue, found flesh. The moan wrenched from her gut as her system erupted.

"Let me go. Let go of my hands. I need to touch you."

"Not yet, not yet." It would end too soon if she touched him now. He hadn't known he could arouse himself to a frenzy just by arousing her. He wanted her weak and wrecked and wailing.

And he wanted to take, take, take.

When he felt her go fluid beneath him, when he felt release pour through her and leave her lax, it still wasn't enough.

He tore the panties away, feeling a dark satisfaction at hearing the delicate fabric rip. Then he drove her back to madness with his mouth.

Finally, when she thought there could be no more, he filled her. Her hands slipped off his damp shoulders, her mouth lifted urgently to his.

And she wrapped herself around him like a vine.

"Mon amour. Mon coeur," she murmured mindlessly as they tumbled over the brink. *"Toujours mon amour."*

They slept, sprawled over each other like exhausted children. And when they woke, steamed the walls in his narrow shower as they took each other again under the hot spray.

Realizing he was taking an unprecedented step—a day off—Camilla packed a picnic and cajoled him into sharing a very late lunch by the pond.

She didn't have to do much cajoling. Picnics, he thought, were romantic. And romance was the current name of the game.

She looked happy, he mused. Relaxed. Her face glowed, her eyes were soft. If he'd been an artist, he'd have painted her now and titled it Camilla Content.

He didn't feel foolish—or not very—telling her so.

"That's just what I am. I love this place." She stretched out on the bank, stared up at the powder-puff clouds. "It's so quiet, it seems as though there's no one else in the world." She turned her head to smile at him. "Perfect for a hermit."

"I'm not a hermit." He polished off the last of the fancy

triangular shaped sandwiches she'd put together. "I just don't like people around."

"I like people." She rolled onto her stomach. "They're often so much kinder than you expect," she added, thinking of Sarah. "But sometimes, if you don't have a place to be alone—or to be quiet—you forget that and only see the demands, the responsibilities, the obligations people mete out."

"If you don't have a place to be alone, you don't get anything done."

"You have such purpose, your own purpose. That's a gift. Not everyone does." Her eyes clouded. "Some of us fumble around looking for one, and end up with so many we realize, all at once, we haven't got any at all."

"You don't strike me as a fumbler."

"Hmm. Sometimes efficiency is just as much of a flaw. Without that quiet time, you stop seeing the flaws, and the virtues. You can forget, not just who you are, but who you want to be." She smiled up at him, then turned over again to rest her head on his lap. "So I like this spot, because it's helped me remember."

"And who are you, Camilla?"

She understood he wanted an answer—a real one. But she found she couldn't speak and irrevocably change this moment. So she evaded. "A woman who won't forget again." She picked up a plum, took a bite, then held it up to him. "I like being alone with you, Delaney."

And she would give them the rest of the lovely, lazy day before Camilla de Cordina joined them.

He wanted to be patient, but patience wasn't his best skill. He'd thought, been sure, she'd been ready to confide in him. What did a man have to do to pry that woman open? he wondered. Most people spilled their guts at the least provocation.

But she just made vague philosophical statements, an occasional wistful one. And clammed up.

It was grating, but he was going to have to press. To do that he was going to have to make it clear that they were… that he was…

He'd never in his life told a woman he loved her. He'd gotten through his entire adult life without it being an issue, much less a problem. Now it was both.

He could march into the kitchen and blurt it out and be done with it. He equated it to ripping off a bandage in one painful jerk. Or he could ease them both into it, stage by stage—like lowering yourself into a cold pool inch by inch so your body adjusted to the shock.

I like having you around, he could say. Maybe you should just plan on staying.

He could let that settle awhile then move up to the I-care-about-you level. She'd have something to say about that. She *always* had something to say. Who would have believed he'd like listening to her so much?

But in any case, he thought, drawing himself back to the point, when they'd finished hashing through all that, he could just finish it off.

"I love you." He winced at his own muttered voice, shot a look toward the kitchen. It didn't even *sound* like him, he decided. The words didn't seem to fit his mouth.

"I love you," he tried again, and exhaled. Easier that time.

"Now, tell me what kind of trouble you're in, I'll take care of it and we'll move on."

Simple, he decided. Direct and supportive. Women liked supportive.

God. He was going to need a good shot of whiskey to get through it.

* * *

"I know it's late." Cocking the receiver on her shoulder, Camilla looked down at her wrist before she remembered her watch was gone. A quick glance at the kitchen clock had her calculating that it was after one in the morning in Cordina. No wonder she'd woken Marian.

"No problem. I was only sleeping."

"I'm sorry. Really. I just had to tell someone."

"Okay, let me pull myself together. Are you coming home?"

"Soon. I promise."

"You missed the first fitting for your ball gown. Your dressmaker is seriously displeased."

"Ball gown?" She drew a blank before it clicked in. "Oh, the Autumn Ball. There's plenty of time. Marian, I'm in love."

"You say that now, but if you'd heard the woman gnashing her teeth, you'd…what? What?"

"I'm in love. It's wonderful. It's terrifying. It's the most incredible thing that's ever happened to me. He's perfect. Oh, he's the most irritating man half the time, but I *like* that. And he's so smart and so funny—and very committed to his work."

"Camilla."

"And he's very attractive. I know that's just surface, but isn't it nice to fall in love with the inner man and have the outer man be gorgeous?"

"Camilla."

"He's in love with me, too. He's coming around to that, though it might take just a little while longer to—"

"Camilla!"

"Yes?"

"Who is he?"

"Oh, he's the man I've been working for here. Delaney Caine."

"The archaeologist? You fell for Indiana Jones?"

"I'm serious, Marian."

"Well, does he at least look like Indiana Jones?"

"No. Hmm, actually perhaps a little. But that's not the point. This isn't a game or a movie, it's my life. And this is something I want, something that feels very right."

"I can hear that. Cam, I'm so happy for you. When will I meet him?"

"I don't know exactly." Gnawing over the question, she wrapped the phone cord around her fingers. "That's part of the problem. After I explain things, then I hope we can make arrangements for him to meet the family."

"Explain things?" There was a long pause. "You mean you haven't told him who you are?"

"Not yet. I didn't expect this to happen, did I? I couldn't anticipate it. And then I wanted…" She trailed off warily as she heard Del heading into the kitchen.

"Camilla, how could you let things go so far and not tell him? If the man's in love with you—"

"I don't know that," she murmured in French. "Not for certain. I didn't intend for it to be complicated."

She cleared her throat as Del took the whiskey bottle from the pantry. It wasn't possible to ask him to hurry, or to cut Marian off, so she continued the conversation in French, keeping her voice as mild as she could manage.

"Marian, I had a right to my privacy. I could hardly stay here, if I'd announced I was a member of the Royal Family. The whole point of this was not to be Camilla de Cordina for a few weeks."

"The point seems to have changed."

"Yes, I know that, but I'd hardly be staying here if people knew who I was. The cabin would be surrounded by the media, and that, if you recall, was what sent me off in the first place."

"If you think the man would call reporters—"

"No. No, of course I don't think that. And I didn't call to argue with you, Marian. I did what I had to do, what I thought best, for me. As to the rest." She slanted a look toward Del as he poured whiskey into a glass. "I'll deal with it."

"I'm your friend, Camilla. I love you. I just don't want to see you hurt or disappointed. Or exploited."

"I don't intend to be. Tell the family I'll be home soon."

"And your dressmaker?"

Camilla sighed. "Inform Madam Monique that Her Highness will not disgrace her at the Autumn Ball. Go back to sleep, Marian."

She hung up, opened the refrigerator for a cold drink while Del stood swirling his whiskey in the glass. "I hope you don't mind me using the phone."

"No, I don't mind."

"I reversed the charges."

"Good. I'd probably have gotten a jolt if I'd noticed a call to Cordina on my phone bill next month."

"Yes, I imagine so. I…" She trailed off, and the hand that had lifted for a glass fell to her side again.

"Je parle francais aussi." Del lifted the whiskey to his lips as she turned to face him. "Your Highness."

Chapter 9

She knew her color faded. She could feel it drain and leave her face cold and stiff. Just as she could feel her heart leap into her throat and fill it with pounding.

Because of it she instinctively straightened her spine.

"I see. You didn't mention it."

"Must've slipped my mind," he said evenly. "Like being a member of the royal family of Cordina slipped yours. Just one of those stray details."

"My lineage never slips my mind. It isn't allowed to. Delaney—"

"So what's all this?" He gestured with the glass. "Your little version of the princess and the pauper? Taking a few weeks, slumming with the hoi polloi."

"You know better. You can't think that."

"Let's see, what should I think?" He lifted the whiskey again, splashed more in the glass. He couldn't precisely pinpoint why he wanted to heave the bottle against the wall.

Or more, why he resisted. "What, are you hiding out from a lover? One a little too anxious to get his hands on the crown jewels?"

"That's unfair. I have no lover but you."

"Not for the past couple of weeks anyway. You should've told me I was having sex with a princess. It might've added a nice flair."

Her lips wanted to tremble, so she firmed them into a hard line. "And that's unkind."

"You want fair? You want kind?" His voice changed from dangerously soft to viciously sharp. "You've got the wrong guy, sister. Somebody plays me for a fool, I get pissed."

"I didn't play you. I never intended to—"

"To what? Cut the crap, Camilla. You don't do anything you don't intend. You came in here because you wanted to play pretend for a while, and amuse yourself with the locals while you were at it."

"That's not true." Her temper started to build to match his. "And it insults both of us."

"You're insulted." He slammed the glass down before he did throw it. "You come into my place and pretend to be someone you're not. You lie about who you are. About what you are. Virginia farm girl, my ass."

"My father has a farm in Virginia." She shouted back because she was too frightened to do otherwise. "I've lived there half the year all of my life."

"And the other half in the palace. Well, I guess the tiara suits you better than a straw hat."

"Yes. No!" Struggling through the anger and panic, she dragged a hand through her hair. "We have a farm in Cordina. My mother—"

"Your 'French' mother," he said coolly.

"You said France, I said Europe." But it was weak, and

she knew it. "Delaney, I'm exactly the same person I was ten minutes ago. I only wanted the privacy of—"

"Privacy? Give me a break. You slept with me. You made damn certain you'd sleep with me. What, looking for a change of pace from the purebreds? You get points for nailing stray Americans on your little adventure?"

Her color came up now, flaming into her cheek. "How dare you! You're crude and vile, and it's despicable to turn something lovely into something cheap. I won't have this discussion, nor explain myself to you while you're in this impossible mood. Move aside."

"You don't give commands here, Princess." He grabbed her arm before she could stalk by him. "You used me."

"No." Tears wanted to brim, wanted to fall. "Not the way you mean. Del, I only wanted a place to be. I only wanted some time."

"You got a hell of a lot more, didn't you? Playtime's over, Your Highness. You're going to do more than explain yourself."

"Let me go." She drew on all of her composure and command, and eyed him coldly. "I have nothing more to say to you now. Let me go."

"Oh, I will. All the way. I guess we've said all there is. You can pack your bags and run away, since that seems to be your pattern."

The temper and shame that warred within her were no match for the grief. "You want me to go?"

"You got what you came for, didn't you? I'll make it easy for you and get the hell out of your way."

Her breath hitched as he started for the door. "Del. Please, don't. I love you."

The pain stabbed through him. The words snarled out of him as he tossed them at her, though they were pure truth.

"You're breaking my heart, sister," he said, "try that line on someone who's stupid enough to believe it. And get the hell away from me." He left and slammed the door behind him.

He tromped through the forest for an hour, thinking vicious thoughts and cursing all women. He stalked the woods another hour as the flames of his temper banked to a smoldering rage.

In love with him? What a crock. She had a lot of nerve pulling that routine on him. She'd been about to pour on the tears, too. He'd seen that coming. Thank God he'd gotten out of there before the floods hit.

He just couldn't stand weeping females.

Well, she'd pulled every other trick out of her hat. Excuse me, he thought bitterly, make that crown. Why not tears?

And for what? So she could have a couple weeks to indulge herself. Cinderella in the wilderness?

He stopped, rubbing at the ache in his gut as he stared out over the pond.

I love this place.

He could hear her saying it, see the easy pleasure in her face as she lay on the grass beside him.

So she had an appreciation of nature. Big deal.

Haven't you ever needed to just breathe?

He remembered her saying that, too. That first day, standing beside him with all that tension in her face, in her voice. As if she'd been standing on the edge of something and fighting to hold her ground instead of leaping over.

Okay, so maybe she had some problems. Who didn't? But that didn't excuse what she'd done. It had all been a pretense, right from the beginning. And she'd let him fall in love with her—let him fall into that cage without warning him it had a trap door to nowhere.

She had to pay for that.

He turned, headed back toward the cabin. Okay, he'd let her explain—not that he was buying any of it. Then...

Then he'd figure out what the hell to do next.

With his head down and his hands in his pockets, he didn't notice her car was gone until he was nearly at the back door. For nearly a full minute he stared blankly at the spot where it had last been parked.

Then he was bolting into the cabin, charging up the stairs.

Her clothes were gone. He flung open both closets as if she might have put them back in the spare room just to make him sweat. She'd even taken the pots and tubes from the medicine cabinet.

On a tearing fury, he searched the cabin for a note. But there was nothing.

He couldn't say she'd gone without a trace. She'd left the candles, the little bottles springing with wildflowers. Her scent, everywhere, was already haunting him.

So, she'd pulled up stakes, he thought. Just because he'd yelled at her and told her she could pack and run away. If the woman couldn't stand up to a fight...

No, better this way, he reminded himself. No point in dragging it out. She was heading back to where she belonged to where she'd been headed all along, and he could get back to work without having her distract him every five minutes.

He prowled over to his notes, picked up one at random. After tossing it down again, he dropped onto the couch to brood.

She'd come back. He talked himself into that, particularly when he got just a little drunk. She was just off in a snit, that was all. Women had snits, didn't they?

His two hours stomping through the woods was a natural expression of justifiable aggravation. He didn't go off in snits.

In the morning, suffering from a surprisingly nasty hangover, he convinced himself he didn't want her to come back. He liked his life the way it had been before she'd plunged into it. And he didn't like, not one damn bit, this sensation of loss and misery. Which was, no question about it, completely her fault.

By the second day, he was edgy and busily working himself into a temper again. She had absolutely no business running off before he'd finished yelling at her. But it was just like her, wasn't it, to stick that chin out, shoot that nose in the air and flounce off. He should've recognized it as princess behavior from the get-go.

When she cooled off and came back, he had a great deal to say to her.

Why the hell hadn't she come back?

Didn't matter to him, he reminded himself and struggled to concentrate on his work. He had plenty to do to keep himself occupied while she was off sulking. In fact, maybe he'd just pack up and take himself back to the dig. It was where he belonged anyway.

And it gave him a hard, rude jolt to realize he'd planned to take her with him. He'd wanted to show her the place, to watch that interest and intellect shine in her eyes when she got her first look at his pet project.

He'd wanted to share that with her—and that was terrifying. He'd wanted to share everything with her. He couldn't believe how much that hurt.

Just as he sat, unsteady in the knowledge that she really wasn't coming back, he heard a car coming down the lane.

He *knew* it! He sprang up, fueled with relief, pleasure, fury, and had reached the door in one leap before he stopped himself. This was not the way to handle it, he decided, or her. He'd *wander* out, casually. Then he'd let her apologize.

Feeling smug, and generous, he stepped outside. Everything inside him sank when he saw it wasn't Camilla climbing out of the car. It was his parents.

"Surprise!" Alice Caine ran toward the porch in her ancient and sturdy boots. Her hair, a streaky mess of mousebrown and gray was, as always falling untidily from beneath a scarred bush hat. She was trim as a girl, with a face splattered with freckles and lined from a life in the sun.

She leaped on her son, gave him a slurpy, smacking kiss on the cheek, then immediately turned to her husband. "Niles, let the boy get the bags. What's the point in having a big, strong son if you can't use him as slave labor? How's the shoulder, Del?" she asked him. "And the rest of it?"

"Fine. It's fine. I wasn't expecting you."

"If you had been, it wouldn't be a surprise." She tipped down her dark, wire-rim glasses. Though she grinned, she was sharp enough to have seen her son's shocked disappointment when he'd stepped out on the sagging porch. "Got some coffee?"

"Sure. Sure." Ashamed of himself, he bent down—she was such a little thing—and gave her a quick hug.

"Drove three hundred fifteen miles today." Mumbling in his public school English accent, Niles Caine finished noting the mileage in his tattered book as he crossed to his son. "Made good time."

He was a big man, tall and dashingly handsome at sixty-seven. His hair, a mop of it, had gone shining silver, and his eyes, green as his son's, were jewel sharp in his tanned face. He tucked the book into the pocket of his faded shirt, then gave Del a crushing bear hug. "How's the shoulder?"

"Fine. Better. What's up with your dig?"

"Oh, we're just taking a break. Clear the mind." Alice said it airily, one warning look at her husband, as she strode into the house. She stopped dead, fisted her hands on her narrow hips. "Del. You've got a woman."

"What?"

"Look at this. Flowers." She arched her brow at the wild-flowers tucked into bottles. "Scents," she added, sniffing a bowl of potpourri. "Clean." She ran a fingertip over a table-top. "Definitely a female on the premises. Where is she?"

"She's not here."

Ah, Alice thought. Poor baby. "Niles, my hero, would you run into town and get me some ice cream?"

"Run into town?" He stared at her. "I've just got here. I haven't so much as sat down yet."

"You can sit down in the car on the drive to town."

"Woman, if you wanted ice cream, why didn't you say so when we were still in the bloody car?"

"I didn't want any then. Something with chocolate." She rose on her toes to kiss his scowling mouth. "I've such a yen for chocolate."

"Flighty, fluttering females," he muttered, and stomped back out to the car.

Alice simply walked to the couch, sat and propped her boots on the table. Smiling, she patted the cushion beside her. "Sit. Coffee can wait. Tell me about the woman."

"There's nothing to tell. She was here, she was a constant annoyance. Now she's gone."

Cranky, wounded bear, she thought indulgently. Just like his father. "Sit." Her voice firmed—she knew how to handle her men. "Why did she leave you?"

"She didn't leave me." His pride pricked, he dropped onto the couch. "She was just working for me, temporarily. Very temporarily," he muttered.

And at his mother's long, patient silence, he cracked. "I kicked her out. If she's too stubborn to come back... I don't need her underfoot anyway."

"There now." She patted his head. "Tell Mommy all about the horrible girl."

"Cut it out." But his lips twitched.

"Was she ugly?"

"No."

"Stupid then."

He sighed. "No."

"A cheap floozy."

Now he laughed. "Mom."

"That's it then." She slapped a hand on his thigh. "A cheap floozy taking advantage of my poor, sweet-natured, naive little boy. Why, I'll fix her wagon. What's her name? I'll hunt her down like a dog."

"She's fairly easy to find," he murmured. "Her name's Camilla. Her Royal Highness Camilla de Cordina. I could strangle her."

Alice tossed her sunglasses and her hat on the table. "Tell me," she said. So he did.

She listened while he worked himself back and forth through temper, into misery and back into temper again. So often, she noted, he had to leap up to pace the room just to keep up with himself.

His description of Camilla—except for the irritating, interfering nuisance portion—jibed with the lovely note she'd received some days before from Her Serene Highness Gabriella.

A gracious—and clever—note, Alice mused, one that acknowledged Gabriella's gratitude to Delaney for his hospitality to her daughter. Alice hadn't been sure if having anyone consider her son hospitable was more of a surprise than learning he was being so with a member of Cordina's Royal Family.

But she was a woman accustomed to thinking on her feet, and adjusting in midstride when necessary. The contents of the note had caused Alice to drag her husband from the Arizona dig and head home to see for herself just what was what.

Now that she'd seen, she had a very good idea just what was what.

What came through, in huge, neon letters to her mother's view, was that her son was completely, pitifully in love.

And it was about damn time.

"So she left," Del finished. "That's for the best all around."

"Probably so," Alice agreed calmly. "It was shortsighted of her to deceive you. Certainly she should've felt comfortable—frankly even obliged—to be forthcoming with you after you told her your own lineage."

"Huh?"

"Obviously a viscount is lower in rank—considerably—from a princess, but she should've had the courtesy to trust you as you trusted her." Delighted by her son's blank face, Alice crossed her booted feet at the ankle. "You did tell her your father is Earl of Brigston—and you are Viscount Brigston."

"It didn't come up," Delaney said, then added with more heat "Why would I?" as his mother simply watched him coolly. "Who remembers anyway? I never use it."

Unless it suits you, Alice thought. But it was enough, she decided, that she'd planted that little seed. "There's your father, back with the ice cream. Let's have some with our coffee."

* * *

She gave her son a day, partly because she simply enjoyed him, and partly because she knew he had to chew on things. She debated how she'd tell him she'd been in communication with Camilla's mother.

"He might get his back up all over again," she mused as she cast her line into the pond. "It would be so like him." At her husband's grunt, she turned to where he sat, papers scattered over his lap and the ground. "Pay attention, Niles."

"Hmm? What? Damn it, Alice, I'm working."

"Your son's work."

"Just leave him alone. A man should handle his own affairs without any interference."

"Hah. So you said to me thirty-three years ago this coming winter. Look where it got you."

"Got me you, didn't it?"

She grinned out over the water. Two peas in a pod, she decided. Her men were two very stubborn peas.

Before she could decide how best to handle things, the matter was taken out of her hands. Del swooped through the woods, making enough racket to scare away every fish for ten miles, and scooped her right off her feet.

"We've got new funding."

"Good thing, because we're not getting any fish for dinner." Still she hugged him. "That's wonderful, Del. Who?"

"I don't have the details—just got the call from the university. I've got to get back to the dig. Sorry to run out on you like this."

"Don't be." She tucked her tongue in her cheek. She saw how it would work now. Perfectly. "Give us a call once you're settled."

"Will. Have to pack."

* * *

That evening, while her son was—very likely—steaming over the idea that his funding was being generated by the interest and influence of a young princess, Alice sat and composed a tidy and formal note to Her Serene Highness Gabriella de Cordina.

The Earl and Countess of Brigston, along with their son, Lord Delaney, Viscount of Brigston, were very pleased to accept her gracious invitation to the Autumn Ball in Cordina.

"It's insulting." Camilla waved the latest communication from Del. "Rude and insulting and just like him."

Gabriella sat calmly, fixing simple pearls at her ears. Guests who had been invited to stay at the palace for a time before and after the ball, would be arriving shortly. "It sounded perfectly polite and informative to me, darling."

And she found it very telling that in the month she'd been back in Cordina her daughter had lost none of the heat where Delaney Caine was concerned.

"That's because you don't know him," Camilla raged on. "Insufferable is what it is. Reporting to me as if I were some sort of accountant. Dollars and cents, that's all. He doesn't tell me anything about the finds—the things he'd know I'd want to know. And see how he signs them? Dr. Delaney Caine. As if we were strangers. He's detestable."

"So you've said." Gabriella turned on the chair of her dressing table. Her hair was swept back from a face her husband told her grew more lovely with each year.

She didn't believe him, but it was nice to hear. Her eyes, the same tawny gold as her daughter's were quietly sober and showed none of the humor and anticipation she felt.

"I'm sure he's grateful for your help in funding the project, Camilla. You parted on such bad terms, he probably feels awkward as well."

"He should feel awkward. He should feel sorry and small." She whirled around her mother's lovely room. Stared out the window at the stunning view of the gardens, the bright blue sea beyond. "I didn't get the funding for him in any case. I got it for the project. The work's the priority. It's an important find and it deserves to be completed."

And her daughter's interest in the work hadn't waned in the weeks since she'd been back. If anything, Gabriella reflected, it had increased. She'd spent hours with books, had gone to the university to speak to professors who were knowledgeable, had raided their library for more books and documents on archaeology.

She'd neglected none of her duties. It simply wasn't in Camilla's makeup to do so. There were times Gabriella wished she were less dedicated. Even though she'd been worried, she'd been pleased when Camilla had taken those weeks for herself.

Her own heart had hurt when her little girl had come home with hers broken. She was grateful their relationship was such that Camilla had confided in her. About falling in love—and becoming Delaney's lover. It helped a woman, Gabriella knew, to talk to a woman.

And now, though she knew her daughter suffered, part of her rejoiced that Camilla's heart was constant. She was still very much in love. Her mother, with a little help, intended to see she got what she wanted. Even if it meant a little— very little, she assured herself—finagling.

She rose, crossing to her daughter to lay her hands on her shoulders, a kiss on the back of her head. "Love isn't always polite."

"He doesn't love me." Camilla hurt still, sharply. "Mama,

he looked at me with such contempt, turned me out of his life with less compassion than you would a stray dog."

And should answer for it, Gabriella thought fiercely. She was counting on her daughter to see that he did. "You weren't honest with him."

"I was trying to be honest with myself. If I was wrong, there still should've been room for... It doesn't matter." She straightened her shoulders. "I have my interests and duties, and he has his. I wish this ball were over and done."

"When it is, you'll go on your first dig. It'll be exciting for you."

"My mind's full of it." Ruthlessly she folded Del's formal letter, set it aside. As she would, she promised herself, set thoughts of him aside. "Imagine me, studying artifacts from the Lower Paleolithic in France. Dr. Lesuer has been so generous, so forthcoming. I'll enjoy working with his team and learning from him. But now, I'm behind schedule. Sarah Lattimer will be here in a couple hours. I believe I told you about Sarah—the shop keeper from Vermont who was so kind to me?"

"Yes, you did. I'm looking forward to meeting her."

"I want her to have a spectacular time. Aunt Eve's going to give her a tour and she'll have a chance to meet Uncle Alex before the ladies tea tomorrow."

"I need you to greet some of my personal guests with me—the Earl and Countess of Brigston and their son. They should be here within thirty minutes. I'm entertaining them in the Gold Parlor on arrival."

"Yes, I remember." She glanced at her watch. "I don't suppose you could have Adrienne fill in for me."

"Your sister's in the nursery with young Armand and the baby. I won't keep you above fifteen minutes," Gabriella promised.

"I'll be there. I'll just adjust a few things in my schedule." She started out, came back and picked up Del's letter. "I need to have this filed," she murmured, and hurried away.

Exactly twenty-nine minutes later, Camilla dashed down the main staircase. Preparations for the Autumn Ball—and all the events leading up to and following it—were well underway. The *regisseur,* the palace manager, would overlook no details. And should he, her aunt's eagle eye would scope them out.

Her Royal Highness, Princess Eve de Cordina was Chatelaine of the palace, and a woman who stood beside her husband as he ruled the country. But she often had her own opinions about matters of state, and had her own career apart from her royal duties. Her Hamilton Company of players was a world-renowned theatrical group and she was also a respected playwright.

Her example served to remind Camilla that with ambition, work and brains, a woman could do anything. Even be on time—barely—to meet guests when her plate was overfull.

She was nearly at the base of the steps when the man jogging up to her caught her by the shoulders. He was handsome as sin and smelled comfortably of horses.

"What's the hurry?"

"Uncle Bennett. I didn't even know you'd arrived." She kissed her mother's youngest brother on the cheek. "And already visited the stables."

"Bry and Thadd are still out there," he said, referring to his two young sons. "Hannah's around here somewhere. She wanted to talk to Eve. And look at you." He ruffled her short hair. "Very chic."

"How was your trip to England?"

"Successful. I found the perfect mare to breed with my stallion."

"I want to see her and all the rest of you—but later. I'm late."

"What's this about some American who needs a good ass-kicking?"

She rolled her eyes. "You've already seen my father."

"On the way in from the stables. I volunteered to hold his coat."

"I don't think you'll have the chance. I don't see the ass he'd like to kick being within striking distance any time in the near future. *A bientôt.*"

"But—" Puzzled, Bennett watched her dash off. Someone had their information skewed, he mused, then began to smile as he climbed up the steps, hoping to search out his brother and harass him for details.

Knowing Reeve MacGee, Bennett doubted that Camilla's father had the wrong data.

Camilla slowed to a dignified if brisk walk as she moved through the palace. Flowers, fresh and elaborate, speared and spilled out of vases and urns. Her heels clicked efficiently on the sparkling marble floors.

The occasional servant paused to bow or curtsy. She greeted most by name, but continued on. She hated being late.

By the time she made it to the Gold Parlor, she was. By six minutes. Because she heard the low murmur of voices, she took another moment to smooth her skirt, her hair, take a breath and fix a welcoming smile on her face.

When she stepped in, she saw her mother was already seated in one of the conversation areas, pouring tea from one of the Meissen china pots into cups for a middle-aged couple.

The woman caught her attention first. Such an intriguing

look, Camilla thought. Lovely in a unique way, and casually disheveled. She wouldn't have called the baggy tweeds fashionable, but they certainly suited the woman.

The man rose as she approached. She started to speak, to apologize for her tardiness in greeting them. Then couldn't speak at all. He was, she thought, an older and more distinguished version of Del.

She needed to find a way to get the man off her mind, she ordered herself, when she started seeing pieces of him in dashing and dignified English earls.

"Camilla, I'd like to introduce you to the Earl and Countess of Brigston. Lord and Lady Brigston, my daughter, Her Royal Highness Camilla de Cordina."

"Lord and Lady Brigston, I apologize for not being here with my mother to welcome you to Cordina. Please, sit and be comfortable. I hope you enjoyed your trip."

"We're delighted to be here, Your Highness." Alice smiled as she curtseyed, then shook hands with Camilla. "As is our son. May I present Lord Delaney, Viscount Brigston."

Her thoughts whirled as Del moved from the far window and crossed the room toward her. Her heart beat too quickly—first with the sheer joy of seeing him, and then with confusion. And lastly, with anger.

Viscount Brigston, she thought. What was this? How did the American scientist become a British aristocrat? The nerve of him.

She inclined her head, coolly, then lifted her chin. "My Lord," she said in a tone frigid as winter.

"Madam," he returned, and with annoyance clear in his eyes, took her offered hand and kissed it.

She got through it. Camilla was too proud, and too innately well mannered not to. But the following thirty minutes were torture. She held up her part in conversation. Which was more, she thought darkly, than Del managed. He barely grumbled monosyllables, and only when directly addressed.

Why did he have to look so big and handsome and *male?* The suit and tie should have dwarfed him somehow, or tamed him by a few degrees. It did neither.

"My son," Alice said at one point, "is delighted and grateful for your assistance in funding the Bardville Project, madam. Isn't that right, Del?"

He shifted in his chair. "I've relayed my appreciation, and the team's, to Her Highness via letters and reports."

"Yes, I received one of your…letters just this morning, Lord Delaney." Camilla smiled with her eyes frosted. "How odd you didn't mention you'd be traveling, and so soon, to Cordina."

He wouldn't have been here if he'd had any choice, he thought. His mother had hounded him like a she-wolf and all but dragged him to the plane by his ear. "I wasn't entirely sure my schedule would permit the trip."

"We're so pleased it did," Gabriella broke in, warned by the battle-light in her daughter's eyes. When Camilla's temper rose too high, her tongue could be lethal. And rash. "So that we can, in some small way, repay you for the hospitality you offered Camilla in your home in Vermont. A lovely part of America, I'm told. I regret never having seen it for myself."

It was a toss-up, Gabriella decided, who looked more shocked by her easy mention of their prior relationship, the princess or the viscount.

Both gaped at her while she sipped her tea. She thought—was nearly certain—she heard the countess muffle a squeak of laughter.

Now, she would see how long the two of them could manage to continue to behave like polite strangers.

"Camilla has developed a keen interest in your field, my lord," Gabriella continued. "It's always rewarding for a mother to see her child so enthusiastic."

"And equally rewarding for a child to entertain her mother," Camilla said with a perfectly pleasant smile—one with an edge only her mother could see. "What an... interesting surprise for you to have invited Lord Delaney and his parents without mentioning the plans to me."

"I hoped it would be, and that you'd be pleased to offer Cordinian hospitality." It was said lightly, but with underlying firmness.

"Of course. Nothing could please me more than repaying Lord Delaney for...everything."

"I'm sure you'd like to rest a bit after your journey," Gabriella said to Niles and Alice as she rose. "Camilla, perhaps you could show Lord Delaney the gardens."

"I'm not—" Del began, then ground his teeth at his mother's killing glare. "I wouldn't want to put you out."

"It's no trouble at all." Gabriella laid a hand, a heavy one, on Camilla's shoulder as she passed.

Trapped, Camilla got to her feet, braced herself as her mother breezily led Del's parents away then turned to face him. "First, let me make it perfectly clear that I had no idea you would be here, and if I had I would have done everything possible to be absent from this welcoming party."

"That's clear. If I could've gotten out of making this trip, I would have. Believe me."

"Second," she continued in the same cool and mannered tone, "I have no more desire to show you the gardens than you have to see them. However, I've less desire to distress my mother or your parents. Ten minutes should do it. I'm sure we can tolerate each other for that length of time. My lord," she said in a hiss.

"Don't start on me." He rose as well, then found himself talking to her back as she strode to the terrace doors on the other side of the room.

When she sailed out, he jammed his hands into his pockets and followed. It was going to be, he thought, a very long four days.

Chapter 10

In the third floor guest wing, Alice paused at the entrance to the suite of rooms they'd been given for their stay in Cordina.

It was time, she decided, to test her impressions and instincts regarding Gabriella de Cordina.

"I wonder, ma'am, if I might have a moment of your time. In private."

"Of course." Gabriella had been calculating her options and considering how best to handle her guest since she'd first set eyes on the woman. In her opinion, Alice Caine preferred the direct approach. And so, when possible, did she. "We'll use my sitting room. It's very comfortable, very private."

As she led Alice through the palace, to the family quarters, she spoke of the history of the building, the art collection. She kept up the polite tour chatter until they were comfortably behind closed doors in her elegant rose and blue sitting room.

"May I offer you some refreshment, Lady Brigston?"

"No, ma'am, thank you." Alice took a seat, folded her hands. "We are, obviously, both aware of the relationship between our children, and the unfortunate way that relationship was left late last summer," she began.

"Yes. Your son was very kind to provide my daughter with shelter."

"I beg your pardon, but that's nonsense. He didn't do it out of kindness, or at least only partially. He isn't unkind, he's just boneheaded."

Gabriella sat back. "Lady Brigston… Alice," she responded warmly, pleased that her judgment about the woman had been on target. "I wasn't certain I was doing the right thing for Camilla by inviting your family—and by not telling her of the invitation or about your son's title. It was self-serving of me. I wanted to give her time to search her heart, and I wanted to gauge her reaction for myself when she saw your son again. The minute I did, I knew I'd done the right thing after all."

"You saw the way they looked at each other—well, before their backs went up."

"Yes, I did. They love each other, and they're both letting pride get in the way."

"It's more than pride with Del. He's so much like his father. Toss him some old bones, and he can give you chapter and verse on the woman who owned them three thousand years ago. Give him a flesh and blood female, and he's clueless. It's not that he's stupid, ma'am—"

"Brie," Gabriella interrupted.

Alice took a breath, settled more comfortably in the chair. Like her son, she knew the formalities of protocol—and like her son found them mildly foolish. She was glad Her Serene Highness felt the same way. "Brie. He's not stupid. He's just a Caine. Through and through."

"I don't like to interfere in the lives of my children," Gabriella began.

"Neither do I. Technically."

They said nothing for a moment, then both began to smile. "Why don't we have a small glass of brandy," Gabriella suggested.

It helped, Alice thought, when you could see the woman your son loved in her mother's eyes. And you liked them both. "Oh, why don't we?"

Pleased, Gabriella rose to fetch the decanter and pour the snifters herself. "I do have an idea, which while not—technically—interfering, may help things along a bit. My sons would call it double-teaming."

"I'm all ears."

Ten minutes later, Alice nodded. "I like your style. Good thing, since we're going to be in-laws." She glanced toward the window when she heard raised voices. "That's Del—booms like a bull when he's mad."

They rose together, moved out to the balcony. In tune they linked arms as they looked down on their children. "They're arguing," Gabriella said with emotion thickening her voice.

"It's great, isn't it?"

"We shouldn't eavesdrop."

"We're just standing here, taking some air. We can't help it if they're shouting at each other."

"I suppose not."

Even as she inched out a bit more, Gabriella heard her sitting room door open and slam shut.

"Is that jackass Caine here yet?"

Mortified, Gabriella closed her eyes, then turned back

as her husband came to the open doorway. "Reeve," she murmured.

"You must be Camilla's father." Delighted, Alice stepped forward, pumped his hand. "I'm the jackass's mother. We were just pretending not to eavesdrop while they yell at each other in the garden. Care to join us?"

He stared, a tall man with silver shot black hair, as his wife began to laugh helplessly. "Well, hell," was all he said.

She hadn't intended to argue. In fact, Camilla had ordered herself not to rise to any bait he might cast. The jackass. She swept him along garden paths as if they were on a forced march, and took none of the pleasure she normally did in the scents, the textures, the charm.

"We're particularly proud of our rose garden. There are more than fifty varieties represented, including the climbing specimens trained on the fifteen arbors in what is called *La Promenade de Rose.* The less formal beds at the far edges add charm, I think, to elegance."

"I don't give a hang about the roses."

"Very well, we'll continue on to the walled garden. It's a particularly lovely spot where—"

"Let's just cut it out." He took her arm, pulled her around.

"I have not given you leave to touch me, sir."

"Tell that to somebody who hasn't seen you naked."

Her color came up—fire under cream—but her voice remained cold. "Nor do I care to be reminded of my previous poor judgment."

"Is that what it comes down to, poor judgment on your part?"

"You're the one who ended it."

"You're the one who took off."

"You told me to go!"

"Like you ever listened to a damn thing I said. If you'd been honest with me from the beginning—"

"You dare?" Incensed, she yanked her arm free. "Honesty, *Lord* Delaney?"

He had the grace to flush. "That has nothing to do with anything. I didn't tell you I had chicken pox when I was ten, either, and it's just as relevant."

"Your title is hardly a rash."

"It's just a title, something I inherited from my father. It doesn't—"

"Ah! Titles, lineages, don't count when they're yours, only when their mine. You asinine jerk."

"Just watch it. Just watch it," he ordered. "It's not the same, and you know it. I don't think of myself that way. I don't use the damn thing, and don't remember it's there half the time. I don't live in a palace and—"

"Neither do I! I live on a farm! This is my uncle's home. You say you don't think of your title half the time. I have no choice but to think of mine every day—with every public move, and most private ones. I wanted time, a little time to live as you live, to have what you take for granted. Freedom. So I took it," she said passionately. "Right or wrong, I took what I needed because I was afraid I might…"

"Afraid of what?"

"It doesn't matter now. It's no longer an issue. We'll consider it bad luck all around that I ended up where I ended up during that storm."

She drew herself in. "Now, I won't embarrass my uncle or the rest of my family by arguing with one of his guests, however insufferable. While you're here, I suggest we do our best to stay out of each other's way." She turned her back on him. "I have nothing more to say to you."

"Some hospitality—Cordinian style."

Shocked to the bone, she whirled back. "My mother—" she nearly choked. "My mother offered you and your family an invitation to our country, to her brother's home. You will receive every courtesy—publicly—from my family and from me. In private..." What hissed through her teeth was an insult more usually heard in a French gutter than a palace garden. Del only raised his eyebrows.

"Nice mouth, Your Highness."

"And now, there is nothing more to be said between us."

"I've got plenty to say to you, sister."

His tone, the term, made sentimental tears want to rise in her throat. Turning her back on him, she did what she could to force them back. "Sir, you are dismissed."

"Oh, stuff a sock in it." Out of patience, he spun her back around. Then froze when he saw the sparkle of tears. "What are you doing? Stop that. If you think you're going to pull out the waterworks to make me feel like a heel, think again."

He took a deliberate step back from her as he searched his pockets. "Look, God. I don't have a handkerchief, so snuffle it back."

"Go away." She was no less appalled than he when a tear spilled over. "Go inside, go back to America, or go to hell. But go away."

"Camilla." Undone, he stepped toward her again.

"Your Highness." Formal in company, and avidly curious, Marian stepped onto the garden path. "I beg your pardon, but Miss Lattimer has arrived. She's been shown to her rooms."

"Sarah?" Surprised, Del stared at Camilla. "You invited Sarah to the palace."

"Yes. I'll be right in, Marian. Thank you. If you'd please show Lord Delaney to his rooms, or anywhere else he'd like to go? Please excuse me, my lord."

"My lord?" Marian studied him carefully when Camilla walked quickly away. She was torn between wanting to level him for hurting her dearest friend, and sighing with sympathy over the misery so plain on his face. "May I show you the rest of the gardens?"

"No, thanks. Unless you've got a handy pond or fountain I can soak my head in."

Marian only smiled. "I'm sure we can accommodate you."

He wondered if he'd be doing everyone a favor if he did leave. His mother would be furious, his father baffled. And they would both be embarrassed, but Camilla would, obviously, be relieved.

And he wouldn't have to see her, look at her and try not to remember how she'd looked wearing jeans and a T-shirt while she fried up eggs. Not that she looked anything like that now.

She was polished and sparkling and elegant as the diamonds he'd seen winking at her ears. And just, he tried to convince himself, as cold.

But it occurred to him that he couldn't let her chase him off—the way he'd chased her. He'd stay, if for no other reason than to prove to her what spine was.

It wasn't hard not to get in her way. The palace was a far cry from a five-room cabin in the Vermont woods.

And he couldn't claim not to be enjoying himself, on some level. He liked her brothers, her cousins. It was like watching a pack of handsome, elegant wolves run just short of wild.

As an only child, he'd never been exposed to big, boisterous families. Which, he soon discovered, was what they were under the titles and polish. A family. Closely knit enough that he had trouble remembering who was sibling, who was cousin.

Several of them talked him into going down to the stables—and a hell of a horse palace it was. The minute they discovered he could ride, he was mounted up.

That was how he met Alexander, Cordina's ruler, and his brother, Prince Bennett, Camilla's uncles. And her father, Reeve MacGee.

"Sir." One of the young men—he thought it was Dorian—grinned and made formal introductions.

Del shifted in the saddle. He'd been taught, of course, but months—years—passed without him needing the protocol. He didn't like having to dig it up—and cared less for the sensation of being dissected by three pair of coolly measuring eyes.

"Welcome to Cordina, Lord Brigston," Alex said in a smooth, faintly aloof voice. "And my home."

"Thank you, sir." Del managed what passed for a bow while mounted on a skittish horse.

"We're pleased to have you, and to repay you in some way for the hospitality you showed my niece." There was a subtle and keen edge under the courtesy. Alex made certain of it.

"That horse wants a run," Bennett said because he felt a tug of sympathy. Poor bastard, he thought. Outnumbered. "You look like you can handle him."

Del felt the quick slice of Alex's words—like a nick from a honed fencing sword. He preferred shifting his gaze to the more friendly brother. "He's a beauty."

"We'll let you enjoy your ride. I'd be interested to speak with you regarding your work," Alexander added. "As it's become so much a passion of Princess Camilla's."

"At your convenience, sir."

Alex nodded, then continued to walk his mount toward

the stables. After a glance of some pity, Bennett followed behind him. Reeve turned his mount until he was side by side with Del.

"You," he said, pointing at his sons, his nephews. "Take off." Then, turning to Del, he continued, "It's time you and I had a little chat," he said as the echo of hooves faded in the race up the hill. "I'm wondering if you can come up with a good reason why I shouldn't just snap your neck."

Well, Del thought, at least there was no need for protocol and politics now. The man looked like he could give the neck-snapping a good shot. He was fit, broad-shouldered, and his hands appeared to be rough and ready.

And he looked to Del more like a soldier than any farmer he'd ever come across.

"I doubt it," Del decided. "You want to do it here, or somewhere more secluded where you can dump me in a shallow grave?"

Reeve's smile was thin. "Let's take a ride. You make a habit out of taking stray young women into your house, Caine?"

"No. She was the first. I can promise she'll be the last."

The day was warm, but breezy. Del hated the fact that he was sweating. The man had eyes like lasers.

"You want me to believe you took her in out of the goodness of your heart. You had no idea who she was—even though her face is plastered on magazine covers, in newspapers, on television screens all over the world. You had no intention of exploiting her, of using her influence for your own gain. Or of trading off the press with stories about how you took her to bed."

"Just a damn minute." Del reined to a stop, and now it was his gaze that bored heat. "I don't use women. I sure as hell couldn't have used her if I'd tried because she'd have kicked me in the teeth for it. I don't have time for gossip magazines or television, and I wasn't expecting to find some runaway princess stranded on the side of the road in a storm. She said she was low on funds so I gave her a place to stay and a job. I didn't ask her a lot of questions or pay much attention."

"Well, enough attention, apparently, to take her to bed."

"That's right. And that's nobody's business but ours. You want to kick my ass over that, you go ahead. But you start accusing me of taking what we had between us and turning it into some cheap splash for the media, I'm kicking yours right back."

Right answer, Reeve thought. Exactly right. He shifted in the saddle. The boy had guts, he decided, pleased. But that was no reason not to torture him. "What are your intentions toward my daughter?"

The angry flush faded until Del was sheet pale. "My— my— What?"

"You heard the question, son. Roll your tongue back in your mouth and answer it."

"I don't have any. She won't even speak to me. I'm staying out of her way."

"Just when I was beginning to think you weren't a complete jackass after all." Reeve swung his mount around again. "Give that horse a good gallop," he advised. "And don't fall off and break your stiff neck."

As he rode back to the stables, Reeve thought the conversation might not have been precisely what his wife had meant when she'd asked him to have a man-to-man talk with Del. But it had certainly been satisfying.

Camilla would have enjoyed a good gallop herself. But the ladies' tea required her attention and her presence. As the weather was fine, the party was spread over the south terrace and the rose garden so that guests could enjoy the views of the Mediterranean and the fragrance of flowers.

Her aunt had opted for casual elegance so the pretty tables were covered with warm peach cloths and set with glass dishes of deep cobalt. More flowers, cheerful tropical blooms, spilled out of shallow bowls while white-coated staff poured flutes of champagne as well as cups of tea. Each lady was presented with a silver compact etched with the royal seal.

A harpist plucked strings quietly in the shade of an arbor tumbled with white roses.

Her aunt Eve, Camilla thought, knew how to set her stage.

Women in floaty dresses wandered the garden or gathered in groups. Knowing her duty, Camilla moved through the guests while she nursed a single glass of champagne. She smiled, exchanged pleasantries, chatted, and shoved all thoughts of Del into a corner of her mind, then ruthlessly locked it.

"I've barely had a moment with you." Eve slid an arm through Camilla's and drew her aside.

She was a small woman with a lovely tumble of raven hair that provided a exquisite frame for her diamond-shaped face. Her eyes, a deep and bold blue, sparkled as she nudged Camilla toward the terrace wall.

"Not enough time now," she said in a voice that still carried a hint of her native Texas drawl, "but later I want to hear about your adventure. Every little detail."

"Mother's already told you."

"Of course." With a laugh, Eve kissed Camilla's cheek. Gabriella had done more then tell her—she had enlisted Eve's help in the matter of prying and poking. "But that's secondhand information. I like going to the source."

"I've been waiting for Uncle Alex to call me out on the carpet."

Eve lifted an eyebrow. "That worries you?"

"I hate upsetting him."

"If I worried about that, I'd spend my life biting my nails." Lips pursed, Eve glanced at her perfect manicure. "Nope. He has to be what he is," she added more soberly, and looked out to the sea that lay blue against the edges of her adopted country. "So much responsibility. He was born for it—and bred for it. As you've been, honey. But he trusts you—completely. And he's very interested in your young man."

"He's not my young man."

"Ah. Well." She remembered, very well, when she'd tried to convince herself Alex, heir to Cordina, wasn't hers. "Let's say he's interested in Lord Delaney's work—and your interest in that work."

"Aunt Chris was a tremendous help," Camilla added, glancing over toward Eve's older sister. She wasn't technically Camilla's aunt, but their family was a very inclusive one.

"Nothing she likes better than a good campaign. That comes from marrying the Gentleman from Texas. The senator was very pleased to discuss the Bardville Research Project with his associates in Florida."

"After Aunt Chris talked him into it, and I'm very grateful to her. She looks wonderful, by the way."

"Like a newlywed," Eve agreed. "After five years of marriage. She always said she was holding out for the perfect man. I'm glad she found him. Whether it takes fifty years or five minutes," she said, giving Camilla's hand a quick squeeze, "when it's right, you know it. And when you know it and you're smart, you don't take no for an answer. Something like that is worth fighting for. Well, back to work."

Camilla stopped by the tables, found a precious three minutes to speak with her young cousin Marissa. She watched her sister, Adrienne, sit and with apparently good cheer, talk with an elderly Italian countess who was deaf as a post.

Hannah, her uncle Bennett's wife, gestured her over to a shady table where she sat enjoying tea and scones with Del's mother.

"Lady Brigston and I have a number of mutual acquaintances," Hannah explained. "I've been badgering her about her work, and now I'm dreaming about running off to dig for dinosaur bones."

There had been a time when, as a British agent, adventure had been Hannah's lifework. But as a princess, and mother of two active sons, she'd traded one kind of adventure for another.

As an agent, she'd had to deliberately downplay her looks and bury her love of fashion, now she could indulge them. Her dark blond hair was sleeked back in a twist. Her sleeveless tea dress showed off athletic arms and was the same vivid green as her eyes.

"I'd like that myself." Smiling, Camilla obeyed Hannah's signal and sat. "Though I imagine it's hard, tedious work. You must love it," she said to Alice.

"It's what I always wanted to do—even as a child. Other girls collected dolls. I collected fossils."

"It's so rewarding," Camilla commented, "to know, always, what you want, and be able to work toward it."

"Indeed." Alice inclined her head. "And tremendously exciting, I'd think, to discover an advocation along the way—and work toward it."

"Oh. Would you excuse me a moment?" Recognizing her cue, Hannah rose. "I need to speak with Mrs. Cartwright." She exchanged a quick and telling look with Alice—and got out of the way.

"Your family, if I may say so, Your Highness, is wonderful."

"Thank you. I agree with you."

"I'm, as a rule, more comfortable in the company of men. Simply don't have much in common with females. So fussy about the oddest things, to my mind."

The hand she waved had nails that were short and unpainted. She wore only a simple gold band on her ring finger. "But I feel very much at home with your mother, your aunts," she went on. "It's no wonder I'm already so fond of you."

"Thank you," Camilla said again, a little flustered. "That's very kind."

"Are you very angry with my son?"

"I—"

"Not that I blame you," Alice went on before Camilla could formulate a diplomatic answer. "He can be such a... what's the word I'm looking for? Oh, yes. Bonehead. Such a bonehead. He gets it from his father, so he really can't help it. He must've given you a terrible time."

"No. Not at all."

"No need to be tactful." She patted Camilla's hand. "It's just we two, and I know my boy in and out. Terrible manners—partially my fault, I can't deny it. I never was one to bother about the niceties. Outrageous temper—that's his father's—always booming around. Forgets why half the time after the explosion—which is annoying and frustrating to the other party. Don't you think?"

"Yes—" With a half laugh, Camilla shook her head.

"Lady Brigston, you're putting me in an awkward position. Let me say I admire your son's work—his approach to it and his passion for it. On a personal level, we have what you might call a conflict in styles."

"You have been well raised, haven't you?" Gabriella had warned her it wouldn't be easy to chip through the composure. "Do you mind if I tell you a little story? There was once a young American girl, barely twenty-one with her college degree hot in her hand. She had a fire in her belly, one burning ambition. Paleontology. Most thought her mad," she added with a twinkle. "After all what was a young woman doing fiddling around with dinosaur bones? She wheedled her way onto a dig—this particular dig because the man in charge was someone who's work—his approach to it and his passion for it—she admired."

She paused, smiled and sipped her tea. "She read his books, read articles on or by him. He was, to her, a great hero. Imagine her reaction when he turned out to be this big, irritable, impatient man who barely acknowledged her existence—and then mostly to complain about it."

"He is like his father," Camilla murmured.

"Oh, the spitting image," Alice acknowledged with some pride. "They sniped at each other, this rude man and this brash young woman. She did most of the sniping as he was so thickheaded most of her best shots just bounced off his skull. It was utterly infuriating."

"Yes," Camilla said almost to herself. "Infuriating."

"He was fascinating. So brilliant, so handsome, so—apparently—disinterested in her. Though he began to soften, just a little, toward her as she was damn good at the work and had a sharp, seeking mind. Caine men admire a sharp, seeking mind."

"Apparently."

"She fell madly in love with him, and after getting over being annoyed with herself over that, she put that sharp mind to work. She pursued him, which flustered him. He found all manner of reasons why this shouldn't be. He was fifteen years older, he didn't have time for females and so on. She had a few quibbles herself. This Earl of Brigston business just didn't fit into her Yankee system very well. It might have discouraged her, but she was stubborn—and she knew, in her heart, he had feelings for her. And since the title came with the man, and she wanted the man, she decided she could live with it. So what could she do but seduce him?"

Because Alice looked at Camilla for agreement, Camilla nodded obediently. "Naturally."

"He stammered and stuttered and looked, for a delightful few moments, like a panicked horse caught in a stable fire. But she had her way with him. And three weeks later, they were married. It seems to be working out well," she added with a little smile.

"She was an admirable young woman."

"Yes, she was. And she gave birth to an admirable, if knot-headed son. Do you love him?"

"Lady Brigston—"

"Oh, please, call me Alice. I look at you, and I see a young woman, so bright, so fresh, so unhappy. I know my place, but I'm looking at Camilla, not Her Royal Highness."

"He sees the title, and forgets the woman who holds it."

"If you want him, don't let him forget. You put flowers in his house," she said, quietly now. "I never remember to do that sort of thing myself. You know he kept them, after you'd gone."

Tears swam into her eyes. "He just didn't notice them."

"Yes. He did. Part of him wants to step away from you

and bury himself in his work again. I imagine both of you—being strong, capable young people—will do very well if you go your separate ways. But I wonder what the two of you might do, might make, if you break through this barrier of pride and hurt and come together. Don't you?"

Yes, Camilla thought. Constantly. "I told him I loved him," she murmured, "and he turned me away."

With a hiss of breath, Alice sat back. "What an ass. Well then, I have one piece of advice. Camilla. Make him crawl a little—it'll be good for him—before he tells you the same. I have no doubt you can manage it."

Del suffered through a formal, and to his mind interminable, dinner party. He was seated between the deaf Italian countess and Camilla's sister, Adrienne. The single advantage was that Camilla's father was seated well across the enormous dining room.

It would, he decided, be more difficult for her dad to stab him with his dinner knife that way.

By the time the main course was served, he'd reversed his initial impression of Adrienne as a vapid if ornamental girl. She was, he realized, simply an incredibly sweet-natured woman who was both blissfully happy and quietly charming.

Her help with the countess saved his sanity. And when Adrienne glanced at him, a quick sparkle in her eyes, he saw some of Camilla's sly humor.

He found himself telling her about some of his work as she asked questions specifically designed to encourage it. It didn't occur to him until later that her talent was in drawing people out.

"No wonder Camilla's so fascinated." Adrienne smiled. She had, he'd noted, her mother's soothing voice and her father's sizzling blue eyes. "She always enjoyed puzzles—and that's your work, really, isn't it? A complex puzzle. I was never very good at them. Will you go back to Florida soon?"

"Yes, very soon." He shouldn't be here at all, he told himself.

"When my children are a bit older, we'll take them there. To Disney World." She looked across the table at her husband.

It was that look he'd think of later as well. The sheer contentment in it. The look that had been missing from Camilla's face, he thought, except for the briefest of times.

It had been there. He remembered it being there, when she'd stretched out on the bank of his pond. *Camilla Content,* he'd called her. And then she'd been gone.

Chapter 11

For a princess she worked like a horse. It made it difficult for a man to manage five minutes alone with her to apologize.

Del wasn't sure exactly what he was apologizing for, but he was beginning to think she had one coming.

Guilt—a taste he didn't care for—had been stuck in his throat since he'd seen that tear run down her cheek. Adding to it were various members of her family who were so bloody friendly, or gracious—or both at the same time—he was beginning to feel like a jackass.

Even her mother had cornered him. If that was an acceptable definition of being taken gently aside to be given a warm and graceful expression of her gratitude for opening his home to her daughter.

"I know she's a grown woman," Gabriella said as she stood with him on a rise overlooking the gem-blue waters of the Mediterranean. "And a capable one. But I'm a mother, and we tend to worry."

"Yes, madam." He agreed, though he'd never considered his mother much of a worrier.

"I worried less when I knew she was with someone trustworthy and kind—who she obviously respected." Gabriella continued to smile, even when he—quite visibly—winced. "I'd been concerned about her for some time."

"Concerned?"

"She'd been working too hard for too long. Since the death of my father, and her own blossoming, you could say, there have been more demands on her time, her energies."

"Your daughter has considerable energy."

"Yes, as a rule. I'm afraid she's been more exposed to the appetites of the media in the last year or two than anyone could be prepared for."

Could he understand? Gabriella wondered. Could anyone who hadn't lived it? She hoped he could.

"She's lovely, as you know, and vibrant—as well as the oldest female of her generation of the family. The media's pursuit of her has been voracious, and I'm afraid it cost her, emotionally. Even physically. I know what it's like. I used to slip away myself. There are times the need to be away, even from something dear to your heart, is overwhelming. Don't you think?"

"Yes. I have Vermont."

Her face went soft, and bright. Yes, she thought, he could understand. "And I had my little farm. Until, I think, very recently, Camilla hadn't found her place to be away. To be quiet, even if it was just inside her mind. Thank you." She rose up and kissed his cheek. "Thank you for helping her find it."

He might have felt lower, Del thought when they parted, if he crawled on his belly and left a slimy trail behind him.

He had to talk to Camilla. Reasonably. Rationally. There were questions now, and he wanted them answered. It seemed only right a man should have some answers before he did that crawling.

But every time he made some subtle inquiry about her, he was told she was in a meeting, taking an appointment, engaged with her personal assistant.

He wanted to think all this meant manicures or shopping or whatnot, until Adrienne corrected him. "I'm sorry, were you looking for Camilla?"

"No." It felt awkward lying to that soft, pretty smile. "Not exactly, madam. I haven't seen her this morning."

Adrienne cuddled her baby daughter. "She's doing double duty, I'm afraid. My oldest isn't feeling quite well, and I don't like to leave him. She's filling in for me at the hospital. I was scheduled to visit the pediatric ward, but with little Armand so fussy, I wanted to be close."

"Ah... I hope he's all right."

"He's napping now, and seems much better. I thought I'd bring the baby out for some sunshine before I went back up to check on him. But Camilla should be back in an hour. No," she corrected. "She has an appointment with Mama regarding the Arts Center afterward. I know she normally deals with correspondence midafternoon, though where she'll find the time today is beyond me."

She kept the soft smile on her face and the delighted laughter inside. The poor man, she thought, was so frustrated. And so in love with her sister.

"Is there something I can do for you?"

"No. No, madam, thank you."

"I believe Dorian escaped down to the stables," she said

kindly. "Several of the guests are making use of the horses, if you'd like to join them."

He didn't, but wished he had when he was summoned by Prince Alexander.

"Lord Brigston, I hope you haven't been neglected since your arrival."

"Not at all, Your Highness."

The office reflected the man, Del thought. Both were elegant, male and polished by tradition. The prince exuded power along with dignity. His hair was black as night and threaded with silver. His aristocratic face was honed to sharp angles. Dark, his eyes were equally sharp and very direct.

"Since the Princess Camilla has expressed such a keen interest, I've studied some of your work. My family's interests," he said in a tone smooth as a polished dagger, "are mine. Tell me more about this current project of yours."

Though he resented being made to feel like a student auditioning, Del obliged. He understood perfectly, and knew he was meant to understand, that he was being measured and judged.

When, in twenty minutes, he was graciously dismissed, Del wasn't certain if he'd passed the audition or if he should keep a wary eye out for the executioner.

But he did know the back of his neck prickled as the image of an ax poised above it hovered in his mind.

Any man, he decided, who considered—however remotely considered—becoming involved with a member of the Royal Family of Cordina needed his head examined. While it was still safely on his shoulders.

Del had always considered himself perfectly sane.

To stay that way, he decided to escape for a couple of hours. It wasn't a simple matter. A man couldn't just call a damn cab to come pick him up at the palace. There was procedure, protocol, policy. In the end, Camilla's older brother Kristian casually offered him the use of a car—and a driver if he liked.

Del took the car and skipped the driver.

And came as close to falling in love with a place not his own as he'd ever in his life.

There was something stunning about it—the tiny country on the sea. It made him think of jewels—old and precious ones passed down from generation to generation.

The land rose in tiers of hills from the lap of the sea. Houses, pink and white and dull gold tumbled up and down those rises, jutted out on the promontory, as if they'd been carved there. Flowers—he'd been paying more attention to them since Camilla—grew in abundance and with such a free and casual air they added immense charm to the drama of rock and cliff. The fronds of regal palms fluttered in a constant balmy breeze.

The sense of age appealed to him. Generation by generation, century by century, this small gem had survived and gleamed, and clung to its heart without giving way to the frenzied rush of urbanity, without exploiting its vast and staggering views with skyscrapers.

He imagined it had changed here and there over time. No place remained the same, and that was the beauty of man. And when man had wisdom along with invention, he managed to find a way to preserve the heart while feeding the mind.

The Bissets, who had ruled here for four centuries, had obviously been wise.

He stopped on the drive back, along the winding, rising road, to study the place of princes. It was only just, he supposed, that the palace stood on the highest point. It faced the sea, its white stones rising from the cliff. It spread, even rambled with its battlements, its parapets and towers harking proudly back to another age. Another time.

Wars, he thought, and royalty. Historic bedfellows.

Even in modern times a small, ugly little war had been fought here. When he'd been a boy a self-styled terrorist had attempted to assassinate members of the Royal Family. Camilla's mother had been kidnapped. Her aunt, then simply Eve Hamilton, had been shot.

He realized now that he hadn't considered that, or how such a history so close to the heart could and did affect Camilla.

Still, she hadn't let it stop her from striking out on her own, alone, he thought now. It didn't stop her from coming back here, to the castle on the hill, and taking up her family duties.

The country, the family, was at peace now. But peace was a fragile thing.

He imagined those who lived inside understood the palace had been built for defense. And his archaeologist's eye could see how cagey the design. There could be no attack from the sea, no force that could breech the sheer rock walls of the cliffs. And the height, the hills made it all but impregnable.

Its port made it rich.

It had also been built for beauty. He considered the quest for beauty a very human need.

Standing where he was, he wouldn't have thought of it as a home, but only as a symbol. But he had been inside, beyond those iron gates. However powerful, or symbolic, or aesthetically potent, it was a home.

Perhaps she lived a part of her life on a farm in Virginia, but this place, this palace, this country, was very much her home.

It had to be obvious to both of them that it couldn't be his.

When he drove back through the gates, passed the bold red uniforms of the palace guards, a cloud of depression came with him.

"He's in a horrible mood," Alice confided to Gabriella when they stole five minutes in the music room. They huddled close, as conspirators should. "Apparently he went out for a drive and came back brooding and snarly. It's a good sign."

"Camilla's been distracted and out of sorts all afternoon. It's going perfectly. Oh, and my spies tell me Delaney asked about her several times this morning."

"The best thing was her being so busy and unavailable. Give that boy time to think."

"He won't be able to think when he sees her tonight. Oh, Alice, she looks so beautiful in her gown. I was at her last fitting, and she's just spectacular."

"They're going to make us beautiful grandchildren," Alice said with a sigh.

He didn't like wearing black tie. There were so many pieces to it, why a man needed all those pieces where a shirt and pants did the job was beyond him.

But he'd made up his mind to leave in the morning, so that was something. He'd already come up with the necessary excuse for his early departure—an urgent e-mail from the site.

No one would know the difference.

He'd fulfill his obligation tonight—for his parents—find a way to apologize or at least come to terms with Camilla. And then get back to reality as soon as possible. He wasn't a man for palaces. Digging under one maybe—now that could be interesting.

All he had to do was survive the sticky formality of one more evening. He was sure he could manage to slip out early from that event as well. In the morning, he'd pay his respects to his hosts, then get the hell out of Dodge.

Only one little chore had to be done first. He had to—in all good conscience—express his appreciation for the help in funding to Camilla. Face-to-face, and without the stiffness he'd fallen back on in correspondence.

That had been small of him and unworthy of her gesture.

Dressed, and wanting nothing more than to get the entire ordeal over with, he joined his parents in their sitting room.

"Well, hell, look at you." It was a rare event to see his mother elegantly attired. He grinned, circling his finger so that she turned. The simple black gown showed off her trim, athletic figure, and the Brigston pearls added panache.

"You're a babe," he decided and made her laugh.

"I figure I can stand these shoes for about an hour and a half, after that, it's anybody's guess." She walked over to straighten her husband's formal tie.

"Don't fuss, Alice. I'm getting rid of the damn thing at the first opportunity." Still Niles smiled as he leaned down to kiss her cheek. "But the boy's right. You are a babe."

"This 'do' will be crawling with babes. Speaking of which," Alice said casually to her son, "have you seen Camilla today?"

"No."

"Ah, well. You'll see her tonight."

"Right." With hundreds of people around, he thought. How the hell would he manage to say what he had to say— once he figured out what that was—when they were surrounded? "Let's get this over with," Del suggested.

"God. Just like your father." Resigned, Alice took each of her men by the arm.

Guests were formally announced, then escorted to the receiving line. The bows and curtsies went on endlessly in Del's estimation. Then he got his first look at Camilla, and forgot everything else.

She wore a gown the same tawny gold as her eyes. In it, she was iridescent. Luminous. It left her shoulders bare, nipped in to a tiny waist, then simply flowed out with what seemed like miles of skirt that shimmered like sun-drenched water in the elegant light of countless chandeliers.

White and yellow diamonds sparkled at her ears, dripped in complex tiers toward the swell of her breast. And fired in the tiara set on the glossy cap of her hair.

She was, in that moment, the embodiment of the fairy-tale princess. Beauty, grace and elegance, and all of them bone-deep.

He had never felt so much the frog.

But he thought—hoped—he'd managed to roll his eyes back into his head by the time he reached her.

"My lord."

"Madam." He took the hand she offered, sliding his thumb over her knuckles. Had this woman actually scrambled eggs for him? If this was reality, maybe all the rest had been some complex fantasy.

"I hope you'll enjoy your evening."

"I wasn't planning on it."

Her polite smile never wavered. "Then I hope you don't find it overly tedious."

"I need five minutes," he murmured.

"I'm afraid this is an inconvenient time. Let go of my hand," she said in an undertone as his grip tightened. "People are watching."

"Five minutes," he said again and their eyes locked, then he reluctantly moved up the line.

Her heart might have raced, but she continued to stand, smile and greet guests. The combination of willpower and breeding stopped her from giving into the towering urge to crane her neck and find Del in the crowd moving into the ballroom. Curiosity pierced with a splinter of hope made her almost ill by the time her aunt and uncle opened Cordina's Autumn Ball.

He'd looked at her—hadn't he—as he had at odd moments in the cabin. As if she were the center of his thoughts.

But, as she and her cousin Luc crossed the floor for their first dance, she had no time for private thoughts.

When the palace opened its doors for a ball, it opened them wide and with brilliant ceremony. Glamour was allowed full sway here and given the satin edge of pomp. Waterfalls of chandeliers showered light on dazzling gowns, glittering jewels, banks of sumptuous flowers. Frothy champagne bubbled in crystal.

On the terrace beyond there was the seductive glow of candles and torchères. Hundreds of antique mirrors lined the walls and threw back reflection after reflection of gorgeously gowned women and elegantly garbed men as they spun around the polished floor.

Jewels flashed, and music soared.

Camilla danced, for duty and for pleasure, and then for love with her father.

"I watched you and Mama."

"Watched us what?"

"Dancing just a bit ago. And I thought, look at them." She pressed her cheek to his. "How can anyone look anywhere but at them. They're so beautiful."

"Did I ever tell you about the first time I saw her?"

Camilla leaned back to laugh into his eyes. "A million times. Tell me again."

"It was her sixteenth birthday. A ball, very much like this. She wore a pale green dress, not so different from what you're wearing now. All those billowing skirts that make a woman look like a fantasy. Diamonds in her hair, the way they're in yours tonight. I fell in love with her on the spot, though I didn't see her again for ten years. She was the most exquisite thing I'd ever laid eyes on."

He looked down at her daughter. "Now I'm dancing with the second most exquisite thing."

"Daddy." She took her hand from his shoulder to touch his face. "I love you so much. I'm sorry you were mad at me."

"I wasn't mad, baby. Worried, but not mad. Now as far as that jackass you were with—"

"Daddy."

The warning light in her eye had him glaring right back at her. "I have one thing to say about him. He has potential."

"You don't really know—" She broke off, narrowed her eyes suspiciously. "Is this a trap?"

"I used to worry that some slick-talking pretty boy was going to come along and sweep you off before you realized he was a jerk. Well, you certainly can't call Caine slick-talking or pretty."

"No, indeed."

"And since you already know he's a jerk, you're in good shape," he added, making her laugh. "I want you happy, Cam. Even more than I want to keep my little girl all to myself."

"You're going to make me cry."

"No, you won't cry." He drew her close again. "You're made of sterner stuff than that."

"I love him, Daddy."

"I know." Reeve's eyes met Del's across the crowds of dancers. "Poor son of a bitch doesn't have a prayer. You go get him, honey. And if he doesn't come around quick enough, let me know. I'd still like a reason to kick his ass."

"Make up your mind, Delaney."

"About what?"

Alice took the wine she'd asked him to fetch. "Whether you're just going to scowl at Camilla half the night, or ask her to dance."

"She hasn't stopped dancing for two minutes all night, has she?"

"It's part of her job. Or do you think she likes dancing with that pizza-faced young man with the buck teeth who's stepping all over her feet? Go. Dance with her."

"If you think I'm lining up with half the men in this place—"

"I'd say you'd lost your wits," Alice finished. "Go, cut in. Another minute with that clumsy boy and she'll have a permanent limp."

"All right, all right." Put that way, it was like doing her a favor. Sort of like riding to the rescue, he decided as he saw—quite clearly—the wince flicker over her face as her feet were stomped on again.

Feeling more heroic with each step, Del threaded through the dancers. He tapped Camilla's partner on the shoulder, and moved in so smoothly he surprised himself.

"Cutting in." He whirled Camilla away before the boy could do more than gawk and stammer.

"That was rude."

"Did the trick. How're your feet?"

Her lips twitched. "Other than a few broken toes, holding up, thank you. You dance quite well, my lord."

"Been a while, but it comes back to you, madam. Either way, I couldn't be worse than your last partner. Figured you needed a break."

"Rescuing the damsel in distress?" She arched her eyebrows. "Really, twice in one lifetime. Be careful or you'll make it a habit. You said you needed five minutes with me—and that was nearly two hours ago. Did you change your mind?"

"No." But he was no longer clear on what to do with five minutes. Not now that he was holding her again. "I wanted to… About the project. The funding."

"Ah." Disappointment sank into her belly. "If it's business, I'll see that Marian schedules an appointment for you tomorrow."

"Camilla. I wanted to thank you."

She softened, just a little. "You're welcome. The project's important to me, too, you know."

"I guess I get that. Now." He had only to angle his head, dip it a little, and his mouth could be on hers. He wanted, more than anything, to have one long taste of her again. Even if it was the last time. "Camilla—"

"The dance is finished." But her gaze stayed locked with his, and her voice was thick. "You have to let me go."

He knew that. He knew exactly that. But not quite yet. "I need to talk to you."

"Not here. For heaven's sake, if you don't let me go you'll have your name splashed all over the papers tomorrow." She smiled, gaily.

"I don't give a damn."

"You haven't lived with it all your life, as I have. Please, step back. If you want to talk, we'll go out on the terrace."

When he relaxed his grip, she eased away, then spoke clearly and in the friendliest of tones for all the pricked ears nearby. "It's warm. I wonder, Lord Delaney, if you'd join me for some fresh air? And I'd love a glass of champagne."

"No problem."

She slid an arm through his as they walked off the dance floor. "My brothers tell me you ride very well. I hope you'll continue to enjoy the stables while you're here." She kept up the casual chatter as he lifted a flute of champagne from a silver tray and offered it.

"Do you ride, madam?"

"Certainly." She sipped, strolled toward the open terrace doors. "My father breeds horses on his farm. I've ridden all my life."

A number of other guests had spilled out onto the terrace. Before Camilla could walk to the rail, Del simply tugged her arm, the wine sloshing to the rim of her glass as he steered her briskly toward the wide stone steps.

"Slow down." She paused at the top. "I can't jog down stairs in this dress. I'll break my neck."

He took her glass from her, then stood restlessly by as she gracefully lifted her billowing skirts with her free hand. At the base of the steps, he set the champagne—barely touched—on the closest table, then continued to pull her down one of the garden paths.

"Stop dragging me along," she hissed. "People will—"

"Oh, lighten up," he snapped.

She grit her teeth as she struggled to maintain her dignity. "See how light you are when gossipmongers in ten countries are tossing your name around tomorrow. In any case, I'm wearing three-inch heels and five miles of skirt. Just slow down."

"I don't listen to gossip, so I won't hear them tossing my name around. And if I slow down too long, somebody's going to jump out of some corner with something for you to do. Or to fawn and scrape. Or just say something so they can say they've spoken to you. I want five damn minutes alone with you."

The retort that rose to her lips faded away.

Sparkling silver luminaries lighted a path that was already streamed with moonlight. She could smell the romance of night jasmine and roses, hear it in the pulse and pound of the sea. And her own heart.

Her lover wanted to be alone with her.

He didn't stop until the music was barely more than a murmur in the distance. "Camilla."

She held her breath. "Delaney."

"I wanted to—" She wore moonlight like pearls, he thought, too dazzled to be astonished by the poetic turn of mind. Her skin was sheened with it. Her eyes glowed. The diamonds in her hair sparked, reminding him there was heat inside the elegance.

He tried again. "I wanted to apologize for... To tell you—"

She didn't know who moved first. It didn't seem to matter. All that mattered was they were in each other's arms. Their mouths met, once, twice. Frantically. Then a third time, long and deep.

"I missed you." He pulled her closer, rocking when she was locked against him. "God, I missed you."

The words seemed to pour into her. "Don't let go. Don't let me go."

"I didn't think I'd ever see you again." He turned his

head to race kisses over her face. "I didn't mean to ever see you again."

"I wasn't ever going to see you again first," she said with a laugh. "Oh, I was so angry when I got that letter. That stiff, formal, nasty letter: 'We of the Bardville Research Project wish to express our sincere appreciation.' I could've murdered you."

"You should've seen the first draft." He eased back enough to grin at her. "It was a lot...pithier."

"I'd probably have preferred it." She threw her arms around his neck. "Oh, I'm so happy. I've been trying to figure out how to live without you. Now I won't have to. After we're married, you can teach me how to read one of those lab reports with all those symbols. I never could..."

She trailed off because he'd gone so completely still. Her soaring heart fell back to earth with a rude and painful thud. "You don't love me." Her voice was quiet, scrupulously calm as she eased out of his arms. "You don't want to marry me."

"Let's just slow down, okay? Marriage—" His throat closed up on the word. "Let's be sensible, Camilla."

"Of course. All right, let's." Now her tone was terrifyingly pleasant. "Why don't you go first?"

"There are... There are issues here," he began, frantically trying to clear his jumbled brain long enough to think.

"Very well." She folded her hands. "Issue number one?"

"Cut that out. You just cut that out." He paced down the path, back again. "I have a very demanding, time-consuming profession."

"Yes."

"When I'm in the field, I usually live in a trailer that makes the cabin look like a five-star hotel."

"Yes?"

He bared his teeth, but snagged his temper back at the

last minute. "You can't stand there, with that palace at your back while you're wearing a damn crown and tell me you don't see there's a problem."

"So, issue one is our different lifestyles and separate responsibilities."

"In a nutshell. And neatly glossing over the tiaras and glass slippers. Yeah."

"Glass slippers?" That snapped it. "Is that how you see me, and my life—as one ball after the next, one magic pumpkin ride? I have just as vital a role in the world in my glass slippers as you do in your work boots."

"I'm not saying you don't. That's the whole point." He tugged his formal tie loose and dragged it off. "This isn't what I do. I can't strap myself up like a penguin every time I turn around because you have a social obligation. But you should have someone who would. And I'm not asking you to chuck your diamonds to live in camp in the middle of nowhere. It's ridiculous. It would never work."

"That's where you're wrong. My father was a cop who wanted to farm. Who wanted, more than anything, peace and quiet and to work on the land. My mother was—is—a princess. When they met she was the chatelaine of this place. She had taken up the responsibility as hostess, as ambassador, as symbolic female head of this country when her mother died. But you see, they loved each other so they found a way to give to each other what they needed, to accept the responsibilities and obligations each brought with them, and to make a life together."

Her chin was up now, her eyes glittering. "They make me proud. And I'm determined to be every bit the woman my mother is. But you, you with your excuses and your pitiful issues, you're not half the man my father is. *He* had courage and spine and romance. He isn't intimidated by a crown because he respects and understands the woman who wears it."

She swept up her skirts again. "I would have lived in your trailer and still have been a princess. My duty to my name—and yours—would never be shirked. It's you who doubt you could live in this palace and still be a man."

Dal

Chapter 12

He hated one single fact the most. She was right. Under all the issues and trappings and complications, he'd been… well, he didn't like the term intimidated. Leery, he decided as he stalked around the gardens as he was wont to stalk around his forest in Vermont. He was leery of linking himself with the princess.

He'd been paying attention in the weeks they'd been apart. He'd seen her face and name splashed over the media. He'd read the stories about her personal life, the speculations about her romantic liaisons.

He knew damn well she wasn't and hadn't been having some hot affair with a French actor as all the articles had trumpeted. She'd been too busy having one with a half-American archaeologist.

Besides, anyone who knew her could see the actor wasn't her type. Too smooth for Camilla.

And that was part of it. The stories, the innuendoes, the

outright fabrications were, for the most part, written by people who didn't know her. Who didn't understand how hard she was willing to work, or her devotion to her mother's country. Her great love of her family, and theirs for her.

They saw an image. The same one he'd let himself be blinded by.

But damn it all to hell and back, the woman had leaped from possible, tentative relationship into marriage so quickly it had been like a sucker punch to the jaw. She didn't give a guy a chance to test his footing.

All or nothing with her, he thought darkly as he jammed his hands into his pockets and reviewed the situation.

First, he finally figures out he's in love with her, then he gets poked in the eye with the fact she's been lying to him. Before he can clear his vision on that, she's long gone. So what that he'd told her to go.

Now, after he'd realized the whole situation was totally impossible, she had to stand there looking like something out of a dream and make him see just how much he'd be losing. And just when he'd started to think maybe, maybe, with time and effort, they could get back what they'd had, she kicked him square in the teeth with marriage.

Yeah, give her a month in a trailer in Florida, toss in a few tropical storms, knee-deep mud, bugs the size of baseballs, and…

She'd be great. He stopped dead in his tracks. She'd be fantastic. She was the kind of woman you could plunk down anywhere, in any situation and she'd find a way. She just kept hacking and prodding and fiddling until she found the way.

Because that was Camilla.

He'd fallen for that, he realized. Before he'd fallen for the looks, the style, the heat, he'd lost his head over her sheer determination to find the answers.

And he was letting a minor detail like royal blood stand in his way.

He wanted the woman, and the princess came along with her. Not half the man her father was? Oh, she'd tried to slice him up with that one. He didn't have courage, backbone. He had no romance?

He'd give her some romance that would knock her out of her glass slippers.

He turned, stormed halfway back to the ballroom before he stopped himself. That, he realized, was just the sort of thing he was going to have to avoid. If this relationship was going to have a chance in hell of working he was going to have to think ahead. A man went charging into a palace ball, tossed a princess over his shoulder and started carting her off, he was going to get them both exactly the sort of press she hated.

And likely end up tossed in some dark, damp dungeon for his trouble.

What a man had to do was work out a clear, rational plan—and carry it out where there were no witnesses.

So he sat down on a marble bench and began to do precisely that.

He got rope at the stables. There were times, he was forced to admit, where being a viscount came in handy. Stable hands were too polite to question the eccentricities of Lord Delaney.

He had to wait until the last waltz was over, and guests were tucked in to bed or were on the other side of the palace gates. That only gave him more time to work out logistics—and to wonder what his parents would do if he ended up breaking his idiotic neck.

He knew where her room was now. That had been a simple matter of subtly pumping Adrienne. He could only be grateful her windows overlooked the gardens where there were plenty of shadows. Though he doubted any guards who patrolled the area would be looking for a man dangling several stories up by a rope.

Even when that man swore bitterly when he swung, nearly face first, into those white stone walls. Rappelling down from the parapet had seemed a lot easier in theory than in fact. He was fairly proficient at it from his work, but climbing down a building at night was considerably different. The cold reality had him swinging in the wind with scraped knuckles and strained temper.

He didn't mind the height so much, unless he thought about the possibility of it being his last view. And all, he mused as he tried for a foothold on a stone balcony rail, because she'd pinched at his ego.

Just couldn't wait until morning. Oh, no, he thought as his foot skidded and he went swinging again. That would've been too easy, too ordinary. Too sane. Why have a civilized conversation in broad daylight and tell a woman you love her and want to marry her when you can do something really *stupid* like commit suicide on the bricks below her bedroom window?

That made a statement.

He managed to settle his weight on the rail, and catch his breath. And the rising wind swept in a brisk September rain.

"Perfect." He glanced up to the heavens. "That just caps it."

While the sudden downpour had rain streaming into his

eyes, he swung out again, kicked lightly off the wall, and worked his way down to Camilla's private terrace.

The first bolt of lightning crashed over the sea as he dropped down, thankfully, to solid stone. He fought with the knot of the thoroughly wet rope he'd looped around. It took him two drenching minutes to free himself. Dumping the rope, he pushed his sopping hair out of his eyes and marched to her terrace doors.

Found them locked.

For a moment he only stood, staring at them. What the hell did she lock the balcony doors for? he wondered with rising irritation. She was three stories up, in a damn palace with guards everywhere.

How often did she have some idiot climb down the wall and drop on her terrace?

She'd drawn the curtains, too, so he couldn't see a bloody thing. He considered, with a spurt of cheerfulness, the satisfaction of kicking in the doors.

There was a certain style to that, he thought. A certain panache. However, that would likely be squashed when alarms started to scream.

Here he was, wet as a drowned rat, on her terrace. And the only way to get in was to knock.

It was mortifying.

So he didn't knock so much as hammer.

Inside, Camilla was using a book as an excuse not to sleep. Every fifteen minutes or so, she actually read a sentence. For the most part, one single fact played over and over in her head.

She'd handled everything badly.

There was no way around it. When she stepped back to look at the big picture, Del had reacted exactly as she'd expect him to react. She had leaped, heart first, into an assumption of marriage.

She'd have been insulted if he'd been the one doing the assuming.

Did love make everyone stupid and careless, or was it just her?

She sighed, turned a page in the book without particular interest. She'd bungled everything, she decided, right from the beginning. Oh, he'd helped. He was such a…what had his mother said? Bonehead. Yes, he was such a bonehead—but she *loved* that about him.

But the blame was squarely on her head.

She hadn't been honest with him, and her reasons for holding back now seemed weak and selfish. His anger, and yes, his hurt, had so shattered her that she'd turned tail and run rather than standing her ground.

Then he'd come to her. Was she so steeped in her own self-pity that she refused to acknowledge that no matter how much pressure had been put on him, he'd never have traveled to Cordina unless he'd wanted to see her?

Even tonight he'd taken a step. Instead of taking one in return, she'd recklessly leaped. She'd taken for granted that he'd simply fall in line. Obviously she was too used to people doing so. Wasn't that one of the reasons she'd taken a holiday from being the princess? Had she learned nothing from those weeks as just plain Camilla?

It wasn't just marriage that had caused him to balk. It was the package that came with it. She closed her eyes. She could do nothing about that—would do nothing even if she could. Her family, her blood, her heritage were essential parts of her.

And yet, she wouldn't want a man who shrugged off the

complexities of her life. She couldn't love a man who enjoyed the fact that they'd be hounded by the press.

So where did that leave her? Alone, she thought, looking around her lovely, lonely room. Because she'd pushed away the only man she loved, the only man she wanted, by demanding too much, too fast.

No. She slammed the book shut. She wouldn't accept that. Accepting defeat was what had sent her running from the cabin. She wasn't going to do that again. There *had* to be an answer. There had to be a compromise. She would... no. She took a deep breath. *They* would find it.

She tossed the covers aside. She'd go to his room now, she decided. She'd apologize for the things she'd said to him and tell him...*ask* him if there was a way they could start again.

Before she could leap out of bed, the pounding on her terrace doors had her jumping back with her heart in her throat. She grabbed the Georgian silver candle-stick from her nightstand as a weapon, and was on the point of snatching up the phone to call security.

"Open the damn door."

She heard the voice boom out, followed by a vicious crack of thunder. Astonished, still gripping her makeshift weapon, she crossed to the doors, and nudged the curtains aside.

She saw him in a flash of lightning. The furious face, the dripping hair, the sopping tuxedo shirt. For a moment she could do nothing but stare with her mouth open.

"Open the damn door," he repeated loudly. "Or I kick it in."

Too stunned to do otherwise, she fumbled with latch and lock. Then she staggered back three steps when he pushed the doors open.

"What?" She could do no more than croak it out as he stood, glaring at her and dripping on the priceless rug.

"You want romance, sister." He grabbed the candle-stick out of her numb fingers and tossed it aside. It looked a little too heavy to risk any accidents, and he had enough bruises for one night.

"Del." She backed up another two steps as he stepped forward. "Delaney. How did you...your hand's bleeding."

"You want backbone? You want adventure? Maybe a little insanity thrown in?" He grabbed her shoulders, lifted her straight to her toes. "How's this?"

"You're all wet," was all she could say.

"You try climbing down the side of a castle in a rain-storm, see what shape you end up in."

"Climb?" She barely registered being pushed across the room. "You climbed down the wall? Have you lost your mind?"

"Damn right. And you know what the guy gets when he breaches the castle walls? He gets the princess."

"You can't just—"

But he could. She discovered very quickly that he could. Before she could clear sheer shock from her system, his mouth was hot on hers. And shock didn't have a chance against need. A thrill swept through her as he dragged her—oh my—to the bed.

He was wet and bleeding and in a towering temper. And he was all hers. She locked her arms around his neck, slid her fingers into that wonderful and dripping hair, and gladly offered him the spoils of war.

Her mouth moved under his, answering his violent kiss with all the joy, all the longing that raged inside her.

The storm burst through the open doors as she released him long enough to tug at his sodden shirt. It landed, some-where, with a wet plop.

He was surprised his clothes didn't simply steam off him.

The heat of his temper paled with the fire that she brought to his blood. So soft, so fragrant, so wonderfully willing. Her face was wet now with the rain he'd brought in with him. He could've lapped it—and her—up like cream.

Undone, he buried his face against her throat. "I need you, damn it. I can't get past it."

"Then have me." Her breath hitched as his hands roamed over her. "Take me."

He lifted his head, looked down at her. Her eyes were dark now, tawny as a cat's. And as her hands came up to frame his face, she smiled. "I've waited so long for you," she murmured. "And I didn't even know."

To prove it, she drew his mouth down to hers again.

Everything he felt for her, about her, from her, bloomed in the kiss. She trembled from it, and the quiet hum in her throat had his pulse bounding.

That long, white throat fascinated him. The strong slope of her shoulders was a wonder. Damp with rain now, the thin night slip she wore clung provocatively to her body. He took his mouth, his hands over the wet silk first, then the hot, damp flesh beneath.

She moved under him. A graceful arch, a quick shiver. Slowly first, savoring first, he explored, exploited. Excited. When her breathing was thick, her eyes dreamily closed, he dragged her to her knees and ravaged.

He'd catapulted her from quiet pleasure to reckless demand so that she floundered. Drowned in him. Those hard hands that had been so blissfully gentle were now erotically rough. Bowing back, she surrendered to that hungry mouth. Moaned his name as he tore reason to shreds.

She went wild in his arms. As her need pitched to meet his, she tore and tugged at his clothes. Kneeling on the bed, they clung, flesh to flesh, heart raging against heart.

Once more, in a flash of lightning, their eyes met. Held. In his, at last, she saw all she needed to see. And it was she who shifted, taking him in. Wrapping her legs around him to take him deep until they both trembled.

"Je t'aime." She said it clearly though her body quaked. "I love you. I can't help myself."

Before he could speak, her mouth covered his. What was left of his control snapped, whipping his body toward frenzy. She met him, beat for frantic beat. When she closed around him, he swallowed her cry of release. And emptied himself.

"Camilla." He couldn't think past her name, even as he slid down her body to nestle between her breasts. He felt her fingers stroke through his hair and wanted nothing more than to close his eyes and stay steeped in her for the rest of his life.

But his gaze skimmed toward the terrace—and the rain cheerfully blowing in the open doors and soaking floor and rug.

"I didn't close the doors. We're starting to flood. Just stay."

As he rolled away, she watched him lazily. Then she bolted up as he started to cross the room. "No! Wait." She scrambled out of bed, snatched the robe that had been draped over the curved back of her settee. "Someone might see," she muttered, then, with her robe modestly closed, hurried to close the doors herself.

Control, he thought as he watched her draw the drapes. Even now. A princess couldn't walk around naked in front of the windows—not even her own. And certainly couldn't have a man do so.

She turned, saw him eyeing her speculatively. "The guards. Guests," she began, then dropped her gaze. "I'll get some towels."

While she walked into the adjoining bath, he untangled his damp tuxedo pants. They were ruined, he decided, and would be miserably uncomfortable. But if they were going to have a conversation, he wanted to be wearing something besides his heart on his sleeve.

She came back, got down on her hands and knees and began mopping the floor. It made him smile. Made him remember her in his cabin.

"I have to be practical, Delaney."

His brows drew together at the strained edge in her voice. "I understand that."

"Do you?" She hated herself for wanting to weep now.

"Yes, I do. I admire the way you manage to be practical, self-sufficient—and royal."

Her head came up slowly. She eased back to sit on her heels, and the look of surprise on her face was enough to have him shoving his hands in his wet pockets. "I admire you," he said again. "I'm not good with words, these kinds of words. Damn it, do you think I'm an idiot? That I don't have a clue what kind of juggling act you—your whole family—has to perform to be who you are and manage to have any sort of life along with it?"

"No." Looking away from him again, she folded the damp portion of the rug back, then dried the floor beneath it. "No, I believe you understand—as much as you can. Maybe more than another man might. I think that's why, in some ways, we're at odds."

"Why don't you look at me when you talk to me?"

Struggling for composure, she pressed her lips together. But her gaze was level when she lifted her head again. "It's difficult for me. Excuse me a moment." She rose, and shoulders straight as a soldier's, carried the damp towels back to the bath.

Women, Del thought, were a hell of a lot of work.

She came back, went to a small cabinet and took out a decanter. "I think some brandy would help. I was wrong," she began as she poured two snifters. "Tonight in the garden, I was wrong to say those things to you. I apologize."

"Oh, shut up." Out of patience, he snatched a snifter out of her hand.

"Can't you at least pretend to be gracious?"

"Not when you're being stupid. If I want an apology, you'll know it." She'd beat him to the damn apology. Wasn't it just like her? He paced away and though he didn't care for it, took a slug of the brandy. "When you're wrong, I'll let you know it."

He spun back, temper alive on his face. "You hurt me." It infuriated him to admit it.

"I know. The things I said—"

"Not that. That just pissed me off." He dragged a hand through his hair. "You lied to me, Camilla. Or the next thing to it. I started counting on you. And I don't mean to clean up after me. I started thinking about you—about us—a certain way. Then it all blew up in my face."

"I handled it badly. It was selfish—I was selfish," she corrected. "I wanted some time—then more time—to just be. I ran. I told myself it wasn't running away, but it was. Last summer, it was all suddenly too heavy, too close. I couldn't..."

"Just be?"

"I couldn't just be," she said, quietly. "Last summer there was an incident with the press. Not much more, really, no less than so many others the past few years. But it had been building up inside me, all of it until it just got to be too much. I couldn't eat. I wasn't sleeping well, I couldn't concentrate on what I was meant to do. I..."

"No, don't stop. Tell me."

"This incident," she said carefully, "wasn't so different from others. But while it was happening I could hear myself screaming. Inside. I thought—I knew—that unless I got away for a while, the next time it happened, the screams wouldn't be just inside. I was afraid I was having some sort of breakdown."

"Camilla, for God's sake."

"I should've spoken with my family." She looked back at him because she'd heard that unspoken question in his shocked tone. "They would have understood, supported me, given me time and room. But I just couldn't bring myself to confess such a weakness. Poor Camilla, who's been given every privilege in life, and more—so much more—the unquestioning love from family, is suddenly too delicate, too fragile to deal with the responsibilities and difficulties of her rank and position."

"That's malarkey."

The term made her laugh a little. And steadied her. "It didn't feel like it at the time. It felt desperate. I was losing myself. I don't know if you can understand that because you know yourself so intimately. But I felt hounded and hunted, and at the same time so unsteady about who I was, inside. What I wanted to do with my life beyond what I was supposed to do, beyond duty. I had no passion for anything, and there's a horrible kind of emptiness to that."

He could imagine it—the pressures, the demands—and the nerves of steel it took to be who she was. The courage, he thought, it had taken to break from all that to find the woman inside.

"So you took off, with a couple suitcases in a rental car, to find it?"

"More or less. And I did find it, though as I said, in the end, I handled it badly."

"We handled it badly," he corrected. "I was over my head with you, and that was when I thought you were a weird rich chick in some kind of trouble. When I found out, I figured you'd used me for some kind of a lark."

She paled. "It was never—"

"I know that now. I know it. I had feelings for you I've never had for anyone else. I'd worked myself up to tell you— and came into the kitchen and heard you talking on the phone."

"To Marian." Eyes closed, Camilla let out a long breath. "The timing," she murmured, "couldn't have been worse. I'm surprised you didn't throw me out bodily."

"Thought about it." He waited until her eyes opened, met his again. "It felt better when I sat around feeling sorry for myself. It took me a while to start considering what it's like for you. The people, the press, the protocol. It's pretty rough."

"It's not all that bad. It's just that sometimes you have to—"

"Breathe," he finished.

"Yes." Tears swam into her eyes. "Yes."

"Don't do that. I can't have a rational conversation if you start dripping. Look, I mean it. Plug the dam. I've never told a woman I love her, and I'm sure as hell not going to do it for the first time when she's blubbering."

"I'm not blubbering." But her voice broke on a sob as joy leaped into her. She yanked open a drawer, tugged out a lace-trimmed hankie and wiped at tears. She wanted to leap again, just leap. But this time, she knew to keep quiet. "So, tell me."

"I'll get to it. You're not fragile, Camilla."

"Not as a rule, no."

"Cordina's crown jewel. I've been catching up on some magazines," he said when she stared at him. "A jewel has to have substance to keep its shine. You've got substance."

"That," she managed to say, "is the most flattering thing you've ever said to me."

"That's just because you're used to men telling you you're beautiful. And I like your family."

"My family?"

"Yeah. Your mother's an amazing woman. I like your brothers, your cousins. Still haven't quite figured out—for sure—which is which, but, I like them. And your sister's sweet." He paused. "I meant that in a good way."

"Yes." Camilla smiled a little. "She is, very sweet."

"Your aunts, uncles, they're interesting people. Admirable. I guess that's where you get it. Had some trouble with your father. But I figure if I had a daughter and some guy was… Well, it's natural for him to want to kick my ass for putting hands on what's his."

"He likes you."

"He'd like to roast me over a slow fire."

"He thinks you have potential."

Del snorted, paced, then glanced back at her. "Does he?"

"Yes. Of course if you make me unhappy, that slow fire could still be arranged. But I don't mean to pressure you."

"You're a clever girl, Princess. Sharp, sexy mind. I could get past that face of yours, but your mind kept hooking me in." He gestured to the thick book on archaeology resting on her nightstand. "So you stayed interested?"

"Yes. I want to learn. I really loved working with you."

"I know."

"I find the work fascinating. Not just because of you, you know. I want to learn for me first. I needed something for myself. Something that pulled at me, from the inside. Something beyond what's expected—must be expected of me because of my position. I wanted to find my passion, and thanks to you I did. I'm making arrangements to join Dr. Lesuer on a project in France."

"Yeah, Lower Paleolithic." Del shrugged. "He's good. Hell of a teacher, too. He's got patience. I don't. It'd probably be less complicated to work with him. Then again, it'd be a shame for you to miss following through on Bardville."

She took a deep breath. "Are you suggesting that I join the project?"

"I've been thinking about outfitting a new site trailer. The old one's a dump. And I need to oversee a lot of lab work. It'd probably be practical to rent a house near the university. Maybe buy something."

The pressure in her chest was unbearable. It was wonderful. "It's understood in my family that when one of us takes a career, or makes a personal commitment, his or her official duties can be adjusted. Tell me."

"Listen, I'm going to complain every time I have to gear up in some fancy suit—and you'll probably throw my own title in my face when I do," he said, walking to her.

"Naturally."

"But I'll carry my weight on what you bring to the deal, and you'll carry yours on what I bring."

She closed her eyes briefly. "Are you asking me to ma—"

He cut her off with a quick, warning sound. "You've got some looks, don't you?" He lifted her chin and cupped her face. "Some fabulous looks. You know, I don't care how many times this face of yours is splashed over magazines. I don't care about the gossip and bull written in them, either. That kind of stuff doesn't matter to me. We know who we are."

Tears clogged her throat, shimmered in her eyes again. Nothing, nothing he might have said could have told her more clearly he believed in her. "Oh, Delaney."

"I don't have a ring for you right now."

"I don't care about that."

"I do." Funny, he thought as he lifted her hand, studied those elegant fingers, that he would feel it was important. "I want you to wear my ring." His gaze shifted to hers and held.

"If you don't want me to cry again, you'll hurry up."

"Okay, okay. Try to give a woman a little romance."

"You climbing down the palace walls is about all the romance I can take for one night. Thanks all the same."

He grinned. "I'm crazy about you. Every bit of you, but especially your smart mouth."

"That's lovely. But I could probably stand just a little more romance than that, if you can manage it."

"I love you." He took her face in his hands. This time when a tear slid down her cheek, he didn't mind. "Camilla. I love who you are. I love who we are when we're together. I love the woman who mopped my kitchen floor, and I love the woman I waltzed with tonight."

Joy soared inside her. "Both sides of that woman love all the sides of you. You make me happy."

"Marry me. Make a life with me. You won't always be comfortable, but you sure as hell won't be bored."

"I'll marry you." She touched her lips to his cheek. "And work with you." And the other. "Live with you. And love you. Always," she murmured as their lips met.

"Come back with me." He pulled her close and just held on. "We'll work out the details—whatever has to be done. I don't want to go back without you."

"Yes. I'll arrange it." She tightened her grip. "We'll arrange it."

"I'll carve out some time off—whatever we need to deal with whatever we have to deal with."

"Don't worry." Here, she thought, was her passion, her contentment and her love all wrapped in one. "We'll work it all out. When there's a question, we'll find the answer."

She rested her head on his shoulder, smiling as she felt his lips brush over her hair. The most important question, she thought, had been asked. And answered.

* * * * *

UNFINISHED BUSINESS

For Laura Sparrow—
old friends are the best friends.

Chapter 1

What am I doing here?

The question rolled around in Vanessa's mind as she drove down Main Street. The sleepy town of Hyattown had changed very little in twelve years. It was still tucked in the foothills of Maryland's Blue Ridge Mountains, surrounded by rolling farmland and thick woods. Apple orchards and dairy cows encroached as close as the town limits, and here, inside those limits, there were no stoplights, no office buildings, no hum of traffic.

Here there were sturdy old houses and unfenced yards, children playing and laundry flapping on lines. It was, Vanessa thought with both relief and surprise, exactly as she had left it. The sidewalks were still bumpy and cracked, the concrete undermined by the roots of towering oaks that were just beginning to green. Forsythia were spilling their yellow blooms, and azaleas held just the hint of the riotous color to come. Crocuses, those vanguards of spring, had been overshadowed by spears of daffodils and early tulips. People continued, as they had in her childhood, to fuss with their lawns and gardens on a Saturday afternoon.

Some glanced up, perhaps surprised and vaguely interested to see an unfamiliar car drive by. Occasionally someone waved—out of habit, not because they recognized her. Then they bent to their planting or mowing again. Through her open window Vanessa caught the scent of freshly cut grass, of hyacinths and earth newly turned. She could hear the buzzing of power mowers, the barking of a dog, the shouts and laughter of children at play.

Two old men in fielders' caps, checked shirts and work pants stood in front of the town bank gossiping. A pack of young boys puffed up the slope of the road on their bikes. Probably on their way to Lester's Store for cold drinks or candy. She'd strained up that same hill to that same destination countless times. A hundred years ago, she thought, and felt the all-too-familiar clutching in her stomach.

What am I doing here? she thought again, reaching for the roll of antacids in her purse. Unlike the town, she had changed. Sometimes she hardly recognized herself.

She wanted to believe she was doing the right thing. Coming back. Not home, she mused. She had no idea if this was home. Or even if she wanted it to be.

She'd been barely sixteen when she'd left—when her father had taken her from these quiet streets on an odyssey of cities, practice sessions and performances. New York, Chicago, Los Angeles and London, Paris, Bonn, Madrid. It had been exciting, a roller coaster of sights and sounds. And, most of all, music.

By the age of twenty, through her father's drive and her talent, she had become one of the youngest and most successful concert pianists in the country. She had won the prestigious Van Cliburn Competition at the tender age of eighteen, over competitors ten years her senior. She had played for royalty and dined with presidents. She had, in her single-minded pursuit of her career, earned a reputation as a brilliant and temperamental artist. The coolly sexy, passionately driven Vanessa Sexton.

Now, at twenty-eight, she was coming back to the home of her childhood, and to the mother she hadn't seen in twelve years.

The burning in her stomach as she pulled up to the curb was so familiar she barely noticed it. Like the town that surrounded it, the home of her youth was much the same as when she'd left it. The sturdy brick had weathered well, and the shutters were freshly painted a deep, warm blue. Along the stone wall that rose above the sidewalk were bushy peonies that would wait another month or more to bloom. Azaleas, in bud, were grouped around the foundation.

Vanessa sat, hands clutching the wheel, fighting off a desperate need to drive on. Drive away. She had already done too much on impulse. She'd bought the Mercedes convertible, driven up from her last booking in D.C., refused dozens of offers for engagements. All on impulse. Throughout her adult life, her time had been meticulously scheduled, her actions carefully executed, and only after all consequences had been considered. Though impulsive by nature, she had learned the importance of an ordered life. Coming here, awakening old hurts and old memories, wasn't part of that order.

Yet if she turned away now, ran away now, she would never have the answers to her questions, questions even she didn't understand.

Deliberately not giving herself any more time to think, she got out of the car and went to the trunk for her suitcases. She didn't have to stay if she was uncomfortable, she reminded herself. She was free to go anywhere. She was an adult, a well-traveled one who was financially secure. Her home, if she chose to make one, could be anywhere in the world. Since her father's death six months before, she'd had no ties.

Yet it was here she had come. And it was here she needed to be—at least until her questions were answered.

She crossed the sidewalk and climbed the five concrete steps. Despite the trip-hammer beating of her heart, she held herself straight. Her father had never permitted slumped shoulders. The presentation of self was as important as the presentation of music. Chin up, shoulders straight, she started up the walk.

When the door opened, she stopped, as if her feet were rooted in the ground. She stood frozen as her mother stepped onto the porch.

Images, dozens of them, raced into her mind. Of herself on the first day of school, rushing up those steps full of pride, to see her mother standing at the door. Sniffling as she limped up the walk after falling off her bike, her mother there to clean up the scrapes and kiss away the hurt. All but dancing onto the porch after her first kiss. And her mother, a woman's knowledge in her eyes, struggling not to ask any questions.

Then there had been the very last time she had stood here. But she had been walking away from the house, not toward it. And her mother hadn't been on the porch waving goodbye.

"Vanessa."

Loretta Sexton stood twisting her hands. There was no gray in her dark chestnut hair. It was shorter than Vanessa remembered, and fluffed around a face that showed very few lines. A rounder face, softer, than Vanessa recalled. She seemed smaller somehow. Not shrunken, but more compact, fitter, younger. Vanessa had a flash of her father. Thin, too thin, pale, old.

Loretta wanted to run to her daughter, but she couldn't. The woman standing on the walk wasn't the girl she had lost and longed for. She looks like me, she thought, battling back tears. Stronger, more sure, but so much like me.

Bracing herself, as she had countless times before stepping onto a stage, Vanessa continued up the walk, up the creaking wooden steps, to stand in front of her mother. They were nearly the same height. That was something that jolted them both. Their eyes, the same misty shade of green, held steady.

They stood, only a foot apart. But there was no embrace.

"I appreciate you letting me come." Vanessa hated the stiffness she heard in her own voice.

"You're always welcome here." Loretta cleared her throat, cleared it of the rush of emotional words. "I was sorry to hear about your father."

"Thank you. I'm glad to see you're looking well."

"I…" What could she say? What could she possibly say that could make up for twelve lost years? "Did you…run into much traffic on the way up?"

"No. Not after I got out of Washington. It was a pleasant ride."

"Still, you must be tired after the drive. Come in and sit down."

She had remodeled, Vanessa thought foolishly as she followed her mother inside. The rooms were lighter, airier, than she remembered. The imposing home she remembered had become cozy. Dark, formal wallpaper had been replaced by warm pastels. Carpeting had been ripped up to reveal buffed pine floors that were accented by colorful area rugs. There were antiques, lovingly restored, and there was the scent of fresh flowers. It was the home of a woman, she realized. A woman of taste and means.

"You'd probably like to go upstairs first and unpack." Loretta stopped at the stairs, clutching the newel. "Unless you're hungry."

"No, I'm not hungry."

With a nod, Loretta started up the stairs. "I thought you'd like your old room." She pressed her lips together as she reached the landing. "I've redecorated a bit."

"So I see." Vanessa's voice was carefully neutral.

"You still have a view of the backyard."

"I'm sure it's fine."

Loretta opened a door, and Vanessa followed her inside.

There were no fussily dressed dolls or grinning stuffed animals. There were no posters tacked on the walls, no carefully framed awards and certificates. Gone was the narrow bed she had once dreamed in, and the desk where she had fretted over French verbs and geometry. It was no longer a room for a girl. It was a room for a guest.

The walls were ivory, trimmed in warm green. Pretty priscillas hung over the windows. There was a four-poster bed, draped with a watercolor quilt and plumped with pillows. A glass vase of freesias sat on an elegant Queen Anne desk. The scent of potpourri wafted from a bowl on the bureau.

Nervous, Loretta walked through the room, twitching at the quilt, brushing imaginary dust from the dresser. "I hope you're comfortable here. If there's anything you need, you just have to ask."

Vanessa felt as if she were checking into an elegant and exclusive hotel. "It's a lovely room. I'll be fine, thank you."

"Good." Loretta clasped her hands together again. How she longed to touch. To hold. "Would you like me to help you unpack?"

"No." The refusal came too quickly. Vanessa struggled with a smile. "I can manage."

"All right. The bath is just—"

"I remember."

Loretta stopped short, looked helplessly out the window. "Of course. I'll be downstairs if you want anything." Giving in to her need, she cupped Vanessa's face in her hands. "Welcome home." She left quickly, shutting the door behind her.

Alone, Vanessa sat on the bed. Her stomach muscles were like hot, knotted ropes. She pressed a hand against her midsection, studying this room that had once been hers. How could the town have seemed so unchanged, and this room, her room, be so different? Perhaps it was the same with people. They might look familiar on the outside, but inside they were strangers.

As she was.

How different was she from the girl who had once lived here? Would she recognize herself? Would she want to?

She rose to stand in front of the cheval glass in the corner. The face and form were familiar. She had examined herself carefully before each concert to be certain her appearance was perfect. That was expected. Her hair was to be groomed—swept up or back, never loose—her face made up for the stage, but never heavily, her costume subtle and elegant. That was the image of Vanessa Sexton.

Her hair was a bit windblown now, but there was no one to see or judge. It was the same deep chestnut as her mother's. Longer, though, sweeping her shoulders from a side part, it could catch fire from the sun or gleam deep and rich in moonlight. There was some fatigue around her eyes, but there was nothing unusual in that. She'd been very careful with her makeup that morning, so there was subtle color along her high cheekbones, a hint of it over her full, serious mouth. She wore a suit in icy pink with a short, snug jacket and a full skirt. The waistband was a bit loose, but then, her appetite hadn't been good.

And all this was still just image, she thought. The confident, poised and assured adult. She wished she could turn back the clock so that she could see herself as she'd been at sixteen. Full of hope, despite the strain that had clouded the household. Full of dreams and music.

With a sigh, she turned away to unpack.

When she was a child, it had seemed natural to use her room as a sanctuary. After rearranging her clothes for the third time, Vanessa reminded herself that she was no longer a child. Hadn't she come to find the bond she had lost with her mother? She couldn't find it if she sat alone in her room and brooded.

As she came downstairs, Vanessa heard the low sound of a radio coming from the back of the house. From the kitchen, she remembered. Her mother had always preferred popular music to the classics, and that had always irritated Vanessa's father. It was an old Presley ballad now—rich and lonely. Moving toward the sound, she stopped in the doorway of what had always been the music room.

The old grand piano that had been crowded in there was gone. So was the huge, heavy cabinet that had held reams and reams of sheet music. Now there were small, fragile-looking chairs with needlepoint cushions. A beautiful old tea caddy sat in a corner. On it was a bowl filled with some thriving leafy green plant. There were watercolors in narrow frames on the walls, and there was a curvy Victorian sofa in front of the twin windows.

All had been arranged around a trim, exquisite rosewood spinet. Unable to resist, Vanessa crossed to it. Lightly, quietly, only for herself, she played the first few chords of a Chopin étude. The action was so stiff that she understood the piano was new. Had her mother bought it after she'd received the letter telling her that her daughter was coming back? Was this a gesture, an attempt to reach across the gap of twelve years?

It couldn't be so simple, Vanessa thought, rubbing at the beginnings of a headache behind her eyes. They both had to know that.

She turned her back on the piano and walked to the kitchen.

Loretta was there, putting the finishing touches on a salad she'd arranged in a pale green bowl. Her mother had always liked pretty things, Vanessa remembered. Delicate, fragile things. Those leanings showed now in the lacy place mats on the table, the pale rose sugar bowl, the collection of Depression glass on an open shelf. She had opened the window, and a fragrant spring breeze ruffled the sheer curtains over the sink.

When she turned, Vanessa saw that her eyes were red, but she smiled, and her voice was clear. "I know you said you weren't hungry, but I thought you might like a little salad and some iced tea."

Vanessa managed an answering smile. "Thank you. The house looks lovely. It seems bigger somehow. I'd always heard that things shrunk as you got older."

Loretta turned off the radio. Vanessa regretted the gesture, as it meant they were left with only themselves to fill the silence. "There were too many dark colors before," Loretta told her. "And too much heavy furniture. At times I used to feel as though the furniture was lurking over me, waiting to push me out of a room." She caught herself, uneasy and embarrassed. "I saved some of the pieces, a few that were your grandmother's. They're stored in the attic. I thought someday you might want them."

"Maybe someday," Vanessa said, because it was easier. She sat down as her mother served the colorful salad. "What did you do with the piano?"

"I sold it." Loretta reached for the pitcher of tea. "Years ago. It seemed foolish to keep it when there was no one to play it. And I'd always hated it." She caught herself again, set the pitcher down. "I'm sorry."

"No need. I understand."

"No, I don't think you do." Loretta gave her a long, searching look. "I don't think you can."

Vanessa wasn't ready to dig too deep. She picked up her fork and said nothing.

"I hope the spinet is all right. I don't know very much about instruments."

"It's a beautiful instrument."

"The man who sold it to me told me it was top-of-the-line. I know you need to practice, so I thought… In any case, if it doesn't suit, you've only to—"

"It's fine." They ate in silence until Vanessa fell back on manners. "The town looks very much the same," she began, in a light, polite voice. "Does Mrs. Gaynor still live on the corner?"

"Oh yes." Relieved, Loretta began to chatter. "She's nearly eighty now, and still walks every day, rain or shine, to the post office to get her mail. The Breckenridges moved away, oh, about five years ago. Went south. A nice family bought their house. Three children. The youngest just started school this year. He's a pistol. And the Hawbaker boy, Rick, you remember? You used to babysit for him."

"I remember being paid a dollar an hour to be driven crazy by a little monster with buckteeth and a slingshot."

"That's the one." Loretta laughed. It was a sound, Vanessa realized, that she'd remembered all through the years. "He's in college now, on a scholarship."

"Hard to believe."

"He came to see me when he was home last Christmas. Asked about you." She fumbled again, cleared her throat. "Joanie's still here."

"Joanie Tucker?"

"It's Joanie Knight now," Loretta told her. "She married young Jack Knight three years ago. They have a beautiful baby."

"Joanie," Vanessa murmured. Joanie Tucker, who had been her best friend since her earliest memory, her confidante, wailing wall and partner in crime. "She has a child."

"A little girl. Lara. They have a farm outside of town. I know she'd want to see you."

"Yes." For the first time all day, Vanessa felt something click. "Yes, I want to see her. Her parents, are they well?"

"Emily died almost eight years ago."

"Oh." Vanessa reached out instinctively to touch her mother's hand. As Joanie had been her closest friend, so had Emily Tucker been her mother's. "I'm so sorry."

Loretta looked down at their joined hands, and her eyes filled. "I still miss her."

"She was the kindest woman I've ever known. I wish I had—" But it was too late for regrets. "Dr. Tucker, is he all right?"

"Ham is fine." Loretta blinked back tears, and tried not to be hurt when Vanessa removed her hand. "He grieved hard, but his family and his work got him through. He'll be so pleased to see you, Van."

No one had called Vanessa by her nickname in more years than she could count. Hearing it now touched her.

"Does he still have his office in his house?"

"Of course. You're not eating. Would you like something else?"

"No, this is fine." Dutifully she ate a forkful of salad.

"Don't you want to know about Brady?"

"No." Vanessa took another bite. "Not particularly."

There was something of the daughter she remembered in that look. The slight pout, the faint line between the brows. It warmed Loretta's heart, as the polite stranger had not. "Brady Tucker followed in his father's footsteps."

Vanessa almost choked. "He's a doctor?"

"That's right. Had himself a fine, important position with some hospital in New York. Chief resident, I think Ham told me."

"I always thought Brady would end up pitching for the Orioles or going to jail."

Loretta laughed again, warmly. "So did most of us. But he turned into quite a respectable young man. Of course, he was always too handsome for his own good."

"Or anyone else's," Vanessa muttered, and her mother smiled again.

"It's always hard for a woman to resist the tall, dark and handsome kind, especially if he's a rogue, as well."

"I think *hood* was the word."

"He never did anything really bad," Loretta pointed out. "Not that he didn't give Emily and Ham a few headaches. Well, a lot of headaches." She laughed. "But the boy always looked out for his sister. I liked him for that. And he was taken with you."

Vanessa sniffed. "Brady Tucker was taken with anything in skirts."

"He was young." They had all been young once, Loretta thought, looking at the lovely, composed stranger who was her daughter. "Emily told me he mooned around the house for weeks after you…after you and your father went to Europe."

"It was a long time ago." Vanessa rose, dismissing the subject.

"I'll get the dishes." Loretta began stacking them quickly. "It's your first day back. I thought maybe you'd like to try out the piano. I'd like to hear you play in this house again."

"All right." She turned toward the door.

"Van?"

"Yes?"

Would she ever call her "Mom" again? "I want you to know how proud I am of all you've accomplished."

"Are you?"

"Yes." Loretta studied her daughter, wishing she had the courage to open her arms for an embrace. "I just wish you looked happier."

"I'm happy enough."

"Would you tell me if you weren't?"

"I don't know. We don't really know each other anymore."

At least that was honest, Loretta thought. Painful, but honest. "I hope you'll stay until we do."

"I'm here because I need answers. But I'm not ready to ask the questions yet."

"Give it time, Van. Give yourself time. And believe me when I say all I ever wanted was what was best for you."

"My father always said the same thing," she said quietly.

"Funny, isn't it, that now that I'm a grown woman I have no idea what that is."

She walked down the hall to the music room. There was a gnawing, aching pain just under her breastbone. Out of habit, she popped a pill out of the roll in her skirt pocket before she sat at the piano.

She started with Beethoven's "Moonlight" sonata, playing from memory and from the heart, letting the music soothe her. She could remember playing this piece, and countless others, in this same room. Hour after hour, day after day. For the love of it, yes, but often—too often—because it was expected, even demanded.

Her feelings for music had always been mixed. There was her strong, passionate love for it, the driving need to create it with the skill she'd been given. But there had always also been the equally desperate need to please her father, to reach that point of perfection he had expected. That unattainable point, she thought now.

He had never understood that music was a love for her, not a vocation. It had been a comfort, a means of expression, but never an ambition. On the few occasions she had tried to explain it, he had become so enraged or impatient that she had silenced herself. She, who was known for her passion and temper, had been a cringing child around one man. In all her life, she had never been able to defy him.

She switched to Bach, closed her eyes and let herself drift. For more than an hour she played, lost in the beauty, the gentleness and the genius, of the compositions. This was what her father had never understood. That she could play for her own pleasure and be content, and that she had hated, always hated, sitting on a stage ringed by a spotlight and playing for thousands.

As her emotions began to flow again, she switched to

Mozart, something that required more passion and speed. Vivid, almost furious, the music sang through her. When the last chord echoed, she felt a satisfaction she had nearly forgotten.

The quiet applause behind her had her spinning around. Seated on one of the elegant little chairs was a man. Though the sun was in her eyes and twelve years had passed, she recognized him.

"Incredible." Brady Tucker rose and crossed to her. His long, wiry frame blocked out the sun for an instant, and the light glowed like a nimbus around him. "Absolutely incredible." As she stared at him, he held out a hand and smiled. "Welcome home, Van."

She rose to face him. "Brady," she murmured, then rammed her fist solidly into his stomach. "You creep."

He sat down hard as the air exploded out of his lungs. The sound of it was every bit as sweet to her as the music had been. Wincing, he looked up at her. "Nice to see you, too."

"What the hell are you doing here?"

"Your mother let me in." After a couple of testing breaths, he rose. She had to tilt her head back to keep her eyes on his. Those same fabulous blue eyes, in a face that had aged much too well. "I didn't want to disturb you while you were playing, so I just sat down. I didn't expect to be sucker punched."

"You should have." She was delighted to have caught him off guard, and to have given him back a small portion of the pain he'd given her. His voice was the same, she thought, deep and seductive. She wanted to hit him again just for that. "She didn't mention that you were in town."

"I live here. Moved back almost a year ago." She had that same sexy pout. He fervently wished that at least that much could have changed. "Can I tell you that you look terrific, or should I put up my guard?"

How to remain composed under stress was something she'd learned very well. She sat, carefully smoothing her skirts. "No, you can tell me."

"Okay. You look terrific. A little thin, maybe."

The pout became more pronounced. "Is that your medical opinion, Dr. Tucker?"

"Actually, yes." He took a chance and sat beside her on the piano stool. Her scent was as subtle and alluring as moonlight. He felt a tug, not so much unexpected as frustrating. Though she sat beside him, he knew she was as distant as she had been when there had been an ocean between them.

"You're looking well," she said, and wished it wasn't so true. He still had the lean, athletic body of his youth. His face wasn't as smooth, and the ruggedness maturity had brought to it only made it more attractive. His hair was still a rich, deep black, and his lashes were just as long and thick as ever. And his hands were as strong and beautiful as they had been the first time they had touched her. A lifetime ago, she reminded herself, and settled her own hands in her lap.

"My mother told me you had a position in New York."

"I did." He was feeling as awkward as a schoolboy. No, he realized, much more awkward. Twelve years before, he'd known exactly how to handle her. Or he'd thought he did. "I came back to help my father with his practice. He'd like to retire in a year or two."

"I can't imagine it. You back here," she elaborated. "Or Doc Tucker retiring."

"Times change."

"Yes, they do." She couldn't sit beside him. Just a residual of those girlish feelings, she thought, but she rose anyway. "It's equally hard to picture you as a doctor."

"I felt the same way when I was slogging through medical school."

She frowned. He was wearing jeans and a sweatshirt and running shoes—exactly the kind of attire he'd worn in high school. "You don't look like a doctor."

"Want to see my stethoscope?"

"No." She stuck her hands in her pockets. "I heard Joanie was married."

"Yeah—to Jack Knight, of all people. Remember him?"

"I don't think so."

"He was a year ahead of me in high school. Football star. Went pro a couple of years, then bunged up his knee."

"Is that the medical term?"

"Close enough." He grinned at her. There was still a little chip in his front tooth that she had always found endearing. "She'll be crazy to see you again, Van."

"I want to see her, too."

"I've got a couple of patients coming in, but I should be done by six. Why don't we have some dinner, and I can drive you out to the farm?"

"I don't think so."

"Why not?"

"Because the last time I was supposed to have dinner with you—dinner and the senior prom—you stood me up."

He tucked his hands in his pockets. "You hold a grudge a long time."

"Yes."

"I was eighteen years old, Van, and there were reasons."

"Reasons that hardly matter now." Her stomach was beginning to burn. "The point is, I don't want to pick up where we left off."

He gave her a considering look. "That wasn't the idea."

"Good." That was just one more thing she could damn

him for. "We both have our separate lives, Brady. Let's keep it that way."

He nodded, slowly. "You've changed more than I'd thought."

"Yes, I have." She started out, stopped, then looked over her shoulder. "We both have. But I imagine you still know your way out."

"Yeah," he said to himself when she left him alone. He knew his way out. What he hadn't known was that she could still turn him inside out with one of those pouty looks.

Chapter 2

The Knight farm was rolling hills and patches of brown and green field. The hay was well up, she noted, and the corn was tender green shoots. A gray barn stood behind a trio of square paddocks. Nearby, chickens fussed and pecked at the ground. Plump spotted cows lolled on a hillside, too lazy to glance over at the sound of an approaching car, but geese rushed along the bank of the creek, excited and annoyed by the disturbance.

A bumpy gravel lane led to the farmhouse. At the end of it, Vanessa stopped her car, then slowly alighted. She could hear the distant putting of a tractor and the occasional yip-yipping of a cheerful dog. Closer was the chatter of birds, a musical exchange that always reminded her of neighbors gossiping over a fence.

Perhaps it was foolish to feel nervous, but she couldn't shake it. Here in this rambling three-story house, with its leaning chimneys and swaying porches, lived her oldest and closest friend—someone with whom she had shared every thought, every feeling, every wish and every disappointment.

But those friends had been children—girls on the threshold of womanhood, where everything is at its most intense and emotional. They hadn't been given the chance to grow apart. Their friendship had been severed quickly and completely. Between that moment and this, so much—too much—had happened to both of them. To expect to renew those ties and feelings was both naive and overly optimistic.

Vanessa reminded herself of that, bracing herself for disappointment, as she started up the cracked wooden steps to the front porch.

The door swung open. The woman who stepped out released a flood of stored memories. Unlike the moment when she had started up her own walk and seen her mother, Vanessa felt none of the confusion and grief.

She looks the same, was all Vanessa could think. Joanie was still sturdily built, with the curves Vanessa had envied throughout adolescence. Her hair was still worn short and tousled around a pretty face. Black hair and blue eyes like her brother, but with softer features and a neat Cupid's-bow mouth that had driven the teenage boys wild.

Vanessa started to speak, searched for something to say. Then she heard Joanie let out a yelp. They were hugging, arms clasped hard, bodies swaying. The laughter and tears and broken sentences melted away the years.

"I can't believe—you're here."

"I've missed you. You look… I'm sorry."

"When I heard you—" Shaking her head, Joanie pulled back, then smiled. "Oh, God, it's good to see you, Van."

"I was almost afraid to come." Vanessa wiped her cheek with her knuckles.

"Why?"

"I thought you might be polite and offer me some tea and wonder what we were supposed to talk about."

Joanie took a rumpled tissue out of her pocket and blew her nose. "And I thought you might be wearing a mink and diamonds and stop by out of a sense of duty."

Vanessa gave a watery laugh. "My mink's in storage."

Joanie grabbed her hand and pulled her through the door. "Come in. I might just put that tea on, after all."

The entryway was bright and tidy. Joanie led Vanessa into a living room of faded sofas and glossy mahogany, of chintz curtains and rag rugs. Evidence that there was a baby in the house was found in teething rings, rattles and stuffed bears. Unable to resist, Vanessa picked up a pink-and-white rattle.

"You have a little girl."

"Lara." Joanie beamed. "She's wonderful. She'll be up from her morning nap soon. I can't wait for you to see her."

"It's hard to imagine." Vanessa gave the rattle a shake before setting it down again. It made a pretty, musical sound that had her smiling. "You're a mother."

"I'm almost used to it." She took Vanessa's hand again as they sat on the sofa. "I still can't believe you're here. Vanessa Sexton, concert pianist, musical luminary and globe-trotter."

Vanessa winced. "Oh, please, not her. I left her in D.C."

"Just let me gloat a minute." She was still smiling, but her eyes, eyes that were so like her brother's, were searching Vanessa's face. "We're so proud of you. The whole town. There would be something in the paper or a magazine, something on the news—or an event like that PBS special last year. No one would talk about anything else for days. You're Hyattown's link to fame and fortune."

"A weak link," Vanessa murmured, but she smiled. "Your farm, Joanie—it's wonderful."

"Can you believe it? I always thought I'd be living in one of those New York lofts, planning business lunches and fighting for a cab during rush hour."

"This is better." Vanessa settled back against the sofa cushions. "Much better."

Joanie toed off her shoes, then tucked her stockinged feet under her. "It has been for me. Do you remember Jack?"

"I don't think so. I can't remember you ever talking about anyone named Jack."

"I didn't know him in high school. He was a senior when we were just getting started. I remember seeing him in the halls now and then. Those big shoulders, and that awful buzz haircut during the football season." She laughed and settled comfortably. "Then, about four years ago, I was giving Dad a hand in the office. I was doing time as a paralegal in Hagerstown."

"A paralegal?"

"A former life," Joanie said with a wave of her hand. "Anyway, it was during Dad's Saturday office hours, and Millie was sick— You remember Millie?"

"Oh, yes." Vanessa grinned at the memory of Abraham Tucker's no-nonsense nurse.

"Well, I jumped into the breach for the weekend appointments, and in walks Jack Knight, all six foot three, two hundred and fifty pounds of him. He had laryngitis." A self-satisfied sigh escaped her. "There was this big, handsome hulk trying to tell me, in cowboy-and-Indian sign language, that no, he didn't have an appointment, but he wanted to see the doctor. I squeezed him in between a chicken pox and an earache. Dad examined him and gave him a prescription. A couple hours later he was back, with these raggedy-looking violets and a note asking me to the movies. How could I resist?"

Vanessa laughed. "You always were a soft touch."

Joanie rolled her big blue eyes. "Tell me about it. Before I knew it, I was shopping for a wedding dress and learning about fertilizer. It's been the best four years of my life." She shook her head. "But tell me about you. I want to hear everything."

Vanessa shrugged. "Practice, playing, traveling."

"Jetting off to Rome, Madrid, Mozambique—"

"Sitting on runways and in hotel rooms," Vanessa finished for her. "It isn't nearly as glamorous as it might look."

"No, I guess partying with famous actors, giving concerts for the queen of England and sharing midnight schmoozes with millionaires gets pretty boring."

"Schmoozes?" Vanessa had to laugh. "I don't think I ever schmoozed with anyone."

"Don't burst my bubble, Van." Joanie leaned over to brush a hand down Vanessa's arm. All the Tuckers were touchers, Vanessa thought. She'd missed that. "For years I've had this image of you glittering among the glittery. Celebing among the celebrities, hoitying among the toity."

"I guess I've done my share of hoitying. But mostly I've played the piano and caught planes."

"It's kept you in shape," Joanie said, sensing Vanessa's reluctance to talk about it. "I bet you're still a damn size four."

"Small bones."

"Wait until Brady gets a load of you."

Her chin lifted a fraction. "I saw him yesterday."

"Really? And the rat didn't call me." Joanie tapped a finger against her lips. There was laughter just beneath them. "So, how did it go?"

"I hit him."

"You—" Joanie choked, coughed, recovered. "You hit him? Why?"

"For standing me up for his senior prom."

"For—" Joanie broke off when Vanessa sprang to her feet and began pacing.

"I've never been so angry. I don't care how stupid it sounds. That night was so important to me. I thought it would be the most wonderful, the most romantic night of my life. You know how long we shopped for the perfect dress."

"Yes," Joanie murmured. "I know."

"I'd been looking forward to that night for weeks and weeks." On a roll now, she swirled around the room. "I'd just gotten my license, and I drove all the way into Frederick to get my hair done. I had this little sprig of baby's breath behind my ear." She touched the spot now, but there was no sentiment in the gesture. "Oh, I knew he was unreliable and reckless. I can't count the number of times my father told me. But I never expected him to dump me like that."

"But, Van—"

"I didn't even leave the house for two days after. I was so sick with embarrassment, so hurt. And then, with my parents fighting. It was—oh, it was so ugly. Then my father took me to Europe, and that was that."

Joanie bit her lip as she considered. There were explanations she could offer, but this was something Brady should straighten out himself. "There might be more to it than you think" was all she said.

Recovered now, Vanessa sat again. "It doesn't matter. It was a long time ago." Then she smiled. "Besides, I think I got the venom out when I punched him in the stomach."

Joanie's lips twitched in sisterly glee. "I'd like to have seen that."

"It's hard to believe he's a doctor."

"I don't think anyone was more surprised than Brady."

"It's odd he's never married…" She frowned. "Or anything."

"I won't touch 'anything,' but he's never married. There are a number of women in town who've developed chronic medical problems since he's come back."

"I'll bet," Vanessa muttered.

"Anyway, my father's in heaven. Have you had a chance to see him yet?"

"No, I wanted to see you first." She took Joanie's hands. "I'm so sorry about your mother. I didn't know until yesterday."

"It was a rough couple of years. Dad was so lost. I guess we all were." Her fingers tightened, taking comfort and giving it. "I know you lost your father. I understand how hard it must have been for you."

"He hadn't been well for a long time. I didn't know how serious it was until, well…until it was almost over." She rubbed a hand over her stomach as it spasmed. "It helped to finish out the engagements. That would have been important to him."

"I know." She was starting to speak again when the intercom on the table crackled. There was a whimper, a gurgle, followed by a stream of infant jabbering. "She's up and ready to roll." Joanie rose quickly. "I'll just be a minute."

Alone, Vanessa stood and began to wander the room. It was filled with so many little, comforting things. Books on agriculture and child-rearing, wedding pictures and baby pictures. There was an old porcelain vase she remembered seeing in the Tucker household as a child. Through the window she could see the barn, and the cows drowsing in the midday sun.

Like something out of a book, she thought. Her own faded wish book.

"Van?"

She turned to see Joanie in the doorway, a round, dark-haired baby on her hip. The baby swung her feet, setting off the bells tied to her shoelaces.

"Oh, Joanie. She's gorgeous."

"Yeah." Joanie kissed Lara's head. "She is. Would you like to hold her?"

"Are you kidding?" Van came across the room to take the baby. After a long suspicious look, Lara smiled and began to kick her feet again. "Aren't you pretty?" Van murmured. Unable to resist, she lifted the baby over her head and turned in a circle while Lara giggled. "Aren't you just wonderful?"

"She likes you, too." Joanie gave a satisfied nod. "I kept telling her she'd meet her godmother sooner or later."

"Her godmother?" Confused, Vanessa settled the baby on her hip again.

"Sure." Joanie smoothed Lara's hair. "I sent you a note right after she was born. I knew you couldn't make it back for the christening, so we had a proxy. But I wanted you and Brady to be her godparents." Joanie frowned at Vanessa's blank look. "You got the note, didn't you?"

"No." Vanessa rested her cheek against Lara's. "No, I didn't. I had no idea you were even married until my mother told me yesterday."

"But the wedding invitation—" Joanie shrugged. "I guess it could have gotten lost. You were always traveling around so much."

"Yes." She smiled again while Lara tugged at her hair. "If I'd known… I'd have found a way to be here if I'd known."

"You're here now."

"Yes." Vanessa nuzzled Lara's neck. "I'm here now. Oh, God, I envy you, Joanie."

"Me?"

"This beautiful child, this place, the look in your eyes when you talk about Jack. I feel like I've spent twelve years in a daze, while you've made a family and a home and a life."

"We've both made a life," Joanie said. "They're just different ones. You have so much talent, Van. Even as a kid I was awed by it. I wanted so badly to play like you." She laughed and enveloped them both in a hug. "As patient as you were, you could barely get me through 'Chopsticks.'"

"You were hopeless but determined. And I'm so glad you're still my friend."

"You're going to make me cry again." After a sniffle, Joanie shook her head. "Tell you what, you play with Lara for a few minutes and I'll go fix us some lemonade. Then we can be catty and gossip about how fat Julie Newton got."

"Did she?"

"And how Tommy McDonald is losing his hair." Joanie hooked an arm through Vanessa's. "Better yet, come in the kitchen with me. I'll fill you in on Betty Jean Baumgartner's third husband."

"Third?"

"And counting."

There was so much to think about. Not just the funny stories Joanie had shared with her that day, Vanessa thought as she strolled around the backyard at dusk. She needed to think about her life and what she wanted to do with it. Where she belonged. Where she wanted to belong.

For over a decade she'd had little or no choice. Or had lacked the courage to make one, she thought. She had done what her father wanted. He and her music had been the only constants. His drive and his needs had been so much more passionate than hers. And she hadn't wanted to disappoint him.

Hadn't dared, a small voice echoed, but she blocked it off. She owed him everything. He had dedicated his life to her career. While her mother had shirked the responsibility, he had taken her, he had molded her, he had taught her. Every hour she had worked, he had worked. Even when he had become desperately ill, he had pushed himself, managing her career as meticulously as ever. No detail had ever escaped his notice—just as no flawed note had escaped his highly critical ear. He had taken her to the top of her career, and he had been content to bask in the reflected glory.

It couldn't have been easy for him, she thought now. His own career as a concert pianist had stalled before he'd hit thirty. He had never achieved the pinnacle he'd so desperately strived for. For him, music had been everything. Finally he'd been able to see those ambitions and needs realized in his only child.

Now she was on the brink of turning her back on everything he had wanted for her, everything he had worked toward. He would never have been able to understand her desire to give up a glowing career. Just as he had never been able to understand, or tolerate, her constant terror of performing.

She could remember it even now, even here in the sheltered quiet of the yard. The gripping sensation in her stomach, the wave of nausea she always battled back, the throbbing behind her eyes as she stood in the wings.

Stage fright, her father had told her. She would outgrow it. It was the one thing she had never been able to accomplish for him.

Yet, despite it, she knew she could go back to the concert stage. She could endure. She could rise even higher if she focused herself. If only she knew it was what she wanted.

Perhaps she just needed to rest. She sat on the lawn glider and sent it gently into motion. A few weeks or a few months of quiet, and then she might yearn for the life she had left behind. But for now she wanted nothing more than to enjoy the purple twilight.

From the glider she could see the lights glowing inside the house, and the neighboring houses. She had shared a meal with her mother in the kitchen—or had tried to. Loretta had seemed hurt when Vanessa only picked at her food. How could she explain that nothing seemed to settle well these days? This empty, gnawing feeling in her stomach simply wouldn't abate.

A little more time, Vanessa thought, and it would ease. It was only because she wasn't busy, as she should be. Certainly she hadn't practiced enough that day, or the day before. Even if she decided to cut back professionally, she had no business neglecting her practice.

Tomorrow, she thought, closing her eyes. Tomorrow was soon enough to start a routine. Lulled by the motion of the glider, she gathered her jacket closer. She'd forgotten how quickly the temperature could dip once the sun had fallen behind the mountains.

She heard the whoosh of a car as it cruised by on the road in front of the house. Then the sound of a door closing. From somewhere nearby, a mother called her child in from play. Another light blinked on in a window. A baby cried. Vanessa smiled, wishing she could dig out the old tent she and Joanie had used and pitch it in the backyard. She could sleep there, just listening to the town.

She turned at the sound of a dog barking, then saw the

bright fur of a huge golden retriever. It dashed across the neighboring lawn, over the bed where her mother had already planted her pansies and marigolds. Tongue lolling, it lunged at the glider. Before Vanessa could decide whether to be alarmed or amused, it plopped both front paws in her lap and grinned a dog's grin.

"Well, hello there." She ruffled his ears. "Where did you come from?"

"From two blocks down, at a dead run." Panting, Brady walked out of the shadows. "I made the mistake of taking him to the office today. When I went to put him in the car, he decided to take a hike." He paused in front of the glider. "Are you going to punch me again, or can I sit down?"

Vanessa continued to pet the dog. "I probably won't hit you again."

"That'll have to do." He dropped down on the glider and stretched out his legs. The dog immediately tried to climb in his lap. "Don't try to make up," Brady said, pushing the dog off again.

"He's a pretty dog."

"Don't flatter him. He's already got an inflated ego."

"They say people and their pets develop similarities," she commented. "What's his name?"

"Kong. He was the biggest in his litter." Hearing his name, Kong barked twice, then raced off to chase the shadows. "I spoiled him when he was a puppy, and now I'm paying the price." Spreading his arms over the back of the glider, he let his fingers toy with the ends of her hair. "Joanie tells me you drove out to the farm today."

"Yes." Vanessa knocked his hand away. "She looks wonderful. And so happy."

"She is happy." Undaunted, he picked up her hand to play

with her fingers. It was an old, familiar gesture. "You got to meet our godchild."

"Yes." Vanessa tugged her hand free. "Lara's gorgeous."

"Yeah." He went back to her hair. "She looks like me."

The laugh came too quickly to stop. "You're still conceited. And will you keep your hands off me?"

"I never was able to." He sighed, but shifted away an inch. "We used to sit here a lot, remember?"

"I remember."

"I think the first time I kissed you, we were sitting here, just like this."

"No." She folded her arms across her chest.

"You're right." As he knew very well. "The first time was up at the park. You came to watch me shoot baskets."

She brushed casually at the knee of her slacks. "I just happened to be walking through."

"You came because I used to shoot without a shirt and you wanted to see my sweaty chest."

She laughed again, because it was absolutely true. She turned to look at him in the shadowy light. He was smiling, relaxed. He'd always been able to relax, she remembered. And he'd always been able to make her laugh.

"It—meaning your sweaty chest—wasn't such a big deal."

"I've filled out some," he said easily. "And I still shoot hoops." This time she didn't seem to notice when he stroked her hair. "I remember that day. It was at the end of the summer, before my senior year. In three months you'd gone from being that pesty little Sexton kid to Sexy Sexton with a yard of the most incredible chestnut hair, and these great-looking legs you used to show off in teeny little shorts. You were such a brat. And you made my mouth water."

"You were always looking at Julie Newton."

"No, I was pretending to look at Julie Newton while I looked at you. Then you just happened to stroll by the court that day. You'd been to Lester's Store, because you had a bottle of soda. Grape soda."

She lifted a brow. "That's quite a memory you've got."

"Hey, these are the turning points in our lives. You said, 'Hi, Brady. You look awful hot. Want a sip?'" He grinned again. "I almost took a bite out of my basketball. Then you flirted with me."

"I did not."

"You batted your eyes."

She struggled with a giggle. "I've never batted my eyes."

"You batted them then." He sighed at the memory. "It was great."

"As I remember it, you were showing off, doing layups and hook shots or whatever. Macho stuff. Then you grabbed me."

"I remember grabbing. You liked it."

"You smelled like a gym locker."

"I guess I did. It was still my most memorable first kiss."

And hers, Vanessa thought. She hadn't realized she was leaning back against his shoulder and smiling. "We were so young. Everything was so intense, and so uncomplicated."

"Some things don't have to be complicated." But sitting there with her head feeling just right on his shoulder, he wasn't so sure. "Friends?"

"I guess."

"I haven't had a chance to ask you how long you're staying."

"I haven't had a chance to decide."

"Your schedule must be packed."

"I've taken a few months." She moved restlessly. "I may go to Paris for a few weeks."

He picked up her hand again, turning it over. Her hands had always fascinated him. Those long, tapering fingers, the baby-smooth palms, the short, practical nails. She wore no rings. He had given her one once—spent the money he'd earned mowing grass all summer on a gold ring with an incredibly small emerald. She'd kissed him senseless when he'd given it to her, and she'd sworn never to take it off.

Childhood promises were carelessly broken by adults. It was foolish to wish he could see it on her finger again.

"You know, I managed to see you play at Carnegie Hall a couple of years ago. It was overwhelming. You were overwhelming." He surprised them both by bringing her fingers to his lips. Then hastily dropped them. "I'd hoped to see you while we were both in New York, but I guess you were busy."

The jolt from her fingertips was still vibrating in her toes. "If you had called, I'd have managed it."

"I did call." His eyes remained on hers, searching, even as he shrugged it off. "It was then I fully realized how big you'd become. I never got past the first line of defense."

"I'm sorry. Really."

"It's no big deal."

"No, I would have liked to have seen you. Sometimes the people around me are too protective."

"I think you're right." He put a hand under her chin. She was more beautiful than his memory of her, and more fragile. If he had met her in New York, in less sentimental surroundings, would he have felt so drawn to her? He wasn't sure he wanted to know.

Friends was what he'd asked of her. He struggled to want no more.

"You look very tired, Van. Your color could be better."

"It's been a hectic year."

"Are you sleeping all right?"

Half-amused, she brushed his hand aside. "Don't start playing doctor with me, Brady."

"At the moment I can't think of anything I'd enjoy more, but I'm serious. You're run-down."

"I'm not run-down, just a little tired. Which is why I'm taking a break."

But he wasn't satisfied. "Why don't you come into the office for a physical?"

"Is that your new line? It used to be 'Let's go parking down at Molly's Hole.'"

"I'll get to that. Dad can take a look at you."

"I don't need a doctor." Kong came lumbering back, and she reached down for him. "I'm never sick. In almost ten years of concerts, I've never had to cancel one for health reasons." She buried her face in the dog's fur when her stomach clenched. "I'm not going to say it hasn't been a strain coming back here, but I'm dealing with it."

She'd always been hardheaded, he thought. Maybe it would be best if he simply kept an eye—a medical eye— on her for a few days. "Dad would still like to see you— personally, if not professionally."

"I'm going to drop by." Still bent over the dog, she turned her head. In the growing dark, he caught the familiar gleam in her eye. "Joanie says you've got your hands full with women patients. I imagine the same holds true of your father, if he's as handsome as I remember."

"He's had a few…interesting offers. But they've eased off since he and your mother hooked up."

Dumbfounded, Vanessa sat up straight. "Hooked up? My mother? Your father?"

"It's the hottest romance in town." He flicked her hair behind her shoulder. "So far."

"My mother?" she repeated.

"She's an attractive woman in her prime, Van. Why shouldn't she enjoy herself?"

Pressing a hand against her stomach, she rose. "I'm going in."

"What's the problem?"

"No problem. I'm going in. I'm cold."

He took her by the shoulders. It was another gesture that brought a flood of memories. "Why don't you give her a break?" Brady asked. "God knows she's been punished enough."

"You don't know anything about it."

"More than you think." He gave her a quick, impatient shake. "Let go, Van. These old resentments are going to eat you from the inside out."

"It's easy for you." The bitterness poured out before she could control it. "It's always been easy for you, with your nice happy family. You always knew they loved you, no matter what you did or didn't do. No one ever sent you away."

"She didn't send you away, Van."

"She let me go," she said quietly. "What's the difference?"

"Why don't you ask her?"

With a shake of her head, she pulled away. "I stopped being her little girl twelve years ago. I stopped being a lot of things." She turned and walked into the house.

Chapter 3

Vanessa had slept only in snatches. There had been pain. But she was used to pain. She masked it by coating her stomach with liquid antacids, by downing the pills that had been prescribed for her occasional blinding headaches. But most of all, she masked it by using her will to ignore.

Twice she had nearly walked down the hall to her mother's room. A third time she had gotten as far as her mother's door, with her hand raised to knock, before she had retreated to her own room and her own thoughts.

She had no right to resent the fact that her mother had a relationship with another man. Yet she did. In all the years Vanessa had spent with her father, he had never turned to another woman. Or, if he had, he had been much too discreet for her to notice.

And what did it matter? she asked herself as she dressed the next morning. They had always lived their own lives, separate, despite the fact that they shared a house.

But it did matter. It mattered that her mother had been content all these years to live in this same house without contact with her only child. It mattered that she had been able to start a life, a new life, that had no place for her own daughter.

It was time, Vanessa told herself. It was time to ask why.

She caught the scent of coffee and fragrant bread as she reached the bottom landing. In the kitchen she saw her mother standing by the sink, rinsing a cup. Loretta was dressed in a pretty blue suit, pearls at her ears and around her throat. The radio was on low, and she was humming even as she turned and saw her daughter.

"Oh, you're up." Loretta smiled, hoping it didn't look forced. "I wasn't sure I'd see you this morning before I left."

"Left?"

"I have to go to work. There're some muffins, and the coffee's still hot."

"To work?" Vanessa repeated. "Where?"

"At the shop." To busy her nervous hands, she poured Vanessa a cup of coffee. "The antique shop. I bought it about six years ago. The Hopkinses' place, you might remember. I went to work for them when—some time ago. When they decided to retire, I bought them out."

Vanessa shook her head to clear it of the grogginess. "You run an antique shop?"

"Just a small one." She set the coffee on the table. The moment they were free, her hands began to tug at her pearl necklace. "I call it Loretta's Attic. Silly, I suppose, but it does nicely. I closed it for a couple of days, but… I can keep it closed another day or so if you'd like."

Vanessa studied her mother thoughtfully, trying to imagine her owning a business, worrying about inventory and bookkeeping. Antiques? Had she ever mentioned an interest in them?

"No." It seemed that talk would have to wait. "Go ahead."

"If you like, you can run down later and take a look." Loretta began to fiddle with a button on her jacket. "It's small, but I have a lot of interesting pieces."

"We'll see."

"Are you sure you'll be all right here alone?"

"I've been all right alone for a long time."

Loretta's gaze dropped. Her hands fell to her sides. "Yes, of course you have. I'm usually home by six-thirty."

"All right. I'll see you this evening, then." She walked to the sink to turn on the faucet. She wanted water, cold and clear.

"Van."

"Yes?"

"I know I have years to make up for." Loretta was standing in the doorway when Vanessa turned. "I hope you'll give me a chance."

"I want to." She spread her hands. "I don't know where either of us is supposed to start."

"Neither do I." Loretta's smile was hesitant, but less strained. "Maybe that's its own start. I love you. I'll be happy if I can make you believe that." She turned quickly and left.

"Oh, Mom," Vanessa said to the empty house. "I don't know what to do."

"Mrs. Driscoll." Brady patted the eighty-three-year-old matron on her knobby knee. "You've got the heart of a twenty-year-old gymnast."

She cackled, as he'd known she would. "It's not my heart

I'm worried about, Brady. It's my bones. They ache like the devil."

"Maybe if you'd let one of your great-grandchildren weed that garden of yours."

"I've been doing my own patch for sixty years—"

"And you'll do it another sixty," he finished for her, setting the blood pressure cuff aside. "Nobody in the county grows better tomatoes, but if you don't ease up, your bones are going to ache." He picked up her hands. Her fingers were wiry, not yet touched by arthritis. But it was in her shoulders, in her knees, and there was little he could do to stop its march.

He completed the exam, listening to her tell stories about her family. She'd been his second-grade teacher, and he'd thought then she was the oldest woman alive. After nearly twenty-five years, the gap had closed considerably. Though he knew she still considered him the little troublemaker who had knocked over the goldfish bowl just to see the fish flop on the floor.

"I saw you coming out of the post office a couple of days ago, Mrs. Driscoll." He made a notation on her chart. "You weren't using your cane."

She snorted. "Canes are for old people."

He lowered the chart, lifted a brow. "It's my considered medical opinion, Mrs. Driscoll, that you *are* old."

She cackled and batted a hand at him. "You always had a smart mouth, Brady Tucker."

"Yeah, but now I've got a medical degree to go with it." He took her hand to help her off the examining table. "And I want you to use that cane—even if it's only to give John Hardesty a good rap when he flirts with you."

"The old goat," she muttered. "And I'd look like an old goat, too, hobbling around on a cane."

"Isn't vanity one of the seven deadly sins?"

"It's not worth sinning if it isn't deadly. Get out of here, boy, so I can dress."

"Yes, ma'am." He left her, shaking his head. He could hound her from here to the moon and she wouldn't use that damn cane. She was one of the few patients he couldn't bully or intimidate.

After two more hours of morning appointments, he spent his lunch hour driving to Washington County Hospital to check on two patients. An apple and a handful of peanut butter crackers got him through the afternoon. More than one of his patients mentioned the fact that Vanessa Sexton was back in town. This information was usually accompanied by smirks, winks and leers. He'd had his stomach gouged several times by teasing elbows.

Small towns, he thought as he took five minutes in his office between appointments. The people in them knew everything about everyone. And they remembered it. Forever. Vanessa and he had been together, briefly, twelve years before, but it might as well have been written in concrete, not just carved in one of the trees in Hyattown Park.

He'd forgotten about her—almost. Except when he'd seen her name or picture in the paper. Or when he'd listened to one of her albums, which he'd bought strictly for old times' sake. Or when he'd seen a woman tilt her head to the side and smile in a way similar to the way Van had smiled.

But when he had remembered, they'd been memories of childhood. Those were the sweetest and most poignant. They had been little more than children, rushing toward adulthood with a reckless and terrifying speed. But what had happened between them had remained beautifully innocent. Long, slow kisses in the shadows, passionate promises, a few forbidden caresses.

Thinking of them now, of her, shouldn't make him ache. And yet he rubbed a hand over his heart.

It had seemed too intense at the time, because they had faced such total opposition from her father. The more Julius Sexton had railed against their blossoming relationship, the closer they had become. That was the way of youth, Brady thought now. And he had played the angry young man to perfection, he remembered with a smirk. Defying her father, giving his own a lifetime of headaches. Making threats and promises as only an eighteen-year-old could.

If the road had run smoothly, they would probably have forgotten each other within weeks.

Liar, he thought with a laugh. He had never been so in love as he had been that year with Vanessa. That heady, frantic year, when he had turned eighteen and anything and everything had seemed possible.

They had never made love. He had bitterly regretted that after she had been swept out of his life. Now, with the gift of hindsight, he realized that it had been for the best. If they had been lovers, how much more difficult it would be for them to be friends as adults.

That was what he wanted, all he wanted, he assured himself. He had no intention of breaking his heart over her a second time.

Maybe for a moment, when he had first seen her at the piano, his breath had backed up in his lungs and his pulse had scrambled. That was a natural enough reaction. She was a beautiful woman, and she had once been his. And if he had felt a yearning the night before, as they had sat on the glider in the growing dusk, well, he was human. But he wasn't stupid.

Vanessa Sexton wasn't his girl anymore. And he didn't want her for his woman.

"Dr. Tucker." One of the nurses poked a head in the door. "Your next patient is here."

"Be right there."

"Oh, and your father said to stop by before you leave for the day."

"Thanks." Brady headed for examining room 2, wondering if Vanessa would be sitting out on the glider that evening.

Vanessa knocked on the door of the Tucker house and waited. She'd always liked the Main Street feeling of the home, with its painted porch and its window boxes. There were geraniums in them now, already blooming hardily. The screens were in the open windows. As a girl, she had often seen Brady and his father removing the storms and putting in the screens—a sure sign that winter was over.

There were two rockers sitting on the porch. She knew Dr. Tucker would often sit there on a summer evening. People strolling by would stop to pass the time or to relay a list of symptoms and complaints.

And every year, over the Memorial Day weekend, the Tuckers would throw a backyard barbecue. Everyone in town came by to eat hamburgers and potato salad, to sit under the shade of the big walnut tree, to play croquet.

He was a generous man, Dr. Tucker, Vanessa remembered. With his time, with his skill. She could still remember his laugh, full and rich, and how gentle his hands were during an examination.

But what could she say to him now? This man who had been such a larger-than-life figure during her childhood? This man who had once comforted her when she'd wept over her parents' crumbling marriage? This man who was now involved with her mother?

He opened the door himself, and stood there studying her. He was tall, as she remembered. Like Brady, he had a wiry, athletic build. Though his dark hair had turned a steely gray, he looked no older to her. There were lines fanning out around his dark blue eyes. They deepened as he smiled.

Unsure of herself, she started to offer him a hand. Before she could speak, she was caught up in a crushing bear hug. He smelled of Old Spice and peppermint, she thought, and nearly wept. Even that hadn't changed.

"Little Vanessa." His powerful voice rolled over her as he squeezed. "It's good to have you home."

"It's good to be home." Held against him, she believed it. "I've missed you." It came with a rush of feeling. "I've really missed you."

"Let me have a look at you." Still standing in the doorway, he held her at arm's length. "My, my, my…" he murmured. "Emily always said you'd be a beauty."

"Oh, Dr. Tucker, I'm so sorry about Mrs. Tucker."

"We all were." He rubbed her hands briskly up and down her arms. "She always kept track of you in the papers and magazines, you know. Had her heart set on you for a daughter-in-law. More than once she said to me, 'Ham, that's the girl for Brady. She'll straighten him out.'"

"It looks like he's straightened himself out."

"Mostly." Draping an arm over her shoulder, he led her inside. "How about a nice cup of tea and a piece of pie?"

"I'd love it."

She sat at the kitchen table while he brewed and served. The house hadn't changed on the inside, either. It was still neat as a pin. It was polished and scrubbed, with Emily's collection of knickknacks on every flat surface.

The sunny kitchen looked out over the backyard, with its big trees leafing and its spring bulbs blooming. To the right was the door that led to the offices. The only change she saw was the addition of a complicated phone and intercom system.

"Mrs. Leary still makes the best pies in town." He cut thick slabs of chocolate meringue.

"And she still pays you in baked goods."

"Worth their weight in gold." With a contented sigh, he sat across from her. "I guess I don't have to tell you how proud we all are of you."

She shook her head. "I wish I could have gotten back sooner. I didn't even know Joanie was married. And the baby." She lifted her teacup, fully comfortable for the first time since her return. "Lara's beautiful."

"Smart, too." He winked. "Of course, I might be a tad prejudiced, but I can't remember a smarter child. And I've seen my share of them."

"I hope to see a lot of her while I'm here. Of all of you."

"We're hoping you'll stay a good long time."

"I don't know." She looked down at her tea. "I haven't thought about it."

"Your mother hasn't been able to talk about anything else for weeks."

Vanessa took a smidgen of the fluffy meringue. "She seems well."

"She is well. Loretta's a strong woman. She's had to be."

Vanessa looked up again. Because her stomach had begun to jump, she spoke carefully. "I know she's running an antique shop. It's hard to imagine her as a businesswoman."

"It was hard for her to imagine, but she's doing a good job of it. I know you lost your father a few months ago."

"Cancer. It was very difficult for him."

"And for you."

She moved her shoulders. "There was little I could do…

little he would allow me to do. Basically he refused to admit he was ill. He hated weaknesses."

"I know." He laid a hand on hers. "I hope you've learned to be more tolerant of them."

He didn't have to explain. "I don't hate my mother," she said with a sigh. "I just don't know her."

It was a good answer. One he appreciated. "I do. She's had a hard life, Van. Any mistakes she made, she's paid for more times than any one person should have to. She loves you. She always has."

"Then why did she let me go?"

His heart went out to her, as it always had. "That's a question you'll have to ask her yourself. And one she needs to answer."

With a little sigh, Vanessa sat back. "I always did come to cry on your shoulder."

"That's what shoulders are for. Mostly I was vain enough to think I had two daughters."

"You did." She blinked the tears away and took a soothing drink of tea. "Dr. Tucker, are you in love with my mother?"

"Yes. Does that upset you?"

"It shouldn't."

"But?"

"It's just that it's difficult for me to accept. I've always had such a clear picture of you and Mrs. Tucker as a set. It was one of my constants. My parents...as unhappy as they were together, for as long as I can remember..."

"Were your parents," he said quietly. "Another permanent set."

"Yes." She relaxed a little, grateful that he understood. "I know that's not reasonable. It's not even reality. But..."

"It should be," he finished for her. "My dear child, there is far too much in life that's unfair. I had twenty-eight years with Emily, and had planned for twenty-eight more. It wasn't to be. During the time I had with her, I loved her absolutely. We were lucky enough to grow into people each of us could continue to love. When she died, I thought that a part of my life was over. Your mother was Emily's closest and dearest friend, and that was how I continued to look at Loretta, for several years. Then she became mine—my closest and dearest friend. I think Emily would have been pleased."

"You make me feel like a child."

"You're always a child when it comes to your parents." He glanced down at her plate. "Have you lost your sweet tooth?"

"No." She laughed a little. "My appetite."

"I didn't want to sound like an old fogy and tell you you're too thin. But you are, a bit. Loretta mentioned you weren't eating well. Or sleeping well."

Vanessa raised a brow. She hadn't realized her mother had noticed. "I suppose I'm keyed up. The last couple of years have been pretty hectic."

"When's the last time you had a physical?"

Now she did laugh. "You sound like Brady. I'm fine, Dr. Tucker. Concert tours makes you tough. It's just nerves."

He nodded, but promised himself that he'd keep an eye on her. "I hope you'll play for me soon."

"I'm already breaking in the new piano. In fact, I should get back. I've been skimping on my practice time lately."

As she rose, Brady came through the connecting door. It annoyed him to see her there. It wasn't bad enough that she'd been in his head all day. Now she was in his kitchen. He nodded to her, then glanced down at the pie.

"The dependable Mrs. Leary." He grinned at his father. "Were you going to leave any for me?"

"She's my patient."

"He always hoards the goodies," Brady said to Vanessa,

dipping a finger in the meringue on her plate. "You wanted to see me before I left?"

"You wanted me to look over the Crampton file." Ham tapped a finger on a folder on the counter. "I made some notes."

"Thanks."

"I've got some things to tie up." He took Vanessa by the shoulders and kissed her soundly. "Come back soon."

"I will." She'd never been able to stay away.

"The barbecue's in two weeks. I expect you to be here."

"I wouldn't miss it."

"Brady," he said as he left, "behave yourself with that girl."

Brady grinned as the door closed. "He still figures I'm going to talk you into the backseat of my car."

"You did talk me into the backseat of your car."

"Yeah." The memory made him restless. "Any coffee?"

"Tea," she said. "With lemon verbena."

With a grunt, he turned and took a carton of milk from the refrigerator. "I'm glad you stopped by to see him. He's crazy about you."

"The feeling's mutual."

"You going to eat that pie?"

"No, I was just—" he sat down and dug in "—leaving."

"What's your hurry?" he asked over a forkful.

"I'm not in a hurry, I just—"

"Sit down." He poured an enormous glass of milk.

"Your appetite's as healthy as ever, I see."

"Clean living."

She should go, really. But he looked so relaxed, and re-laxing, sitting at the table shoveling in pie. Friends, he'd said. Maybe they *could* be friends. She leaned back against the counter.

"Where's the dog?"

"Left him home. Dad caught him digging in the tulips yesterday, so he's banished."

"You don't live here anymore?"

"No." He looked up and nearly groaned. She was leaning on the counter in front of the window, the light in her hair. There was the faintest of smiles playing on that full, serious mouth of hers. The severe tailoring of her slacks and shirt made her seem that much softer and feminine. "I, ah…" He reached for the milk. "I bought some land outside of town. The house is going up slow, but it's got a roof."

"You're building your own house?"

"I'm not doing that much. I can't get away from here long enough to do much more than stick up a couple of two-by-fours. I've got a couple of guys hammering it together." He looked at her again, considering. "I'll drive you out some time so you can take a look."

"Maybe."

"How about now?" He rose to put his dishes in the sink.

"Oh, well… I really have to get back…."

"For what?"

"To practice."

He turned. Their shoulders brushed. "Practice later."

It was a challenge. They both knew it, both understood it. They were both determined to prove that they could be in each other's company without stirring up old yearnings.

"All right. I'll follow you out, though. That way you won't have to come back into town."

"Fine." He took her arm and led her out the back door.

He'd had a secondhand Chevy sedan when she'd left town. Now he drove a sporty four-wheel drive. Three miles out of town, when they came to the steep, narrow lane, she saw the wisdom of it.

It would be all but impassable in the winter, she thought as her Mercedes jolted up the graveled incline. Though the leaves were little more than tender shoots, the woods were thick. She could see the wild dogwoods blooming white. She narrowly avoided a rut. Gravel spit out from under her wheels as she negotiated the last sweeping turn and came to a halt behind Brady.

The dog came racing, barking, his tail fanning in the breeze.

The shell of the house was up. He wasn't contenting himself with a cabin in the woods, she noted. It was a huge, spreading two-story place. The windows that were in place were tall, with half-moon arches over them. What appeared to be the skeleton of a gable rose up from the second story. It would command a majestic view of the distant Blue Mountains.

The grounds, covered with the rubble of construction, sloped down to a murmuring creek. Rain would turn the site into a mud pit, she thought as she stepped from her car. But, oh, when it was terraced and planted, it would be spectacular.

"It's fabulous." She pushed back her hair as the early evening breeze stirred it. "What a perfect spot."

"I thought so." He caught Kong by the collar before he could leap on her.

"He's all right." She laughed as she bent down to rub him. "Hello, fella. Hello, big boy. You've got plenty of room to run around here, don't you?"

"Twelve acres." He was getting that ache again, just under his heart, watching her play with his dog. "I'm going to leave most of it alone."

"I'm glad." She turned a full circle. "I'd hate to see you

manicure the woods. I'd nearly forgotten how wonderful they are. How quiet."

"Come on." He took her hand, held it. "I'll give you the tour."

"How long have you had the land?"

"Almost a year." They walked across a little wooden bridge, over the creek. "Watch your step. The ground's a mess." He looked down at her elegant Italian flats. "Here." He hoisted her up and over the rubble. She felt the bunching of his arm muscles, he the firm length of her legs.

"You don't have to—" He set her down, hastily, in front of a pair of atrium doors. "Still Mr. Smooth, aren't you?"

"You bet."

Inside there was subflooring and drywall. She saw power tools, sawhorses and piles of lumber. A huge stone fireplace was already built into the north wall. Temporary stairs led to the second level. The scent of sawdust was everywhere.

"The living room," he explained. "I wanted plenty of light. The kitchen's over there."

He indicated a generous space that curved off the main room. There was a bay window over the sink that looked out into the woods. A stove and refrigerator were nestled between unfinished counters.

"We'll have an archway to keep in tune with the windows," he went on. "Then another will lead around to the dining room."

She looked up at the sky through a trio of skylights. "It seems very ambitious."

"I only intend to do it once." Taking her hand again, he led her around the first floor. "Powder room. Your mother found me this great pedestal sink. The porcelain's in perfect shape. And this is a kind of a den, I guess. Stereo equipment, books." When he narrowed his eyes, he could see the finished product perfectly. And oddly, so could she. "Do you remember Josh McKenna?"

"Yes. He was your partner in crime."

"Now he's a partner in a construction firm. He's doing all these built-ins himself."

"Josh?" She ran a hand over a shelf. The workmanship was beautiful.

"He designed the kitchen cabinets, too. They're going to be something. Let's go up. The stairs are narrow, but they're sturdy."

Despite his assurances, she kept one hand pressed against the wall as they climbed. There were more skylights, more arches. The eyebrow windows, as he called them, would go over the bed in the master suite, which included an oversize bathroom with a tiled sunken tub. Though there were a mattress and a dresser in the bedroom, the bath was the only finished room. Vanessa stepped off subflooring onto ceramic.

He'd chosen cool pastels with an occasional vivid slash of navy. The huge tub was encircled by a tiled ledge that sat flush against another trio of windows. Vanessa imagined soaking there with a view of the screening woods.

"You've pulled out all the stops," she commented.

"When I decided to move back, I decided to do it right." They continued down the hall, between the studded walls. "There are two more bedrooms on this floor, and another bath. I'm going to use glass brick in that one. The deck will run all around, then drop down to the second level on the west side for sunset." He took her up another flight of splattered steps into the gable. "I'm thinking about putting my office up here."

It was like a fairy tale, Vanessa thought, circular in shape, with more arching windows. Everywhere you stood there was a lofty view of the woods and the mountains beyond.

"I could live right here," she said, "and feel like Rapunzel."

"Your hair's the wrong color." He lifted a handful. "I'm glad you never cut it. I used to dream about this hair." His gaze shifted to hers. "About you. For years after you left, I used to dream about you. I could never figure it out."

She turned away quickly and walked to one of the windows. "When do you think you'll have it finished?"

"We're shooting for September." He frowned at her back. He hadn't thought of her when he'd designed the house, when he'd chosen the wood, the tiles, the colors. Why was it that now that she was here it was as if the house had been waiting for her? As if he'd been waiting for her? "Van?"

"Yes," she answered, keeping her back to him. Her stomach was in knots, her fingers were twisted. When he said nothing else, she forced herself to turn, made her lips curve. "It's a fabulous place, Brady. I'm glad you showed it to me. I hope I get the chance to see it when it's done."

He wasn't going to ask her if she was going to stay. He didn't want to know. He couldn't let it matter. But he knew that there was unfinished business between them, and he had to settle it, at least in his own mind.

He crossed to her slowly. He saw the awareness come into her eyes with his first step. She would have backed away if there had been anywhere to go.

"Don't," she said when he took her arms.

"This is going to hurt me as much as it does you."

He touched his lips to hers, testing. And felt her shudder. Her taste, just that brief taste, made him burn. Again he kissed her, lingering over it only seconds longer. This time he heard her moan. His hands slid up her arms to cup her face. When his mouth took hers again, the testing was over.

It did hurt. She felt the ache through every bone and muscle. And damn him, she felt the pleasure. A pleasure she had lived without for too long. Greedy for it, she pulled him closer and let the war rage frantically inside her.

She was no longer kissing a boy, however clever and passionate that boy had been. She wasn't kissing a memory, no matter how rich and clear that memory had been. It was a man she held now. A strong, hungry man who knew her much too well.

When her lips parted for his, she knew what he would taste like. As her hands dug into his shoulders, she knew the feel of those muscles. With the scent of sawdust around them, and the light gentle through the glass, she felt herself rocked back and forth between the past and present.

She was all he remembered, and more. He had always been generous, always passionate, but there seemed to be more innocence now than there had been before. It was there, sweet, beneath the simmer of desire. Her body trembled even as it strained against his.

The dreams he thought he had forgotten flooded back. And with them the needs, the frustrations, the hopes, of his youth.

It was her. It had always been her. And yet it had never been.

Shaken, he pulled back and held her at arm's length. The color had risen over her cheekbones. Her eyes had darkened, clouded, in that way that had always made him churn. Her lips were parted, soft, unpainted. His hands were lost, as they had been countless times before, in her hair.

And the feeling was the same. He could have murdered her for it. Twelve years hadn't diluted the emotion she could pull out of him with a look.

"I was afraid of that," he murmured. He needed to keep

sane, he told himself. He needed to think. "You always could stop my heart, Vanessa."

"This is stupid." Breathless, she stepped back. "We're not children anymore."

He dipped his hands in his pockets. "Exactly."

She ran an unsteady hand through her hair. "Brady, this was over a long time ago."

"Apparently not. Could be we just have to get it out of our systems."

"My system's just fine," she told him. It was a lie. "You'll have to worry about your own. I'm not interested in climbing into the backseat with you again."

"That might be interesting." He surprised himself by smiling, and meaning it. "But I had more comfortable surroundings in mind."

"Whatever the surroundings, the answer's still no."

She started toward the steps, and he took her by the arm. "You were sixteen the last time you said no." Slowly, though impatience simmered through him, he turned her to face him. "As much as I regret it, I have to say you were right. Times have changed, and we're all grown up now."

Her heart was beating too fast, she thought. His fault. He had always been able to tie her into knots. "Just because we're adults doesn't mean I'll jump in your bed."

"It does mean that I'll take the time and make the effort to change your mind."

"You are still an egotistical idiot, Brady."

"And you still call me names when you know I'm right." He pulled her close for a hard, brief kiss. "I still want you, Van. And this time, by God, I'm going to have you."

She saw the truth of it in his eyes before she jerked away. She felt the truth of it inside herself. "Go to hell."

She turned and rushed down the stairs.

He watched from the window as she raced across the bridge to her car. Even with the distance, he heard her slam the door. It made him grin. She'd always had a devil of a temper. He was glad to see it still held true.

Chapter 4

She pounded the keys. Tchaikovsky. The first piano concerto. The first movement. Hers was a violently passionate interpretation of the romantic theme. She wanted the
violence, wanted to let it pour out from inside her and into
the music.

He'd had no right. No right to bring everything back. To
force her to face feelings she'd wanted to forget. Feelings
she'd forgotten. Worse, he'd shown her how much deeper,
how much more raw and intense, those feelings could be
now that she was a woman.

He meant nothing to her. Could be nothing more to her
than an old acquaintance, a friend of her childhood. She
would not be hurt by him again. And she would never—
never—allow anyone to have the kind of power over her
that Brady had once had.

The feelings would pass, because she would make them
pass. If there was one thing she had learned through all these

years of work and travel, it was that she and she alone was responsible for her emotions.

She stopped playing, letting her fingers rest on the keys. While she might not have been able to claim serenity, she was grateful that she had been able to exorcise most of the anger and frustration through her music.

"Vanessa?"

She turned her head to see her mother standing in the doorway. "I didn't know you were home."

"I came in while you were playing." Loretta took a step forward. She was dressed as she had been that morning, in her sleek suit and pearls, but her face showed a hesitant concern. "Are you all right?"

"Yes, I'm fine." Vanessa lifted a hand to push back her hair. Looking at her mother, she felt flushed, untidy and vulnerable. Automatically, defensively, she straightened her shoulders. "I'm sorry. I guess I lost track of the time."

"It doesn't matter." Loretta blocked off the urge to move closer and smooth her daughter's hair herself. "Mrs. Driscoll stopped by the shop before I closed. She mentioned that she saw you going into Ham Tucker's house."

"She still has an eagle eye, I see."

"And a big nose." Loretta's smile was hesitant. "You saw Ham, then."

"Yes." Vanessa turned on the stool, but didn't rise. "He looks wonderful, almost unchanged. We had some pie and tea in the kitchen."

"I'm glad you had a chance to visit with him. He's always been so fond of you."

"I know." She took a bracing breath. "Why didn't you tell me you were involved with him?"

Loretta lifted a hand to her pearls and twisted the strand nervously. "I suppose I wasn't sure how to bring it up. To explain. I thought you might be…might feel awkward about seeing him again if you knew we were…" She let her words trail off, certain the word *dating* would be out of place at her age.

Vanessa merely lifted a brow. "Maybe you thought it was none of my business."

"No." Her hand fell to her side. "Oh, Van…"

"Well, it isn't, after all." Slowly, deliberately, Vanessa patched up the cracks in her shield. "You and my father had been divorced for years before he died. You're certainly free to choose your own companions."

The censure in her daughter's voice had Loretta's spine straightening. There were many things, many, that she regretted, that had caused her shame. Her relationship with Abraham Tucker wasn't one of them.

"You're absolutely right," she said, her voice cool. "I'm not embarrassed, and I certainly don't feel guilty, about seeing Ham. We're adults, and both of us are free." The tilt of her chin as she spoke was very like her daughter's. "Perhaps I felt odd about what started between us, because of Emily. She had been my oldest and dearest friend. But Emily was gone, and both Ham and I were alone. And maybe the fact that we both had loved Emily had something to do with our growing closer. I'm very proud that he cares for me," she said, color dotting her cheeks. "In the past few years, he's given me something I've never had from another man. Understanding."

She turned and hurried up the stairs. She was standing in front of her dresser, removing her jewelry, when Vanessa came in.

"I apologize if I seemed too critical."

Loretta slapped the pearls down on the wood. "I don't want you to apologize like some polite stranger, Vanessa.

You're my daughter. I'd rather you shouted at me. I'd rather you slammed doors or stormed into your room the way you used to."

"I nearly did." She walked farther into the room, running a hand over the back of a small, tufted chair. Even that was new, she thought—the little blue lady's chair that so suited the woman who was her mother. Calmer now, and more than a little ashamed, she chose her next words carefully. "I don't resent your relationship with Dr. Tucker. Really. It surprised me, certainly. And what I said before is true. It's none of my business."

"Van—"

"No, please." Vanessa held up a hand. "When I first drove into town, I thought nothing had changed. But I was wrong. It's difficult to accept that. It's difficult to accept that you moved on so easily."

"Moved on, yes," Loretta said. "But not easily."

Vanessa looked up, passion in her eyes. "Why did you let me go?"

"I had no choice," Loretta said simply. "And at the time I tried to believe it was what was best for you. What you wanted."

"What I wanted?" The anger she wanted so badly to control seeped out as bitterness. "Did anyone ever ask me what I wanted?"

"I tried. In every letter I wrote you, I begged you to tell me if you were happy, if you wanted to come home. When you sent them back unopened, I knew I had my answer."

The color ran into and then out of Vanessa's face as she stared at Loretta. "You never wrote me."

"I wrote you for years, hoping that you might find the compassion to open at least one."

"There were no letters," Vanessa said, very deliberately, her hands clenching and unclenching.

Without a word, Loretta went over to an enameled trunk at the foot of her bed. She drew out a deep box and removed the lid. "I kept them," she said.

Vanessa looked in and saw dozens of letters, addressed to her at hotels throughout Europe and the States. Her stomach convulsing, she took careful breaths and sat on the edge of the bed.

"You never saw them, did you?" Loretta murmured. Vanessa could only shake her head. "He would deny me even such a little thing as a letter." With a sigh, Loretta set the box back in the trunk.

"Why?" Vanessa's throat was raw. "Why did he stop me from seeing your letters?"

"Maybe he thought I would interfere with your career." After a moment's hesitation, Loretta touched her shoulder. "He was wrong. I would never have stopped you from reaching for something you wanted and deserved so much. He was, in his way, protecting you and punishing me."

"For what?"

Loretta turned and walked to the window.

"Damn it, I have a right to know." Fury had her on her feet and taking a step forward. Then, with an involuntary gasp, she was clutching her stomach.

"Van?" Loretta took her shoulders, moving her gently back to the bed. "What is it?"

"It's nothing." She gritted her teeth against the grinding pain. It infuriated her that it could incapacitate her, even for a moment, in front of someone else. "Just a spasm."

"I'm going to call Ham."

"No." Vanessa grabbed her arm. Her long musician's fingers were strong and firm. "I don't need a doctor. It's just stress." She kept one hand balled at her side and struggled to get past the pain. "And I stood up too fast." Very carefully, she relaxed her hand.

"Then it won't hurt to have him look at you." Loretta draped an arm over her shoulders. "Van, you're so thin."

"I've had a lot to deal with in the last year." Vanessa kept her words measured. "A lot of tension. Which is why I've decided to take a few months off."

"Yes, but—"

"I know how I feel. And I'm fine."

Loretta removed her arm when she heard Vanessa's dismissive tone. "All right, then. You're not a child anymore."

"No, I'm not." She folded her hands in her lap as Loretta rose. "I'd like an answer. What was my father punishing you for?"

Loretta seemed to brace herself, but her voice was calm and strong when she spoke. "For betraying him with another man."

For a moment, Vanessa could only stare. Here was her mother, her face pale but set, confessing to adultery. "You had an affair?" Vanessa asked at length.

"Yes." Shame rushed through her. But she knew she could deal with it. She'd lived with shame for years. "There was someone… It hardly matters now who it was. I was involved with him for almost a year before you went to Europe."

"I see."

Loretta gave a short, brittle laugh. "Oh, I'm sure you do. So I won't bother to offer you any excuses or explanations. I broke my vows, and I've been paying for it for twelve years."

Vanessa lifted her head, torn between wanting to understand and wanting to condemn. "Did you love him?"

"I needed him. There's a world of difference."

"You didn't marry again."

"No." Loretta felt no regret at that, just a vague ache, as from an old scar that had been bumped once too often. "Marriage wasn't something either of us wanted at the time."

"Then it was just for sex." Vanessa pressed her fingers against her eyes. "You cheated on your husband just for sex."

A flurry of emotions raced over Loretta's face before she calmed it again. "That's the least common denominator. Maybe, now that you're a woman, you'll understand, even if you can't forgive."

"I don't understand anything." Vanessa stood. It was foolish to want to weep for something that was over and done. "I need to think. I'm going for a drive."

Alone, Loretta sat on the edge of the bed and let her own tears fall.

She drove for hours, aimlessly. She spent most of the time negotiating curving back roads lined with budding wildflowers and arching trees. Some of the old farms had been sold and subdivided since she'd been here last. Houses and yards crisscrossed over what had once been sprawling corn or barley fields. She felt a pang of loss on seeing them. The same kind of pang she felt when she thought of her family.

She wondered if she would have been able to understand the lack of fidelity if it had been some other woman. Would she have been able to give a sophisticated little shrug and agree that the odd affair was just a part of life? She wasn't sure. She hadn't been raised to see a sanctified state. And it wasn't some other woman. It was her mother.

It was late when she found herself turning into Brady's lane. She didn't know why she'd come here, come to him, of all people. But she needed someone to listen. Someone who cared.

The lights were on. She could hear the dog barking from

inside the house at the sound of her car. Slowly she retraced the steps she had taken that evening. When she had run from him, and from her own feelings. Before she could knock, Brady was at the door. He took a long look at her through the glass before pulling it open.

"Hi."

"I was out driving." She felt so completely stupid that she took a step back. "I'm sorry. It's late."

"Come on in, Van." He took her hand. The dog sniffed at her slacks, wagging his tail. "Want a drink?"

"No." She had no idea what she wanted. She looked around, aware that she'd interrupted him. There was a step-ladder against a wall, and a portable stereo set too loud. Rock echoed to the ceiling. She noted there was a fine coat of white dust on his hands and forearms, even in his hair. She fought a ridiculous urge to brush it out for him. "You're busy."

"Just sanding drywall." He walked over to turn off the music. The sudden silence made her edgy. "It's amazingly therapeutic." He picked up a sheet of sandpaper. "Want to try it?"

She managed to smile. "Maybe later."

He stopped by the refrigerator to pull out a beer. He gestured with it. "Sure?"

"Yes. I'm driving, and I can't stay long."

He popped the top and took a long drink. The cold beer eased through the dust in his throat—and through the knot that had lodged there when he saw her walking to his door. "I guess you decided not to be mad at me anymore."

"I don't know." Hugging her arms, Vanessa walked to the far window. She wished she could see the moon, but it was hiding behind a bank of clouds. "I don't know what I feel about anything."

He knew that look, that set of her shoulders, that tone of voice. It had been the same years before, when she would escape from one of the miserable arguments between her parents. "Why don't you tell me about it?"

Of course he would say that, she thought. Hadn't she known he would? And he would listen. He always had. "I shouldn't have come here," she said with a sigh. "It's like falling back into an old rut."

"Or slipping into a comfortable pair of shoes." He winced a little at his own words. "I don't think I like that much better. Look, do you want to sit down? I can dust off a sawhorse, or turn over a can of drywall compound."

"No. No, I couldn't sit." She continued to stare out the window. All she could see was her own pale reflection ghosted on the glass. "My mother told me she'd had an affair before my father took me to Europe." When he didn't respond, she turned to study his face. "You knew."

"Not at the time." The hurt and bewilderment on her face had him crossing to her to brush at her hair. "Not long after you were gone, it came out." He shrugged. "Small towns."

"My father knew," Vanessa said carefully. "My mother said as much. That must have been why he took me away the way he did. And why she didn't come with us."

"I can't comment on what went on between your parents, Van. If there are things you need to know, you should hear them from Loretta."

"I don't know what to say to her. I don't know what to ask." She turned away again. "In all those years, my father never said a thing about it."

That didn't surprise him, but he doubted Julius's motives had been altruistic. "What else did she tell you?"

"What else is there to tell?" Vanessa countered.

Brady was silent for a moment. "Did you ask her why?"

"I didn't have to." She rubbed a chill from her arms. "She told me she didn't even love the man. It was just physical. Just sex."

He contemplated his beer. "Well, I guess we should drag her out in the street and shoot her."

"It's not a joke," Vanessa said, whirling around. "She deceived her husband. She cheated on him while they were living together, while she was pretending to be part of a family."

"That's all true. Considering the kind of woman Loretta is, it seems to me she must have had some very strong reasons." His eyes stayed on hers, calm and searching. "I'm surprised it didn't occur to you."

"How can you justify adultery?"

"I'm not. But there are very few situations that are simple black and white. I think once you get over the shock and the anger, you'll ask her about those gray areas."

"How would you feel if it was one of your parents?"

"Lousy." He set the beer aside. "Want a hug?"

She felt the tears rise to burn the backs of her eyes. "Yes," she managed, and went gratefully into his arms.

He held her, his arms gentle, his hands easy as they stroked along her back. She needed him now, he thought. And the need was for friendship. However tangled his emotions were, he could never refuse her that. He brushed his lips over her hair, enchanted by the texture, the scent, the warm, deep color. Her arms were tight around him. Her head was nestled just beneath his.

She still fitted, he thought. She was still a perfect fit.

He seemed so solid. She wondered how such a reckless boy could have become such a solid, dependable man. He was giving her, without her even having asked, exactly what she needed. Nothing more, nothing less.

Her eyes closed, she thought how easy, how terrifyingly easy, it would be to fall in love with him all over again.

"Feeling any better?"

She didn't know about better, but she was definitely feeling. The hypnotic stroke of his hands up and down her spine, the steady rhythm of his heart against hers.

She lifted her head, just enough to see his eyes. There was understanding in them, and a strength that had developed during the time she had been without him.

"I can't make up my mind whether you've changed or whether you're the same."

"Some of both." Her scent was waltzing through his system. "I'm glad you came back."

"I didn't mean to." She sighed again. "I wasn't going to get near you again. When I was here before, I was angry because you made me remember—and what I remembered was that I'd never really forgotten."

If she looked at him that way five more seconds, he knew, he'd forget she'd come looking for a friend. "Van... you should probably try to straighten this out with your mother. Why don't I drive you home?"

"I don't want to go home tonight." Her words echoed in her head. She had to press her lips tightly together before she could form the next words. "Let me stay here with you."

The somewhat pleasant ache that had coursed through him as he'd held her turned sharp and deadly. With his movements slow and deliberate, he put his hands on her shoulders and stepped back.

"That's not a good idea." When her mouth turned into a pout, he nearly groaned.

"A few hours ago, you seemed to think it was a very good idea." She shrugged his hands off her shoulders before she turned. "Apparently you're still a lot of talk and no action."

He spun her around quickly, threats hovering on his tongue. As she watched, the livid fury in his eyes died to a smolder. "You still know what buttons to push."

She tilted her head. "And you don't."

He slipped a hand around her throat. "You're such a brat." When she tossed back her head, he was tempted to give her throat just one quick squeeze. He reminded himself that he was a doctor. "It would serve you right if I dragged you upstairs and made love to you until you were deaf, dumb and blind."

She felt a thrill of excitement mixed with alarm. What would it be like? Hadn't she wondered since the first moment she'd seen him again? Maybe it was time to be reckless.

"I'd like to see you try."

Desire seared through him as he looked at her, her head thrown back, her eyes hooded, her mouth soft and sulky. He knew what it would be like. Damn her. He'd spent hours trying not to imagine what now came all too clearly to his mind. In defense he took a step backward.

"Don't push it, Van."

"If you don't want me, why—?"

"You know I do," he shouted at her as he spun away. "Damn it, you know I always have. You make me feel like I'm eighteen and itchy again." When she took a step forward, he threw up a hand. "Just stay away from me." He snatched up his beer and took a long, greedy swallow. "You can take the bed," he said more calmly. "I've got a sleeping bag I can use down here."

"Why?"

"The timing stinks." He drained the beer and tossed the empty bottle into a five-gallon drum. It shattered. "By God, if we're going to have another shot at this, we're going to do it right. Tonight you're upset and confused and unhappy. You're angry with your mother, and you're not going to hate me for taking advantage of all of that."

She looked down at her hands and spread them. He was right. That was the hell of it. "The timing's never been right for us, has it?"

"It will be." He put a hand on either side of her face. "You can count on it. You'd better go up." He dropped his hands again. "Being noble makes me cranky."

With a nod, she started toward the stairs. At the base, she stopped and turned. "Brady, I'm really sorry you're such a nice guy."

He rubbed at the tension at the back of his neck. "Me, too."

She smiled a little. "No, not because of tonight. You're right about tonight. I'm sorry because it reminds me how crazy I was about you. And why."

Pressing a hand to the ache in his gut, he watched her go upstairs. "Thanks a lot," he said to himself. "That's just what I needed to hear to make sure I don't sleep at all tonight."

Vanessa lay in Brady's bed, tangled in Brady's sheets. The dog had deserted him to sleep at her feet. She could hear the soft canine snoring as she stared into the deep, deep country dark.

Would she—could she—have gone through with her invitation to come to this bed with him? A part of her yearned to. A part of her that had waited all these years to feel as only he could make her feel.

Yet, when she had offered herself to him, she had done so recklessly, heedlessly, and in direct opposition to her own instinct for survival.

She had walked away from him just this evening, angry,

even insulted, at his cocky insistence that they would become lovers. What kind of sense did it make for her to have come back to him in emotional turmoil and rashly ask to do just that?

It made no sense at all.

He had always confused her, she thought as she turned restlessly in his bed. He had always been able to make her ignore her own common sense. Now that she was sleeping—or trying to—alone, her frustration was tempered by gratitude that he understood her better than she understood herself.

In all the years she had been away, in all the cities where she had traveled, not one of the men who had escorted her had tempted her to open the locks she had so firmly bolted on her emotions.

Only Brady. And what, for God's sake, was she going to do about it?

She was sure—nearly sure—that if things stayed as they were she would be able to leave painlessly when the time came. If she could think of him as a friend, a sometimes maddening friend, she could fly off to pick up her career when she was ready. But if he became her lover, her first and only lover, the memory might haunt her like a restless ghost throughout her life.

And there was more, she admitted with a sigh. She didn't want to hurt him. No matter how angry he could make her, no matter how deeply he had, and could, hurt her, she didn't want to cause him any real pain.

She knew what it was like to live with that kind of pain, the kind that spread and throbbed, the kind that came when you knew someone didn't care enough. Someone didn't want you enough.

She wouldn't do to Brady what had been done to her.

If he had been kind enough to allow her to hide in his home for a few hours, she would be kind enough to repay the favor by making sure they kept a reasonable distance between them.

No, she thought grimly, she would not be his lover. Or any man's. She had her mother's example before her. When her mother had taken a lover, it had ruined three lives. Vanessa knew her father had never been happy. Driven, yes. Obsessed with his daughter's career. And bitter, Vanessa thought now. Oh, so bitter. He had never forgiven his wife for her betrayal. Why else had he blocked the letters she had sent to her daughter? Why else had he never, never spoken her name?

As the gnawing in her stomach grew sharper, she curled up tight. Somehow she would try to accept what her mother had done, and what she hadn't done.

Closing her eyes, she listened to the call of an owl in the woods, and the distant rumble of thunder on the mountain.

She awoke at first light to the patter of rain on the roof. It sent music playing in her head as she shifted. Though she felt heavy with fatigue, she sat up, hugging her knees as she blinked at the gloom.

The dog was gone, but the sheets at her feet were still warm from him. It was time for her to go, as well.

The big tiled tub was tempting, but she reminded herself to be practical and turned instead to the glassed-in corner shower. In ten minutes she was walking quietly downstairs.

Brady was flat on his stomach in his twisted sleeping bag, his face buried in a ridiculously small pillow. With his dog sitting patiently beside him, he made a picture that turned her heart upside down.

Kong grinned and thumped his tail as she came to the

bottom of the steps. She put a warning finger to her lips. Kong obviously wasn't up on sign language, as he let out two sharp, happy barks, then turned to lick Brady's face wherever he could reach.

Swearing, Brady shoved the dog's face away from his. "Let yourself out, damn it. Don't you know a dead man when you see one?"

Undaunted, Kong sat on him.

"Here, boy." Vanessa walked to the door and opened it. Delighted to have his needs understood, Kong bounded outside into the pattering rain. When she looked back, Brady was sitting up, the sleeping bag pooled around his waist. Bleary-eyed, he scowled at her.

"How come you look so damn good?"

The same could be said about him, she thought. As he'd claimed, he'd filled out a bit. His naked chest looked rock-firm, his shoulders leanly muscled. Because her nerves were beginning to jump, she concentrated on his face.

Why was it he looked all the more attractive with a night's stubble and a surly set to his mouth?

"I used your shower. I hope you don't mind." When he just grunted, she worked up a smile. If she felt this awkward now, she wondered, how would she have felt if he'd joined her in the bed? "I appreciate the night's sanctuary, Brady. Really. Why don't I pay you back by making some coffee?"

"How fast can you make it?"

"Faster than room service." She slipped past him to the adjoining kitchen. "I learned to keep a travel pot with me in hotels." She found a glass pot and a plastic cone filter. "But I think this is a little out of my league."

"Put some water in the kettle. I'll walk you through it."

Grateful for the occupation, she turned on the tap. "I'm sorry about all this," she said. "I know I dumped on you last night, and you were very…" She turned, and her words trailed off. He was standing now, tugging jeans over his hips. Her mouth went bone-dry.

"Stupid," he finished for her. Metal rasped on metal as he pulled up the zipper. "Insane."

"Understanding," she managed. He started toward her. Her feet knocked up against the unfinished counter as she took a hasty step in retreat.

"Don't mention it," he said. "And I do mean don't mention it. I've had an entire sleepless night to regret it."

She lifted a hand to his cheek, then hastily dropped it when she saw his eyes darken. "You should have told me to go home. It was childish of me not to. I'm sure my mother was worried."

"I called her after you went up."

She looked down at the floor. "You're much kinder than I am."

He didn't want her gratitude, he thought. Or her embarrassment. Annoyed, he passed her a paper filter. "You put this in the cone and put the cone on the glass pot. Six scoops of coffee in the filter, then pour the hot water through. Got it?"

"Yes." There was no need for him to be so snotty when she was trying to thank him.

"Terrific. I'll be back in a minute."

She set her hands on her hips as he padded upstairs. An exasperating man, she thought. Sweet and compassionate one minute, surly and rude the next. With a half laugh, she turned back to scowl at the teakettle. And wasn't that just the combination that had always fascinated her? At least she was no longer a naive girl certain he would turn into a prince.

Determined to finish what she had started, she measured out the coffee. She loved the rich morning aroma of it, and wished she hadn't had to stop drinking it. Caffeine, she thought with a wistful sigh. It no longer seemed to agree with her.

She was pouring the boiling water over the coffee when Brady came back. His hair was damp, she noted. And there was the lingering scent of soap around him. Because her mind was set to be friendly, she smiled at him.

"That had to be the quickest shower on record."

"I learned to be quick when I was an intern." He took a long, deep sniff of the coffee. It was his bad luck that he could also smell his shampoo on her hair. "I'm going to feed Kong," he said abruptly, and left her alone again.

When he returned, she was smiling at the coffee, which had nearly dripped through. "I remember one of these in your kitchen on Main Street."

"My mother always made drip coffee. The best."

"Brady, I haven't told you how sorry I am. I know how close you were."

"She never gave up on me. Probably should have more than once, but she never did." His eyes met Vanessa's. "I guess mothers don't."

Uncomfortable, Vanessa turned away. "I think it's ready." When he reached for two mugs, she shook her head. "No, I don't want any, thanks. I've given it up."

"As a doctor, I can tell you that's commendable." He poured a full mug. "As a human being, I have to ask how you function."

She smiled. "You just start a little slower, that's all. I have to go."

He simply put a hand on the counter and blocked her way. There was rain on his hair now, and his eyes were very clear. "You didn't sleep well."

"I'd say that makes two of us."

He took a casual sip of his coffee as he completed a thorough study of her face. The fatigue he saw was due to more than one restless night. "I want you to do something for me."

"If I can."

"Go home, pull the covers over your head, and tune out until noon."

Her lips curved. "I might just do that."

"If those shadows under your eyes aren't gone in forty-eight hours, I'm going to sic my father on you."

"Big talk."

"Yeah." He set the mug aside and then, leaning his other hand on the counter, effectively caged her. "I seem to remember a comment last night about no action."

Since she couldn't back up, she held her ground. "I was trying to make you mad."

"You did." He leaned closer until their thighs met.

"Brady, I don't have the time or patience for this. I have to go."

"Okay. Kiss me goodbye."

Her chin tilted. "I don't want to."

"Sure you do." His mouth whispered over hers before she could jerk her head back. "You're just afraid to."

"I've never been afraid of you."

"No." He smiled an infuriating smile. "But you've learned to be afraid of yourself."

"That's ridiculous."

"Prove it."

Seething, she leaned forward, intent on giving him a brief, soulless kiss. But her heart was in her throat almost instantly. He used no pressure, only soft, soft persuasion. His lips were warm and mobile against hers, his tongue cleverly tracing the shape of her mouth before dipping inside to tease and tempt.

On a breathless murmur, she took her hands up and over his naked chest to his shoulders. His skin was damp and cool.

He nipped gently at her lips, drowning in the taste of her. Using all his control, he kept his tensed hands on the counter. He knew that if he touched her now, even once, he wouldn't stop.

She would come to him. He had promised himself that as he'd sweated through the night. She would come to him, and not because of a memory, not because of grief. Because of need.

Slowly, while he still had some control, he lifted his head and backed away. "I want to see you tonight, Van."

"I don't know." She put a hand to her spinning head.

"Then you think about it." He picked up his mug again, surprised the handle didn't shatter in his grip. "You can call me when you make up your mind."

Her confusion died away, to be replaced by anger. "I'm not playing games."

"Then what the hell are you doing?"

"I'm just trying to survive." She snatched up her purse and ran out into the rain.

Chapter 5

Bed sounded like a wonderful idea, Vanessa decided as she pulled up in front of the house. Maybe if she drew down the shades, put the music on low and willed herself to relax, she would find the sleep she had lost the night before. When she felt more rested, she might have a clearer idea of what to say to her mother.

She wondered if a few hours' sleep would help her resolve her feelings about Brady.

It was worth a shot.

She stepped out of the car and rounded the hood to the sidewalk. When she heard her name called, she turned. Mrs. Driscoll was lumbering toward her, clutching her purse and a stack of mail. A huge, wood-handled black umbrella was tight in her fist. Vanessa's smile came naturally as she moved forward to greet her.

"Mrs. Driscoll. It's good to see you again."

Only a little winded, Mrs. Driscoll peered out of sharp little eyes. "Heard you were back. Too skinny."

With a laugh, Vanessa bent to kiss her leathery cheek. As always, her former teacher smelled of lavender sachet. "You look wonderful."

"Take care of yourself." She sniffed. "That snippy Brady tells me I need a cane. He thinks he's a doctor. Hold on to this." Bossy by nature, she shoved the umbrella into Vanessa's hand. She opened her purse to stuff her mail inside, stubbornly keeping her balance. The rain made her bones ache all the more, but she had always loved to walk in it. "It's about time you came home. You staying?"

"Well, I haven't—"

"About time you gave your mother some attention," she interrupted, leaving Vanessa with nothing to say. "I heard you playing when I walked to the bank yesterday, but I couldn't stop."

Vanessa struggled with the heavy umbrella, and with her manners. "Would you like to come in, have some tea?"

"Too much to do. You still play real nice, Vanessa."

"Thank you."

When Mrs. Driscoll took the umbrella back, Vanessa thought the little visit was over. She should have known better. "I've got a grandniece. She's been taking piano lessons in Hagerstown. Puts a strain on her ma, having to haul her all that way. Figured now that you're back, you could take over."

"Oh, but I—"

"She's been taking them nigh on a year, an hour once a week. She played 'Jingle Bells' real well at Christmas. Did a fair turn on 'Go Tell Aunt Rhody,' too."

"That's very nice," Vanessa managed, beginning to feel

desperate, as well as wet. "But since she's already got a teacher, I wouldn't want to interfere."

"Lives right across from Lester's. Could walk to your place. Give her ma a breather. Lucy—that's my niece, my younger brother's second girl—she's expecting another next month. Hoping for a boy this time, since they've got the two girls. Girls just seem to run in the family."

"Ah…"

"It's hard on her driving clear up to Hagerstown."

"I'm sure it is, but—"

"You have a free hour once a week, don't you?"

Exasperated, Vanessa dragged a hand through her rapidly dampening hair. "I suppose I do, but—"

Violet Driscoll knew when to spring. "How about today? The school bus drops her off just after three-thirty. She can be here at four."

She had to be firm, Vanessa told herself. "Mrs. Driscoll, I'd love to help you out, but I've never given instruction."

Mrs. Driscoll merely blinked her little black eyes. "You know how to play the thing, don't you?"

"Well, yes, but—"

"Then you ought to be able to show somebody else how. Unless they're like Dory—that's my oldest girl. Never could teach her how to crochet. Clumsy hands. Annie's got good hands. That's my grandniece. Smart, too. You won't have any trouble with her."

"I'm sure I won't—I mean, I'm sure she is. It's just that—"

"Give you ten dollars a lesson." A smug smile creased Mrs. Driscoll's face as Vanessa rattled her brain for excuses. "You were always quick in school, Vanessa. Quick and well behaved. Never gave me any grief like Brady. That boy was trouble from the get-go. Couldn't help but like him for it. I'll see that Annie's here at four."

She trundled off, sheltered under the enormous umbrella, leaving Vanessa with the sensation of having been flattened by an antique but very sturdy steamroller.

Piano lessons, she thought on a little groan. How had it happened? She watched the umbrella disappear around the corner. It had happened the same way she had "volunteered" to clean the blackboard after school.

Dragging a hand through her hair, she walked to the house. It was empty and quiet, but she'd already given up on the idea of going back to bed. If she was going to be stuck running scales with a fledgling virtuoso, then she'd better prepare for it. At least it would keep her mind occupied.

In the music room, she went to the gracefully curved new cabinet. She could only hope that her mother had saved some of her old lesson books. The first drawer contained sheet music she considered too advanced for a first-year student. But her own fingers itched to play as she skimmed the sheets.

She found what she was looking for in the bottom drawer. There they were, a bit dog-eared, but neatly stacked. All of her lesson books, from primer to level six. Struck by nostalgia, she sat cross-legged on the floor and began to pore through them.

How well she remembered those first heady days of lessons. Finger exercises, scales, drills, those first simple melodies. She felt an echo of that rush of emotion that had come when she had learned that she had the power to turn those printed notes into music.

More than twenty years had passed since that first day, that first lesson. Her father had been her teacher then, and though he had been a hard taskmaster, she had been a willing student. How proud she had been the first time he had told her she'd done well. Those small and rare words of praise had driven her to work all the harder.

With a sigh, she dipped into the drawer for more books. If young Annie had been taking lessons for a year, she should have advanced beyond the primary level. It was then that she found the thick scrapbook, the one she knew her mother had started years before. With a smile, she opened the first page.

There were pictures of her at the piano. It made her laugh to see herself in pigtails and neat white ankle socks. Sentimentally she paged through photos of her first recital, her early certificates of accomplishment. And here were the awards that had once hung on her walls, the newspaper clippings from when she had won her first regional competition, her first national.

How terrified she'd been. Sweaty hands, buzzing ears, curdling stomach. She'd begged her father to let her withdraw. He'd refused to listen to her fears. And she'd won, Vanessa mused.

It surprised her that the clippings continued. Here was an article from the London *Times,* written a full year after she had left Hyattown. And here a picture of her in Fort Worth after she'd won the Van Cliburn.

There were dozens—no, hundreds—Vanessa realized. Hundreds of pictures, snippets of news, pieces of gossip, magazine articles—many she had never seen herself. It seemed that everything that had ever been printed about her was here, carefully preserved. Everything, Vanessa thought, down to the last interview she had granted before her concerts in D.C.

First the letters, she thought, the book weighing heavily on her thighs, and now this. What was she supposed to think? What was she supposed to feel? The mother she had believed had forgotten her had written her religiously, even when there had been no answer. Had followed every step of her career, though she'd been allowed no part in it.

And, Vanessa added with a sigh, had opened the door to her daughter again without question.

But it didn't explain why Loretta had let her go without a murmur. It didn't explain the years away.

I had no choice.

She remembered her mother's words. But what had she meant? An affair would have destroyed her marriage. There was no doubt of that. Vanessa's father would never have forgiven her. But why had it severed her relationship with her daughter?

She had to know. She would know. Vanessa rose and left the books scattered on the rug. She would know today.

The rain had stopped, and the watery sunlight was already struggling through the clouds. Birdsong competed with the sound of a children's television show that chirped through the window of the house next door. Though it was only a few blocks away, she drove to the antique shop. Under other circumstances she would have enjoyed the walk, but she wanted no interruptions from old friends and acquaintances. The old two-story house was just on the edge of town. The sign that read Loretta's Attic was a graceful arch over the front door.

There was an old-fashioned sleigh in the yard, its metal fittings polished to a gleam. A scarred whiskey barrel was filled to overflowing with petunias, their purple-and-white petals drenched with rain. On either side of the entrance, well-groomed beds spilled over with spring color. A beribboned grapevine wreath hung on the door. When she pushed it open, bells jingled.

"It's circa 1860," she heard her mother say. "One of my

finest sets. I had it refinished locally by a man who does a great deal of work for me. You can see what a wonderful job he does. The finish is like glass."

Vanessa half listened to the exchange coming from the next room. Though she was frustrated to find her mother with a customer, the shop itself was a revelation.

No dusty, cramped antique shop this. Exquisite glass-fronted cabinets displayed china, statuettes, ornate perfume bottles and slender goblets. Wood gleamed on each individual piece. Brass shone. Crystal sparkled. Though every inch of space was utilized, it was more like a cozy family home than a place of business. The scent of rose-and-spice potpourri wafted from a simmer pot.

"You're going to be very happy with that set," Loretta was saying as she walked back into the main room. "If you find it doesn't suit after you get it home, I'll be more than willing to buy it back from you. Oh, Vanessa." After fumbling a moment, she turned to the young executive type beside her. "This is my daughter. Vanessa, this is Mr. Peterson. He's from Montgomery County."

"Damascus," he explained. He looked like a cat who'd been given a whole pitcher of cream. "My wife and I just bought an old farmhouse. We saw that dining room set here a few weeks ago. My wife hasn't been able to talk about anything else. Thought I'd surprise her."

"I'm sure she'll be thrilled."

Vanessa watched as her mother accepted his credit card and went briskly about completing the transaction.

"You've got a terrific place here, Mrs. Sexton," he went on. "If you came over the county line, you'd have to beat off customers."

"I like it here." She handed him his receipt. "I've lived here all my life."

"Cute town." He pocketed the receipt. "After our first dinner party, I can guarantee you some new customers."

"And I can guarantee I won't beat them off." She smiled at him. "Will you need some help Saturday when you pick it up?"

"No, I'll drag a few friends with me." He shook her hand. "Thanks, Mrs. Sexton."

"Just enjoy it."

"We will." He turned to smile at Vanessa. "Nice meeting you. You've got a terrific mother."

"Thank you."

"Well, I'll be on my way." He stopped halfway to the door. "Vanessa Sexton." He turned back. "The pianist. I'll be damned. I just saw your concert in D.C. last week. You were great."

"I'm glad you enjoyed it."

"I didn't expect to," he admitted. "My wife's the classical nut. I figured I'd catch a nap, but, man, you just blew me away."

She had to laugh. "I'll take that as a compliment."

"No, really. I don't know Mozart from Muzak, but I was—well, I guess enthralled's a good word. My wife'll just about die when I tell her I met you." He pulled out a leather-bound appointment book. "Would you sign this for her? Her name's Melissa."

"I'd be glad to."

"Who'd have expected to find someone like you in a little place like this?" He shook his head as she handed the book back to him.

"I grew up here."

"I can guarantee my wife'll be back." He winked at Loretta. "Thanks again, Mrs. Sexton."

"You're welcome. Drive carefully." She laughed a little

after the bells had jingled at his exit. "It's an amazing thing, watching your own child sign an autograph."

"It's the first one I've signed in my hometown." She took a deep breath. "This is a beautiful place. You must work very hard."

"I enjoy it. I'm sorry I wasn't there this morning. I had an early delivery coming."

"It's all right."

Loretta picked up a soft rag, then set it down again. "Would you like to see the rest of the shop?"

"Yes. Yes, I would."

Loretta led the way into the adjoining room. "This is the set your admirer just bought." She ran a fingertip over the top of a gleaming mahogany table. "It has three leaves and will sit twelve comfortably when extended. There's some beautiful carving on the chairs. The buffet and server go with it."

"They're beautiful."

"I bought them at an estate sale a few months ago. They'd been in the same family for over a hundred years. It's sad." She touched one of the glass knobs on the server. "That's why I'm so happy when I can sell something like this to people who will care for it."

She moved to a curved glass china cabinet and opened the door. "I found this cobalt glass at a flea market, buried in a box. Now, the cranberry I got at auction, and paid too much. I couldn't resist it. These saltcellars are French, and I'll have to wait for a collector to take them off my hands."

"How do you know about all of this?" Vanessa asked.

"I learned a lot by working here before I bought it. From reading, from haunting other shops and auctions." She laughed a little as she closed the cabinet door. "And through trial and error. I've made some costly mistakes, but I've also wangled some real bargains."

"You have so many beautiful things. Oh, look at this." Almost reverently, she picked up a Limoges ring box. It was perhaps six inches high and fashioned in the shape of a young girl in a blue bonnet and blue checkered dress. There was a look of smug pleasure on her glossy face. "This is charming."

"I always try to keep in a few Limoges pieces. Whether they're antique or new."

"I have a small collection myself. It's difficult to travel with fragile things, but they always make hotel suites more like home."

"I'd like you to have it."

"I couldn't."

"Please," Loretta said before Vanessa could set it down again. "I've missed a number of birthdays. It would give me a great deal of pleasure if you'd accept it."

Vanessa looked up. They had to turn at least the first corner, she told herself. "Thank you. I'll treasure it."

"I'll get a box for it. Oh, there's the door. I get a lot of browsers on weekday mornings. You can take a look upstairs if you like."

Vanessa kept the little box cupped in her hands. "No, I'll wait for you." Loretta gave her a pleased look before she walked away to greet her customer. When she heard Dr. Tucker's voice join her mother's, Vanessa hesitated, then went in to meet him.

"Well, Van, getting a look at your mother at work?"

"Yes."

He had his arm around her mother's shoulders. Loretta's color had risen. He's just kissed her, Vanessa realized, trying to analyze her feelings. "It's a wonderful place."

"Keeps her off the streets. Of course, I'm going to be doing that myself from now on."

"Ham!"

"Don't tell me you haven't told the child yet." He gave her a quick, impatient squeeze. "Good grief, Loretta, you've had all morning."

"Tell me what?"

With these two, Ham thought, a man had to take the bull by the horns. "It's taken me two years to wear her down, but she finally gave me a yes."

"A yes?" Vanessa repeated.

"Don't tell me you're as thickheaded as your mother?" He kissed the top of Loretta's head and grinned like a boy. "We're getting married."

"Oh." Vanessa stared blankly. "Oh."

"Is that the best you can do?" he demanded. "Why don't you say congratulations and give me a kiss?"

"Congratulations," she said mechanically, and walked over to peck his cheek.

"I said a kiss." He swung his free arm around her and squeezed. Vanessa found herself hugging him back.

"I hope you'll be happy," she managed, and discovered she meant it.

"Of course I will. I'm getting two beauties for the price of one."

"Quite a bargain," Vanessa said with a smile. "When's the big day?"

"As soon as I can pin her down." It hadn't escaped him that Vanessa and Loretta hadn't exchanged a word or an embrace. "Joanie's fixing dinner for all of us tonight," he decided on the spot. "To celebrate."

"I'll be there."

When she stepped back, he grinned wickedly. "After the piano lesson."

Vanessa rolled her eyes. "News travels fast."

"Piano lesson?" Loretta repeated.

"Annie Crampton, Violet Driscoll's grandniece." He gave a hearty laugh as Vanessa wrinkled her nose. "Violet snagged Vanessa this morning."

Loretta smiled. "What time's the lesson?"

"Four. She made me feel like I was the second-grade milk monitor again."

"I can speak to Annie's mother if you'd like," Loretta said.

"No, it's all right. It's only an hour a week while I'm here. But I'd better get back." This was not the time for questions and demands. "I have to put some kind of program together. Thank you again for the box."

"But I haven't wrapped it."

"It's all right. I'll see you at Joanie's, Dr. Tucker."

"Maybe you could call me Ham now. We're family."

"Yes. Yes, I guess we are." It was less effort than she had expected to kiss her mother's cheek. "You're a very lucky woman."

"I know." Loretta's fingers dug into Ham's.

When the bells jingled behind Vanessa, Ham took out a handkerchief.

"I'm sorry," Loretta said as she sniffled into it.

"You're entitled to shed a few. I told you she'd come around."

"She has every reason to hate me."

"You're too hard on yourself, Loretta, and I won't have it."

She merely shook her head as she balled the handkerchief in her hand. "Oh, the choices we make in this life, Ham.

And the mistakes. I'd give anything in the world to have another chance with her."

"Time's all you need to give." He tilted her chin up and kissed her. "Just give her time."

Vanessa listened to the monotonous plunk of the keys as Annie ground out "Twinkle, Twinkle, Little Star." She might have good hands, but so far Vanessa hadn't seen her put them to good use.

She was a skinny girl with pale flyaway hair, a sulky disposition and knobby knees. But her twelve-year old hands were wide-palmed. Her fingers weren't elegant, but they were as sturdy as little trees.

Potential, Vanessa thought as she tried to smile her encouragement. Surely there was some potential buried there somewhere.

"How many hours a week do you practice, Annie?" Vanessa asked when the child had mercifully finished.

"I don't know."

"Do you do your finger exercises every day?"

"I don't know."

Vanessa gritted her teeth. She had already learned this was Annie's standard answer for all questions. "You've been taking lessons regularly for nearly a year."

"I don't—"

Vanessa put up a hand. "Why don't we make this easy? What do you know?"

Annie just shrugged and swung her feet.

Giving up, Vanessa sat beside her on the stool. "Annie— and give me a real answer—do you want to take piano lessons?"

Annie knocked the heels of her orange sneakers together. "I guess."

"Is it because your mother wants you to?"

"I asked if I could." She stared sulkily down at the keys. "I thought I would like it."

"But you don't."

"I kinda do. Sometimes. But I just get to play baby songs."

"Mmm." Sympathetic, Vanessa stroked her hair. "And what do you want to play?"

"Stuff like Madonna sings. You know, good stuff. Stuff like you hear on the radio." She slanted Vanessa a look. "My other teacher said that's not real music."

"All music is real music. We could make a deal."

Suspicion lighted in Annie's pale eyes. "What kind of deal?"

"You practice an hour every day on your finger exercises and the lesson I give you." She ignored Annie's moan. "And I'll buy some sheet music. One of Madonna's songs. I'll teach you to play it."

Annie's sulky mouth fell open. "For real?"

"For real. But only if you practice every day, so that when you come next week I see an improvement."

"All right!" For the first time in nearly an hour, she grinned, nearly blinding Vanessa with her braces. "Wait till I tell Mary Ellen. She's my best friend."

"You've got another fifteen minutes before you can tell her." Vanessa rose, inordinately pleased with herself. "Now, why don't you try that number again?"

Her face screwed up with concentration, Annie began to play. A little incentive, Vanessa thought with a lifted brow, went a long way.

An hour later, she was still congratulating herself. Tutoring the girl might be fun, after all. And she could indulge her own affection for popular music.

Later in her room, Vanessa ran a finger down the Limoges box her mother had given her. Things were changing for her, faster than she had expected. Her mother wasn't the woman she had thought she would find. She was much more human. Her home was still her home. Her friends still her friends.

And Brady was still Brady.

She wanted to be with him, to have her name linked with his as it once had been. At sixteen she had been so sure. Now, as a woman she was afraid, afraid of making a mistake, of being hurt, of losing.

People couldn't just pick up where they had left off. And she could hardly start a new beginning when she had yet to resolve the past.

She took her time dressing for the family dinner. It was to be a festive occasion, and she was determined to be a part of it. Her deep blue dress was cut slimly, with a splash of multicolored beadwork along one shoulder. She left her hair loose, and added braided earrings studded with sapphires.

Before she closed her jewelry box, she took out a ring with a tiny emerald. Unable to resist, she slipped it on. It still fit, she thought, and smiled at the way it looked on her finger. With a shake of her head, she pulled it off again. That was just the sort of sentiment she had to learn to avoid. Particularly if she was going to get through an evening in Brady's company.

They were going to be friends, she reminded herself. Just friends. It had been a long time since she had been able to indulge in the luxury of a friendship. And if she was still attracted to him—well, that would just add a touch of spice, a little excitement. She wouldn't risk her heart, or his, on anything more.

She pressed a hand to her stomach, swearing at the discomfort. Out of her drawer she took an extra roll of antacids. Festive the evening might be, she thought as she took a pill. But it would still be stressful.

It was time she learned to deal with stress better, she told herself as she stared at her reflection. It was time she refused to allow her body to revolt every time she had to deal with something uncomfortable or unpleasant. She was a grown woman, after all, and a disciplined one. If she could learn to tolerate emotional distress, she could certainly overcome the physical.

After checking her watch, she started downstairs. Vanessa Sexton was never late for a performance.

"Well, well." Brady was lounging at the base of the steps. "You're still Sexy Sexton."

Just what she needed, she thought, her stomach muscles knotting. Did he have to look so gorgeous? She glanced at the front door that he'd left open behind him, then back at him.

"You're wearing a suit."

He glanced down at the gray tweed. "Looks like."

"I've never seen you in a suit," she said foolishly. She stopped a step above him. Eye-to-eye. "Why aren't you at Joanie's?"

"Because I'm taking you to Joanie's."

"That's silly. I have my own—"

"Shut up." Taking her shoulders, he hauled her against him for a kiss. "Every time I do that, you taste better."

She had to wait for her heart to flutter back into place. "Look, Brady, we're going to have to set up some ground rules."

"I hate rules." He kissed her again, lingering over it this time. "I'm going to get a real kick out of being related to you." He drew back, grinning. "Sis."

"You're not acting very brotherly," she murmured.

"I'll boss you around later. How do you feel about it?"

"I've always loved your father."

"And?"

"And I hope I'm not hard-hearted enough to begrudge my mother any happiness she might have with him."

"That'll do for now." He narrowed his eyes as she rubbed her temple. "Headache?"

She dropped her hand quickly. "Just a little one."

"Take anything?"

"No, it'll pass. Shouldn't we go?"

"All right." He took her hand to lead her out. "I was thinking…why don't we drop by Molly's Hole on the way home?"

She couldn't help but laugh. "You still have a one-track mind."

He opened the car door for her. "Is that a yes?"

She tilted her head, slanted him a look. "That's an I'll-think-about-it."

"Brat," he muttered as he closed the door.

Ten minutes later, Joanie was bursting through her front door to greet them. "Isn't it great? I can hardly stand it!" She grabbed Vanessa to swing her around. "We're really going to be sisters now. I'm so happy for them, for us!" She gave Vanessa another crushing hug.

"Hey, how about me?" Brady demanded. "Don't I even get a hello?"

"Oh, hi, Brady." At his disgusted look, she laughed and launched herself at him. "Wow! You wore a suit and everything!"

"So I'm told. Dad said we had to dress up."

"And did you ever." She pulled back. "Both of you. Lord, Van, where did you get that dress? Fabulous," she said, before Vanessa could answer. "I'd kill to be able to squeeze my hips into that. Well, don't just stand out here, come on in. We've got a ton of food, champagne, the works."

"Hell of a hostess, isn't she?" Brady commented as Joanie rushed inside, shouting for her husband.

Joanie hadn't exaggerated about the food. There was a huge glazed ham, with a mountain of whipped potatoes, an array of vegetables, fluffy homemade biscuits. The scent of cooling apple pies wafted in from the kitchen. The home's festive air was accented by candles and the glint of crystal wineglasses.

The conversation was loud and disjointed, punctuated by Lara's cheerful banging of her spoon against the tray of her high chair.

Vanessa heard her mother laughing, more freely, more openly, than she could ever remember. And she looked lovely, Vanessa thought, smiling at Ham, leaning over to stroke Lara. It was happiness, she realized. True happiness. In all her memories, she could pull out no picture of her mother's face when it had been truly happy.

As the meal wore on, she nibbled lightly, certain that no one would notice her lack of appetite in the confusion. But when she saw Brady watching her, she forced herself to take another bite, to sip at the iced champagne, to laugh at one of Jack's jokes.

"I think this occasion calls for a toast." Brady rose. He shot Lara a look as she squealed. "You have to wait your turn," he told her, hefting his glass. "To my father, who turned out to be smarter than I always figured. And to his beautiful bride-to-be, who used to look the other way when I'd sneak into the backyard to neck with her daughter." Over the ensuing laughter, glasses were clinked.

Vanessa drank the bubbly wine and hoped she wouldn't pay for it later.

"Anyone for dessert?" Joanie's question was answered by communal moans. "Okay, we'll hold off on that. Jack, you help me clear the table. Absolutely not," she said when Loretta stood to stack plates. "The guest of honor does not do dishes."

"Don't be silly—"

"I mean it."

"All right, then I'll just clean Lara up."

"Fine, then you and Dad can spoil her until we're done here. Not you, either," she added when Vanessa began to clear the table. "You're not doing dishes on your first dinner in my home."

"She's always been bossy," Brady commented when his sister disappeared into the kitchen. "Would you like to go into the living room? We can put on some music."

"No, actually, I'd like some air."

"Good. There's nothing I like better than walking in the twilight with a beautiful woman." He gave her a cocky grin and held out a hand.

Chapter 6

The evening was soft and smelled of rain. There were lilacs blooming, their scent an elegant whisper on the air. She
remembered they had been Joanie's favorite. To the west,
the sun was sinking below the mountains in a blaze of red.
Cows stood slack-hipped in the fading light. They walked
around the side of the house toward a field thick with hay.

"I hear you've taken on a student."

"Mrs. Driscoll gets around."

"Actually, I heard it from John Cory while I was giving
him a tetanus shot. He heard it from Bill Crampton—that's
Annie's father's brother. He runs a repair shop out of his
garage. All the men hang around over there to tell lies and
complain about their wives."

Despite her dragging discomfort, Vanessa had to laugh.
"At least it's reassuring to know the grapevine still works."

"So how'd the lesson go?"

"She has...possibilities."

"How does it feel to be on the other end?"

"Odd. I promised I'd teach her how to play rock."

"You?"

Vanessa bristled. "Music," she said primly, "is music."

"Right." He put a fingertip behind her earlobe so that he could watch the jewels she wore there catch the last light of the setting sun. And so that he could touch her. "I can see it now, Vanessa Sexton on keyboards with a heavy metal band." He considered a minute. "Do you think you could wear one of those metal corsets, or whatever they're called?"

"No, I couldn't, no matter what they're called. And if you're only along to make fun of me, I can walk by myself."

"Touchy." He draped an arm around her shoulders. He was glad the scent of his shampoo was still in her hair. He wondered if any of the men he'd seen her linked with in magazines and newspapers had felt the same way.

"I like Jack," she said.

"So do I." They walked along a fence thick with honeysuckle.

"Joanie seems so happy here, on the farm, with her family. I often wondered about her."

"Did you ever think about me? After you'd left, after you'd hit it so big, did you ever think about me?"

She looked out over the fields. "I suppose I did."

"I kept thinking you would write."

Too much, she thought. Too often. "Time passed, Brady. And at first I was too angry and hurt. At you and at my mother." Because she wanted to lighten the mood, she smiled. "It took me years to forgive you for dumping me the night of the prom."

"I didn't." He swore and stuck his hands in his pockets. "Look, it's a stupid thing and long over, but I'm tired of taking the rap."

"What are you talking about?"

"I didn't dump you, damn it. I'd rented my first tux, bought my first corsage. Pink and yellow roses." Now that he had brought it up, he felt like a total fool. "I guess I was probably as excited about that night as you were."

"Then why did I sit in my room wearing my new dress for two and a half hours?"

He blew out a long breath. "I got arrested that night."

"What?"

"It was a mistake," he said carefully. "But by the time it was straightened out, it was too late to explain. The charges were pretty thin, to say the least, but I hadn't exactly been a Boy Scout up until then."

"But what were you arrested for?"

"Statutory rape." At her astonished look, he shrugged. "I was over eighteen. You weren't."

It took almost a full minute before it could sink in, before she could find her voice. "But that's ridiculous. We never…"

"Yeah." To his undying regret. "We never."

She pulled both hands through her hair as she tried to reason it out. "Brady, it's almost too ludicrous to believe. Even if we had been intimate, it wouldn't have had anything to do with rape. You were only two years older than I was, and we loved each other."

"That was the problem."

She put a hand on her stomach, kneading a deep ache. "I'm sorry, so sorry. How miserable you must have been. And your parents. Oh, God. What a horrible thing for any-one to go through. But who in the world would have had you arrested? Who would have—" She saw his face, and her answer. "Oh, no!" she moaned, turning away. "Oh, God!"

"He was dead sure I'd taken advantage of you. And he was dead sure I would ruin your life." And maybe, Brady thought as he stared out over the fields, he wouldn't have been far off. "The way he put it, he was going to see I paid for the first, and he was going to do what needed to be done to prevent the second."

"He could have asked me," she whispered. "For once in my life, he could have asked me." She shivered against a quick chill. "It's my fault."

"That's a stupid response."

"No," she said quietly. "It's my fault, because I could never make him understand how I felt. Not about you, not about anything." She took a long breath before she looked at Brady again. "There's nothing I can say that can make up for what he did."

"There's nothing you have to say." He put his hands on her shoulders, and would have drawn her back against him if she hadn't held herself so stiff. Instead, he massaged her knotted muscles, patiently, with his competent physician's hands. "You were as innocent as I was, Van. We never straightened it out, because for the first few days I was too mad to try and you were too mad to ask. Then you were gone."

Her vision blurred before she blinked back the tears. She could picture him all too easily—young, rebellious, angry. Afraid. "I don't know what to say. You must have been terrified."

"Some," he admitted. "I was never formally charged, just held for questioning. You remember old Sheriff Grody—he was a hard-edged, potbellied bully. And he didn't like me one little bit. Later I realized he was just taking the opportunity to make me sweat. Someone else might have handled it differently."

There was no use bringing up the way he'd sat in the cell, bone-scared, helplessly angry, waiting to be allowed his phone call, while the sheriff and Sexton consulted in the next room.

"There was something else that happened that night. Maybe it balanced the scales some. My father stood up for me. I'd never known he would stand up for me that way, no questions, no doubts, just total support. I guess it changed my life."

"My father," Vanessa said. "He knew how much that night meant to me. How much you meant to me. All my life I did what he wanted—except for you. He made sure he had his way even there."

"It's a long way behind us, Van."

"I don't think I can—" She broke off on a muffled gasp of pain.

He turned her quickly. "Vanessa?"

"It's nothing. I just—" But the second wave came too sharp, too fast, doubling her over. Moving fast, he scooped her up and headed back for the house. "No, don't. I'm all right. It was just a twinge."

"Breathe slow."

"Damn it, I said it's nothing." Her head fell back as the burning increased. "You're not going to cause a scene," she said between shallow breaths.

"If you've got what I think you've got, you're going to see one hell of a scene."

The kitchen was empty as he came in, so he took the back stairs. At least she'd stopped arguing, Brady thought as he laid her on Joanie's bed. When he switched on the lamp, he could see that her skin was white and clammy.

"I want you to try to relax, Van."

"I'm fine." But the burning hadn't stopped. "It's just stress, maybe a little indigestion."

"That's what we're going to find out." He eased down

beside her. "I want you to tell me when I hurt you." Very gently, he pressed on her lower abdomen. "Have you ever had your appendix out?"

"No."

"Any abdominal surgery?"

"No, nothing."

He kept his eyes on her face as he continued the examination. When he pressed just under her breastbone, he saw the flare of pain in her eyes before she cried out. Though his face was grim, he took her hand soothingly.

"Van, how long have you been having pain?"

She was ashamed to have cried out. "Everyone has pain."

"Answer the question."

"I don't know."

He struggled for patience. "How does it feel now?"

"It's fine. I just want—"

"Don't lie to me." He wanted to curse her as pungently as he was cursing himself. He'd known she wasn't well, almost from the moment he'd seen her again. "Is there a burning sensation?"

Because she saw no choice, she relented. "Some."

It had been just about an hour since they'd eaten, he thought. The timing was right. "Have you had this happen before, after you've had alcohol?"

"I don't really drink anymore."

"Because you get this reaction?"

She closed her eyes. Why didn't he just go and leave her alone? "I suppose."

"Do you get gnawing aches, here, under the breastbone?"

"Sometimes."

"And in your stomach?"

"It's more of a grinding, I guess."

"Like acute hunger pangs."

"Yes." The accuracy of his description made her frown. "It passes."

"What are you taking for it?"

"Just over-the-counter stuff." And enough was enough. "Brady, becoming a doctor's obviously gone to your head. You're making a case out of nothing. I'll take a couple of antacids and be fine."

"You don't treat an ulcer with antacids."

"I don't have an ulcer. That's ridiculous. I'm never sick."

"You listen to me." He propped a hand on either side of her head. "You're going into the hospital for tests—X-rays, an upper G.I. And you're going to do what I tell you."

"I'm not going to the hospital." The very idea of it made her remember the horror of her father's last days. "You're not my doctor."

He swore at her richly.

"Nice bedside manner. Now get out of my way."

"You stay right here. And I mean right here."

She obeyed, only because she didn't know if she could manage to stand. Why now? she wondered as she fought against the pain. Why here? She'd had nasty attacks like this before, but she'd always been alone, and she'd always been able to weather them. And she would weather it this time. Just as she was struggling to sit up, Brady came back with his father.

"Now, what's all this?" Ham said.

"Brady overreacting." She managed to smile, and would have swung her legs off the bed if Brady hadn't stopped her.

"She doubled up with pain when we were outside. There's burning in the abdomen, acute tenderness under the breast-bone."

Ham sat on the bed and began his own gentle probing. His questions ran along the same lines as Brady's, and his face became more and more sober at her answers. At last he sat back.

"Now what's a young girl like you doing with an ulcer?"

"I don't have an ulcer."

"You've got two doctors telling you different. I assume that's your diagnosis, Brady."

"It is."

"Well, you're both wrong." Vanessa struggled to push herself up. Ham merely shifted the pillows behind her and eased her back. With a nod, he looked back at his son.

"Of course, we'll confirm it with X-rays and tests."

"I'm not going in the hospital." She was desperately hanging on to one small bit of control. "Ulcers are for Wall Street brokers and CEOs. I'm a musician, for God's sake. I'm not a compulsive worrier, or someone who lets tension rule my life."

"I'll tell you what you are," Brady said, anger shimmering in his voice. "You're a woman who hasn't bothered to take care of herself, who's too damn stubborn to sit back and admit when she's taken on too much. And you're going to the hospital if I have to hog-tie you."

"Easy there, Dr. Tucker," Ham said mildly. "Van, have you had any vomiting, any traces of blood?"

"No, of course not. It's just a little stress, maybe a little overwork—"

"A little ulcer," he told her firmly. "But I think we can treat it with medication if you're going to hang tough about the hospital."

"I am. And I don't see that I need medication, or two doctors hovering over me."

"Testy," Ham commented. "You'll have medication or the hospital, young lady. Remember, I'm the one who treated you for damn near everything, starting with diaper rash. I think a cimetidine might clear this up," he said to Brady. "As long as she stays away from spicy food and alcohol for the length of the treatment."

"I'd like it better if she had the tests."

"So would I," he agreed. "But short of dosing her with morphine and dragging her in, I think this is the cleanest way to treat it."

"Let me think about the morphine," Brady grumbled, and made his father chuckle.

"I'm going to write you a prescription," he told Vanessa. "You get it filled tonight. You have twenty minutes before the pharmacy in Boonsboro closes."

"I'm not sick," she said, pouting.

"Just humor your soon-to-be-stepfather. I've got my bag downstairs. Brady, why don't you come along with me?"

Outside the door, Ham took his son's arm and pulled him to the head of the stairs. "If the medication doesn't clear it up within three or four days, we'll put some pressure on her to have the tests. Meanwhile, I think the less stress the better."

"I want to know what caused it." Fury vibrated through his voice as he stared at the closed bedroom door.

"So do I. She'll talk to you," Ham said quietly. "Just give her some room. I'm going to tell Loretta. Vanessa won't like that, but I'm going to do it. See that she gets the first dose in her tonight."

"I will. Dad, I'm going to take care of her."

"You always meant to." Ham put a hand on Brady's shoulder. "Just don't push too hard too fast. She's like her mother in that way, tends to pull back when you get close." He hesitated, and though he reminded himself that his son was a grown man, he could only think that the grown man was his son. "Are you still in love with her?"

"I don't know. But this time I'm not going to let her get away until I do."

"Just remember, when a man holds on to something too tight, it slips right through his fingers." He gave Brady's shoulder a final squeeze. "I'll go write that prescription."

When Brady walked back into the bedroom, Vanessa was sitting on the edge of the bed, embarrassed, humiliated, furious.

"Come on." His voice was brisk and unsympathetic. "We can just get to the pharmacy before it closes."

"I don't want your damn pills."

Because he was tempted to throttle her, he dipped his hands into his pockets. "Do you want me to carry you out of here, or do you want to walk?"

She wanted to cry. Instead, she rose stiffly. "I'll walk, thank you."

"Fine. We'll take the back stairs."

She didn't want to be grateful that he was sparing her the explanations and sympathy. She walked with her chin up and her shoulders squared. He didn't speak until he slammed the car door.

"Somebody ought to give you a swift right hook." His engine roared into life. Gravel spit from under the tires.

"I wish you'd just leave me alone."

"So do I," he said fervently. He turned off the lane onto asphalt. By the time he'd hit fifth gear, he was calmer. "Are you still having pain?"

"No."

"Don't lie to me, Van. If you can't think of me as a friend, think of me as a doctor."

She turned to stare out the darkened window. "I've never seen your degree."

He wanted to gather her close then, rest her head on his

shoulder. "I'll show it to you tomorrow." He slowed as they came to the next town. He said nothing until they pulled up at the pharmacy. "You can wait in the car. It won't take long."

She sat, watching him stride under the lights through the big glass windows of the pharmacy. They were having a special on a popular brand of soft drink. There was a tower of two-liter bottles near the window. There were a few stragglers left inside, most of whom obviously knew Brady, as they stopped to chat while he stood by the drug counter. She hated the feeling of being trapped inside the car with the pain gnawing inside her.

An ulcer, she thought. It wasn't possible. She wasn't a workaholic, a worrier, a power-mad executive. And yet, even as she denied it, the grinding ache dragged through her, mocking her.

She just wanted to go home to lie down, to will the pain away into sleep. Oblivion. It would all be gone tomorrow. Hadn't she been telling herself that for months and months?

When he came back, he set the small white bag in her lap before he started the car. He said nothing as she sat back in the seat with her eyes closed. It gave him time to think.

It didn't do any good to snap at her. It did even less good to be angry with her for being sick. But it hurt and infuriated him that she hadn't trusted him enough to tell him she was in trouble. That she hadn't trusted herself enough to admit it and get help.

He was going to see that she got that help now, whether she wanted it or not. As a doctor, he would do the same for a stranger. How much more would he do for the only woman he had ever loved?

Had loved, he reminded himself. In this case, the past tense was vital. And because he had once loved her with all the passion and purity of youth, he wouldn't see her go through this alone.

At the curb in the front of her house, he parked, then walked around the car to open her door. Vanessa climbed out and began the speech she'd carefully planned on the drive.

"I'm sorry if I acted childishly before. And ungrateful. I know you and your father only want to help. I'll take the medication."

"Damn right you will." He took her arm.

"You don't have to come in."

"I'm coming in," he said as he pulled her up the walk. "I'm watching you take the first dose, and then I'm putting you to bed."

"Brady, I'm not an invalid."

"That's right, and if I have anything to say about it, you won't become one."

He pushed open the door—it was never locked—and hauled her directly upstairs. He filled a glass in the bathroom, handed it to her, then opened the bottle of medication and shook out a pill himself.

"Swallow."

She took a moment to scowl at him before she obeyed. "Are you going to charge me for a house call?"

"The first one's for old times' sake." Gripping her arm again, he pulled her into the bedroom. "Now take off your clothes."

Pain or no pain, she tossed back her head. "Aren't you supposed to be wearing a lab coat and a stethoscope when you say that?"

He didn't even bother to swear. Turning, he yanked open a drawer and searched until he found a nightshirt. She would wear silk to bed, he thought, clenching his teeth. Of course she would. After tossing it on the bed, he pushed her around and dragged down her zipper.

"When I undress you for personal reasons, you'll know it."

"Cut it out." Shocked, she caught the dress as it pooled at her waist. He merely tugged the nightshirt over her head.

"I can control my animal lust by thinking of your stomach lining."

"That's disgusting."

"Exactly." He tugged the dress over her hips. The nightshirt drifted down to replace it. "Stockings?"

Unsure if she should be mortified or infuriated, she unrolled them down the length of her legs. Brady gritted his teeth again. No amount of hours in anatomy class could have prepared him for the sight of Vanessa slowly removing sheer stockings in lamplight.

He was a doctor, he reminded himself, and tried to recite the first line of the Hippocratic oath.

"Now get in bed." He pulled down the quilt, then carefully tucked it up to her chin after she climbed in. Suddenly she looked sixteen again. He clung to his professionalism, setting the bottle of pills on her nightstand. "I want you to follow the directions."

"I can read."

"No drinking." A doctor, he repeated to himself. He was a doctor, and she was a patient. A beautiful patient with sinfully soft skin and big green eyes. "We don't use bland diets so much anymore, just common sense. Stay away from spicy foods. You're going to get some relief fairly quickly. In all probability you won't even remember you had an ulcer in a few days."

"I don't have one now."

"Vanessa." With a sigh, he brushed back her hair. "Do you want anything?"

"No." Her hand groped for his before he could rise. "Can you—? Do you have to go?"

He kissed her fingers. "Not for a while."

Satisfied, she settled back. "I was never supposed to let you come up here when we were teenagers."

"Nope. Remember the night I climbed in the window?"

"And we sat on the floor and talked until four in the morning. If my father had known, he would have—" She broke off, remembering.

"Now isn't the time to worry about all that."

"It isn't a matter of worry, really, but of wondering. I loved you, Brady. It was innocent, and it was sweet. Why did he have to spoil that?"

"You were meant for big things, Van. He knew it. I was in the way."

"Would you have asked me to stay?" She hadn't thought she would ask, but she had always wanted to know. "If you had known about his plans to take me to Europe, would you have asked me to stay?"

"Yes. I was eighteen and selfish. And if you had stayed, you wouldn't be what you are. And I wouldn't be what I am."

"You haven't asked me if I would have stayed."

"I know you would have."

She sighed. "I guess you only love that intensely once. Maybe it's best to have it over and done with while you're young."

"Maybe."

She closed her eyes, drifting. "I used to dream that you would come and take me away. Especially before a performance, when I stood in the wings, hating it."

His brows drew together. "Hating what?"

"The lights, the people, the stage. I would wish so hard that you would come and we would go away together. Then I knew you wouldn't. And I stopped wishing. I'm so tired."

He kissed her fingers again. "Go to sleep."

"I'm tired of being alone," she murmured before she drifted off.

He sat, watching her, trying to separate his feelings for what had been from what was. And that was the problem, he realized. The longer he was with her, the more the edges between the past and present blurred.

There was one and only one thing that was clear. He had never stopped loving her.

After touching his lips to hers, he turned off the bedside light and left her to sleep.

Chapter 7

Bundled in her ratty blue terry-cloth robe, her hair tousled and her disposition grim, Vanessa trudged downstairs. Because she'd been hounded, she'd been taking the medication Ham Tucker had prescribed for two days. She felt better. It annoyed her to have to admit it, but she was a long way from ready to concede that she'd needed it.

More, she was embarrassed that it was Brady who had supervised her first dose and tucked her into bed. It hadn't been so bad when they'd been sniping at each other, but when she'd weakened and asked him to stay with her, he'd been kind. Doctor to patient, she reminded herself. But she had never been able to resist Brady when he was kind.

The morning suited her mood. Thick gray clouds, thick gray rain. It was, she thought, a perfect day to sit alone in the house and brood. In fact, it was something to look forward to. Rain, depression, and a private pity party. At least solitary sulking would be a change. She'd had little time to be alone since the night of Joanie's dinner party.

Her mother tended to hover, finding excuses to come home two or three times each workday. Dr. Tucker checked in on her twice a day, no matter how much Vanessa protested. Even Joanie had come by, to cluck and fuss, bringing armfuls of lilacs and bowls of chicken soup. Neighbors peeped in from time to time to measure her progress. There were no secrets in Hyattown. Vanessa was certain she'd had good wishes and advice from all two hundred and thirty-three residents of the town.

Except one.

Not that she cared that Brady hadn't found time to come by. She scowled and tugged at the belt of her robe. In fact, she told herself as her fingers trailed over the newel post, she was glad he had been conspicuously absent. The last thing she wanted was Brady Tucker—Hyattown's own Dr. Kildare—looming over her, poking at her and shaking his head in his best I-told-you-so manner. She didn't want to see him. And she certainly didn't need to.

She hated making a fool of herself, she thought as she scuffed barefoot down the hallway to the kitchen. And what other term was there for all but keeling over in Joanie's backyard? Then being carried to bed and having Brady treat her like some whining patient.

An ulcer. That was ridiculous, of course. She was strong, competent and self-sufficient—hardly ulcer material. But she unconsciously pressed a hand to her stomach.

The gnawing ache she'd lived with longer than she could remember was all but gone. Her nights hadn't been disturbed by the slow, insidious burning that had so often kept her awake and miserable. In fact, she'd slept like a baby for two nights running.

A coincidence, Vanessa assured herself. All she'd needed was rest. Rest and a little solitude. The grueling schedule she'd maintained the past few years was bound to wear even the strongest person down a bit.

So she'd give herself another month—maybe two—of Hyattown's version of peace, quiet and restoration before making any firm career decisions.

At the kitchen doorway, she came to an abrupt halt. She hadn't expected to find Loretta there. In fact, she had purposely waited to come down until after she'd heard the front door open and close.

"Good morning." Loretta, dressed in one of her tidy suits, hair and pearls in place, beamed a smile.

"I thought you'd gone."

"No, I ran up to Lester's for a paper." She gestured toward the newspaper folded neatly beside the single place setting. "I thought you might want to see what's happening in the world."

"Thank you." Exasperated, Vanessa stood where she was. She hated the fact that she still fumbled whenever Loretta made a gentle maternal gesture. She was grateful for the consideration, but she realized it was the gratitude of a guest for a hostess's generosity. And so it left her feeling guilty and disheartened. "You didn't have to bother."

"No bother. Why don't you sit down, dear? I'll fix you some tea. Mrs. Hawbaker sent some of her own chamomile over from her herb garden."

"Really, you don't have to—" Vanessa broke off at the sound of a knock on the back door. "I'll get it."

She opened the door, telling herself she didn't want it to be Brady. She didn't care if it was Brady. Then she told herself she wasn't the least bit disappointed when the visitor turned out to be female.

"Vanessa." A brunette who huddled under a dripping umbrella was smiling at her. "You probably don't remember me. I'm Nancy Snooks—used to be Nancy McKenna, Josh McKenna's sister."

"Well, I—"

"Nancy, come in." Loretta hurried to the door. "Lord, it's really coming down, isn't it?"

"Doesn't look like we'll have to worry about a drought this year. I can't stay." She remained on the stoop, shifting from foot to foot. "It's just that I heard Vanessa was back and giving piano lessons. My boy Scott's eight now."

Vanessa saw the blow coming and braced herself. "Oh, well, I'm not really—"

"Annie Crampton's just crazy about you," Nancy said quickly. "Her mama's my second cousin, you know. And when I was talking it over with Bill—Bill's my husband— we agreed that piano lessons would be real good for Scott. Mondays right after school would work out best for us—if you don't have another student then."

"No, I don't, because—"

"Great. Aunt Violet said ten dollars is what you're charging for Annie. Right?"

"Yes, but—"

"We can swing that. I'm working part-time over to the feed and grain. Scott'll be here sharp at four. Sure is nice to have you back, Vanessa. I gotta go. I'll be late for work."

"You be careful driving in this rain," Loretta put in.

"I will. Oh, and congratulations, Mrs. Sexton. Doc Tucker's the best."

"Yes, he is." Loretta managed to smile without laughing out loud as she shut the door on a whoosh of rain. "Nice girl," she commented. "Takes after her aunt Violet."

"Apparently."

"I should warn you." Loretta walked over to set a cup of tea on the table. "Scott Snooks is a terror."

"It figures." It was too early in the morning to think, Vanessa decided. She sat, dropped her heavy head in her hands. "She wouldn't have trapped me if I'd been awake."

"Of course not. How about some nice French toast?"

"You don't have to fix me breakfast." Vanessa's voice was muffled by her hands.

"No trouble at all." Loretta was humming as she poured milk into a bowl. She'd been cheated out of being a mother for twelve years. There was nothing she'd rather do than pamper her daughter with a hot breakfast.

Vanessa scowled down at her tea. "I don't want to keep you. Don't you have to open the shop?"

Still humming, Loretta broke an egg into the bowl. "The beauty of having your own place is calling your own hours." She added touches of cinnamon, sugar and vanilla. "And you need a good breakfast. Ham says you're on the mend, but he wants you to put on ten pounds."

"Ten?" Vanessa nearly choked on her tea. "I don't need—" She bit off an oath as another knock sounded.

"I'll get it this time," Loretta announced. "If it's another hopeful parent, I'll shoo them away."

But it was Brady who stood dripping on the back stoop this time. Without the shelter of an umbrella, he grinned at Vanessa while rain streamed from his dark hair. Instant pleasure turned to instant annoyance the moment he opened his mouth.

"Morning, Loretta." He winked at Vanessa. "Hi, gorgeous."

With something close to a snarl, Vanessa huddled over her steaming tea.

"Brady, what a nice surprise." After accepting his kiss

on the cheek, Loretta closed the door on the rain. "Have you had breakfast?" she asked as she went back to the stove to soak the bread.

"No, ma'am." He took an appreciative sniff and hoped he was about to. "Is that French toast?"

"It will be in just a minute. You sit down and I'll fix you a plate."

He didn't have to be asked twice. After dragging his hands through his dripping hair and scattering rain all over creation, he joined Vanessa at the table. He flashed her a smile, a cheerful, friendly look that neatly disguised the fact that he was studying her color. The lack of shadows under her eyes gratified him as much as the mutinous expression in them.

"Beautiful day," he said.

Vanessa lifted her gaze to the rain-lashed windows. "Right."

Undaunted by her grudging response, he shifted in his chair to chat with Loretta as she flipped the browning bread in the skillet.

Not a peep from him in two days, Vanessa thought, and now he pops up on the doorstep, big as life and twice as irritating. He hadn't even asked her how she was feeling—not that she wanted to be fussed over, she reminded herself. But he was a doctor—and he was the one who'd come up with that ridiculous diagnosis.

"Ah, Loretta." Brady all but drooled when she set a heaping plate of fragrant bread in front of him. "My father's a lucky man."

"I suppose cooking's the first priority when a Tucker goes looking for a wife," Vanessa said, feeling nasty.

Brady only smiled as he glopped on maple syrup. "It couldn't hurt."

Vanessa felt her temper rise. Not because she couldn't cook. Certainly not. It was the narrow-minded, sexist idea that infuriated her. Before she could think of a suitably withering reply, Loretta set a plate in front of her.

"I can't eat all of this."

"I can," Brady said as he started on his own meal. "I'll finish up what you don't."

"If you two are set, I'd best go open the shop. Van, there's plenty of that chicken soup left that Joanie brought over yesterday. It'll heat up fine in the microwave for lunch. If this rain keeps up, I'll probably be home early. Good luck with Scott."

"Thanks."

"Scott?" Brady asked, as Loretta went out.

Vanessa merely propped her elbows on the table. "Don't ask."

Brady waited until Loretta had left them alone before rising to help himself to coffee. "I wanted to talk to you about the wedding."

"The wedding?" She looked over. "Oh, the wedding. Yes, what about it?"

"Dad's been applying a little Tucker pressure. He thinks he's got Loretta convinced to take the plunge over the Memorial Day weekend."

"Memorial Day? But that's next week."

"Why wait?" Brady said after a sip, echoing his father's sentiments. "That way they can use the annual picnic as a kind of town wedding reception."

"I see." But it was so soon, Vanessa thought frantically. She hadn't even adjusted to being with her mother again, to living in the same house with her, and now… But it wasn't her decision, she reminded herself. "I suppose they'll move into your father's house."

"I think that's the plan." He sat again. "They've been kicking around the idea of renting this one eventually. Does that bother you?"

She concentrated on cutting a neat slice of the bread. How could she know? She hadn't had time to find out if it was home or not. "No, I suppose not. They can hardly live in two houses at once."

Brady thought he understood. "I can't see Loretta selling this place. It's been in your family for years."

"I often wondered why she kept it."

"She grew up here, just as you did." He picked up his coffee again. "Why don't you ask her what she plans to do about it?"

"I might." She moved her shoulders restlessly. "There's no hurry."

Because he knew her, he let it go at that. "What I really wanted to talk to you about was a wedding present. Obviously they won't need a toaster or a set of china."

"No." Vanessa frowned down at her plate. "I suppose not."

"I was thinking—I ran it by Joanie and she likes the idea. Why don't we pool our resources and give them a honeymoon? A couple weeks in Cancún. You know, a suite overlooking the Caribbean, tropical nights, the works. Neither one of them has ever been to Mexico. I think they'd get a charge out of it."

Vanessa looked up at him again. It was a lovely idea, she decided. And it was typical of him to have thought of it. "As a surprise?"

"I think we can pull it off. Dad's been trying to juggle his schedule to get a week free. I can sabotage that so he'll think he can only manage a couple of days. Getting the tickets, making some reservations, that's the easy part. Then we have to pack their bags without getting caught."

Warming to the idea, she smiled. "If your father has the same stars in his eyes my mother does, I think we can manage that. We could give them the tickets at the picnic, then bundle them into a limo. Is there a limo service around here?"

"There's one in Frederick. I hadn't thought of that." He pulled out a pad to make a note.

"Get them the bridal suite," Vanessa said. When he looked up and grinned, she shrugged. "If we're going to do it, let's do it right."

"I like it. One limo, one bridal suite, two first-class tickets. Anything else?"

"Champagne. A bottle in the limo, and another in the room when they arrive. And flowers. Mom likes gardenias." She stopped abruptly as Brady continued to write. She'd called Loretta "Mom." It had come out naturally. It sounded natural. "She—she used to like gardenias."

"Terrific." He slipped the pad back in his jacket pocket. "You didn't leave me any."

Baffled, she followed his gaze to her own empty plate. "I... I guess I was hungrier than I thought."

"That's a good sign. Any burning?"

"No." Off balance, she rose to take her plate to the sink. "Any pain?"

"No. I told you before, you're not my doctor."

"Um-hmm." He was standing behind her when she turned. "We'll just figure I'm taking Doc Tucker's appointments today. Let's have a little vertical examination." Before she could move aside, he pressed gentle fingers to her abdomen. "Hurt?"

"No, I told you I—"

He pressed firmly under her breastbone. She winced. "Still tender?"

"A little."

He nodded. When he'd touched that spot two days before, she'd nearly gone through the roof. "You're coming along nicely. Another few days and you can even indulge in a burrito."

"Why is it that everyone who comes in here is obsessed with what I eat?"

"Because you haven't been eating enough. Understandable, with an ulcer."

"I don't have an ulcer." But she was aching from his touch—for an entirely different reason. "And would you move?"

"Right after you pay your bill." Before she could object or respond, he pressed his lips to hers, firmly, possessively. Murmuring her name, he took her deeper, until she was clinging to him for balance. The floor seemed to drop away from her feet so that he, and only he, was touching her. His thighs against hers, his fingers knotted in her hair, his mouth, hungry and impatient, roaming her face.

She smelled of the morning, of the rain. He wondered what it would be like to love her in the gloomy light, her sigh whispering against his cheek. And he wondered how much longer he would have to wait.

He lifted his head, keeping his hands in her hair so that her face was tilted toward his. In the misty green of her eyes, he saw himself. Lost in her. Gently now, and with an infinite care that stilled her wildly beating heart, he touched his lips to hers again.

Her arms tightened around him, strengthening, even as every bone in her body seemed to melt. She tilted her head so that their lips met in perfect alignment, with equal demand.

"Vanessa—"

"Don't say anything, not yet." She pressed her mouth to his throat and just held on. She knew she would have to think, but for now, for just a moment, she wanted only to feel.

His pulse throbbed, strong and fast, against her lips. His body was firm and solid. Gradually his hands relaxed their desperate grip and stroked through her hair. She became aware of the hiss and patter of rain, of the cool tiles under her bare feet, of the morning scents of coffee and cinnamon.

But the driving need would not abate, nor would the confusion and fear that blossomed inside her.

"I don't know what to do," she said at length. "I haven't been able to think straight since I saw you again."

Her murmured statement set off dozens of new fires. His hands moved up to her shoulders and gripped harder than he had meant them to. "I want you, Van. You want me. We're not teenagers anymore."

She stepped back as far as his hands would allow. "It's not easy for me."

"No." He studied her as he struggled to examine his own emotions. "I'm not sure I'd want it to be. If you want promises—"

"No," she said quickly. "I don't want anything I can't give back."

He'd been about to make them, hundreds of them. With an effort, he swallowed them all, reminding himself that he'd always moved too fast when it involved Vanessa. "What can you give back?"

"I don't know." She lifted her hands to his and squeezed

before she stepped away. "God, Brady, I feel as though I'm slipping in and out of the looking glass."

"This isn't an illusion, Van." It was a struggle to keep from reaching for her again. But he knew that what his father had told him was true. When you held too tight, what you wanted most slipped through your fingers. "This is just you and me."

She studied him, the eyes so blue against the dark lashes, the damp, untidy hair, the stubborn set of his jaw, the impossibly romantic shape of his mouth. It was so easy to remember why she had loved him. And so easy to be afraid she still did.

"I won't pretend I don't want to be with you. At the same time, I want to run the other way, as fast as I can." Her sigh was long and shaky. "And hope like hell you catch up with me. I realize my behavior's been erratic since I've come home, and a big part of that is because I never expected to find you here, or to have all these old feelings revived. And that's part of the problem. I don't know how much of what I feel for you is just an echo and how much is real."

He found himself in the frustrating position of competing with himself. "We're different people now, Van."

"Yes." She looked at him, her eyes level and almost calm. "When I was sixteen, I would have gone anywhere with you, Brady. I imagined us together forever, a house, a family."

"And now?" he said carefully.

"Now we both know things aren't that simple, or that easy. We're different people, Brady, with different lives, different dreams. I had problems before—we both did. I still have them." She lifted her hands, let them fall. "I'm not sure it's wise to begin a relationship with you, a physical relationship, until I resolve them."

"It's more than physical, Vanessa. It's always been more."

She nodded, taking a moment to calm a fresh flood of emotion. "All the more reason to take it slowly. I don't know what I'm going to do with my life, with my music. Having an affair will only make it that much more difficult for both of us when I leave."

Panic. He tasted it. When she left again, it would break his heart. He wasn't sure that particular organ would survive a second time. "If you're asking me to turn off my feelings and walk away, I won't." In one swift movement, he pulled her against him again. The hell with what was right. "And neither will you."

She felt the thrill race up her spine, those twin sprinters—excitement and alarm. The ghost of the boy she had known and loved was in his eyes, reckless, relentless. She'd never been able to resist him.

"I'm asking you to let me sort this through." If he wanted to use anger, then she would match him blow for blow. "The decision's mine, Brady," she said, jerking away. "I won't be pressured or threatened or seduced. Believe me, it's all been tried before."

It was the wrong switch to pull. His eyes, already hot, turned to blue fire. "I'm not one of your smooth, well-mannered lovers, Van. I won't pressure or threaten or seduce. When the time comes, I'll just take."

Challenged, she tossed her head back. "You won't take anything I don't give. No man does. Oh, I'd like to toss those smooth, well-mannered lovers in your face." She gave him a shove as she walked past him to the stove. "Just to see you squirm. But I'll do better than that." She whirled back, hair flying. "I'll tell you the truth. There haven't been any lovers. Because I haven't wanted there to be." Insolent and mocking, she leaned against the stove. "And if I decide I don't want you, you'll just have to join the ranks of the disappointed."

No one. There had been no one. Almost before he could absorb it, she was hurling her final insult. He bristled, took a step toward her, then managed to stop himself. If he touched her now, one of them would crawl. He didn't want it to be him. He stalked to the back door, and had wrenched it open before he got his temper under control enough to realize that his retreat was exactly what she'd wanted.

So he'd throw her a curve.

"How about going to the movies tonight?"

If he'd suggested a quick trip to the moon, she would have been no less surprised. "What?"

"The movies. Do you want to go to the movies?"

"Why?"

"Because I have a craving for popcorn," he snapped. "Do you want to go or not?"

"I... Yes," she heard herself say.

"Fine." He slammed the door behind him.

Life was a puzzle, Vanessa decided. And she was having a hard time fitting the pieces together. For a week she'd been whirled into wedding and picnic plans. Coleslaw and potato salad, long-stemmed roses and photographers. She was dead sure it was a mistake to try to coordinate a town picnic with an intimate family wedding. It was like trying to juggle bowling balls and feathers.

As the final week passed, she was too busy and too confused to notice that she felt better than she had in years. There was the secret honeymoon, and Joanie's enthusiastic bubbling over every aspect of the upcoming nuptials. There were flowers to be ordered and arranged—and a hundred hamburger patties to make.

She went out with Brady almost every night. To the movies, to dinner. To a concert. He was such an easy and amusing companion that she began to wonder if she had dreamed the passion and anger in the gloomy kitchen.

But each night when he walked her to the door, each night when he kissed her breathless, she realized he was indeed giving her time to think things through. Just as he was making certain she had plenty to think about.

The night before the wedding, she stayed at home. But she thought of him, even as she and Loretta and Joanie bustled around the kitchen putting last-minute touches on a mountain of food.

"I still think the guys should be here helping," Joanie muttered as she slapped a hamburger patty between her hands.

"They'd just be in the way." Loretta molded another hunk of meat into shape. "Besides, I'm too nervous to deal with Ham tonight."

Joanie laughed. "You're doing fine. Dad's a basket case. When he came by the farm today, he asked me three times for a cup of coffee. He had one in his hand the whole time."

Pleased, Loretta chuckled. "It's nice to know he's suffering, too." She looked at the kitchen clock for the fifth time in five minutes. Eight o'clock, she thought. In fourteen hours she would be married. "I hope it doesn't rain."

Vanessa, who'd been deemed an amateur, looked up from her task of arranging the patties in layers between waxed paper. "The forecast is sunny and high seventies."

"Oh, yes." Loretta managed a smile. "You told me that before, didn't you?"

"Only fifty or sixty times."

Her brows knitted, Loretta looked out the window. "Of course, if it did rain, we could move the wedding indoors. It would be a shame to have the picnic spoiled, though. Ham enjoys it so."

"It wouldn't dare rain," Joanie stated, taking the forgotten patty from the bride-to-be's hands. Unable to resist, she tucked her tongue in her cheek. "It's too bad you had to postpone your honeymoon."

"Oh, well." With a shrug, Loretta went back to work. She didn't want to show her disappointment. "Ham just couldn't manage to clear his schedule. I'll have to get used to that sort of thing, if I'm going to be a doctor's wife." She pressed a hand to her nervous stomach. "Is that rain? Did I hear rain?"

"No," Vanessa and Joanie said in unison.

With a weak laugh, Loretta washed her hands. "I must be hearing things. I've been so addled this past week. Just this morning I couldn't find my blue silk blouse—and I've misplaced the linen slacks I got on sale just last month. My new sandals, too, and my good black cocktail dress. I can't think where I might have put them."

Vanessa shot Joanie a warning look before her friend could chuckle. "They'll turn up."

"What? Oh, yes…yes, of course they will. Are you sure that's not rain?"

Exasperated, Vanessa put a hand on her hip. "Mom, for heaven's sake, it's not rain. There isn't going to be any rain. Go take a hot bath." When Loretta's eyes filled, Vanessa rolled her eyes. "I'm sorry. I didn't mean to snap at you."

"You called me 'Mom,'" Loretta said, her breath hitching. "I never thought you would again." As tears overflowed, she rushed from the room.

"Damn it." Vanessa leaned her hands on the counter. "I've been working overtime to keep the peace all week, and I blow it the night before the wedding."

"You didn't blow anything." Joanie put a hand on her shoulder and rubbed. "I'm not going to say it's none of my business, because we're friends, and tomorrow we'll be family. I've watched you and Loretta walk around each other ever since you got back. And I've seen the way she looks at you when your back is turned, or when you leave a room."

"I don't know if I can give her what she wants."

"You're wrong," Joanie said quietly. "You can. In a lot of ways you already have. Why don't you go upstairs, make sure she's all right? I'll give Brady a call and have him help me load most of this food up and take it down to Dad's."

"All right."

Vanessa went upstairs quietly, slowly, trying to work out the right things to say. But when she saw Loretta sitting on the bed, nothing seemed right.

"I'm sorry." Loretta dabbed at her eyes with a tissue. "I guess I'm overly emotional tonight."

"You're entitled." Vanessa hesitated in the doorway. "Would you like to be alone?"

"No." Loretta held out a hand. "Would you sit awhile?"

Unable to refuse, Vanessa crossed the room to sit beside her mother.

"For some reason," Loretta began, "I've been thinking about what you were like as a baby. You were so pretty. I know all mothers say that, but you were. So bright and alert, and all that hair." She reached out to touch the tips of Vanessa's hair. "Sometimes I would just sit and watch you as you slept. I couldn't believe you were mine. As long as I can remember, I wanted to have a home and children. Oh, I wanted to fill a house with children. It was my only ambition." She looked down at the tissue she had shredded. "When I had you, it was the happiest day of my life. You'll understand that better when you have a baby of your own."

"I know you loved me." Vanessa chose her words carefully. "That's why the rest was so difficult. But I don't think this is the time for us to talk about it."

"Maybe not." Loretta wasn't sure it would ever be the time for a full explanation. One that might turn her daughter away again, just when she was beginning to open her heart. "I just want you to know that I understand you're trying to forgive, and to forgive without explanations. That means a great deal to me." She took a chance and gripped her daughter's hand. "I love you now even more than I did that first moment, when they put you into my arms. No matter where you go or what you do, I always will."

"I love you, too." Vanessa brought their joined hands to her cheek for a moment. "I always have." And that was what hurt the most. She rose and managed to smile. "I think you should get some sleep. You want to look your best tomorrow."

"Yes. Good night, Van."

"Good night." She closed the door quietly behind her.

Chapter 8

Vanessa heard the hiss at her window and blinked groggily awake. Rain? she thought, trying to remember why it was so important there be no rain that day.

The wedding, she thought with a start, and sat straight up. The sun was up, she realized as she shook herself. It was streaming through her half-opened window like pale gold fingers. But the hiss came again—and a rattle.

Not rain, she decided as she sprang out of bed. Pebbles. Rushing to the window, she threw it all the way up.

And there he was, standing in her backyard, dressed in ripped sweats and battered sneakers, his legs spread and planted, his head back and a fistful of pebbles in his hand.

"It's about time," Brady whispered up at her. "I've been throwing rocks at your window for ten minutes."

Vanessa leaned an elbow on the sill and rested her chin in her palm. "Why?"

"To wake you up."

"Ever hear of a telephone?"

"I didn't want to wake your mother."

She yawned. "What time is it?"

"It's after six." He glanced over to see Kong digging at the marigolds and whistled the dog to him. Now they both stood, looking up at her. "Well, are you coming down?"

She grinned. "I like the view from here."

"You've got ten minutes before I find out if I can still shimmy up a drainpipe."

"Tough choice." With a laugh, she shut the window. In less than ten minutes, she was creeping out the back door in her oldest jeans and baggiest sweater. Thoughts of a romantic assignation were dispelled when she saw Joanie, Jack and Lara.

"What's going on?" she demanded.

"We're decorating." Brady hefted a cardboard box and shoved it at her. "Crepe paper, balloons, wedding bells. The works. We thought we'd shoot for discreet and elegant here for the ceremony, then go all out down at Dad's for the picnic."

"More surprises." The box weighed a ton, and she shifted it. "Where do we start?"

They worked in whispers and muffled laughter, arguing about the proper way to drape crepe paper on a maple tree. Brady's idea of discreet was to hang half a dozen paper wedding bells from the branches and top it off with balloons. But it wasn't until they had carted everything down the block to the Tuckers that he really cut loose.

"It's a reception, not a circus," Vanessa reminded him. He had climbed into the old sycamore and was gleefully shooting out strips of crepe paper.

"It's a celebration," he replied. "It reminds me of when

we'd roll old Mr. Taggert's willow every Halloween. Hand me some more pink."

Despite her better judgment, Vanessa obeyed. "It looks like a five-year-old did it."

"Artistic expression."

With a muttered comment, Vanessa turned. She saw that Jack had climbed on the roof and was busily anchoring a line of balloons along the gutter. While Lara sat on a blanket with a pile of plastic blocks and Kong for company, Joanie tied the last of the wedding bells to the grape arbor. The result of their combined efforts wasn't elegant, and it certainly wasn't artistic. But it was terrific.

"You're all crazy," Vanessa decided when Brady jumped from the tree to land softly beside her. He smelled lightly of soap and sweat. "What's next? A calliope and a snake charmer?"

He reached into a box and drew out another roll of white and a roll of pink. "The mall was out of calliopes, but we've still got some of this left."

Vanessa thought a moment, then grinned. "Give me the tape." With it in her hand, she raced to the house. "Come on," she said, gesturing to Brady. "Give me a boost."

"A what?"

"I need to get up on your shoulders." She got behind him and leaped up nimbly to hook her legs around his waist. "Try to stand still," she muttered as she inched her way upward. He tried not to notice that her thighs were slender and only a thin layer of denim away. "Now I need both rolls."

They juggled the paper and tape between them.

"I like your knees," Brady commented, turning his head to nip at one.

"Just consider yourself a stepladder." She secured the tips

of the streamers to the eaves of the house. "Move back, but slowly. I'll twist as you go."

"Go where?"

"To the back of the yard—to that monstrosity that used to be a sycamore tree."

Balancing her and craning his neck behind him to be sure he didn't step on an unwary dog—or his niece—or in a gopher hole, he walked backward. "What are you doing?"

"I'm decorating." She twisted the strips of pink and white together, letting the streamer droop a few inches above Brady's head. "Don't run into the tree." When they reached it, she hooked her feet around Brady's chest and leaned forward. "I just have to reach this branch. Got it."

"Now what?"

"Now we do another from the tree to the other side of the house. Balance," she said, leaning forward to look at him. "That's artistic."

When the deed was done, and the last scrap of colored paper used, she put her hands on her hips and studied the results. "Nice," she decided. "Very nice—except for the mess you made of the sycamore."

"The sycamore is a work of art," he told her. "It's riddled with symbolism."

"It looks like Mr. Taggert's willow on Halloween," Joanie chimed in as she plucked up Lara and settled her on her hip. "One look at that and he's going to know who rolled it in toilet paper every year." She grinned up at Vanessa, who was still perched on Brady's shoulders. "We'd better run. Only two hours until countdown." She poked a finger in Brady's chest. "You're in charge of Dad until we get back."

"He's not going anywhere."

"I'm not worried about that. He's so nervous he might tie his shoelaces together."

"Or forget to wear shoes at all," Jack put in, taking Joanie's arm to lead her away. "Or he could wear his shoes and forget his pants, all because you were standing here worrying about it so you didn't get home and change and get back in time to nag him."

"I don't nag," she said with a chuckle as he pulled her along. "And, Brady, don't forget to check with Mrs. Leary about the cake. Oh, and—" The rest was muffled when Jack clamped a hand over her mouth.

"And I used to put my hands over my ears," Brady murmured. He twisted his head to look up at Vanessa. "Want a ride home?"

"Sure."

He trooped off, still carrying her, through the neighboring yards. "Putting on weight?" He'd noticed she was filling out her jeans very nicely.

"Doctor's orders." She gave his hair an ungentle tug. "So watch your step."

"Purely a professional question. How about I give you an exam?" He turned his head to leer at her.

"Look out for the—" She ducked down so that the clotheslines skimmed over her head. "You might have walked around it."

"Yeah, but now I can smell your hair." He kissed her before she could straighten up again. "Are you going to make me some breakfast?"

"No."

"Coffee?"

She chuckled as she started to squirm down his back. "No."

"Instant?"

"No." She was laughing when her feet hit the ground.

"I'm going to take a long, hot shower, then spend an hour primping and admiring myself in the mirror."

He gathered her close, though the dog was trying to wiggle between them. "You look pretty good right now."

"I can look better."

"I'll let you know." He tipped her face up to his. "After the picnic, you want to come by, help me look at paint chips?"

She gave him a quick, impulsive kiss. "I'll let you know," she said before she dashed inside.

Loretta's nerves seemed to have transferred to her daughter. While the bride calmly dressed for her wedding day, Vanessa fussed with the flower arrangements, checked and rechecked the bottle of champagne that had been set aside for the first family toast, and paced from window to window looking for the photographer.

"He should have been here ten minutes ago," she said when she heard Loretta start downstairs. "I knew it was a mistake to hire Mrs. Driscoll's grandson's brother-in-law. I don't understand why—" She turned, breaking off when she saw her mother.

"Oh. You look beautiful."

Loretta had chosen a pale, pale green silk with only a touch of ecru lace along the tea-length hem. It was simple—simply cut, simply beautiful. On an impulse, she'd bought a matching picture hat, and she'd fluffed her hair under the brim.

"You don't think it's too much?" She reached up, her fingers skimming the hat. "It is just a small, informal wedding."

"It's perfect. Really perfect. I've never seen you look better."

"I feel perfect." She smiled. As a bride should, she was glowing. "I don't know what was wrong with me last night.

Today I feel perfect. I'm so happy." She shook her head quickly. "I don't want to cry. I spent forever on my face."

"You're not going to cry," Vanessa said firmly. "The photographer— Oh, thank God, he's just pulling up outside. I'll— Oh, wait. Do you have everything?"

"Everything?"

"You know, something old, something new?"

"I forgot." Struck by bridal superstition, Loretta started a frantic mental search. "The dress is new. And these…" She touched a finger to her pearls. "These were my mother's— and her mother's, so they're old."

"Good start. Blue?"

Color rose in Loretta's cheeks. "Yes, actually, under the dress. I have, ah… My camisole has little blue ribbons down the front. I suppose you think I'm foolish buying fancy lingerie."

"No, I don't." Vanessa touched her mother's arm, and was surprised by the quick impulse she had to hug her. Instead, she stepped back. "That leaves borrowed."

"Well, I—"

"Here." Vanessa unclasped the thin gold braided bracelet she wore. "Take this, and you'll be all set." She peeked out the window again. "Oh, here comes Doc Tucker and the rest of them." With a laugh, she waved. "They look like a parade. Go into the music room until I can hustle them outside."

"Van." Loretta was still standing, holding the bracelet in her hand. "Thank you."

Vanessa waited until her mother was out of sight before opening the door. Mass confusion entered. Joanie was arguing with Brady about the proper way to pin a boutonniere. Jack claimed his wife had tied his tie so tight that he couldn't breathe, much less talk. Ham paced the length of the house and back again before Vanessa could nudge him outside.

"You brought the dog," Vanessa said, staring at Kong, who had a red carnation pinned jauntily to his collar.

"He's family," Brady claimed. "I couldn't hurt his feelings."

"Maybe a leash?" she suggested.

"Don't be insulting."

"He's sniffing at Reverend Taylor's shoes."

"With any luck, that's all he'll do to Reverend Taylor's shoes." He turned back to her as she stifled a giggle. "You were right."

"About what?"

"You can look better."

She was wearing a thin, summery dress with yards of skirt in a bold floral print. Its snug contrasting bodice was a rich teal blue, with a bandeau collar that left the curve of her shoulders bare. The gold rope around her neck, and her braided earrings, matched the bracelet she had given Loretta.

"So can you." In a natural movement, she reached up to straighten the knot in the dark blue tie he was wearing with an oyster-colored suit. "I guess we're all set."

"We're still missing something."

She looked around quickly. The baskets of flowers were in place. Joanie was brushing imaginary dust off her father's sleeve while Reverend Taylor cooed over Lara and tried to avoid Kong. The wedding bells were twirling slowly in the light breeze.

"What?"

"The bride."

"Oh, Lord. I forgot. I'll go get her." Turning, Vanessa raced into the house. She found Loretta in the music room, sitting on the piano stool taking long, deep breaths. "Are you ready?"

She took one more. "Yes." Rising, she walked through the house. But at the back door she paused and groped for Vanessa's hand. Together they crossed the lawn. With each step, Ham's smile grew wider, her mother's hand steadier. They stopped in front of the minister. Vanessa released her mother's hand, stepped back and took Brady's.

"Dearly beloved…" the minister began.

She watched her mother marry under the shade of the maple with paper wedding bells swaying.

"You may kiss the bride," the minister intoned. A cheer went up from neighboring yards where people had gathered. The camera clicked as Ham brought Loretta close for a long, full-bodied kiss that brought on more whistles and shouts.

"Nice job," Brady said as he embraced his father.

Vanessa put her confused emotions on hold and turned to hug her mother. "Best wishes, Mrs. Tucker."

"Oh, Van."

"No crying yet. We've still got lots of pictures to take."

With a squeal, Joanie launched herself at them both. "Oh, I'm so happy." She plucked Lara from Jack's arms. "Give your grandma a kiss."

"Grandma," Loretta whispered, and with a watery laugh she swung Lara into her arms. "Grandma."

Brady laid an arm over Vanessa's shoulders. "How do you feel, Aunt Van?"

"Amazed." She laughed up at him as Mrs. Driscoll's grandson's brother-in-law scurried around snapping pictures. "Let's go pour the champagne."

Two hours later, she was in the Tucker backyard, hauling a tray of hamburger patties to the grill.

"I thought your father always did the honors," she said to Brady.

"He passed his spatula down to me." He had his suit coat off now, his sleeves rolled up and his tie off. Smoke billowed up from the grill as meat sizzled. He flipped a patty expertly.

"You do that very well."

"You should see me with a scalpel."

"I'll pass, thanks." She shifted to avoid being mowed down by two running boys. "The picnic's just like I remember. Crowded, noisy and chaotic."

People milled around in the yard, in the house, even spilled out along the sidewalks. Some sat at the long picnic tables or on the grass. Babies were passed from hand to hand. The old sat in the shade waving at flies as they gossiped and reminisced. The young ran in the sunshine.

Someone had brought a huge portable stereo. Music poured from the rear corner of the yard, where a group of teenagers had gathered to flirt.

"We'd have been there just a few years back," Brady commented.

"You mean you're too old to hang around a boom box now?"

"No. But they think I am. Now I'm Dr. Tucker—as opposed to my father, who's Doc Tucker—and that automatically labels me an adult." He skewered a hot dog. "It's hell growing up."

"Being dignified," she added as he popped it into a bun and slathered on mustard.

"Setting an example for the younger generation. Say 'ah,'" he told her, then shoved the hot dog in her mouth.

She chewed and swallowed in self-defense. "Maintaining a certain decorum."

"Yeah. You've got mustard on your mouth. Here." He grabbed her hand before she could wipe it off. "I'll take care of it." He leaned down and slid the tip of his tongue over the corner of her mouth. "Very tasty," he decided, then nipped lightly at her bottom lip.

"You're going to burn your burgers," she murmured.

"Quiet. I'm setting an example for the younger generation."

Even as she chuckled, he covered her mouth fully with his, lengthening the kiss, deepening it, drawing it out, until she forgot she was surrounded by people. And so did he.

When he released her, she lifted a hand to her spinning head and tried to find her voice.

"Just like old times," someone shouted.

"Better," Brady said quietly, and would have pulled her close again, but for a tap on his shoulder.

"Let that girl go and behave yourself, Brady Tucker." Violet Driscoll shook her head at the pair of them. "You've got hungry people here. If you want to smooch with your girl, you just wait till later."

"Yes, ma'am."

"Never had a lick of sense." She winked at Vanessa as she started back to the shade. "But he's a handsome so-and-so."

"She's right." Vanessa tossed back her hair.

"I'm a handsome so-and-so?"

"No, you've never had a lick of sense."

"Hey!" he called after her. "Where are you going?"

Vanessa shot him a long, teasing look over her shoulder and kept walking.

It was like old times, Vanessa thought as she stopped to talk to high school friends and watched children race and shout and gobble down food. Faces had aged, babies had been born, but the mood was the same. There was the smell of good food, the sounds of laughter and of a cranky baby being lulled to sleep. She heard arguments over the Orioles' chances for a pennant this year, talk about summer plans and gardening tips.

She could smell the early roses blooming and see the tangle of morning glories on the trellis next door.

When Brady found her again, she was sitting on the grass with Lara.

"What're you doing?"

"Playing with my niece." They both lifted their heads to smile at him.

Something shifted inside him. Something fast and unexpected. And something inevitable, he realized. Seeing her smiling up at him, a child's head on her shoulder, sunlight pouring over her skin. How could he have known he'd been waiting, almost his entire life, for a moment like this? But the child should be his, he thought. Vanessa and the child should be his.

"Is something wrong?" she asked.

"No." He brought himself back with a long, steadying breath. "Why?"

"The way you were staring at me."

He sat beside her, touched a hand to her hair. "I'm still in love with you, Vanessa. And I don't know what the hell to do about it."

She stared. Even if she could have latched on to the dozens of emotions swirling through her, she couldn't have put any into words. It wasn't a boy she was looking at now. He was a man, and what he had spoken had been said deliberately. Now he was waiting for her to move, toward him or away. But she couldn't move at all.

Lara bounced in her lap and squealed, shattering the silence. "Brady, I—"

"There you are." Joanie dropped down beside them.

"Whoops," she said as the tension got through to her. "I'm sorry. I guess it's bad timing."

"Go away, Joanie," Brady told her. "Far away."

"I'd already be gone, since you've asked so nicely, but the limo's here. People are already heading around front to stare at it. I think it's time to see the newlyweds off."

"You're right." Almost using Lara as a shield, Vanessa scrambled to her feet. "We don't want them to miss their plane." She braced herself and looked at Brady again. "You've got the tickets?"

"Yeah, I got them." Before she could skirt around him, he cupped her chin in his hand. "We've still got unfinished business, Van."

"I know." She was grateful her voice could sound so calm when her insides were knotted. "Like Joanie said, it's bad timing." With Lara on her hip, she hurried off to find her mother.

"What's all this about a limo?" Ham demanded as Joanie began unrolling his pushed-up sleeves. "Did somebody die?"

"Nope." Joanie fastened the button on his cuff. "You and your new wife are going on a little trip."

"A trip?" Loretta repeated, as Vanessa handed her her purse.

"When newlyweds take a trip," Brady explained, "it's called a honeymoon."

"But I've got patients all next week."

"No, you don't." With Brady and Jack on either side of Ham, and Vanessa and Joanie flanking Loretta, they led the baffled bride and groom to the front of the house.

"Oh, my" was all Loretta could say as she spotted the gleaming white stretch limo.

"Your plane leaves at six." Brady took an envelope out of his pocket and handed it to his father. *"Vaya con Dios."*

"What is all this?" Ham demanded. Vanessa noted with a chuckle that old shoes and cans were already being tied to the bumper. "My schedule—"

"Is cleared." Brady gave Ham a slap on the back. "See you in a couple weeks."

"A couple weeks?" His eyebrows shot up. "Where the hell are we going?"

"South of the border," Joanie chimed in, and gave her father a hard, smacking kiss. "Don't drink the water."

"Mexico?" Loretta's eyes widened. "Are we going to Mexico? But how can we— The shop. We haven't any luggage."

"The shop's closed," Vanessa told her. "And your luggage is in the trunk." She kissed Loretta on each cheek. "Have a good time."

"In the trunk?" Her baffled smile widened. "My blue silk blouse?"

"Among other things."

"You all did this." Despite the persistent photographer, Loretta began to cry. "All of you."

"Guilty." Brady gave her a huge hug. "Bye, Mom."

"You're a sneaky bunch." Ham had to take out his handkerchief. "Well, Loretta, I guess we've got ourselves a honeymoon."

"Not if you miss your plane." Joanie, always ready to worry, began to push them toward the limo. "Don't sit in the sun too long. It's much more intense down there. Oh, and whatever you buy, make sure you shop around and bargain first. You can change your money at the hotel—there's a phrase book in the carry-on. And if you need—"

"Say goodbye, Joanie," Jack told her.

"Oh, shoot." She rubbed her knuckles under her damp eyes. "Bye. Wave bye-bye, Lara."

"Oh, Ham. Gardenias." Loretta began to weep again.

With shouts and waves from the entire town, the limo began to cruise sedately down Main Street, followed by the clang and thump of cans and shoes, and an escort of running children.

"There they go," Joanie managed, burying her face in Jack's shoulder. He patted her hair.

"It's okay, honey. Kids have to leave home sometime. Come on, I'll get you some potato salad." He grinned at Brady as he led her away.

Vanessa cleared the lump in her throat. "That was quite a send-off."

"I want to talk to you. We can go to your house or mine."

"I think we should wait until—"

"We've already waited too long."

Panicked, she looked around. How was it that they were alone again so quickly? "The party— You have guests."

"Nobody'll miss us." With a hand on her arm, he turned toward his car.

"Dr. Tucker, Dr. Tucker!" Annie Crampton was racing around the corner of the house. "Come quick! Something's wrong with my grandpa!"

He moved quickly. By the time Vanessa reached the backyard, he was already kneeling beside the old man, loosening his collar.

"Pain," the old man said. "In my chest...can't breathe."

"I got Dad's bag," Joanie said as she passed it to Brady. "Ambulance is coming."

Brady just nodded. "Take it easy, Mr. Benson." He took a small bottle and a syringe out of the bag. "I want you to stay calm." He continued to talk as he worked, calming and soothing with his voice. "Joanie, get his file," he murmured.

Feeling helpless, Vanessa put an arm around Annie's shoulders and drew her back. "Come on, Annie."

"Is Grandpa going to die?"

"Dr. Tucker's taking care of him. He's a very good doctor."

"He takes care of my mom." She sniffled and wiped at her eyes. "He's going to deliver the baby and all, but Grandpa, he's real old. He fell down. He just got all funny-looking and fell down."

"Dr. Tucker was right here." She stroked Annie's flyaway hair. "If he was going to get sick, it was the best place for it. When he's better, you can play your new song for him."

"The Madonna song?"

"That's right." She heard the wail of an ambulance. "They're coming to take him to the hospital."

"Will Dr. Tucker go with him?"

"I'm sure he will." She watched as the attendants hurried out with a stretcher. Brady spoke to them briskly, giving instructions. She saw him put his hands on Annie's mother's shoulders, speaking slowly, calmly, while she looked up at him with trust and tears in her eyes. When Brady started after the stretcher, Vanessa gave Annie a last squeeze.

"Why don't you go sit with your mother for a minute? She'll be scared." How well she knew, Vanessa thought. She remembered the fear and despair she had felt when they had taken her own father. Turning, she rushed after Brady.

"Brady." She knew she couldn't waste his time. When he turned, she saw the concern, the concentration and the impatience in his eyes. "Please let me know how—what happens."

He nodded, then climbed in the rear of the ambulance with his patient.

* * *

It was nearly midnight when Brady pulled up in front of his house. There was a sliver of a moon, bone-white against a black sky studded with stars as clear as ice. He sat where he was for a moment, letting his muscles relax one by one. With his windows down he could hear the wind sighing through the trees.

The fatigue of an eighteen-hour-day had finally caught up with him on the drive home. He was grateful Jack had brought his car to the hospital. Without it, he would have been tempted to stretch out in the lounge. Now all he wanted was to ease his tired body into a hot tub, turn on the jets and drink a cold beer.

The lights were on downstairs. He was glad he'd forgotten to turn them off. It was less depressing to come home to an empty house if the lights were on. He'd detoured into town on the way home and driven by Vanessa's. But her lights had been out.

Probably for the best, he thought now. He was tired and edgy. Hardly the mood for patient, sensible talk. Maybe there was an advantage to letting her stew over the fact that he was in love with her.

And maybe there wasn't. He hesitated, his hand on the door. What the hell was wrong with him, he wondered. He'd always been a decisive man. When he'd decided to become a doctor, he'd gone after his degree with a vengeance. When he'd decided to leave his hospital position in New York and come home to practice general medicine, he'd done so without a backward glance or a whisper of regret.

Life-altering decisions, certainly. So why the hell couldn't he decide what to do about Vanessa?

He was going back to town. If she didn't answer her door, he would climb up the damn rainspout and crawl in her bedroom window. One way or the other, they were going to straighten this mess out tonight.

He'd already turned away and started back to his car when the door to the house opened.

"Brady?" Vanessa stood in the doorway, the light at her back. "Aren't you coming in?"

He stopped dead and stared at her. In a gesture of pure frustration, he dragged a hand through his hair. Was it any wonder he couldn't decide what to do about her? She'd never been predictable. Kong raced out of the house, barking, and jumped on him.

"Jack and Joanie dropped us off." Vanessa stood, twisting the doorknob back and forth. "I hope you don't mind."

"No." With the dog racing in circles around him, he started back to the house. Vanessa stepped back, out of reach.

"I brought some leftovers from the picnic. I didn't know if you'd have a chance to get any dinner."

"No, I didn't."

"Mr. Benson?"

"Stabilized. It was shaky for a while, but he's tough."

"I'm glad. I'm so glad. Annie was frightened." She rubbed her hands on her thighs, linked her fingers together, pulled them apart, then stuck them in the pockets of her skirt. "You must be exhausted—and hungry. There's plenty of food in the fridge. The, ah, kitchen looks wonderful." She gestured vaguely. "The new cabinets, the counters, everything."

"It's coming along." But he made no move toward it. "How long have you been here?"

"Oh, just a couple of hours." Five, to be exact. "You had some books, so I've been reading."

"Why?"

"Well, to pass the time."

"Why are you here, Van?"

She bent to stroke the dog. "That unfinished business you mentioned. It's been a long day, and I've had plenty of time to think."

"And?"

Why didn't he just sweep her away, carry her upstairs? And shut her up. "And I… About what you said this afternoon."

"That I'm in love with you."

She cleared her throat as she straightened. "Yes, that. I'm not sure what I feel—how I feel. I'm not sure how you feel, either."

"I told you how I feel."

"Yes, but it's very possible that you think you feel that way because you used to—and because falling back into the same routine, the same relationship—with me—is familiar, and comfortable."

"The hell it is. I haven't had a comfortable moment since I saw you sitting at the piano."

"Familiar, then." She began to twist the necklace at her throat. "But I've changed, Brady. I'm not the same person I was when I left here. We'll never be able to pretend those years away. So, no matter how attracted we are to each other, it could be a mistake to take it any further."

He crossed to her, slowly, until they were eye to eye. He was ready to make a mistake. More than ready. "Is that what you were waiting here to tell me?"

She moistened his lips. "Partly."

"Then I'll have my say."

"I'd like to finish first." She kept her eyes level. "I came here tonight because I've never been able to get you completely out of my mind. Or my…" Heart. She wanted to say it, but couldn't. "My system," she finished. "I've never stopped caring about you, or wondering. Because of something we had no control over, we were cheated out of growing up enough to make the decision to move apart or to become lovers." She paused, but only for a moment. "I came here tonight because I realized I want what was taken away from us. I want you." She stepped closer and put her arms around him. "Is that clear enough?"

"Yeah." He kissed her gently. "That's clear enough."

She smiled at him. "Make love with me, Brady. I've always wanted you to."

With their hands joined, they walked upstairs together.

Chapter 9

She had already been upstairs while she had waited for him to come home—smoothing and straightening the covers on the bed, fluffing the pillows, standing and looking at the room and wondering what it would be like to walk into it with him.

He turned on the lamp beside the bed. It was a beautiful old rose-tinted globe that sat on a packing crate. The floors were unfinished, the walls spackled with drywall mud. The bed was only a mattress on the floor beneath the windows. It was the most beautiful room she'd ever seen.

He wished he could have given her candles and roses, a huge four-poster with satin sheets. All he could give her was himself.

And suddenly he was as nervous as a boy on his first date.

"The atmosphere's a little thin in here."

"It's perfect," she told him.

He took her hands and raised them to his lips. "I won't hurt you, Van."

"I know." She kissed his hands in turn. "This is going to sound stupid, but I don't know what to do."

He lowered his mouth to hers, testing, tempting. "You'll catch on."

Her lips curved as her hands slid up his back. "I think you're right." With an instinct that was every bit as potent as experience, she let her head fall back, let her hands glide and press and wander.

Her lips parted for his, and she tasted his little groan of pleasure. Then she shivered with pleasure of her own as his strong, clever hands skimmed down her body, his thumb brushing down the side of her breast, his fingers kneading at her waist, his palm cupping her hip, sliding down her thigh, before its upward journey.

She pressed against him, delighting in the shower of sensations. When his teeth scraped lightly down her throat, over her bare shoulder, she murmured his name. Like the wind through the trees, she sighed for him, and swayed. Pliant and willing, she waited to be molded.

Her absolute trust left him shaken. No matter how hot her passion, she was innocent. Her body might be that of a woman, but she was still as untouched as the girl he had once loved and lost. He wouldn't forget it. As the need flamed inside him, he banked it. This time it would be for her. All for her.

Compassion and tenderness were as much a part of his nature as his recklessness. He showed her only the gentle side now, as he eased the snug top down to her hips. He kissed her, soothing her with murmurs even as his hands set off millions of tiny explosions as they tugged her dress to the floor.

She wore a swatch of white lace that seemed to froth over the swell of her breasts before skimming down to nip at her waist. For his own pleasure, he held her at arm's length and just looked.

"You stop my heart," he told her.

With unsteady hands, she reached out to unbutton his shirt. Though her breath was already ragged, she kept her eyes on his as she slid the shirt from his shoulders and let it fall to join her dress on the floor. With her heart pounding wildly in her ears, she linked her arms around his neck.

"Touch me." She tilted her head back, offered her mouth. "Show me."

Though the kiss was hard, demanding, ruthless, he forced his hands to be gentle. Her own were racing over him, bringing a desperate edge to an already driving need. When he lowered her onto the bed, he watched her eyes close on a sigh, then open again, clouded with desire.

He dipped his head to absorb her taste on his tongue as it skimmed along the verge of lace, as it slid beneath to tease her taut nipples. Her hips ached and her fingers dug into his back as the pleasure rocketed through her.

With a flick of the wrist, he unsnapped her garters, then sent her churning as he slowly peeled down her stockings, blazing the newly bared flesh with his lips. It seemed he found every inch of her, every curve, fascinating. His gentle fingers played over her, everywhere, until the music roared in her head.

As patient as he was ruthless, he drove her closer and closer to the edge she'd never seen. Her body was like a furnace, pumping out heat, pulsing with needs as sharp as his. He drove himself mad watching her, seeing the way everything she felt, each new sensation he brought to her, raced over her face, into her eyes.

Desire. Passion. Pleasure. Excitement. They flowed from him to her, then back again. Familiar. Oh, yes. They recognized each other. That brought comfort. Yet it was new, unique, gloriously fresh. That was the adventure.

He reveled in the way her skin flowed through his hands, the way her body tensed and arched at his touch. The way the lamplight slanted over her, over his hands as he peeled the last barrier of lace away.

Naked, she reached for him, tugging frantically at his slacks. Because he knew his own needs were tearing his control to shreds, he cupped her in his hand and sent her flying over the last line.

She cried out, stunned, helpless, her eyes glazing over, as her hand slipped limply from his shoulder. Even as she shuddered, he eased into her, slowly, gently, murmuring her name again and again as the blood roared in his ears and pushed him to take his pleasure quickly. Love demanded gentleness.

She lost her innocence sweetly, painlessly, and with simple joy.

She lay in Brady's bed, tangled in Brady's sheets. A sparrow heralded the dawn. During the night, the dog had crept in to take his rightful place at the foot of the bed. Lazily Vanessa opened her eyes.

Brady's face was barely an inch from hers, and she had to ease back and blink to focus on him. He was deep in sleep, his arm heavy around her waist, his breathing slow and even. Now, completely relaxed and vulnerable, he looked more like the boy she remembered than the man she was beginning to know.

She loved. There was no doubt in her mind that she loved.

Her heart nearly burst with it. But did she love the boy or the man?

Very gently, she brushed at the hair on his forehead. All she was really sure of was that she was happy. And, for now, it was enough.

More than enough, she thought as she slowly stretched. During the night he had shown her how beautiful making love could be when two people cared about each other. And how exciting it could be when needs were met and desires reached. Whatever happened tomorrow, or a year from to-morrow, she would never forget what they had shared.

Lightly, not wanting to wake him, she touched her lips to his. Even that quiet contact stirred her. Hesitant, curious, she trailed her fingertips over his shoulders, down the length of his back. The need grew and spread inside her.

As dreams went, Brady thought, this was one of the best. He was under a warm quilt in the first light of day. Vanessa was in bed beside him. Her body was pressed against his, shifting gently, arousing quickly. Those beautiful, talented fingers were stroking along his skin. That soft, sulky mouth was toying with his. When he reached for her, she sighed, arching under his hand.

Everywhere he touched she was warm and smooth. Her arms were around him, strong silken ropes that trapped him gloriously against her. When she said his name, once, then twice, the words slipped under the gauzy curtain of his fantasy. He opened his eyes and saw her.

This was no dream. She was smiling at him. Those misty green eyes were heavy with sleep and passion. Her body was slim and soft and curved against his.

"Good morning," she murmured. "I wasn't sure if you—"

He closed his mouth over hers. Dream and reality melded seductively as he slipped inside her.

* * *

The sunlight was stronger when she lay over him, her head on his heart, her body still pulsing.

"You were saying?"

"Hmm." The effort to open her eyes seemed wasted, so she kept them closed. "Was I?"

"You weren't sure if I what?"

She sifted through her thoughts. "Oh. I wasn't sure if you had any morning appointments."

He continued to comb his fingers through her hair. "It's Sunday," he reminded her. "Office is closed. But I have to run into the hospital and check on Mr. Benson and a couple of other patients. How about you?"

"Nothing much. Some lesson plans, now that I have ten students."

"Ten?" There was more snicker than surprise in his voice.

She shifted then, folding her arms over his chest and resting her chin on them. "I was ambushed at the picnic yesterday."

"Ten students." He grinned at her. "That's quite a commitment. Does that mean you're planning to settle in town again?"

"At least for the summer. I haven't decided whether I'll agree to a fall tour."

So he had the summer to convince her, he thought. "How about dinner?"

She narrowed her eyes. "We haven't even had breakfast yet."

"I mean tonight. We could have our own picnic with the leftovers. Just you and me."

Just you and me. "I'd like that."

"Good. Now why don't we start the day off right?"

After a chuckle, she pressed her lips to his chest. "I thought we already had."

"I meant you could wash my back." Grinning, he sat up and dragged her out of bed.

Vanessa discovered she didn't mind being alone in the house. After Brady dropped her off, she changed into jeans and a short-sleeved sweatshirt. She wanted to spend the day at the piano, planning the lessons, practicing and, if her current mood held, composing.

There had never been enough time for composing on tour, she thought as she tied her hair back. But now she had the summer. Even if ten hours a week would be taken up by lessons, and nearly that many again by planning them, she had plenty of time to indulge in her first love.

Her first love, she repeated with a smile. No, that wasn't composing. That was Brady. He had been her first love. Her first lover. And it was more than probable he would be her last.

He loved her. Or believed he did. He would never have used the words unless he believed it. Nor could she, Vanessa reflected. She had to be sure of what was best for herself, for him, for everyone, before she risked her heart with those three words.

Once she said them, he wouldn't let go again. However much he had mellowed over the years, however responsible he had become, there was still enough of that wild and willful boy in him to have him tossing her over his shoulder and carrying her off. While that fantasy might have its appeal, a daydream appeal, she was too sensible a woman to tolerate it in reality.

The past was done, she thought. Mistakes had been made. She wouldn't risk the future.

She didn't want to think about tomorrow. Not yet. She wanted only to think of, and enjoy, today.

As she started toward the music room, the phone rang. She debated just letting it ring—a habit she'd developed in hotel rooms when she hadn't wanted to be disturbed. On the fifth ring, she gave in and answered.

"Hello."

"Vanessa? Is that you?"

"Yes. Frank?" She recognized the voice of her father's nervous and devoted assistant.

"Yes. It's me—I," he corrected.

Vanessa could all but see him running a soothing hand over the wide bald spot on top of his head. "How are you, Frank?"

"Fine. Fine. Oh—how are you?"

"I'm fine, too." She had to smile. Though she knew her father had tolerated Frank Margoni only because the man would work an eighty-hour week without complaint, Vanessa was fond of him. "How's the new protégé?"

"Protégé—? Oh, you mean Francesco. He's brilliant, really brilliant. Temperamental, of course. Throws things. But then, he's an artist. He's going to be playing at the benefit in Cordina."

"Princess Gabriella's benefit? The Aid to Handicapped Children?"

"Yes."

"I'm sure he'll be wonderful."

"Oh, of course. No doubt. Certainly. But, you see, the princess…she's terribly disappointed that you won't perform. She asked me—" there was an audible gulp "—personally, if I would persuade you to reconsider."

"Frank—"

"You'd stay at the palace, of course. Incredible place."

"Yes, I know. Frank, I haven't decided if I'm going to perform again."

"You know you don't mean that, Vanessa. With your gift—"

"Yes, *my* gift," she said impatiently. "Isn't it about time I realized it is mine?"

He was silent a moment. "I know your father was often insensitive to your personal needs, but that was only because he was so aware of the depth of your talent."

"You don't have to explain him to me, Frank."

"No...no, of course I don't."

She let out a long sigh. It wasn't fair to take out her frustrations on the hapless Frank Margoni, as her father always had. "I understand the position you're in, Frank, but I've already sent my regrets, and a donation, to Princess Gabriella."

"I know. That's why she contacted me. She couldn't get ahold of you. Of course, I'm not officially your manager, but the princess knew our connection, so..."

"If I decide to tour again, Frank, I'll depend on you to manage me."

"I appreciate that, Vanessa." His glum voice brightened perceptibly. "And I realize that you've needed some time for yourself. The last few years—grueling, I know. But this benefit is important." He cleared his throat with three distinct clicks. "And the princess is very stubborn."

Reluctantly Vanessa smiled. "Yes, I know."

"It's only one performance," he continued, sensing a weak spot. "Not even a full concert. You'll have carte blanche on the material. They'd like you to play two pieces, but even one would make such a tremendous difference. Your name on the program would add so much." He paused only long enough to suck in a breath. "It's a very worthy cause."

"When is the benefit?"

"Next month."

She cast her eyes to the ceiling. "Next month. It's practically next month already, Frank."

"The third Saturday in June."

"Three weeks." She let out a long breath. "All right, I'll do it. For you, and for Princess Gabriella."

"Vanessa, I can't tell you how much I—"

"Please don't." She softened the order with a laugh. "It's only one night."

"You can stay in Cordina as long as you like."

"One night," she repeated. "Send me the particulars here. And give my best to Her Highness."

"I will, of course. She'll be thrilled. Everyone will be thrilled. Thank you, Vanessa."

"It's all right, Frank. I'll see you in a few weeks."

She hung up and stood silent and still. Odd, but she didn't feel tensed and keyed up at the thought of a performance. And a huge one, she considered. The theater complex in Cordina was exquisite and enormous.

What would happen if she clutched in the wings this time? She would get through it somehow. She always had. Perhaps it was fate that she had been called now, when she was teetering on some invisible line. To go forward, or backward, or to stay.

She would have to make a decision soon, she thought as she walked to the piano. She prayed it would be the right one.

She was playing when Brady returned. He could hear the music, romantic and unfamiliar, flowing through the open windows. There was the hum of bees in the flowers, the purr of a lawn mower, and the music. The magic of it.

He saw a woman and a young child standing on the side-walk, listening.

She had left the door open for him. He had only to push the screen to be inside. He moved quietly. It seemed he was stepping through the liquid notes.

She didn't see him. Her eyes were half-closed. There was a smile on her face, a secret smile. As if whatever images she held in her mind were pouring out through her fingers and onto the keys.

The music was slow, dreamy, enriched by an underlying passion. He felt his throat tighten.

When she finished, she opened her eyes and looked at him. Somehow she had known he would be there when the last note died away.

"Hello."

He wasn't sure he could speak. He crossed to her and lifted her hands. "There's magic here. It astonishes me."

"Musician's hands," she said. "Yours are magic. They heal."

"There was a woman standing on the sidewalk with her little boy. I saw them when I drove up. She was listening to you play, and there were tears on her cheeks."

"There's no higher compliment. Did you like it?"

"Very much. What was it called?"

"I don't know. It's something I've been working on for a while. It never seemed right until today."

"You wrote it?" He looked at the music on the piano and saw the neatly written notes on the staff paper. "I didn't know you composed."

"I'm hoping to do more of it." She drew him down to sit beside her. "Aren't you going to kiss me hello?"

"At least." His lips were warm and firm on hers. "How long have you been writing?"

"For several years—when I've managed to sneak the time. Between traveling, rehearsals, practice and performances, it hasn't been much."

"But you've never recorded anything of your own."

"None of it's really finished. I—" She stopped, tilted her head. "How do you know?"

"I have everything you've ever recorded." At her smug smile, he continued. "Not that I actually play any of them." He gave an exaggerated yelp when her elbow connected with his ribs. "I suppose that's the sign of a temperamental artist."

"That's *artiste* to you, philistine."

"Why don't you tell this philistine about your composing?"

"What's to tell?"

"Do you like it?"

"I love it. It's what I like best."

He was playing with her fingers. "Then why haven't you finished anything?" He felt the tension the moment it entered her.

"I told you. There hasn't been time. Touring isn't all champagne and caviar, you know."

"Come on." Keeping her hands in his, he pulled her to her feet.

"Where are we going?"

"In here, where there's a comfortable couch. Sit." He eased her down, then put his hands on her shoulders. His eyes were dark and searching on her face. "Talk to me."

"About what?"

"I wanted to wait until you were recovered." He felt her stiffen, and shook his head. "Don't do that. As your friend, as a doctor, and as the man who loves you, I want to know what made you ill. I want to make sure it never happens again."

"You've already said I've recovered."

"Ulcers can reoccur."

"I didn't have an ulcer."

"Can it. You can deny it all you want—it won't change the facts. I want you to tell me what's been going on the last few years."

"I've been touring. Performing." Flustered, she shook her head. "How did we move from composing to all this?"

"Because one leads to the other, Van. Ulcers are often caused by emotion. By frustrations, angers, resentments that are bottled up to fester instead of being aired out."

"I'm not frustrated." She set her chin. "And you, of all people, should know I don't bottle things up. Ask around, Brady. My temper is renowned on three continents."

He nodded, slowly. "I don't doubt it. But I never once remember you arguing with your father."

She fell silent at that. It was nothing more than the truth.

"Did you want to compose, or did you want to perform?"

"It's possible to do both. It's simply a matter of discipline and priorities."

"And what was your priority?"

Uncomfortable, she shifted. "I think it's obvious it was performing."

"You said something to me before. You said you hated it."

"Hated what?"

"You tell me."

She pulled away to rise and pace the room. It hardly mattered now, she told herself. But he was sitting here, watching her, waiting. Past experience told her he would dig and dig until he uncovered whatever feelings she wanted to hide.

"All right. I was never happy performing."

"You didn't want to play?"

"No," she corrected. "I didn't want to perform. I have

to play, just as I have to breathe, but…" She let her words trail off, feeling like an imbecile. "It's stage fright," she snapped. "It's stupid, it's childish, but I've never been able to overcome it."

"It's not stupid or childish." He rose, and would have gone to her, but she was already backing away. "If you hated performing, why did you keep going on? Of course," he said, before she could answer.

"It was important to him." She sat on the arm of a chair, then stood again, unable to settle. "He didn't understand. He'd put his whole life into my career. The idea that I couldn't perform, that it frightened me—"

"That it made you ill."

"I was never ill. I never missed one performance because of health."

"No, you performed despite your health. Damn it, Van, he had no right."

"He was my father. I know he was a difficult man, but I owed him something."

He was a selfish son of a bitch, Brady thought. But he kept his silence. "Did you ever consider therapy?"

Vanessa lifted her hands. "He opposed it. He was very intolerant of weakness. I suppose that was his weakness." She closed her eyes a moment. "You have to understand him, Brady. He was the kind of man who would refuse to believe what was inconvenient for him. And, as far as he was concerned, it just ceased to exist." Like my mother, she thought with a weary sigh. "I could never find the way to make him accept or even understand the degree of the phobia."

"I'd like to understand."

She cupped her hands over her mouth a moment, then let them fall. "Every time I would go to the theater, I would tell myself that this time, this time, it wouldn't happen. This time I wouldn't be afraid. Then I would stand in the wings, shaking and sick and miserable. My skin would be clammy, and the nausea would make me dizzy. Once I started playing, it would ease off. By the end I'd be fine, so I would tell myself that the next time..." She shrugged.

He understood, too well. And he hated the idea of her, of anyone, suffering time after time, year after year. "Did you ever stop to think that he was living his life through you?"

"Yes." Her voice was dull. "He was all I had left. And, right or wrong, I was all he had. The last year, he was so ill, but he never let me stop, never let me care for him. In the end, because he had refused to listen, refused the treatments, he was in monstrous pain. You're a doctor—you know how horrible terminal cancer is. Those last weeks in the hospital were the worst. There was nothing they could do for him that time. So he died a little every day. I went on performing, because he insisted, then flying back to the hospital in Geneva every chance I had. I wasn't there when he died. I was in Madrid. I got a standing ovation."

"Can you blame yourself for that?"

"No. But I can regret." Her eyes were awash with it.

"What do you intend to do now?"

She looked down at her hands, spread her fingers, curled them into her palms. "When I came back here, I was tired. Just worn out, Brady. I needed time—I still do—to understand what I feel, what I want, where I'm going." She stepped toward him and lifted her hands to his face. "I didn't want to become involved with you, because I knew you'd be one more huge complication." Her lip curved a little. "And I was right. But when I woke up this morning in your bed, I was happy. I don't want to lose that."

He took her wrists. "I love you, Vanessa."

"Then let me work through this." She went easily into his arms. "And just be with me."

He pressed a kiss to her hair. "I'm not going anywhere."

Chapter 10

"That was the last patient, Dr. Tucker."

Distracted, Brady looked up from the file on his desk and focused on his nurse. "What?"

"That was the last patient." She was already swinging her purse over her shoulder and thinking about putting her feet up. "Do you want me to lock up?"

"Yeah. Thanks. See you tomorrow." He listened with half an ear to the clink of locks and the rattle of file drawers. The twelve-hour day was almost at an end. The fourth twelve-hour day of the week. Hyattown was a long way from New York, but as far as time served was concerned, Brady had found practicing general medicine in a small town as demanding as being chief resident in a major hospital. Along with the usual stream of patients, hospital rounds and paperwork, an outbreak of chicken pox and strep throat had kept him tied to his stethoscope for over a week.

Half the town was either scratching or croaking, he

thought as he settled down to his paperwork. The waiting room had been packed since the end of the holiday weekend. As the only doctor in residence, he'd been taking office appointments, making house calls, doing rounds. And missing meals, he thought ruefully, wishing they still stocked lollipops, rather than balloons and plastic cars, for their younger patients.

He could get by with frozen microwave meals and coffee for a few days. He could even get by with only patches of sleep. But he couldn't get by without Vanessa. He'd barely seen her since the weekend of the wedding—since the weekend they had spent almost exclusively in bed. He'd been forced to cancel three dates. For some women, he thought, that alone would have been enough to have them stepping nimbly out of a relationship.

Better that she knew up front how bad it could get. Being married to a doctor was being married to inconvenience. Canceled dinners, postponed vacations, interrupted sleep.

Closing the file, he rubbed his tired eyes. She was going to marry him, he determined. He was going to see to that. If he ever wangled an hour free to set the stage and ask her.

He picked up the postcard on the corner of his desk. It had a brilliant view of the sun setting on the water, palm trees and sand—and a quickly scrawled note from his father on the back.

"You'd better be having a good time, Dad," Brady mused as he studied it. "Because when you get back, you're going to pay up."

He wondered if Vanessa would enjoy a tropical honeymoon. Mexico, the Bahamas, Hawaii. Hot, lazy days. Hot, passionate nights. Moving too fast, he reminded himself. You couldn't have a honeymoon until you had a wedding.

And you couldn't have a wedding until you'd convinced your woman she couldn't live without you.

He'd promised himself he would take it slowly with Vanessa. Give her all the romance they'd missed the first time around. Long walks in the moonlight. Champagne dinners. Evening drives and quiet talks. But the old impatience pulled at him. If they were married now, he could drag his weary bones home. She'd be there. Perhaps playing the piano. Or curled up in bed with a book. In the next room, there might be a child sleeping. Or two.

Much too fast, Brady warned himself. But he hadn't known, until he'd seen her again, how much he'd wanted that basic and traditional home. The woman he loved, and the children they made between them. Christmas mornings and Sunday afternoons.

Leaning back, he let his eyes close. He could picture it perfectly. Too perfectly, he admitted. He knew his vision left questions unanswered and problems unresolved. They were no longer children who could live on dreams. But he was too tired to be logical. Too needy to be sensible.

Vanessa stood in the doorway and watched him with a mixture of surprise and awe. This was Brady, she reminded herself. Her Brady. But he looked so different here, so professional, in his white lab coat with the framed diplomas and certificates surrounding him. There were files neatly stacked on his desk, and there was an ophthalmoscope in his pocket.

This wasn't the wild youth hell-bent on giving the world a left jab. This was a settled, responsible man who had hundreds of people depending on him. He had already made his niche.

And where was hers? she wondered. He had made his choices and found his place. She was still floundering. Yet, however much she flailed or stumbled, she was always drawn to him. Always back to him.

With a faint smile on her face, she stepped into the office. "You've got another appointment, Dr. Tucker."

"What?" His eyes snapped open. He stared at her as dream and reality merged. She was standing on the other side of his desk, her hair pulled back, in a breezy cotton blouse and slacks.

"I was going to say code blue, or red alert, one of those things you hear on TV, but I didn't know which would fit." She put the basket she carried on the desk.

"I'd settle for 'Hi.'"

"Hi." With a quick laugh, she looked around the office. "I almost didn't come in," she told him. "When I came to the door, you looked so...intimidating."

"Intimidating?"

"Like a doctor. A real doctor," she said on another laugh. "The kind who uses needles and makes terrifying noncommittal noises and scribbles things on charts."

"Hmm," Brady said. "Ah."

"Exactly."

"I can take off the lab coat."

"No, actually, I think I like it. As long as you promise not to whip out a tongue depressor. I saw your nurse as she was leaving. She said you were through for the day."

"Just." The rest of the paperwork would have to wait. "What's in the basket?"

"Dinner—of sorts. Since you wouldn't make a house call, I decided to see if you could fit me into your office schedule."

"It's an amazing coincidence, but I've just had a cancellation." The fatigue simply drained away as he looked at her. Her mouth was naked, and there was a dusting of freckles across the bridge of her nose. "Why don't you sit down and tell me what the problem is?"

"Well." Vanessa sat in the chair in front of the desk. "You see, doctor, I've been feeling kind of light-headed. And absentminded. I forget what I'm doing in the middle of doing it and catch myself staring off into space."

"Hmmm."

"Then there have been these aches. Here," she said, and put a hand on her heart.

"Ah."

"Like palpitations. And at night…" She caught her lower lip between her teeth. "I've had these dreams."

"Really?" He came around to sit on the corner of the desk. There was her scent, whispery light, to flirt with him. "What kind of dreams?"

"They're personal," she said primly.

"I'm a doctor."

"So you say." She grinned at him. "You haven't even asked me to take off my clothes."

"Good point." Rising, he took her hand. "Come with me."

"Where?"

"Your case warrants a full examination."

"Brady—"

"That's Dr. Brady to you." He hit the lights in examining room 1. "Now about that ache."

She gave him a slow, measured look. "Obviously you've been dipping into the rubbing alcohol."

He merely took her by the hips and boosted her onto the examining table. "Relax, sweetie. They don't call me Dr. Feelgood for nothing." He took out his ophthalmoscope and directed the light into her eyes. "Yes, they're definitely green."

"Well, that's a relief."

"You're telling me." He set the instrument aside. "Okay, lose the blouse and I'll test your reflexes."

"Well..." She ran her tongue over her teeth. "As long as I'm here." She let her fingers wander down the buttons, unfastening slowly. Under it she wore sheer blue silk. "I'm not going to have to wear one of those paper things, am I?"

He had to catch his breath as she peeled off the blouse. "I think we can dispense with that. You look to be in excellent health. In fact, I can say without reservation that you look absolutely perfect."

"But I have this ache." She took his hand and pressed it to her breast. "Right now my heart's racing. Feel it?"

"Yeah." Gently he absorbed the feeling of silk and flesh. Her flesh. "I think it's catching."

"My skin's hot," she murmured. "And my legs are weak."

"Definitely catching." With a fingertip he slid a thin silk strap from her shoulder. "You may just have to be quarantined."

"With you, I hope."

He unhooked her slacks. "That's the idea."

When she toed off her sandals, the other strap slithered down her shoulders. Her voice was husky now, and growing breathless. "Do you have a diagnosis?"

He eased the slacks down her hips. "Sounds like the rocking pneumonia and the boogie-woogie flu."

She'd arched up to help him remove her slacks, and now she just stared. "What?"

"Too much Mozart."

"Oh." She twined her arms around his shoulders. It seemed like years since she'd been able to hold him against her. When his lips found the little hollow near her collarbone, she smiled. "Can you help me, Doctor?"

"I'm about to do my damnedest."

His mouth slid over hers. It was like coming home. Her little sigh merged with his as she leaned into him. Dreamily she changed the angle of the kiss and let his taste pour into her. Whatever illness she had, he was exactly the right medicine.

"I feel better already." She nibbled on his lip. "More."

"Van?"

Her heavy eyes opened. While her fingers combed through his hair, she smiled. The light glowed in her eyes. Again he could see himself there, trapped in the misty green. Not lost this time. Found.

Everything he'd ever wanted, ever needed, ever dreamed of, was right here. He felt the teasing pleasure turn to grinding ache in the flash of an instant. With an oath, he dragged her mouth back to his and feasted.

No patience this time. Though the change surprised her, it didn't frighten her. He was her friend, her lover. Her only. There was a desperation and a fervency that thrilled, that demanded, that possessed. As the twin of his emotions rose in her, she pulled him closer.

More, she thought again, but frantically now. She could never get enough of being wanted this wildly. She dragged at his lab coat, even as her teeth scraped over his lip. Desire pumped through her like a drug and had her yanking at his T-shirt before the coat hit the floor. She wanted the feel of his flesh, the heat of it, under her hands. She wanted the taste of that flesh, the succulence of it, under her lips.

The loving he had shown her until now had been calm and sweet and lovely. This time she craved the fire, the dark, the madness.

Control broken, he pushed her back on the narrow padded table, tearing at the wisp of silk. He could tolerate nothing between them now—only flesh against flesh and heart against heart. She was a wonder of slender limbs and subtle curves, of pale skin and delicate bones. He wanted to taste, to touch, to savor every inch.

But her demands were as great as his. She pulled him to her, sliding agilely over him so that her lips could race from his to his throat, his chest, beyond. Rough and greedy, his hands streaked over her, exploiting everywhere, as her questing mouth drove him mad.

His taste. Hot and dark and male, it made her giddy. His form. Firm and hard and muscled, it made her weak. Already damp, his skin slid under her seeking fingers. And she played him deftly, as she would her most passionate concerto.

She feared her heart would burst from its pounding rhythm. Her head spun with it. Her body trembled. Yet there was a power here. Even through the dizziness she felt it swelling in her. How could she have known she could give so much—and take so much?

His pulse thundered under her fingertips. Between his frenzied murmurs, his breath was ragged. She saw the echo of her own passion in his eyes, tasted it when she crushed her mouth to his. For her, she thought as she let herself drown in the kiss. Only for her.

He grasped her hips, fingers digging in. With each breath he took, her scent slammed into his system, potent as any narcotic. Her hair curtained his face, blocking the light and letting him see only her. The faint smile of knowledge was in her eyes. With her every movement, she enticed.

"For God's sake, Van." Her name was part oath, part prayer. If he didn't have her now, he knew he would die from the need.

She shifted, arching back, as she took him into her. For an instant, time stopped, and with it his breath, his thoughts, his life. He saw only her, her hair streaming back like a wild red river, her body pale and gleaming in the harsh light, her face glowing with the power she had only just discovered.

Then it was all speed and sound as she drove them both.

This was glory. She gave herself to it, her arms reaching up before she lost her hands in her own hair. This was wonder. And delight. No symphony had ever been so rousing. No prelude so passionate. Even as sensation shuddered through her, she begged for more.

There was freedom in the greed. Ecstasy in the knowledge that she could take as much as she wanted. Excitement in understanding that she could give just as generously.

Her heart was roaring in her ears. When she groped for his hands, his fingers clamped on to hers. They held tight as they burst over the peak together.

She slid down to him, boneless, her head spinning and her heart racing still. His skin was damp, as hers was, his body as limp. When she pressed her lips to his throat, she could feel the frantic beating of his pulse.

She had done that, Vanessa realized, still dazed. She had taken control and given them both pleasure and passion. She hadn't even had to think, only to act, only to feel. Sailing on this new self-awareness, she propped herself up on an elbow and smiled down at him.

His eyes were closed, his face so completely relaxed that she knew he was next to sleep. His heartbeat, was settling down to a purr, as was hers. Through the contentment, she felt need bloom anew.

"Doctor," she murmured, nibbling at his ear.

"Hmm."

"I feel a lot better."

"Good." He drew in a deep breath, let it out. He figured

that was the most exercise he would be able to handle for days. "Remember, your health is my business."

"I'm glad to hear that." She ran a fingertip down his chest experimentally. And felt muscles jump. "Because I think I'm going to need more treatments." She trailed the tip of her tongue down his throat. "I still have this ache."

"Take two aspirin and call me in an hour."

She laughed, a low, husky sound that had his blood humming again. "I thought you were dedicated." Slowly, seductively, she roamed his face with kisses. "God, you taste good." She lowered her mouth to his and sunk in.

"Vanessa." He could easily have floated off to sleep with her gentle stroking. But when her hand slid downward, contentment turned into something more demanding. He opened his eyes and saw that she was smiling at him. She was amused, he noted. And—pun intended—completely on top of things. "You're asking for trouble," he told her.

"Yeah." She lowered her head again to nip at his lip. "But am I going to get it?"

He answered the question to their mutual satisfaction.

"Good God," he said when he could breathe again. "I'm going to have this table bronzed."

"I think I'm cured." She pushed the hair from her face as she slid to the floor. "For now."

Groaning a little, he swung his legs off the table. "Wait till you get my bill."

"I'm looking forward to it." She handed him his pants, then slithered into her teddy. She didn't know about him, but she'd never think the same way about examining room 1 again. "And to think I came by to offer you some ham sandwiches."

"Ham?" His fingers paused on the snap of his jeans. "As in food? Like meat and bread?"

"And potato chips."

His mouth was already watering. "Consider yourself paid in full."

She shook back her hair, certain that if she felt any better she'd be breaking the law. "I take it to mean you're hungry."

"I haven't eaten since breakfast. Chicken pox," he explained as she pulled on her blouse. "If someone was to offer me a ham sandwich, I'd kiss her feet."

She wiggled her toes. "I like the sound of that. I'll go get the basket."

"Hold it." He took her arm. "If we stay in this room, my nurse is going to get a shock when she opens up tomorrow."

"Okay." She picked up his T-shirt. "Why don't we take it back to my house?" She rubbed the soft cotton against her cheek before handing it to him. "And eat in bed."

"Good thinking."

An hour later, they were sprawled across Vanessa's bed as Brady poured the last drop from a bottle of chardonnay. Vanessa had scoured the house for candles. Now they were set throughout the room, flickering while Chopin played quietly on the bedside radio.

"That was the best picnic I've had since I was thirteen and raided the Girl Scout overnight jamboree."

She scrounged for the last potato chip, then broke it judiciously in half. "I heard about that." There hadn't been time for Girl Scouts with her training. "You were always rotten."

"Hey, I got to see Betty Jean Baumgartner naked. Well, almost naked," he corrected. "She had on a training bra and panties, but at thirteen that's pretty erotic stuff."

"A rotten creep."

"It was hormones." He sipped his wine. "Lucky for you, I've still got plenty." With a satisfied sigh, he leaned back against the pillow. "Even if they're aging."

Feeling foolish and romantic, she bent over to kiss his knee. "I've missed you, Brady."

He opened his eyes again. "I've missed you, too. I'm sorry this week's been so messed up."

"I understand."

He reached out to twine a lock of her hair around his finger. "I hope you do. Office hours alone doubled this week."

"I know. Chicken pox. Two of my students are down with it. And I heard you delivered a baby—boy, seven pounds six ounces—took out a pair of tonsils... Is it pair or set?" she wondered. "Sewed up a gash in Jack's arm, and splinted a broken finger. All that being above and beyond the day-to-day sniffles, sneezes, aches and exams."

"How do you know?"

"I have my sources." She touched his cheek. "You must be tired."

"I was before I saw you. Anyway, it'll ease off when Dad gets back. Did you get a postcard?"

"Yes, just today." She settled back with her wine. "Palm trees and sand, mariachi players and sunsets. It sounds like they're having a wonderful time."

"I hope so, because I intend to switch places with them when they get back."

"Switch places?"

"I want to go away with you somewhere, Van." He took her hand, kissed it. "Anywhere you want."

"Away?" Her nerves began to jump. "Why?"

"Because I want to be alone with you, completely alone, as we've never had the chance to be."

She had to swallow. "We're alone now."

He set his wine aside, then hers. "Van, I want you to marry me."

She couldn't claim surprise. She had known, once he had used the word *love,* that marriage would follow. Neither did she feel fear, as she'd been certain she would. But she did feel confusion.

They had talked of marriage before, when they'd been so young and marriage had seemed like such a beautiful dream. She knew better now. She knew marriage was work and commitment and a shared vision.

"Brady, I—"

"This isn't the way I planned it," he interrupted. "I'd wanted it to be very traditional—to have the ring and a nicely poetic speech. I don't have a ring, and all I can tell you is that I love you. I always have, I always will."

"Brady." She pressed his hand to her cheek. Nothing he could have said would have been more poetic. "I want to be able to say yes. I didn't realize until just this moment how much I want that."

"Then say it."

Her eyes were wide and wet when they lifted to his. "I can't. It's too soon. No," she said, before he could explode. "I know what you're going to say. We've known each other almost our whole lives. It's true. But in some ways it's just as true that we only met a few weeks ago."

"There was never anyone but you," he said slowly. "Every other woman I got close to was only a substitute. You were a ghost who haunted me everywhere I went, who faded away every time I tried to reach out and touch."

Nothing could have moved her or unnerved her more. "My life's turned upside down since I came back here. I never thought I would see you again—and I thought that if I did it wouldn't matter, that I wouldn't feel. But it does matter, and I do feel, and that only makes it more difficult."

She was saying almost what he wanted to hear. Almost. "Shouldn't that make it easier?"

"No. I wish it did. I can't marry you, Brady, until I look into the mirror and recognize myself."

"I don't know what the hell you're talking about."

"No, you can't." She dragged her hands through her hair. "I barely do myself. All I know is that I can't give you what you want. I may never be able to."

"We're good together, Van." He had to fight to keep from holding too tight. "Damn it, you know that."

"Yes." She was hurting him. She could hardly bear it. "Brady, there are too many things I don't understand about myself. Too many questions I don't have the answers to. Please, I can't talk about marriage, about lifetimes, until I do."

"My feelings aren't going to change."

"I hope not."

He reeled himself back, slowly. "You're not going to get away from me this time, Van. If you cut and run, I'll come after you. If you try to sneak off, I'll be right there."

Pride rose instantly to wage war with regret. "You make that sound like a threat."

"It is."

"I don't like threats, Brady." She tossed her hair back in a gesture as much challenge as annoyance. "You should remember I don't tolerate them."

"And you should remember I make good on them." Very deliberately, he took her by the shoulders and pulled her against him. "You belong to me, Vanessa. Sooner or later you're going to get that through your head."

The thrill raced up her spine, as it always did when she

saw that dangerous light in his eyes. But her chin came up. "I belong to myself first, Brady. Or I intend to. You'll have to get that through your head. Then, maybe, we'll have something."

"We have something now." When his mouth came to hers, she tasted the anger, the frustration, and the need. "You can't deny it."

"Then let it be enough." Her eyes were as dark and intent as his. "I'm here, with you. While I am, there's nothing and no one else." Her arms went around him, enfolding. "Let it be enough."

But it wasn't enough. Even as he rolled onto her, as his mouth fastened hungrily on hers, as his blood fired, he knew it wasn't enough.

In the morning, when she woke—alone, with his scent on sheets that were already growing cold—she was afraid it would never be.

Chapter 11

Nice, very nice, Vanessa thought as Annie worked her way through one of her beloved Madonna's compositions. She had to admit it was a catchy tune, bold and sly by turns. She'd had to simplify it a bit for Annie's inexperienced fingers, but the heart was still there. And that was what counted.

Perhaps the improvement in Annie's technique wasn't radical, but there was improvement. And, as far as enthusiasm went, Annie Crampton was her prize student.

Her own attitude had changed, as well Vanessa admitted. She hadn't known she would enjoy quite so much influencing young hearts and minds with music. She was making a difference here—perhaps only a small one so far, but a difference.

Then there was the added benefit of the lessons helping her keep her mind off Brady. At least for an hour or two every day.

"Well done, Annie."

"I played it all the way through." The wonder on Annie's face was worth the few sour notes she had hit. "I can do it again."

"Next week." Vanessa picked up Annie's book just as she heard the front screen slam. "I want you to work on this next lesson. Hi, Joanie."

"I heard the music." She shifted Lara to her other hip. "Annie Crampton, was that you playing?"

Braces flashed. "I played it all the way through. Miss Sexton said I did a good job."

"And you did. I'm impressed—especially because she could never teach me anything beyond 'Heart and Soul.'"

Vanessa placed a hand on Annie's head. "Mrs. Knight didn't practice."

"I do. And my mom says I've learned more in three weeks than I did in three months up at the music store." She flashed a final grin as she gathered up her books. "And it's more fun, too. See you next week, Miss Sexton."

"I really was impressed," Joanie said as Annie slammed out the front door.

"She has good hands." She held out her own for the baby. "Hello, Lara."

"Maybe you could give her lessons one day."

"Maybe." She cuddled the baby.

"So, other than Annie, how are the lessons going? You're up to, what—?"

"Twelve students. And that's my absolute limit." She pressed her nose against Lara's and had the baby giggling. "Absolutely. But, all in all, they're going fairly well. I've learned to check students' hands before they sit at the piano. I never did figure out what Scott Snooks smeared on the keys."

"What did it look like?"

"Green." She laughed and bounced Lara. "Now we have an inspection before each lesson."

"If you can teach Scott Snooks anything other than murder and mayhem, you're a miracle worker."

"That's the challenge." And she was beginning to enjoy it. "If you've got time, I can defrost a can of lemonade."

"Miss Domesticity." Joanie grinned. "No, really, I only have a couple of minutes. Don't you have another student coming?"

"Saved by the chicken pox." With Lara in tow, Vanessa moved to the living room. "What's your hurry?"

"I just stopped by to see if you needed anything in town. Dad and Loretta will be back in a few hours, and I want to see them. Meanwhile, I've got three dozen errands to run. Hardware store, grocery store, the lumber place. I still can't believe Jack sweet-talked me into that one." She plopped into a chair. "I've spent most of the morning picking up behind Lara the Wrecking Crew as she single-handedly totaled the house. And to think I was thrilled when she took her first step."

"I could use some sheet music." Vanessa gently removed Lara's grasping fingers from her necklace. "I tell you what, I'll write down the titles for you, and in exchange I'll babysit."

Joanie shook her head and rubbed a hand over her ear. "Excuse me, did you say babysit?"

"Yes. As in you-can-leave-Lara-with-me-for-a-couple-of-hours."

"A couple of hours," she repeated slowly. "Do you mean I can go to the mall, alone, by myself?"

"Well, if you'd rather not—"

Joanie let out a whoop as she jumped up to kiss Vanessa and Lara in turn. "Lara, baby, I love you. Goodbye."

"Joanie, wait." Laughing, Vanessa sprang up to grab her arm. "I haven't written down the titles for the sheet music."

"Oh, yeah. Right. I guess I got a little too excited." She blew her hair out of her eyes. "I haven't been shopping by myself in... I forget." Her smile faded to a look of dismay. "I'm a terrible mother. I was happy about leaving her behind. No, not happy. Thrilled. Ecstatic. Delirious. I'm a terrible mother."

"No, you're a crazy person, but you're a wonderful mother."

Joanie steadied herself. "You're right, it was just the thrill of going to the hardware store without a stroller and a diaper bag that went to my head. Are you sure you can handle it?"

"We'll have a great time."

"Of course you will." Keen-eyed, she surveyed the living room. "Maybe you should move anything important up a couple of feet. And nail it down."

"We'll be fine." She set Lara on the floor and handed her a fashion magazine to peruse—and tear up. "See?"

"Okay... I nursed her before I left home, and there's an emergency bottle of apple juice in her diaper bag. Can you change a diaper?"

"I've seen it done before. How hard can it be?"

"Well, if you're sure you don't have anything you have to do."

"My evening is free. When the newlyweds get home, I only have to walk a half a block to see them."

"I guess Brady will be coming by."

"I don't know."

Joanie kept her eye on Lara as the baby pushed herself

up and toddled to the coffee table. "Then it hasn't been my imagination."

"What?"

"That there's been a lot of tension between you two the last week or so."

"You're stalling, Joanie."

"Maybe—but I am interested. The couple of times I've seen Brady recently, he's been either snarling or distracted. I don't want you to tell me it was wishful thinking when I hoped you two would get back together."

"He asked me to marry him."

"He— Wow! Oh, that's wonderful! That's terrific!" As Joanie launched herself into Vanessa's arms, Lara began to bang on the table and squeal. "See, even Lara's excited."

"I said no."

"What?" Slowly, Joanie stepped back. "You said no?"

She turned away from the stunned disappointment in Joanie's face. "It's too soon for all of this, Joanie. I've only been back a few weeks, and so much has happened. My mother, your father..." She walked over to move a vase out of Lara's reach. "When I got here, I wasn't even sure how long I would stay, a couple of weeks, maybe a month. I've been considering a tour next spring."

"But that doesn't mean you can't have a personal life. If you want one."

"I don't know what I want." Feeling helpless, she looked back at Joanie. "Marriage is... I don't even know what it means, so how can I consider marrying Brady?"

"But you love him."

"Yes, I think I do." She lifted her hands, fingers spread. "I don't want to make the same mistake my parents did. I need to be sure we both want the same things."

"What do you want?"

"I'm still figuring it out."

"You'd better figure fast. If I know my brother, he won't give you a lot of time."

"I'll take what I need this time." Before Joanie could argue, she shook her head. "You'd better go if you want to get back before my mother and Ham come home."

"Oh, you're right. I'll go get the diaper bag." She paused at the door. "I know we're already stepsisters, but I'm still holding out for sisters-in-law."

Brady knew he was asking for more grief when he started up the walk to Vanessa's house. During the past week, he had tried to keep his distance. When the woman you loved refused to marry you, it didn't do much for your ego.

He wanted to believe she was just being stubborn, and that backing off and playing it light would bring her around. But he was afraid it went much deeper than that. She'd taken a stand. He could walk away, or he could pound down her door. It wouldn't make any difference.

Either way, he needed to see her.

He knocked on the wooden frame of the screen but got no answer. Hardly surprising, he thought, as the banging and crashing from inside would have drowned out any other sound. Maybe she was in a temper, he thought hopefully. Enraged with herself for turning her back on her chance at happiness.

The image appealed to him. He was almost whistling when he opened the screen and walked down the hall.

Whatever he'd been expecting, it hadn't been his niece gleefully banging pots and pans together on the floor while Vanessa, dusted with flour, stood at the counter. Spotting him, Lara hoisted a stainless steel lid and brought it down with a satisfied bang.

"Hi."

With a hand full of celery, Vanessa turned. She expected her heart to do a quick flip-flop when she saw him. It always did. But she didn't smile. Neither did he.

"Oh. I didn't hear you come in."

"I'm not surprised." He reached down to pick up Lara and give her a quick swing. "What are you doing?"

"Babysitting." She rubbed more flour on her nose. "Joanie had to go into town, so I volunteered to watch Lara for a couple of hours."

"She's a handful, isn't she?"

Vanessa blew out a weary breath. She couldn't bear to think about the mess they had left in the living room. "She likes it in here."

He set the baby down, gave her padded bottom a light pat and sent her off to play with a small tower of canned goods. "Wait until she figures out how to rip the labels off. Got anything to drink?"

"Lara's got a bottle of apple juice."

"I wouldn't want to deprive her."

"There's a can of lemonade in the freezer." She went back to chopping celery. "If you want it, you'll have to make it yourself. My hands are full."

"So I see." He opened the freezer. "What are you making?"

"A mess." She brought the knife down with a thunk. "I thought since my mother and Ham were due back soon it would be nice to have a casserole or something. Joanie's already done so much, I wanted to try to—" She set the knife down in disgust. "I'm no good at this. I'm just no good at it. I've never cooked a meal in my life." She whirled as Brady came to the sink to run cold water into a pitcher. "I'm a grown woman, and if it wasn't for room service and pre-packaged meals I'd starve to death."

"You make a great ham sandwich."

"I'm not joking, Brady."

With a wooden spoon, he began to stir the lemonade. "Maybe you should be."

"I came in here thinking I'd try to put myself into this little fantasy. What if I were a doctor's wife?"

He stopped stirring to look at her. "What if you were?"

"What if he were coming home after taking appointments and doing hospital rounds all day? Wouldn't I want to fix him a meal, something we could sit down to together, something we could talk over? Isn't that something he would want? Expect?"

"Why don't you ask him?"

"Damn it, Brady, don't you see? I couldn't make it work."

"All I see is that you're having trouble putting—" He leaned forward to look at the disarray on the counter. "What is this?"

Her mouth moved into a pout. "It's supposed to be a tuna casserole."

"You're having trouble putting a tuna casserole together. And, personally, I hope you never learn how to do it."

"That's not the point."

Struck by tenderness, he brushed at a streak of flour on her cheek. "What is the point?"

"It's a little thing, maybe even a stupid thing. But if I can't even do this—" she shoved and sent an onion scampering down the counter "—how can I work out the bigger ones?"

"Do you think I want to marry you so that I can have a hot meal every night?"

"No. Do you think I want to marry you and feel inept and useless?"

Truly exasperated, he gestured toward the counter. "Because you don't know what to do with a can of tuna?"

"Because I don't know how to be a wife." When her voice rose, she struggled to calm it. Perhaps Lara was too young, and too interested in her pans and cans, to detect an argument, but Vanessa had lived through too many of her own. "And, as much as I care for you, I don't know if I want to be. There's one thing I do well, Brady, and that's my music."

"No one's asking you to give that up, Van."

"And when I go on tour? When I'm gone weeks at a time, when I have to devote endless hours to rehearsals and practicing? What kind of marriage would we have, Brady, in between performances?"

"I don't know." He looked down at his niece, who was contentedly placing cans inside of pots. "I didn't know you were seriously considering going on tour again."

"I have to consider it. It's been a part of my life for too long not to." Calmer now, she went back to dicing vegetables. "I'm a musician, Brady, the same way you're a doctor. What I do doesn't save lives, but it does enrich them."

He pushed an impatient hand through his dark hair. He was in the business of soothing doubts and fears, as much as he was in the business of healing bodies. Why couldn't he soothe Vanessa's?

"I know what you do is important, Van. I admire it. I admire you. What I don't see is why your talent would have to be an obstacle to our being together."

"It's just one of them," she murmured.

He took her arm, slowly turning her to face him. "I want to marry you. I want to have children with you and make a home for them. We can do that here, where we both belong, if you just trust me."

"I need to trust myself first." She took a bracing breath. "I leave for Cordina next week."

His hand slid away from her arm. "Cordina?"

"Princess Gabriella's annual benefit."

"I've heard of it."

"I've agreed to give a performance."

"I see." Because he needed to do something, he opened a cupboard and took out a glass. "And when did you agree?"

"I signed almost two weeks ago."

His fingers tensed on the glass. "And didn't mention it."

"No, I didn't mention it." She wiped her hands on her thighs. "With everything that was happening between us, I wasn't sure how you would react."

"Were you going to wait until you were leaving for the airport, or were you just going to send me a postcard when you got there? Damn it, Van." He barely controlled the urge to smash the glass against the wall. "What the hell kind of games have you been playing with me? Was all this just killing time, lighting up an old flame?"

She went pale, but her voice was strong. "You know better."

"All I know is that you're leaving."

"It's only a single performance, a few days."

"And then?"

She turned to look out the window. "I don't know. Frank, my manager, is anxious to put a tour together. That's in addition to some special performances I've been asked to do."

"In addition," he repeated. "You came here with an ulcer because you could barely make yourself go out onstage, because you pushed yourself too far too often. And you're already talking about going back and doing it again."

"It's something I have to work out for myself."

"Your father—"

"Is dead," she cut in. "He can't influence me to perform. I hope you won't try to influence me not to." She took a calming breath, but it didn't help. "I don't believe I pushed myself too far. I did what I needed to do. All I want is the chance to decide what that is."

As the war inside him continued, Brady wondered if there could be a victor. Or if there would only be victims. "You've been thinking about going back, starting with Cordina, but you never talked to me about it."

"No. However selfish it sounds, Brady, this is something I needed to decide for myself. I realize it's unfair for me to ask you to wait. So I won't." She closed her eyes tight, then opened them again. "Whatever happens, I want you to know that the last few weeks, with you, have meant everything to me."

"The hell with that." It was too much like a goodbye. He yanked her against him. "You can go to Cordina, you can go anywhere, but you won't forget me. You won't forget this."

There was fury in the kiss. And desperation. She fought neither. How could she when their mirror images raged within her? She thought that if her life was to end that instant, she would have known nothing but this wild wanting.

"Brady." She brought her hands to his face. When her brow rested against his, she drew a deep breath. "There has to be more than this. For both of us."

"There is more." With his thumbs under her jaw, he tilted her head back. "You know there is."

"I made a promise to myself today. That I would take the time to think over my life, every year of it, every moment that I remembered that seemed important. And when I had done that, I would make the right decision. No more hesitations or excuses or doubts. But for now you have to let me go."

"I let you go once before." Before she could shake her head, he tightened his grip. "You listen to me. If you leave, like this, I won't spend the rest of my life wishing for you. I'll be damned if you'll break my heart a second time."

As they stood close, their eyes locked on each other's, Joanie strolled into the room.

"Well, some babysitters." With a laugh, she plucked Lara up and hugged her. "I can't believe I actually missed this monster. Sorry it took so long." She smiled at Lara and kept babbling as she fought her way through the layers of tension. "There was a line a mile long at the grocery." She glanced down at the scattered pots and canned goods. "It looks like she kept you busy."

"She was fine," Vanessa managed. "She ate about half a box of crackers."

"I thought she'd gained a couple pounds. Hi, Brady. Good timing." His one-word comment had her rolling her eyes. "I meant I'm glad you're here. Look who I ran into outside." She turned just as Ham and Loretta walked in, arm in arm. "Don't they look great?" Joanie wanted to know. "So tanned. I know tans aren't supposed to be healthy, but they look so good."

"Welcome back." Vanessa smiled, but stayed where she was. "Did you have a good time?"

"It was wonderful." Loretta set a huge straw bag down on the table. There was warm color on her cheeks, on her bare arms. And, Vanessa noted, that same quiet happiness in her eyes. "It has to be the most beautiful place on earth, all that white sand and clear water. We even went snorkeling."

"Never seen so many fish," Ham said as he dropped yet another straw bag on the table.

"Ha!" Loretta gave him a telling look. "He was looking at all those pretty legs under water. Some of those women down there wear next to nothing." Then she grinned. "The men, too. I stopped looking the other way after the first day or two."

"Hour or two," Ham corrected.

She only laughed and dug into her bag. "Look here, Lara. We brought you a puppet." She dangled the colorful dancer from its strings.

"Among a few dozen other things," Ham put in. "Wait until you see the pictures. I even rented one of those underwater cameras and got shots of the, ah, fish."

"It's going to take us weeks to unpack it all. I can't even think about it." With a sigh, Loretta sat down at the table. "Oh, and the silver jewelry. I suppose I went a little wild with it."

"Very wild," Ham added with a wink.

"I want you both to pick out the pieces you like best," she said to Vanessa and Joanie. "Once we find them. Brady, is that lemonade?"

"Right the first time." He poured her a glass. "Welcome home."

"Wait until you see your sombrero."

"My sombrero?"

"It's red and silver—about ten feet across." She grinned over at Ham. "I couldn't talk him out of it. Oh, it's good to be home." She glanced at the counter. "What's all this?"

"I was…" Vanessa sent a helpless look at the mess she'd made. "I was going to try to fix some dinner. I… I thought you might not want to fuss with cooking your first night back."

"Good old American food." Ham took the puppet to dangle it for the giggling Lara. "Nothing would hit the spot better right now."

"I haven't exactly—"

Catching her drift, Joanie moved over to the counter. "Looks like you were just getting started. Why don't I give you a hand?"

Vanessa stepped back, bumped into Brady, then moved away again. "I'll be back in a minute."

She hurried out and took the stairs at a dash. In her room, she sat on the bed and wondered if she was losing her mind. Surely it was a close thing when a tuna casserole nearly brought her to tears.

"Van." Loretta stood with her hand on the knob. "May I come in a minute?"

"I was coming back down. I just—" She started to rise, then sat again. "I'm sorry. I don't want to spoil your homecoming."

"You haven't. You couldn't." After a moment, she took a chance. Closing the door, she walked over to sit on the bed beside her daughter. "I could tell you were upset when we came in. I thought it was just because…well, because of me."

"No. No, not entirely."

"Would you like to talk about it?"

She hesitated so long that Loretta was afraid she wouldn't speak at all.

"It's Brady. No, it's me," Vanessa corrected, impatient with herself. "He wants me to marry him, and I can't. There are so many reasons, and he can't understand. *Won't* understand. I can't cook a meal or do laundry or any of the things that Joanie just breezes right through."

"Joanie's a wonderful woman," Loretta said carefully. "But she's different from you."

"I'm the one who's different, from Joanie, from you, from everyone."

Lightly, afraid to go too far, Loretta touched her hair. "It's not a crime or an abnormality not to know how to cook."

"I know." But that only made her feel more foolish. "It's simply that I wanted to feel self-sufficient and ended up feeling inadequate."

"I never taught you how to cook, or how to run a household. Part of that was because you were so involved with your music, and there wasn't really time. But another reason, maybe the true one, is that I didn't want to. I wanted to have that all to myself. The house, the running of it, was all I really had to fulfill me." She gave a little sigh as she touched Vanessa's rigid arm. "But we're not really talking about casseroles and laundry, are we?"

"No. I feel pressured, by what Brady wants. Maybe by who he wants. Marriage, it sounds so lovely. But—"

"But you grew up in a household where it wasn't." With a nod, Loretta took Vanessa's hand. "It's funny how blind we can be. All the time you were growing up, I never thought what was going on between your father and me affected you. And of course it did."

"It was your life."

"It was our lives," Loretta told her. "Van, while we were away, Ham and I talked about all of this. He wanted me to explain everything to you. I didn't agree with him until right now."

"Everyone's downstairs."

"There have been enough excuses." She couldn't sit, so she walked over to the window. The marigolds were blooming, a brilliant orange and yellow against the smug-faced pansies.

"I was very young when I married your father. Eighteen." She gave a little shake of her head. "Lord, it seems like a lifetime ago. And certainly like I was another person. How he swept me off my feet! He was almost thirty then, and had just come back after being in Paris, London, New York, all those exciting places."

"His career had floundered," Vanessa said quietly. "He'd never talk about it, but I've read—and, of course, there were others who loved to talk about his failures."

"He was a brilliant musician. No one could take that away from him." Loretta turned. There was a sadness in her eyes now, lingering. "But he took it away from himself. When his career didn't reach the potential he expected, he turned his back on it. When he came back home, he was troubled, moody, impatient."

She took a moment to gather her courage, hoping she was doing the right thing. "I was a very simple girl, Van. I had led a very simple life. Perhaps that was what appealed to him at first. His sophistication—his, well, worldliness— appealed to me. Dazzled me. We made a mistake—as much mine as his. I was overwhelmed by him, flattered, infatuated. And I got pregnant."

Shock robbed Vanessa of speech as she stared at her mother. With an effort, she rose. "Me? You married because of me?"

"We married because we looked at each other and saw only what we wanted to see. You were the result of that. I want you to know that when you were conceived, you were conceived in what we both desperately believed was love. Maybe, because we did believe it, it was love. It was certainly affection and caring and need."

"You were pregnant," Vanessa said quietly. "You didn't have a choice."

"There is always a choice." Loretta stepped forward, drawing Vanessa's gaze to hers. "You were not a mistake or an inconvenience or an excuse. You were the best parts of us, and we both knew it. There were no scenes or recriminations. I was thrilled to be carrying his child, and he was just as happy. The first year we were married, it was good. In many ways, it was even beautiful."

"I don't know what to say. I don't know what to feel."

"You were the best thing that ever happened to me, or to your father. The tragedy was that we were the worst thing that ever happened to each other. You weren't responsible for that. We were. Whatever happened afterward, having you made all the difference."

"What did happen?"

"My parents died, and we moved into this house. The house I had grown up in, the house that belonged to me. I didn't understand then how bitterly he resented that. I'm not sure he did, either. You were three then. Your father was restless. He resented being here, and couldn't bring himself to face the possibility of failure if he tried to pick up his career again. He began to teach you, and almost overnight it seemed that all of the passion, all of the energy he had had, went into making you into the musician, the performer, the star he felt he would never be again."

Blindly she turned to the window again. "I never stopped him. I never tried. You seemed so happy at the piano. The more promise you showed the more bitter he became. Not toward you, never toward you. But toward the situation, and, of course, toward me. And I toward him. You were the one good thing we had ever done together, the one thing we could both love completely. But it wasn't enough to make us love each other. Can you understand that?"

"Why did you stay together?"

"I'm not really sure. Habit. Fear. The small hope that somehow we would find out we really did love each other. There were too many fights. Oh, I know how they used to upset you. When you were older, a teenager, you used to run from the house just to get away from the arguing. We failed you, Van. Both of us. And, though I know he did things that were selfish, even unforgivable, I failed you more, because I closed my eyes to them. Instead of making things right, I looked for an escape. And I found it with another man."

She found the courage to face her daughter again. "There is no excuse. Your father and I were no longer intimate, were barely even civil, but there were other alternatives open to me. I had thought about divorce, but that takes courage, and I was a coward. Suddenly there was someone who was kind to me, someone who found me attractive and desirable. Because it was forbidden, because it was wrong, it was exciting."

Vanessa felt the tears burn the back of her eyes. She had to know, to understand. "You were lonely."

"Oh, God, yes." Loretta's voice was choked. She pressed her lips together. "It's no excuse—"

"I don't want excuses. I want to know how you felt."

"Lost," she whispered. "Empty. I felt as though my life were over. I wanted someone to need me again, to hold me. To say pretty things to me, even if they were lies." She shook her head, and when she spoke again her voice was stronger. "It was wrong, Vanessa, as wrong as it was for your father and I to rush together without looking closely." She came back to the bed, took Vanessa's hand. "I want it to be different for you. It will be different. Holding back from something that's right for you is just as foolish as rushing into something that's wrong."

"And how do I know the difference?"

"You will." She smiled a little. "It's taken me most of my life to understand that. With Ham, I knew."

"It wasn't." She was afraid to ask. "It wasn't Ham that you... He wasn't the one."

"All those years ago? Oh, no. He would never have betrayed Emily. He loved her. It was someone else. He wasn't in town long, only a few months. I suppose that made it easier for me somehow. He was a stranger, someone who didn't know me, didn't care. When I broke it off, he moved on."

"You broke it off? Why?"

Of all the things that had gone before, Loretta knew this would be the most difficult. "It was the night of your prom. I'd been upstairs with you. Remember, you were so upset?"

"He had Brady arrested."

"I know." She tightened her grip on Vanessa's hand. "I swear to you, I didn't know it then. I finally left you alone because, well, you needed to be alone. I was thinking about how I was going to give Brady Tucker a piece of my mind when I got ahold of him. I was still upset when your father came home. But he was livid, absolutely livid. That's when it all came out. He was furious because the sheriff had let Brady go, because Ham had come in and raised holy hell."

She let Vanessa's hands go to press her fingers to her eyes. "I was appalled. He'd never approved of Brady—I knew that. But he wouldn't have approved of anyone who interfered with his plans for you. Yet this—this was so far beyond anything I could imagine. The Tuckers were our friends, and anyone with eyes could see that you and Brady were in love. I admit I had worried about whether you would make love, but we'd talked about it, and you'd seemed very sensible. In any case, your father was raging, and I was so angry, so incensed by his insensitivity, that I lost control. I told him what I had been trying to hide for several weeks. I was pregnant."

"Pregnant," Vanessa repeated. "You— Oh, God."

Loretta sprang up to pace the room. "I thought he would go wild, but instead he was calm. Deadly calm." There was no use telling her daughter what names he had called her in that soft, controlled voice. "He said that there was no question about our remaining together. He would file for divorce. And would take you. The more I shouted, begged, threatened, the calmer he became. He would take you because he was the one who would give you the proper care. I was—well, it was obvious what I was. He already had tickets for Paris. Two tickets. I hadn't known about it, but he had been planning to take you away in any case. I was to say nothing, do nothing to stop him, or he would drag me through a custody suit that he would win when it came out that I was carrying another man's bastard." She began to weep then, silently. "If I didn't agree, he would wait until the child was born and file charges against me as an unfit mother. He swore he would make it his life's work to take that child, as well. And I would have nothing."

"But you...he couldn't..."

"I had barely been out of this county, much less the state. I didn't know what he could do. All I knew was that I was going to lose one child, and perhaps two. You were going to go to Paris, see all those wonderful things, play on all those fabulous stages. You would be someone, have something." Her cheeks drenched, she turned back. "As God is my witness, Vanessa, I don't know if I agreed because I thought it was what you would want, or because I was afraid to do anything else."

"It doesn't matter." She rose and went to her mother. "It doesn't matter anymore."

"I knew you would hate me—"

"No, I don't." She put her arms around Loretta and brought her close. "I couldn't. The baby," she murmured. "Will you tell me what you did?"

Grief, fresh and vital, swam through her. "I miscarried,

just shy of three months. I lost both of you, you see. I never had all those babies I'd once dreamed of."

"Oh, Mom." Vanessa rocked as she let her own tears fall. "I'm sorry. I'm so sorry. It must have been terrible for you. Terribly hard."

With her cheek against Vanessa's, she held tight. "There wasn't a day that went by that I didn't think of you, that I didn't miss you. If I had it to do over—"

But Vanessa shook her head. "No, we can't take the past back. We'll start right now."

Chapter 12

She sat in her dressing room, surrounded by flowers, the scent and the color of them. She barely noticed them. She'd hoped, perhaps foolishly, that one of the luscious bouquets, one of the elegant arrangements, had been sent by Brady.

But she had known better.

He had not come to see her off at the airport. He had not called to wish her luck, or to tell her he would miss her while she was gone. Not his style, Vanessa thought as she studied her reflection in the mirror. It never had been. When Brady Tucker was angry, he was angry. He made no polite, civilized overtures. He just stayed mad.

He had the right, she admitted. The perfect right.

She had left him, after all. She had gone to him, given herself to him, made love to him with all the passion and promise a woman could bring to a man. But she had held back the words. And, by doing so, she had held back herself.

Because she was afraid, she thought now. Of making

that dreadful, life-consuming mistake. He would never understand that her caution was as much for him as it was for herself.

She understood now, after listening to her mother. Mistakes could be made for the best of reasons, or the worst of them. It was too late to ask her father, to try to understand his feelings, his reasons.

She only hoped it wasn't too late for herself.

Where were they now, those children who had loved so fiercely and so unwisely? Brady had his life, his skill, and his answers. His family, his friends, his home. From the rash, angry boy he had been had grown a man of integrity and purpose.

And she? Vanessa stared down at her hands, the long, gifted fingers spread. She had her music. It was all she had ever really had that belonged only to her.

Yes, she understood now, perhaps more than she wanted to, her mother's failings, her father's mistakes. They had, in their separate ways, loved her. But that love hadn't made them a family. Nor had it made any of the three of them happy.

So while Brady was setting down his roots in the fertile soil of the town where they had both been young, she was alone in a dressing room filled with flowers, waiting to step onto another stage.

At the knock on her door, she watched the reflection in the dressing room mirror smile. The show started long before the key light clicked on.

"Entrez."

"Vanessa." The Princess Gabriella, stunning in blue silk, swept inside.

"Your Highness." Before she could rise and make her

curtsy, Gabriella was waving her to her seat in a gesture that was somehow imperious and friendly all at once.

"Please, don't get up. I hope I'm not disturbing you."

"Of course not. May I get you some wine?"

"If you're having some." Though her feet ached after a backbreaking day on her feet, she only sighed a little as she took a chair. She had been born royal, and royalty was taught not to complain. "It's been so hectic today, I haven't had a chance to see you, make certain you've been comfortable."

"No one could be uncomfortable in the palace, Your Highness."

"Gabriella, please." She accepted the glass of wine. "We're alone." She gave brief consideration to slipping out of her shoes, but thought better of it. "I wanted to thank you again for agreeing to play tonight. It's so important."

"It's always a pleasure to play in Cordina." The lights around the mirror sent the dozens of bugle beads on Vanessa's white dress dancing. "I'm honored that you wanted to include me."

Gabriella gave a quick laugh before she sipped. "You're annoyed that I bothered you while you were on vacation." She tossed back her fall of red-gold hair. "And I don't blame you. But for this, I've learned to be rude—and ruthless."

Vanessa had to smile. Royalty or not, the Princess Gabriella was easy to be with. "Honored and annoyed, then. I hope tonight's benefit is a tremendous success."

"It will be." She refused to accept less. "Eve— You know my sister-in-law?"

"Yes, I've met Her Highness several times."

"She's American—and therefore pushy. She's been a tremendous help to me."

"Your husband, he is also American?"

Gabriella's topaz eyes lit. "Yes. Reeve is also pushy. This

year we involved our children quite a bit, so it's been even more of a circus than usual. My brother, Alexander, was away for a few weeks, but he returned in time to be put to use."

"You are ruthless with your family, Gabriella."

"It's best to be ruthless with those you love." She saw something, some cloud, come and go in Vanessa's eyes. She would get to that. "Hannah apologizes for not coming backstage before your performance. Bennett is fussing over her."

"Your younger brother is entitled to fuss when his wife is on the verge of delivering their child."

"Hannah was interested in you, Vanessa." Gabriella couldn't resist a smile. "As your name was linked with Bennett's before his marriage."

Along with half the female population of the free world, Vanessa thought, but she kept her smile bland. "His Highness was the most charming of escorts."

"He was a scoundrel."

"Tamed by the lovely Lady Hannah."

"Not tamed, but perhaps restrained." The princess set her glass aside. "I was sorry when your manager informed us that you wouldn't spend more than another day in Cordina. It's been so long since you visited us."

"There is no place I've felt more welcome." She toyed with the petals of a pure white rose. "I remember the last time I was here, the lovely day I spent at your farm, with your family."

"We would love to have you to ourselves again, whenever your schedule permits." Compassionate by nature, she reached out a hand. "You are well?"

"Yes, thank you. I'm quite well."

"You look lovely, Vanessa, perhaps more so because

there's such sadness in your eyes. I understand the look. It faced me in the mirror once, not so many years ago. Men put it there. It's one of their finest skills." Her fingers linked with Vanessa's. "Can I help you?"

"I don't know." She looked down at their joined hands, then up into Gabriella's soft, patient eyes. "Gabriella, may I ask you, what's the most important thing in your life?"

"My family."

"Yes." She smiled. "You had such a romantic story. How you met and fell in love with your husband."

"It becomes more romantic as time passes, and less traumatic."

"He's an American, a former policeman?"

"Of sorts."

"If you had had to give up your position, your, well, birthright, to have married him, would you have done so?"

"Yes. But with great pain. Does this man ask you to give up something that's so much a part of you?"

"No, he doesn't ask me to give up anything. And yet he asks for everything."

Gabriella smiled again. "It is another skill they have."

"I've learned things about myself, about my background, my family, that are very difficult to accept. I'm not sure if I give this man what he wants, for now, that I won't be cheating him and myself in the bargain."

Gabriella was silent a moment. "You know my story, it has been well documented. After I had been kidnapped, and my memory was gone, I looked into my father's face and didn't know him. Into my brothers' eyes and saw the eyes of strangers. However much this hurt me, it hurt them only more. But I had to find myself, discover myself in the most basic of ways. It's very frightening, very frustrating. I'm not a patient or a temperate person."

Vanessa managed another smile. "I've heard rumors."

With a laugh, Gabriella picked up her wine and sipped again. "At last I recognized myself. At last I looked at my family and knew them. But differently," she said, gesturing. "It's not easy to explain. But when I knew them again, when I loved them again, it was with a different heart. Whatever flaws they had, whatever mistakes they had made, however they had wounded me in the past, or I them, didn't matter any longer."

"You're saying you forgot the past."

She gave a quick shake of her head, and her diamonds sizzled. "The past wasn't forgotten. It can't be. But I could see it through different eyes. Falling in love was not so difficult after being reborn."

"Your husband is a fortunate man."

"Yes. I remind him often." She rose. "I'd better leave you to prepare."

"Thank you."

Gabriella paused at the door. "Perhaps on my next trip to America you will invite me to spend a day in your home."

"With the greatest pleasure."

"And I'll meet this man."

"Yes." Vanessa's laugh was quick and easy. "I think you will."

When the door closed, she sat again. Very slowly she turned her head, until she faced herself in the mirror, ringed by bright lights. She saw dark green eyes, a mouth that had been carefully painted a deep rose. A mane of chestnut hair. Pale skin over delicate features. She saw a musician. And a woman.

"Vanessa Sexton," she murmured, and smiled a little.

Suddenly she knew why she was there, why she would

walk out onstage. And why, when she was done, she would go home.

Home.

It was too damn hot for a thirty-year-old fool to be out in the afternoon sun playing basketball. That was what Brady told himself as he jumped up and jammed another basket.

Even though the kids were out of school for the summer, he had the court, and the park, to himself. Apparently children had more sense than a lovesick doctor.

The temperature might have taken an unseasonable hike into the nineties, and the humidity might have decided to join it degree for degree, but Brady figured sweating on the court was a hell of a lot better than brooding alone at home.

Why the hell had he taken the day off?

He needed his work. He needed his hours filled.

He needed Vanessa.

That was something he was going to have to get over. He dribbled into a fast layup. The ball rolled around the rim, then dropped through.

He'd seen the pictures of Vanessa. They'd been all over the damn television, all over the newspaper. People in town hadn't been able to shut up about it—about her—for two days.

He wished he'd never seen her in that glittery white dress, her hair flaming down her back, those gorgeous hands racing over the keys, caressing them, drawing impossible music from them. Her music, he thought now. The same composition she'd been playing that day he'd walked into her house to find her waiting for him.

Her composition. She'd finished it.

Just as she'd finished with him.

He scraped his surgeon's fingers on the hoop.

How could he expect her to come back to a one-horse town, her high school sweetheart? She had royalty cheering her. She could move from palace to palace for the price of a song. All he had to offer her was a house in the woods, an ill-mannered dog and the occasional baked good in lieu of fee.

That was bull, he thought viciously as the ball rammed onto the backboard and careened off. No one would ever love her the way he did, the way he had all of his damn life. And if he ever got his hands on her again, she'd hear about it. She'd need an otolaryngologist by the time her ears stopped ringing.

"Stuff it," he snapped at Kong as the dog began to bark in short, happy yips. He was out of breath, Brady thought as he puffed toward the foul line. Out of shape. And—as the ball nipped the rim and bounced off—out of luck.

He pivoted, grabbed the rebound, and stopped dead in his tracks.

There she was, wearing those damn skimpy shorts, an excuse for a blouse that skimmed just under her breasts, carrying a bottle of grape soda and sporting a bratty smile on her face.

He wiped the sweat out of his eyes. The heat, his mood—and the fact that he hadn't slept in two days—might be enough to bring on a hallucination. But he didn't like it. Not a bit.

"Hi, Brady." Though her heart was jolting against her ribs, she schooled her voice. She wanted it cool and low and just a little snotty. "You look awful hot." With her eyes on his, Vanessa took a long sip from the bottle, ran her tongue over her upper lip and sauntered the rest of the way to him. "Want a sip?"

He had to be going crazy. He wasn't eighteen any-more. But he could smell her. That floaty, flirty scent. He could feel the hard rubber of the ball in his bare hands, and the sweat dripping down his bare chest and back. As he watched, she leaned over to pet the dog. Still bent, she tossed her hair over her shoulder and sent him one of those taunting sidelong smiles.

"Nice dog."

"What the hell are you doing?"

"I was taking a walk." She straightened, then tipped the bottle to her lips again, draining it before she tossed the empty container into the nearby trash bin. "Your hook shot needs work." Her mouth moved into a pout. "Aren't you going to grab me?"

"No." If he did, he wasn't sure if he would kiss her or strangle her.

"Oh." She felt the confidence that had built up all during the flight, all during the interminable drive home, dry up. "Does that mean you don't want me?"

"Damn you, Vanessa."

Battling tears, she turned away. This wasn't the time for tears. Or for pride. Her little ploy to appeal to his sentiment had been an obvious mistake. "You have every right to be angry."

"Angry?" He heaved the ball away. Delighted, the dog raced after it. "That doesn't begin to describe what I'm feeling. What kind of game are you playing?"

"It's not a game." Eyes brilliant, she turned back to him. "It's never been a game. I love you, Brady."

He didn't know if her words slashed his heart or healed it. "You took your damn time telling me."

"I took what I had to take. I'm sorry I hurt you." Any moment now, her breath would begin to hitch, mortifying her. "If you decide you want to talk to me, I'll be at home."

He grabbed her arm. "Don't you walk away from me. Don't you walk away from me ever again."

"I don't want to fight with you."

"Tough. You come back here, stir me up. You expect me to let things go on as they have been. To put aside what I want, what I need. To watch you leave time and time again, with never a promise, never a future. I won't do it. It's all or nothing, Van, starting now."

"You listen to me."

"The hell with you." He grabbed her then, but there was no fumbling in this kiss. It was hot and hungry. There was as much pain as pleasure here. Just as he wanted there to be.

She struggled, outraged that he would use force. But his muscles were like iron, sleeked with the sweat that heat and exercise had brought to his skin. The violence that flamed inside him was more potent than any she had known before, the need that vibrated from him more furious.

She was breathless when she finally tore away. And would have struck him if she hadn't seen the dark misery in his eyes.

"Go away, Van," he said tightly. "Leave me alone."

"Brady."

"Go away." He rounded on her again, the violence still darkening his eyes. "I haven't changed that much."

"And neither have I." She planted her feet. "If you've finished playing the macho idiot, I want you to listen to me."

"Fine. I'm going to move to the shade." He turned away from her, snatching up a towel from the court and rubbing it over his head as he walked onto the grass.

She stormed off after him. "You're just as impossible as you ever were."

After a quick, insolent look, he dropped down under the

shade of an oak. To distract the dog, he picked up a handy stick and heaved it. "So?"

"So I wonder how the hell I ever fell in love with you. Twice." She took a deep, cleansing breath. This was not going as she had hoped. So she would try again. "I'm sorry I wasn't able to explain myself adequately before I left."

"You explained well enough. You don't want to be a wife."

She gritted her teeth. "I believe I said I didn't know how to be one—and that I didn't know if I wanted to be one. My closest example of one was my mother, and she was miserably unhappy as a wife. And I felt inadequate and insecure."

"Because of the tuna casserole."

"No, damn it, not because of the tuna casserole, because I didn't know if I could handle being a wife and a woman, a mother and a musician. I hadn't worked out my own definition of any of those terms." She frowned down at him. "I hadn't really had the chance to be any of them."

"You were a woman and a musician."

"I was my father's daughter. Before I came back here, I'd never been anything else." Impassioned, she dropped down beside him. "I performed on demand, Brady. I played the music he chose, went where he directed. And I felt what he wanted me to feel."

She let out a long breath and looked away, to those distant Blue Mountains. "I can't blame him for that. I certainly don't want to—not now. You were right when you said I'd never argued with him. That was my fault. If I had, things might have changed. I'll never know."

"Van—"

"No, let me finish. Please. I've spent so much time working all this out." She could still feel his anger, but she took heart from the fact that he didn't pull his hand away when she touched it. "My coming back here was the first thing I'd done completely on my own in twelve years. And even that wasn't really a choice. I had to come back. Unfinished business." She looked back at him then, and smiled. "You weren't supposed to be a part of that. And when you were, I was even more confused."

She paused to pluck at the grass, to feel its softness between her fingers. "Oh, I wanted you. Even when I was angry, even when I still hurt, I wanted you. Maybe that was part of the problem. I couldn't think clearly around you. I guess I never have been able to. Things got out of control so quickly. I realized, when you talked about marriage, that it wasn't enough just to want. Just to take."

"You weren't just taking."

"I hope not. I didn't want to hurt you. I never did. Maybe, in some ways, I tried too hard not to. I knew you would be upset that I was going to Cordina to perform."

He was calm again. After the roller-coaster ride she'd taken his emotions on, his anger had burned itself out. "I wouldn't ask you to give up your music, Van. Or your career."

"No, you wouldn't." She rose to walk out of the shade into the sun and he followed her. "But I was afraid I would give up everything, anything, to please you. And if I did, I wouldn't be. I wouldn't be, Brady."

"I love what you are, Van." His hands closed lightly over her shoulders. "The rest is just details."

"No." She turned back. Her eyes were passionate, and her grip was tight. "It wasn't until I was away again that I began to see what I was pulling away from, what I was moving toward. All my life I did what I was told. Decisions were made for me. The choice was always out of my hands. This time *I* decided. I chose to go to Cordina. I chose to perform. And when I stood in the wings, I waited for the fear to come. I waited for my stomach to clutch and the sweat to break out, and the dizziness. But it didn't come." There were tears in her eyes again, glinting in the sunlight. "It felt wonderful. I felt wonderful. I wanted to step out on the stage, into those lights. I wanted to play and have thousands of people listen. *I* wanted. And it changed everything."

"I'm glad for you." He ran his hands up and down her arms before he stepped back. "I am. I was worried."

"It was glorious." Hugging her arms, she spun away. "And in my heart I know I never played better. There was such…freedom. I know I could go back to all the stages, all the halls, and play like that again." She turned back, magnificent in the streaming sunlight. "I know it."

"I am glad for you," he repeated. "I hated thinking about you performing under stress. I'd never be able to allow you to make yourself ill again, Van, but I meant it when I said I wouldn't ask you to give up your career."

"That's good to hear."

"Damn it, Van, I want to know you'll be coming back to me. I know a house in the woods doesn't compare with Paris or London, but I want you to tell me you'll come back at the end of your tours. That when you're here we'll have a life together, and a family. I want you to ask me to go with you whenever I can."

"I would," she said. "I would promise that, but—"

Rage flickered again. "No buts this time."

"But," she repeated, eyes challenging, "I'm not going to tour again."

"You just said—"

"I said I could perform, and I will. Now and then, if a particular engagement appeals, and if I can fit it comfortably into the rest of my life." With a laugh, she grabbed his hands. "Knowing I can perform, when I want, when I choose. That's important to me. Oh, it's not just important, Brady. It's like suddenly realizing I'm a real person. The person I haven't had a chance to be since I was sixteen. Before I went onstage this last time, I looked in the mirror. I knew who I was, I liked who I was. So instead of there being fear when I stepped into the light, there was only joy."

He could see it in her eyes. And more. "But you came back."

"I chose to come back." She squeezed his fingers. "I needed to come back. There may be other concerts, Brady, but I want to compose, to record. And as much as it continues to amaze me, I want to teach. I can do all of those things here. Especially if someone was willing to add a recording studio onto the house he's building."

Closing his eyes, he brought her hands to his lips. "I think we can manage that."

"I want to get to know my mother again—and learn how to cook. But not well enough so you'd depend on it." She waited until he looked at her again. "I chose to come back here, to come back to you. About the only thing I didn't choose to do was love you." Smiling, she framed his face in her hands. "That just happened, but I think I can live with it. And I do love you, Brady, more than yesterday."

She brought her lips to his. Yes, more than yesterday, she realized. For this was richer, deeper, but with all the energy and hope of youth.

"Ask me again," she whispered. "Please."

He was having trouble letting her go, even far enough that he could look down into her eyes. "Ask you what?"

"Damn you, Brady."

His lips were curved as they brushed through her hair. "A few minutes ago, I was mad at you."

"I know." Her sigh vibrated with satisfaction. "I could always wrap you around my little finger."

"Yeah." He hoped she'd keep doing it for the next fifty or sixty years. "I love you, Van."

"I love you, too. Now ask me."

With his hands on her shoulders, he drew her back. "I want to do it right this time. There's no dim light, no music."

"We'll stand in the shade, and I'll hum."

"Anxious, aren't you?" He laughed and gave her another bruising kiss. "I still don't have a ring."

"Yes, you do." She'd come, armed and ready. Reaching into her pocket, she pulled out a ring with a tiny emerald. She watched Brady's face change when he saw it, recognized it.

"You kept it," he murmured before he lifted his gaze to hers. Every emotion he was feeling had suddenly doubled.

"Always." She set it in the palm of his hand. "It worked before. Why don't you try it again?"

His hand wasn't steady. It hadn't been before. He looked at her. There was a promise in her eyes that spanned more than a decade. And that was absolutely new.

"Will you marry me, Van?"

"Yes." She laughed and blinked away tears. "Oh, yes."

He slipped the ring on her finger. It still fit.

* * * * *

Get 4 FREE REWARDS!

We'll send you 2 FREE Books plus 2 FREE Mystery Gifts.

FREE
Value Over
$20

Both the **Romance** and **Suspense** collections feature compelling novels written by many of today's bestselling authors.

YES! Please send me 2 FREE novels from the Essential Romance or Essential Suspense Collection and my 2 FREE gifts (gifts are worth about $10 retail). After receiving them, if I don't wish to receive any more books, I can return the shipping statement marked "cancel." If I don't cancel, I will receive 4 brand-new novels every month and be billed just $7.24 each in the U.S. or $7.49 each in Canada. That's a savings of up to 28% off the cover price. It's quite a bargain! Shipping and handling is just 50¢ per book in the U.S. and $1.25 per book in Canada.* I understand that accepting the 2 free books and gifts places me under no obligation to buy anything. I can always return a shipment and cancel at any time. The free books and gifts are mine to keep no matter what I decide.

Choose one: ☐ **Essential Romance**
(194/394 MDN GQ6M)

☐ **Essential Suspense**
(191/391 MDN GQ6M)

Name (please print)

Address   Apt. #

City   State/Province   Zip/Postal Code

Email: Please check this box ☐ if you would like to receive newsletters and promotional emails from Harlequin Enterprises ULC and its affiliates. You can unsubscribe anytime.

Mail to the **Reader Service:**
IN U.S.A.: P.O. Box 1341, Buffalo, NY 14240-8531
IN CANADA: P.O. Box 603, Fort Erie, Ontario L2A 5X3

Want to try 2 free books from another series? Call 1-800-873-8635 or visit www.ReaderService.com.

---

*Terms and prices subject to change without notice. Prices do not include sales taxes, which will be charged (if applicable) based on your state or country of residence. Canadian residents will be charged applicable taxes. Offer not valid in Quebec. This offer is limited to one order per household. Books received may not be as shown. Not valid for current subscribers to the Essential Romance or Essential Suspense Collection. All orders subject to approval. Credit or debit balances in a customer's account(s) may be offset by any other outstanding balance owed by or to the customer. Please allow 4 to 6 weeks for delivery. Offer available while quantities last.

Your Privacy—Your information is being collected by Harlequin Enterprises ULC, operating as Reader Service. For a complete summary of the information we collect, how we use this information and to whom it is disclosed, please visit our privacy notice located at corporate.harlequin.com/privacy-notice. From time to time we may also exchange your personal information with reputable third parties. If you wish to opt out of this sharing of your personal information, please visit readerservice.com/consumerchoice or call 1-800-873-8635. **Notice to California Residents**—Under California law, you have specific rights to control and access your data. For more information on these rights and how to exercise them, visit corporate.harlequin.com/california-privacy.

STRS20MAX